THE OTHER S
PART I: THE HOMECOMING

The Other Side of England:

PART I: THE HOMECOMING

JOSEPH CANNING

ISBN-13: 978-1535116855
ISBN-10: 1535116854

To Carol

By the same author:

Once Upon An Island

Olive's Boys

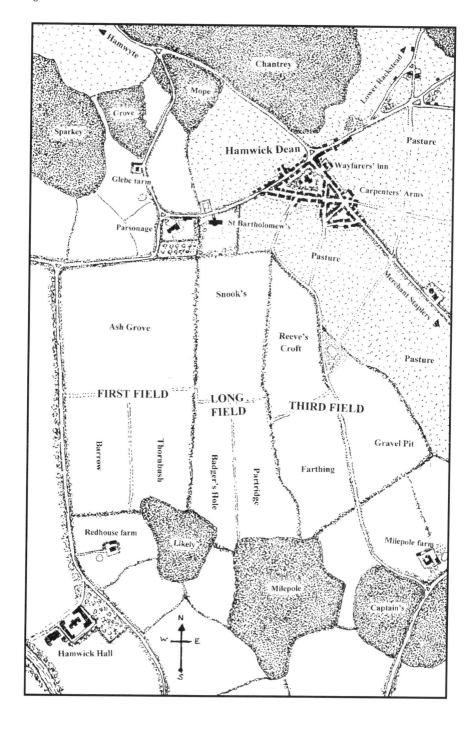

ONE

IN THE EARLY hours of a hoar-frosted late January morning, a ponderous, long-bodied 'fly' wagon, with a loose canvas tilt, pulled by eight horses harnessed in pairs and with the felloes of its wheels hooped by stout iron tyres, trundled into the deserted High Street of the small market town of Hamwyte in the Hundred of the same name in the northern part of the county. It had travelled from the capital, thirty-eight miles distant, at an average pace of two miles an hour, with a load of cloth, calico, tea, spirits, molasses and candles, having left the Red Lion Inn at the Aldwych milestone at nine o'clock on what was by then the previous morning and spent the whole nineteen hours since upon the road.

The heavy frost had descended in the mid-afternoon when the slow-moving 'fly' was barely midway through its journey, coating every standing thing, gate and gatepost, tree-trunk and branch, fence and hedgerow alike, with a dull, silvery rime which, if nothing else, had at least improved the vehicle's progress, hardening the ground and so reducing the prospect of its wheels becoming embedded in the many ruts and quagmires which defaced the high road between the capital and the market town, most particularly the final eight miles from the county town of Melchborough.

At that hour, only the hunched and shivering figure of a stable boy, disturbed by the rumbling of wheels on the gravelled road and thinking the overnight mail had come early, was about in the yard of the old Black Bear Inn, midway along the High Street, as the frost-coated wagoner brought his team to a halt under the lantern hanging over the arched entrance. The wagoner, a grizzled, white-bearded man, who rode not on the cumbersome vehicle itself but upon a pony trotting alongside, now turned and rode back to the rear of the 'fly,' banging with the stock of his long whip against the side and calling out, seemingly to no one in particular: 'Wake up, boys, wake up! You're there!'

After a short while, the heads of two men appeared from under a tarpaulin, blinking sleep from their eyes. Then slowly, stiffly, the figures of two British infantrymen, still wearing the patched and faded red jacket and white trousers uniform of their regiment and carrying their soiled knapsacks, climbed over the tailboard and jumped down, yawning and stretching and rubbing at their stiff and frozen limbs. One was a tall, lean-faced man, some five feet eleven inches in height, in his late twenties, with dark hair and grey eyes and the three chevrons of a sergeant still sewn on his sleeve: the other was stocky, broad-shouldered and barrel-chested, barely above five feet two inches, almost as if his growth had been stunted, no more than twenty-four years of age, with pale blue eyes, a freckled face and cropped red hair. Their uniform, a local might have recognised – had there been anyone other than the sleepy stable boy up at that hour – was of His Majesty's 44th Regiment of Foot, raised partly in that county and partly in Ireland and nicknamed 'the Fighting Fours' by themselves, but churlishly 'the Pompadours' by men of other regiments because of the distinctive 'rose-pompadour' collars, lapels and cuffs on their red jackets.

The wagoner acknowledged their thanks for the ride with a simple nod of his head: then, wrapping his surcoat more tightly about him, he pulled his hat down over his ears, retied a scarf around his mouth, flicked his long whip out over the heads of the front pair of his eight-strong team and, with a gruff 'Walk on,' set the 'fly' rumbling off into the darkness.

'Back at last,' said the taller of the two men, giving a nervous laugh, almost as if he could not believe that he had arrived where he had.

'Aye, back at last,' declared his shorter, red-haired companion, smiling, too. 'Home in Hamwyte again. I never thought I'd see the day!'

'Neither did I,' said the taller sergeant, with a sigh, his breath forming a cloud before his face, 'neither did I.'

The two regarded each other for a moment in that self-conscious way men do sometimes when not knowing what to say or do next: then the smaller, red-haired man reached out and briefly gripped the other's hand. 'I go that way, Jem,' he said, nodding towards the lower end of the town which lay farther along the same High Street, where the low rumbling of the 'fly's' iron-rimmed wheels and the distant barking of a dog now broke the night's silence. 'I have a bed at my sister's for now.'

'I go this way, Will,' answered the other, pointing towards a narrow lane which diverted off the High Street to the right a few yards farther on from where they stood in the glow of the archway lantern. Then in a more sombre, more wistful tone, the taller man said: 'We'll have a drink together sometime, Will, a drink to remember all the others who haven't come home.'

'Aye, we'll do that, Jem, we'll do that,' replied the shorter Will Ponder, nodding solemnly, and, as if to end the moment, he swung his knapsack up on to his shoulder and declared: 'Well, I'm for home – I'll be glad to get out of this cold. I don't envy you your walk, Jem. Good luck. We'll meet again soon.' And with that, he strode off into the darkness, giving a final wave of his hand as he went.

Jem Stebbings watched his friend go: then, gritting his teeth as the frost nipped hard at his exposed nose and ears and ungloved hands, he shouldered his own knapsack and set off down the narrow lane which ran past the back gate of the Black Bear yard. Several darkened houses lined the route for a hundred yards or so before they gave way to open countryside.

After twists and turns of two miles, the road crossed a small hump-back bridge over a gently-flowing river and climbed a long hill, with woods upon either side, to emerge at cross-roads on the crown of a low, flat-topped ridge. This was Jem Stebbings's destination, for atop the ridge lay the village of Hamwick Dean, his home, the home he had not seen for a twelve years, not since he had left it as a youth of seventeen.

For before the 'fly' had brought him into Hamwyte from London, he had come up by coach from Dover with his friend: and before that, he had crossed the Channel from France in a near gale on a pitching barque from Calais, where the second battalion of the 44th Regiment of Foot had been disbanded on the twenty-fourth day of January: and before that, he had trudged for three days to the coast from the British Army's encampment at Versailles outside Paris, where he and his comrades-in-arms had spent six dreary months garrisoning the city following the abdication and flight of the megalomaniac Emperor of the French, Napoleon Bonaparte. And before all that, he had marched day upon day, year upon year in snow and rain and blistering sun to and from a hundred places on the Peninsula of Spain at the whim of his commander-in-chief, the great Duke of Wellington himself, standing with him and seventy thousand others for a final time eight months earlier at a small Belgian village named Waterloo, eight miles south of Brussels.

Had there been any other traveller on the road at that early hour, a farmer perhaps, hunched upon his jolting cart, heading down the long, tree-lined hill on his way early to the Tuesday market at Hamwyte, he might well have been astonished to see the tall, slim, dark-haired soldier come trudging up the same hill as if oblivious to the freezing air, simply placing one foot in front of the other and staring straight ahead, like a man marching for long hours in rank over difficult terrain, with only the back of the man in front on which to fix his gaze. He would have noticed that the rime-encrusted soldier walked with a slight limp and that he swung his left arm more crookedly than his right: and, had he had the wherewithal to think back to the great battle which had been fought the previous June in the Lowlands across the North Sea, he might well have surmised that the soldier had sustained his wounds there as one of the great Duke's gallant army and given him a cheery 'Good morning' in thanks as they passed.

But, at that unearthly hour, the cockerels had yet to crow, the first light of day was still three hours away and the wise were still abed: so there was no one to observe him when soon after six o'clock he reached the cross-roads which mark the entrance to the village, dropped his pack on the small triangle of green by the guidepost and then, as if performing some peculiar jig to unheard music, danced and flapped his arms and stamped his feet in a vain attempt to restore the circulation to his bloodless limbs.

Eventually, having succeeded at least in returning some warmth to his toes and fingers, he picked up his knapsack again, threw it casually over one shoulder and set off down the village's main street, which the locals simply called The Street, since at one time it had been the only one in the village and which was lined on both sides by rows of low plaster-and-weatherboarded labourers' cottages, some with pantiled roofs, some thatched with straw, each with a small garden to its front, but all dark and still. Strangely, he did not turn into the gateway of any of these or knock upon a door, but instead, some fifty yards down, turned into the front yard of the cream-distempered Wayfarers' Inn and began rapping loudly on the knocker without a pause.

In the bedroom above, Caleb Chapman, the landlord of the Wayfarers', was asleep, curled up against the warmth of his wife and happily held there by the weight of the blankets he had laid atop them both the previous evening: and, as might be expected on a hoar-frosted morning, when every breath a man breathed formed a cloud before his face and the very glass of the window panes seemed to have been fractured by the jagged icescape formed upon its surface, he did not take kindly to being disturbed by a loud and incessant knocking at his front door which demanded that he climb from his comfortable hollow and expose himself to the freezing air to answer it. Indeed, so deep in slumber was he that morning that it was a good half-minute before the noise even penetrated his subconscious and brought him to awareness: and it was a further half-minute, as the knocking continued, before grumpily, as might be expected of a man cruelly awakened at so early an hour, he pushed off the weight of the blankets, pulled up his bedsocks, thrust his feet into a pair of worn leather shoes beside the bed and made his way impatiently to the window, where he rubbed hard at the glass with his fingers, for the frost was on the inside as well as the outside.

'Who is it?' demanded his wife, sleepily, propping herself upon one elbow.

'Can't see for sure, it's too dark,' growled the landlord, squinting hard through the small patch of cleared glass. 'He's under the overhang of the porch. Whoever he is, he's making a damned racket. What in God's name does he want at this hour of the morning?'

'There's only one way to find out,' his wife said with a wide yawn and a sigh of the uncaring, falling back on the pillow again and pulling the tops of the blankets up under her chin. 'You'll have to go down and ask him or we'll never get back to sleep because it doesn't sound like he's going to go away, does it?'

In his twenty-two years as the landlord of the Wayfarers' Inn, Caleb Chapman had been awakened in such a fashion and at such an hour only once – during the invasion scare of 1805, two years after the resumption of hostilities against Napoleon following the collapse of the Peace of Amiens when it was thought by some that the French army had landed at Cobwycke, at the head of the Langwater estuary, only ten miles distant: but then the whole village had been awakened that night.

'Hold on! I'm coming, I'm coming,' cried Caleb Chapman, descending the stairs, now with his nightshirt tucked into a pair of breeches, which he had hurriedly pulled on, and a topcoat thrown around his shoulders as a protection against the frigid air. Then, as the insistent knocking continued: 'You don't have to knock so damned loud! I hear you, I hear you! I'm coming.'

'Is that you, Caleb?' came the muffled question from outside, with evident relief in the voice. 'Thank God! I wasn't sure whether you would still be about. Let me in, Caleb, let me in, for pity's sake! I'm freezing to death out here!'

The landlord did not much care for the remark about his still being 'about' – the cheek of the man! As if he were likely to go anywhere else, except perhaps to his grave and, at forty-nine, he was not yet ready even to think about such a thing. The use of his name, however, stirred his interest, but, as he did not recognise the voice and being a naturally cautious man, like most innkeepers, instead of drawing back the bolts, he went first into the large bar parlour to the right of the stairs and peered through the ice-scaped panes of the inn's wide bay window. Whoever was knocking so insistently upon his door at such an ungodly hour, he was not going to let him in till he had discovered who he was and what he wanted, no matter if he did use his name: he could easily have taken that from the white-painted sign above the door: 'Caleb Chapman, licensed victualler, ales and spirits.'

Scraping away the thick grime and ice, he managed to ascertain that the blurred figure was that of a soldier. 'Who are you and what do you want?' he demanded, rapping loudly on the pane with his knuckles to attract the other's attention.

'It's me, Caleb – Jem Stebbings,' answered the soldier, somewhat desperately, turning to the face peering at him through the window and annoyed at the landlord's delay, for by then he had been standing outside the inn for almost four minutes and the severity of the frost had negated all his previous exertions to warm himself. In short, his cheeks, his nose, his ears, his feet and his fingers were all numbed amd bloodless again.

'Jem who?'

'Jem Stebbings,' came the impatient reply, 'Aaron's son. You must remember me, Caleb. I used to live in the village. I've been away at the wars for the past twelve years. Surely you remember me? We used to live in the old Vine Cottage along the Lower Rackstead road. I've been in the army fighting against Boney. I've just got back. I've walked all the way from Hamwyte. Open up, Caleb, for God's sake, it's freezing out here!'

Somewhere in Caleb Chapman's sleep-dulled brain a distant memory stirred: the face of a slim, dark-haired youth, with sallow skin and a broad smile, came into his mind's eye, along with the figures of a man and a woman, the youth's father and mother, to be replaced almost immediately by the memory of a sad double funeral, two coffins in the same grave, all paid for by the parish, with half the village crowding into the churchyard – memories from the past, stirred by a name he had almost forgotten.

With a weary sigh, still wishing the other would go away so he could go back to bed, Caleb Chapman drew back the bolts, turned the heavy key in the great lock and pulled open the door, but only far enough to confirm the identity of a man whose name he had not expected to hear again and to look upon a face which he had never expected to see again.

TWO

THE LAST TIME Caleb Chapman had seen Jem Stebbings was in the December of 1803, as a youth of seventeen years, being escorted by the parish constable of the time, the saddler Isaac Hicken, down the long hill towards Hamwyte with five other youths from the village to join the Melchborough Militia after the hostilities against the French had resumed in the May following the two-year respite afforded by the Peace of Amiens.

Not unnaturally, there had been a great surge of patriotism throughout the land, especially as the 'Corsican Corporal' across the Channel was assembling an army of upwards of a hundred and fifty thousand men in camps at Boulogne, Bruges and Montreuil and also building a 'national flotilla' of invasion barges in ports all along the Channel coast, from Etaples in the Pas-de-Calais to Flushing in Holland, in which to convey his 'Army of England' across the twenty-one miles or so of sea to the Kent coast for the march on London.

The Government, seeking to expand the scope of volunteers, had instructed that all able-bodied males between the ages of seventeen and fifty-five not already in the services be listed as liable for duty in the full-time county militia or in a more local volunteer company of their own making. In some parishes, every able-bodied man offered his services – albeit to serve in the parish volunteer force, as that way they could remain at home and were excluded from joining the full-time county militia, which might be sent anywhere in the country and, worse, was also a source of replacement recruits for the regular army. Thus, the provincial gentry and the middle-classes were allowed to display their martial valour in the local volunteer companies without actually having to take to the field against an enemy.

Counties, however, were still set a quota to fill for the militia and the honest and dutiful patriots who comprised the Vestry of Hamwick Dean, meeting first in the church and then adjourning immediately after prayers to the Wayfarers' Inn, agreed to ballot for six of their own young men to join the hundred in total to be drawn from Hamwyte and the surrounding villages, who were to journey to

Melchborough and fill the ranks of the full-time county militia there, whether they wanted to do so or not, especially as, under an amendment to an earlier Act of Parliament, the fine payable by a parish which did not provide its quota had been increased to forty pounds. The parish constable of the time and the two churchwardens went round the village drawing up a list of every inhabitant, male and female, as the Government had decreed that all men, including the infirm, along with their occupations and family ties, were to be listed and the able-bodied amongst them were then to be classified into four broad categories. First-class candidates for the draft into the militia were men and youths aged between the ages of seventeen and thirty, unmarried and with no children living under ten years of age: second class were men aged between thirty to fifty, unmarried and ditto: third class, were men aged between seventeen to thirty, married with two children under ten years: and fourth class were the remainder aged between seventeen and fifty-five.

With no siblings, no relatives in that region of whom he knew and, therefore, no ties whatsoever, in the view of the Vestry, Jem had fitted perfectly the 'first-class category' as defined by the Government's list. So when the ballot for the 'quota men' was drawn in the Wayfarers' in the early December by the old Squire himself, Sir Evelyn Darcy-Harprigg, as a Justice of the Peace, in the presence of the old parson, the Reverend Henry Burlingham, also a Justice of the Peace, the churchwardens, the parish constable and other members of the Vestry, plus what part of the male population of the village could crowd inside to watch, with the women and girls waiting outside and each mother praying it would not be her son who would have to 'go,' it was not surprising that Jem was one of the six selected – the first name, in fact, 'out of the hat,' so to speak.

After all, he was an orphan, had no permanent home any longer, as the family's rented cottage was needed by a husband and wife with seven children, and he was a potential burden on the poor rate. The hope of the overseer of the poor at that time, Elijah Scoble, in placing him, as 'a poor friendless youth,' with a bricklayer in another parish well away from Hamwick Dean, with whom he would have had to live till the age of twenty, had failed miserably, as had the attempt to have him apprenticed to an ale cask maker and finally to have him taken up by a farmer at a Michaelmas hiring fair on Inworth heath.

In fact, the only man at the fair who had showed any interest had looked him up and down, noted how thin were his arms and how half-starved he looked and had walked on. The alternative, which was for young Jem Stebbings to go as a roundsman, that is, one who would be auctioned to work for various employers around the parish for a week here and a week there, perhaps lodging with them or, more likely, sleeping in their barn, paid a small wage by them and have the remainder made up by the parish, suited no one, particularly with winter coming on. Rather than that, Jem had preferred being balloted into the full-time militia.

With him went the other 'unwanted' of the parish: two predatory nineteen-year-olds, Henry Gabriel and Thomas Coote, both 'unholy bastard begetters' in the words of the Reverend Burlingham and the churchwardens, and both recently returned from two months' detention in the House of Correction at Steadleigh for stealing a goose from the parson's Glebe farm. To be truthful, both had agreed that it was time for them to leave the village and had readily 'consented' to their names being 'drawn' from the ballot since the alternative was marriage to the 'victims' of their lust, paid for by the parish, of course.

The three others were Daniel Day, Enoch Dodds and Henry Pyle, all aged eighteen, family mavericks one and all, of the kind who were known for their indolent and often drunken ways, preferring to sleep half the day and, on rising, to spend the rest of it in one or other of the ale houses around the district, before making one of their frequent night-time sallies into the woods for game, particularly on Darcy-Harprigg land under the misapprehension that, 'The Squire 'on't mind us taking a bird or two!'

Unfortunately for them, Sir Evelyn did mind, very much, and ensured their names were 'balloted' as well: thus, it was these five, along with Jem, who went marching off down the long hill towards Hamwyte one frosty Tuesday morning to take the coach to Melchborough, smiling and waving as they went, with their worldly goods in a carpet bag slung over their shoulders, a two-pounds 'enlistment bonus' given by the Vestry jingling in their pockets, the parish constable and one of the churchwarden's accompanying them to ensure they got on the right coach and the blessings of the parson and the whole populace echoing in their ears. What they did not hear, of course, were the sighs of relief once they were out of sight.

So it was perhaps understandable that, when confronted by an unremembered voice through a wooden door and seeing only the vague shape of its owner through the glass of a frost-coated window pane, Caleb Chapman had not immediately recalled him to mind, especially when it was thought by all who had known him, having heard nothing of him for twelve years, that he most probably had died in battle long before upon some foreign field at a place of which none of them had heard. That and the fact that people had their own lives to lead and forget easily: now, though, he remembered him.

'Jem Stebbings! Of course I remember you! Good gracious, boy, we all thought you was dead and gorn long agoo!' exclaimed the astonished landlord, swinging open the door and stepping back. 'Come in, come in. You look near frozen out there. You picked a fine night to be walking all that way and no mistake. We en't had a frost like this in ten year or more, leastways not round here. T'is the worst I can remember by a long chalk. Come in quick, boy, come in quick, do.'

Jem, the 'boy' who was now a man, needed no second invitation and gratefully followed the stooped and balding landlord as he padded into the large bay-windowed parlour and across the bare floorboards towards a smaller taproom at the rear, relieved and thankful that he had been remembered, but more so that he had found a refuge from the bitter cold outside.

'Gawd, dear me, Jem Stebbings, young Jem Stebbings,' mused Caleb Chapman, as if in disbelief still, pushing open the door of the low-ceilinged taproom, which, being smaller and panelled, was a few degrees warmer than the chill air of the larger parlour, though it was still cold enough for the breath of both to form the same faint clouds in front of their faces before dissolving into the gloom. However, it did have a small fire from the previous night still smouldering amid the ash in its grate.

'Gracious! I never expected to see you again, that I didn't,' continued the landlord, crossing to the hearth and giving the fire a few short, vigorous thrusts with the poker in the hope of stirring it into life, 'though I don't know why you have come back to Hamwick. There en't much hereabouts for a man like yourself. I would have thought a young chap like yourself would have a better life staying in the army, especially now Boney's gorn and there 'on't be no more fighting to be done. There's more life there than here, I would expect.'

'My soldiering days are over, Caleb,' said Jem with a shrug, more of resignation than sadness. 'My battalion, the Second Forty-Fours, has been disbanded. We've done all the fighting we're going to do. We've beaten the Frenchies fair and square, and we've all been given a medal, and now we are being turned out to fend for ourselves. T'is only to be expected, though, I suppose, and I for one cannot say I am upset by it.'

As he spoke, he dropped his knapsack on to one of the rough wooden tables and slumped down upon a bench: already, he could feel the numbness of his nose and ears caused by the bite of the frost beginning to ease and the first painful return of the circulation was flowing again through his frozen fingers.

'I am sorry to wake you so early, Caleb,' went on Jem, 'but I have nowhere else to go and it is fearful cold out there. If you are able, I should like to billet here for a month or two, until I can find my feet, if that is all right with you?'

'Here? For a month or two?' Caleb Chapman raised both eyebrows: he had not had a visitor stay in three or four years and the last one who had taken a bed had remained only a few days. A guest staying a whole month, or perhaps two months, would bring in a tidy sum in bed and board as well as drink, which would be extra, of course, as would the price of a candle and any fire required in his room.

'Aye, Caleb, I hope by then I might be able to find something more permanent – a cottage to rent in the village perhaps. Even our old Vine Cottage, if it is still standing. I have the money to pay any rent asked.'

As he spoke, Jem slipped his hand into the knapsack beside him on the table and drew out a small pouch which jingled. 'I have ten pounds of my army pay here,' he said, emptying several silver coins into his palm and placing six of them in a line upon the table. 'It is prize money they gave us all when we broke up. I am willing to give you five or six shillings here and now to show my intent is honest.'

'Six will do nicely to start,' said Caleb quickly, plumping for the higher figure and scooping up the coins, adding bluntly as he did so: 'I doubt you'll find a cottage so quick about here, though. There en't none to be had lest someone dies and that's the truth of the matter and a great inconvenience it is, too. When Nat Newman, the blacksmith, tried to hire another helper at his forge, the man he got from Lesser Tottle had to give up after two or three months because he had to walk four miles here every morning before five o'clock to start work. He couldn't get a cottage in the village anywhere. You can but try, I suppose, but you might find it a mite easier to take up lodgings with one of the old widow women. They are always on the lookout for a boarder. I am sure you'd find lodgings with one o' they, if you asked, which'd be more permanent, like, than here, as they are always in need of money and t'would be a home of a kind. Till then, you can stay here a month or two, certainly – as long as you like so long as you pays.'

A serious look came to his face as he looked at Jem. 'I don't suppose you are aware of it,' he said sombrely, 'but you are the only one that went from here that has come back.'

He then recounted the sad tale of the other five: Enoch Dodds, Daniel Day and Henry Pyle had all died of disease somewhere in the West Indies, according to a letter someone wrote to the old parson: he let out a snort and rubbed at his nose as if it were itching. 'They three was all in the Forty-Fourth like you, but in the first battalion. I don't suppose you ever come across any on'em at any time, did you? – ' He paused while Jem reminded him he was in the second battalion and, no, he had not come across any of them after they had been taken from the militia, they to the first battalion, he to the second: the first battalion had always been elsewhere.

Of the other two, the 'bastard begetters,' Henry Gabriel and Thomas Coote, from all accounts, they had spent the war patrolling the beaches and marshes on the Isle of Thanet at the mouth of the Thames, still serving with the full-time militia, and had never fired a shot in anger: both had married local Kentish girls from one of the villages there and, in Caleb's estimation, both probably had had to do so. The upshot was that when the militias had been disbanded, the two Hamwick Dean youths had remained there, residents by marriage, though no one in Hamwick Dean was overly bothered that they had not returned, save for the mothers of the two children they had fathered, but then the parish was keeping them.

Caleb Chapman had returned to stoking the reluctant fire. 'You'll find the village is a lot different than when you left it,' he declared, almost as if saddened by the fact. 'The Old Squire, Sir Evelyn, is dead – the whole village and half the county turned out for his funeral. A sad day that was to lose him because he weren't a bad old stick for a squire. Other places had far worse. The old Hall is empty at the moment – has been for a number of years. T'is all tied up in the courts in London, him having no heir, so everything is going to rack and ruin and likely to go on that way what with the slump and the prices of almost anything being so high and everything – '

'Did the Old Squire not have a son?' Jem asked: he seemed to remember that there was a youth of his age who was schooled up in the next county somewhere and who returned to the village on occasions and whom he had seen riding around with his father.

'The son's dead, too,' the stoop-backed landlord said matter-of-factly, pausing to look up. 'Died at sea. Killed at Trafalgar, he was. He were aboard one of the ships that was in the thick of the fighting, so I heard. I knowed the name of it, but I can't remember it. Anyway, he got hisself killed, which did for the Old Squire. That and other things – ' All of a sudden his voice took on a sharp, critical tone. ' – You want to ask your old friend, Dick Dollery, about the Old Squire. I en't saying n'more than that. He'll tell you, I have no doubt – him and Enos Diddams. You ask they two about it, is all I'm saying.' Again he fell silent as if recalling memories: then he heaved a sigh as the flames began to flicker up through the ash and carefully placed some more coals on the fire before straightening again.

'You'll find there's a lot of new people in the village now – a new parson for a start – ' Something in the way he said it told Jem that he was not overly happy with that fact. ' – A new bailiff at Glebe farm –' Again the way he said it indicated he did not approve of that newcomer either. ' – These en't exactly the best o' times to be coming back. That they en't. Things en't like they were. They've changed. The war has made things a lot worse than they was afore it started. These is hard times. Folks is a lot worse off than they used to be. You being away in the army, you wouldn't know of such things, but everything round here has changed or is a-changing. You'll find that out for yourself in time, I expect.'

He did not elaborate further, but asked casually and with obvious intent: 'I take it you have plans now you are back?'

'Oh yes, Caleb, I have plans,' Jem answered the landlord, 'and enough money now to be able to carry them out. That is why I have come back.'

Only as he spoke those words did Jem finally feel that he was indeed back in the village of his birth after twelve years away soldiering for King and Country against the armies of the French, and with the sole desire in his heart to forget the carnage he had witnessed on the battlefields of the Peninsula and the Lowlands of Belgium and to spend the rest of his days in the peace and tranquillity and, he hoped for himself, the prosperity of England's countryside.

THREE

THE FACT that the invasion of England never came was due, of course, to the Royal Navy's valiant victory under Horatio Nelson over the combined French and Spanish fleets under Villeneuve at the Battle of Trafalgar, off Cadiz, southern Spain, in the October of 1805. In order to draw off the Royal Navy, which was powerful enough to defeat any French invasion attempt, the wily Napoleon had instructed the Franco-Spanish fleet to make a feint voyage towards the West Indies: there, they would shake off the British fleet, which inevitably would follow, return up the Channel, join the flotilla of barges at Boulogne and so protect the 'Army of England' as it crossed to Kent. Unfortunately for Napoleon's plans, Admiral Nelson's fleet, having initially fallen for the ruse, finally caught up with Villeneuve's fleet off Cadiz and ended the invasion threat in the great sea battle there.

By then, the 'First Consul for Life' had elevated himself to 'Emperor of the French,' placing the crown on his own head in the December of 1804 because the Pope would not do it and supposedly so he would not owe allegiance to anyone. By then, too, Jem and three of the other Hamwick Dean youths, Enoch Dodds, Daniel Day and Henry Pyle, were privates in the regular army.

Trained militiamen had long been viewed as a ready pool of new recruits: indeed, a third or more of army recruits at that time were former militiamen. So it was no surprise that, after many dreary months on guard duty in a fortified camp built south of the county town, just in case an invasion force came marching north from London, Jem and the others should become the targets of an army recruiting sergeant. A week after taking the enlistment bonus, Jem was on a barque sailing from Falmouth to the pleasant, sun-bathed Channel island of Guernsey as part of a small replacement draft for the second battalion of the 44th of Foot, while his three companions sailed to the West Indies and their doom with another replacement draft for the first battalion.

The second battalion, first raised on the renewal of hostilities, was one of several stationed on the Channel Islands in case the French should take it into their heads to sail across the narrow divide between them and 'liberate' people who did not want to be 'liberated.' Though the French supposedly had laid their plans to invade the islands, they never carried them out either: Bonaparte's attention was always occupied elsewhere on the Continent and Jem and his new comrades-in-arms idled away several hot and glorious summers and warm and damp winters there undisturbed.

Then in the November of 1807, the French, under General Junot, invaded Portugal through Spain and Lisbon fell without a shot being fired: Napoleon wanted the Iberian ports and the Spanish, who supported the French with two divisions of their own, wanted the Portuguese fleet. However, in the spring of 1808, Napoleon sent further troops into Spain, ostensibly heading for Portugal, but the duplicitous 'Corsican Corporal' turned on his Spanish allies, capturing several forts, deposing the monarchy and placing his brother Joseph on the throne. The Spanish rose up against his troops in Madrid and the infamous May massacre occurred: the widespread Spanish revolt which followed finally triggered an insurrection against the French in Portugal in the June.

On the first of August, 1808, a British expeditionary force, under the temporary command of Lieutenant-General Sir Arthur Wellesley, the future Duke of Wellington, landed in Portugal: the bungling half-measures and failures of the small and overstretched British Army on the Continent were about to come to an end and a new phase of the war was beginning, one in which Jem was destined to take part.

However, despite two victories within that month, at Rolica and Vimerio, Wellesley was considered too junior an officer to command the expedition and was replaced. Then, the replacement commanders, Dalrymple and Burrard, controversially granted the beleaguered French, stranded four hundred miles from safety, favourable armistice terms under the Convention of Cintra and allowed them to be evacuated aboard Royal Navy ships to Bayonne along with the booty they had accumulated.

Napoleon himself then took a hand, leading a hundred thousand veterans of the Grande Armée back into Spain, retaking Madrid and routing the Spanish everywhere and forcing a small British force under yet another commander, Sir John Moore, to make its disastrous retreat through the snows of northern Spain to Corunna, where Moore was killed by a cannon shot during the evacuation. It paved the way for Wellesley to return to Portugal in the April of 1809 to command an Anglo-Portuguese force and, after victories at Grijo and Porto in the May, his troops advanced into Spain to join up with a Spanish army. They defeated the French at Talavera, but it was a costly victory, achieved despite Spanish tardiness, recklessness and precipitous flight.

It left Wellesley exposed, so he retreated westwards and, though the devious Spaniards had promised food to the British if they advanced into Spain, not only did they not provide it but they threatened to pillage any of their own towns which sold food to their 'allies.' As a result, Wellesley's men continued to retreat back to Portugal, where, fearing a new French attack, the British commander ordered the construction of a line of a hundred and sixty-two forts along key roads and entrenchments and earthworks to protect Lisbon, the Lines of Torres Vedras.

It was after a French army of around sixty thousand, led by Marshal Masséna, reinvaded Portugal in the July of 1810 that the second battalion of the 44th of Foot, Jem amongst them, sailed for the Iberian Peninsula along with other British troops, landing first at Cadiz and, after a few weeks of doing little, re-embarking in the October for Lisbon, where they were quartered in a convent. A week later, having received their camp equipments, consisting of a camp-kettle and bill-hook to every six men, a blanket, canteen and haversack to each man, the battalion paraded in the city's Grand Square and then, with three days' provisions, marched in sections, to the music of their bugles and drums, to join the main British army inside the Lines.

Jem's mess of six cast lots as to who should be cook for the first day: unluckily, and somewhat suspiciously, the lot fell to Jem, the youngest of that mess, who not only carried the camp-kettle but also his own knapsack containing two shirts, two pairs of stockings, one pair of overalls, two shoe-brushes, a shaving box, one pair of spare shoes and other articles, plus his greatcoat and blanket rolled above the knapsack, a canteen of water slung over one shoulder and on the other a haversack, with beef and bread and sixty rounds of ball-cartridge.

Over the next four years, he was to share in the carrying of that camp-kettle, along with his own equipment, hundreds of times and for hundreds of miles: in fact, in the series of advances and retreats which so marked the Peninsular campaign, Jem and the others of his mess were to cover most, though not all, of the six thousand and more miles which Wellington's army marched and counter-marched, in advance and retreat, as it fought its way back and forth across Spain, eventually to reach Madrid and finally, in 1814, after further setbacks and retirements, to march through the Pyrenees into France itself to besiege the southern city of Toulouse, where they were at the war's end.

In the beginning, Jem, by then twenty-three years of age, was present, along with his comrades-in-arms of the 44th of Foot, at Fuentes d'Onoro on the Spanish-Portuguese border for the three days in May of 1811 when thirty-two thousand British and Portuguese formed up along the deep ravine of the Don Casas stream as forty-five thousand French under Massena launched a frontal assault against the barricaded village. Fortunately for Jem's survival and that of his raw and untested comrades, the 44th of Foot were out on the left of the line, with the Fifth Division, near the destroyed Fort Concepcion, and only their Light Company took part in the ferocious fighting on the third of May when it took a wild bayonet charge by the Light Infantry to reclaim the narrow sloping streets of the village, lost earlier to the massed French.

Thus, when the sun sank at the end of that first day, the village remained in British hands, but so exhausting had the fighting been that both sides spent the whole of the second day recovering. As dawn broke on the third day, however, Massena again sent his massed columns of infantry against the village. The British had taken up positions behind the many low stone walls which, along with the closeness of the buildings and the steep inclines of the streets, prevented the French cavalry from charging them down: and, when the enemy cavalry and infantry, jostling each other, became jammed in the close confines between the houses, they were shot down by musket volley after musket volley.

Out of ammunition and in desperation, the French resorted to the bayonet. Their charge, however, was halted by yet more murderous volleys and, when finally they withdrew, they left thousands of casualties behind. Jem was one of those detailed to dig the burial pits into which the stripped and looted bodies of the French were tossed with no concern for their faith or care for their dignity: they were, after all, the enemy, 'Johnny French,' and as such never to be trusted.

It was not until the April of the following year that Jem's battalion took part fully in a major action when, as part of Brigadier-General Leith's Fifth Division, they marched with an Allied army, some twenty-five thousand strong, to besiege the fortress town of Badajoz. Jem was amongst the many work parties which, in the torrential rain of a Spanish spring, dug trenches, parallels and earthworks to protect the heavy siege artillery which the Duke brought up to smash through the stonework of the curtain wall: and several times he had to throw down his spade, grab his musket and form up as the French made sallies in an attempt to destroy the advancing lines. When the maze of trenches was finally far enough forward, the heavy eighteen-pound and twenty-four-pound howitzers were hauled into place and, in no time at all, they had pounded two breaches in the wall.

Helped by a generous portion of rum, Jem and his comrades were all fired up for the attack on the fifth: but the order was delayed for twenty-four hours to allow another breach to be made and it was not until the sixth that Wellington ordered his regiments forward in a night attack. Again, as luck would have it, Jem's battalion, along with the Portuguese, was part of a diversionary assault to the east and north to escalade the walls of the San Vincente bastion and so they did not take part in the terrible assault on the three breaches.

There, the alerted French garrison poured such a lethal hail of musket fire, supported by grenades, stones, barrels of gunpowder with crude fuses, and even bales of burning hay, down upon the British and Portuguese troops surging forward *en masse* that the breaches were soon filled with dead and wounded and the troops coming up behind had to struggle over them to get forward, only to be mown down in turn by volleys of grape and blasted by shrapnel from the grenades and bombs.

Though they outnumbered the French garrison by almost five to one, the Allied soldiers were being halted everywhere. In just under two hours, two thousand of the attacking force were killed or badly wounded at the main breach alone, while countless more of the Third Division were shot down as they made their diversionary assault. Indeed, so great was the carnage that Wellington was about to call a halt to the attack when his soldiers finally got a foothold on the curtain wall: and first amongst them were the 44th of Foot, who succeeded in taking the San Vicente bastion and were the first to plant their colours atop its walls.

Jem, however, was not with them: he had been shot in the thigh and was lying amongst a heap of dead and dying at the foot of the wall. Thus, he took no part in the orgy of drunkenness, rape and pillage in the town which followed the French surrender as the British and Portuguese troops went on the rampage, enraged by the slaughter all around the curtain wall, where bodies were piled high and, some said, blood flowed like streams in the ditches and trenches. So uncontrollable were they over the next three days that some even turned on any officer who tried to pacify them and they were not brought to order till Wellington ordered a gallows to be erected in the central square and threatened to hang anyone who did not desist.

Fortunately, Jem's wound was not too severe. The ball in his thigh was mostly spent before it struck him and so was not too deeply embedded – that is, it was not below the depth of the surgeon's finger and so was extracted that way. Had it been any deeper, it would have been left inside his body and allowed to work itself into a shallower position before removal, though there was no guarantee it would come out and many a veteran of the Peninsula stood at Waterloo still with a leaden ball inside him from the Spanish campaign: indeed, some, those who lived, would carry them for the rest of their lives.

All in all, Jem reckoned himself luckier than most, certainly luckier than the two who had crawled back to lie alongside him, one who had been bayoneted in the stomach and the other stabbed in the chest by a sword thrust: bayonet, sword or knife wounds left deep puncture wounds and were usually fatal, especially if in the chest or abdomen as there was little the surgeons could do. The best they could do, in fact, was to let the wounds bleed for a while in the hope of cleaning them of dirt and strands of clothing and increase the width of their injuries to boost this. But the two died anyway before either was ready to be sewn up.

So in the June, though still not fully recovered from his wound, Jem was able to join the march to Salamanca, where Wellington's foray into central Spain was blocked by Marmont's army. For weeks on end, the two armies shadowed each other, with Marmont repeatedly threatening Wellington's supply line: so close, in fact, did they march on occasions that Jem, hobbling along mostly at the rear of the battalion with the other walking wounded, expected the French to come into line at any moment and begin firing. By the twenty-second of July, as Marmont's army grew to fifty thousand and the odds turned against him, Wellington had decided to withdraw his British, Portuguese and Spanish force all the way back to Portugal – until, unexpectedly, he saw that Marmont had made a tactical error. He had separated his left flank from his main body and the wily Duke immediately ordered the major part of his army to attack the over-extended French left-wing.

Jem's battalion was in the centre with the Second Brigade of Leith's division before the village and hills of Araphiles. By then, he had been promoted to corporal and had cheered with the rest of them as Packenham's hidden Third Division took two French divisions marching across their front completely by surprise: and when the heavy cavalry crashed into the last of the three French divisions and broke them, Jem had fixed his bayonet with the rest of his comrades and limped forward in support with the other walking wounded till a musket ball struck his arm and he was taken back. So he was not on the field when a young lieutenant of the 44th, the same one who had disciplined him a month previously for giving a 'sloppy salute,' won eternal glory for the regiment by capturing the Imperial Eagle of the French 62nd Regiment of Line.

In the heat of August, the battalion had entered Madrid and then had marched north to take part in the disastrous siege of Burgos during the September and October. In the retreat that followed, all the way back to Portugal, the 44th of Foot had distinguished themselves in the skirmishing at Vila Muriel, but at a high cost so that by the end of October the strength of the battalion had been reduced to just forty-two men of all ranks, amongst them still Jem Stebbings. Despite a draft of forty officers and three hundred and seventy-three men, only a hundred and thirty were truly fit for duty: therefore, in the December, Wellington had ordered six of his companies to return to England to re-organise, while the remaining fit men formed a provisional battalion of four companies, which stayed on in the Peninsula.

Having been twice wounded, though recovered, Jem was amongst those returned to England. He remained in barracks with the regiment without returning to Hamwick Dean and, in the March of 1814, now promoted to sergeant, departed with his comrades-in-arms for Flanders to take part in the disastrous assault on the fortress of Bergen-op-Zoom. The four thousand British stormed into the fortress in four columns: two got in and gained the ramparts with very little loss, but the left column lost so many officers at the head of their men that it fell into disorder, while the right was weakened when a detachment of the First Guards was cut off. Again Jem survived, this time unscathed, but it proved to be an ignominious retreat which, as two decades of war finally ended in the October, fetched up the 44th of Foot at Ostend, where they were billeted on the town in various occupied houses, much to the displeasure of the inhabitants, except the grog shop owners and the brothel keepers, who did a good trade.

FOUR

THEN CAME the panic of the Hundred Days, following Bonaparte's escape from Elba at the beginning of March, 1815, his arrival in Paris, the reforming of his armies, with many of the Old Guard and just-released prisoners-of-war returning to the Eagle, followed by the march north on Brussels. Jem and his comrades-in-arms were hurried from their billets in Ostend and marched eastward, fifty miles in little more than twenty-four hours, through heavy downpours, arriving just in time to join Sir Denis Pack's Ninth Infantry Brigade as part of Sir Thomas Picton's Fifth Division at the strategic Quatre-Bras cross-roads, a short way south of Genappes on the Brussels-Charleroi road, as a hundred thousand French came up in pursuit of Wellington's hastily assembled force of British regiments, German Legionaries and untried and unreliable Belgian and Dutch militias.

The battalion reached Quatre-Bras at about two o'clock, halting to cook their stirabout of oatmeal and water with biscuit. The 44th lay on one side of the road and the Duke of Brunswick's dragoons were on the other: but it was not long before the order to 'Fall in!' was given and the brigade advanced. As they topped a rise in the road, they found the whole countryside ahead swarming with the advancing French and, as Jem and his comrades themselves went down the slope, French skirmishers in the fields of rye five-feet high began picking them off. The men either side of Jem, one named Coxwaite from the village of Gledlang in the same Hundred as Hamwick Dean, another, an Irishman from Donegal named Cullen, fell with a groan and disappeared. However, by file-firing from each company, Jem's battalion managed to clear the rye of the French and, after several further movements, the 44th were detached at the double to rising ground, where they found French cavalry had captured the guns, having driven off the artillerymen: the guns were quickly retaken by the 44th.

The battalion's moment of fame came when an attack by Kellerman's cuirassiers fell upon the 44th's rear so unexpectedly that they had no time to form a square, which was the best way to fend off cavalry. So Lieutenant-Colonel Hamerton instantly decided to receive the cavalry with his battalion in line. 'Rear rank, right about face,' he ordered as Kellerman's cuirassiers came charging up. 'Make ready! Present!'

Jem, who was with his platoon in the rear rank, had been schooled enough in war by then to know how perilous their position was. 'Fire!' came the command: Jem aimed his musket at the breastplate of one of the cavalry with a sabre, a black-moustachioed character who seemed to have his eye fixed upon him alone. The effect of the volley was astonishing: the cuirassiers were immediately thrown into confusion: horses crashed down and men toppled, riders wheeled away and collided with other riders. So great was the confusion that, as the survivors started to flee towards their own position, they rode across the flank of the rest of the 44th, where the lieutenant commanding the Light Company, which had held its fire, now ordered his men to fire upon them with their Baker rifles: and no sooner did the cuirassiers gallop across the proper front of the regiment than the men there did likewise with their muskets. The 'Fighting Fours,' had, by their coolness and steadiness, accomplished a feat of arms which the best-disciplined corps in the world might have hoped in vain to do: they had routed the famed French cavalry while standing in line rather than in the normal square.

Two days later, on the eighteenth, after a six-mile march back towards Brussels in stifling, clammy heat and then a violent thunderstorm, followed by a night bivouacked in a stubbled wheat field, Jem had awoken stiff and chilled to the marrow and soaked to the skin by the night's incessant downpour. All around him, the British troops, who had passed a similarly dismal night, were stirring to the sound of trumpets and preparing their muskets for action by simply discharging them straight up into the air before returning to huddle around the embers of numerous fires, fuelled by uprooted fencing and doors and window frames taken from farm buildings to their rear. Like them, Jem's thoughts that day were more on a desire for better food and a sup of rum to warm him rather than the coming battle, for he and his comrades-in-arms had eaten nothing other than the biscuit and meal and water stirabout they had been given two days previously at Quatre-Bras for the sole reason that the commissariat wagons were enmeshed in the chaos on the roads through the Forest of Soigniés behind them as thousands of peasants fled northwards away from the advancing French.

The Duke of Wellington had taken up a position astride the main Charleroi-Brussels road where it emerges from the forest, south of the village of Mont Sainte-Jean only about eight miles from the Belgian capital itself: there, the road crosses a low ridge and undulates southwards across a shallow valley before rising on the other side to another ridge by Rossommes farm. On the northern Mont-Sainte-Jean ridge, the main Charleroi-Brussels road was crossed at right angles by a sunken lane, steep banked in places and lined then upon both sides by thick straggling beech hedges as it wound its way along two-thirds of the length of the crest between two villages some five miles apart, Braine L'Alleud in the west and d'Ohain in the east.

Some two hundred yards below the crossroads at the centre of Wellington's line stood the high-walled La Haye-Sante farm, on the right side of the road, one of the strategic points, while a mile distant on the southern rise of the valley on the same road stood La Belle Alliance inn, where Napoleon was to take up his position to conduct the French battle.

Wellington's own command position was beneath a tall elm tree atop a high bank at the crossroads, which gave him a good view along most of his line, the main strength of which lay to the west or right of the main road in a south-facing curve down towards the strategic, walled Hougoumont chateau, with dependable British and King's German Legion battalions interspersed amongst the less reliable Belgians and Dutch militias, some of whom a year before had been in Napoleon's armies.

The four hundred and fifty-five officers and men of the 44th of Foot were placed some six hundred yards east or to the left of the crossroads, behind the sunken lane to d'Ohain, part of the reserve Ninth Brigade along with the third battalion of the 1st Royal Scots, the 42nd of Foot or Royal Highland Regiment and the 92nd of Foot or Gordon Highlanders. The brigade, which was under the command of Major-General Sir Denis Pack, was part of the eccentric Sir Thomas Picton's Fifth Division. On the Ninth's right, between them and the crossroads, was the Eighth Brigade, under Brigadier-General Sir James Kempt, comprising the 95th Riflemen, 32nd of Foot or Cornwalls, the 79th of Foot or Cameron Highlanders and the 28th of Foot or North Gloucestershires.

A little way down the slope, in between the two British brigades, two Dutch-Belgian battalions had somewhat foolishly placed themselves in a forward position in a hollow as if deigning the cover of the ridge-top and the thick hedges, while alongside them were three batteries of British and Dutch foot artillery. On the extreme of that flank, on the 44th's left, were three Hanoverian landwehr battalions under a British officer and several squadrons of dragoons facing the fortified Papelotte farm, while lurking behind was General Ponsonby's heavy cavalry brigade of Royal Dragoons, Scots Greys and Inniskilling Dragoons.

It had stopped raining by the time Jem's battalion reached their places in a clover field on the extreme left of the brigade's position, a little behind the Scots and well back from the sunken lane and hedges on the forward slope. Though a heat mist still filled the hollows in the valley, every now and again the sun would burst through the heavy grey clouds overhead and light up the whole countryside. It was during one of these bright bursts that Jem got his first clear view of the thousands of French troops drawn up in great masses on the distant ridge only a mile or so from where he stood. Great columns of infantry were marching steadfastly to their places and squadron after squadron of cuirassiers, with the sun shining on their steel breastplates, along with red- uniformed dragoons, brown-uniformed hussars and green-uniformed Polish lancers, were forming up.

'Holy, Mother of God!' exclaimed Padraig Cannon, a tall, smiling, wavy-haired Irishman from the wilds of County Donegal, instinctively crossing himself. 'This is going to be a rough day and no mistake!'

'Christ, sergeant! Whyever did we join this man's army?' was all a shocked Will Ponder could gasp as he gazed awestruck at all the panoply of the assembled French. 'We'll be lucky if we get through this lot in one piece.'

Will Ponder had served alongside Jem for two years and, sadly, was the last survivor of eight men from the county who had been transferred into the 44th of Foot when the regiment needed new recruits after their losses at Burgos and Vila Muriel: all the others now rested under the dry dirt of Spain.

'Belay that chat,' Jem ordered, 'we've been through worse than this.' However, he said it without much conviction, for he knew as well as every other man there that that day might well be their last.

Sometime around nine o'clock, there was a sudden roll of drums along the whole of the French line and a burst of music from the bands of a hundred battalions was borne to them on the air. Jem recognised the music as the *Marseillaise,* but the sound was soon lost in a sudden uproar of cheering that arose: Napoleon himself was riding along the French front to encourage his troops. Jem and the other Peninsular War veterans exchanged wry smiles: none of them would ever have cheered their coldly autocratic commander in the same way: they respected the hook-nosed Duke, but they did not love him, at least not as the French seemed to love their 'Little Corporal.'

However, like all of the Peninsular veterans, Jem had a far greater faith in the Duke than he did in the Corsican. To his way of thinking, Wellington would never have left a whole army to flounder and die amid the snows of Russia during its disastrous retreat from Moscow while he set off by sledge and coach back to the safety of Paris. No, when it came to generals, he would rather be standing on the Duke's side of the valley any day.

Jem reckoned it must have been about half-past eleven when the battle proper began. Suddenly eighty French cannons, facing them on slightly higher ground across the swampy valley in the enemy's centre, began booming out. At the same time the crash of musketry could be heard in the far distance to the west: the French infantry were attacking Hougoumont chateau on the Allies' right flank in force and, at the same time, attempting to soften up by cannonade their centre and left, where Jem's battalion was standing, as a prelude to a major attack there. Cannonballs began to whiz over their heads and the first agonised cries were heard in the Scots regiments in front to their right. In no time at all, limping figures were being helped to the rear. Then, from nearby, there was a sudden loud rapport as the Allied artillery finally opened up and a great rolling ironic cheer went along the ridge-top.

Jem's battalion and the three Scots battalions were quickly ordered to lie down on the reverse slope of the ridge to gain some protection from the cannonading. Fortunately, the muddy ground of the clover field in which they lay dissipated the effect of the roundshot and shell ploughing up the earth around and sometimes in amongst them: however, men were killed and others maimed. A few yards to Jem's left, a man was decapitated by one cannonball and others had arms and legs scythed off: and several of the Gordon Highlanders, who were lying down immediately to their front, came back through their lines, groaning and covered in blood, helped by their comrades.

How long the cannonading lasted, Jem had no idea. It seemed two or more hours at least: but suddenly it stopped and, on the far ridge, column upon column of close-packed French infantry came marching over the crest and through their lines of guns, down into the shallow valley and up the slope straight towards the Allied positions. Seventeen thousand men of D'Erlon's First Corps, in four divisions, were attacking Wellington's centre and left, which Napoleon considered was the weakest point and also the likely place at which the Prussian army, retreating from the disastrous battle of Ligny two days before, might form a conjunction from the east.

Through the mud and the sodden barley and rye fields, shoulder to shoulder, in bulky, unwieldy columns, with drums beating and preceded by a wall of blue-coated skirmishers extending over hundreds of yards, the four French divisions came resolutely up the slope, one towards La Haye-Sante farm, two towards the centre and the positions of the Eighth and Ninth Brigades and the fourth towards the landwehr battalions and Papelotte farm on the Allied left. Though temporarily checked as the Allied artillery fired grape and roundshot in amongst them and volley after volley of musketry crashed into them, the marching columns regrouped, stepped over the dead bodies of their comrades and came steadily on up the glacis slope through the high rye and barley till they were no more than a hundred yards from the crest.

Suddenly, from out of the smoke to the right, Jem and the others saw the whole Dutch-Belgian brigade come rushing back across the sunken road in full flight.

A great groan went up. 'Bloody foreigners!' snorted Padraig Cannon. 'We'd be better off without them. They'd sooner fight for Boney than fight for us. I wouldn't trust one mother's son of them.'

Smoke from the artillery as well as the musketry obscured much of what was happening in front from Jem's view. In fact, the head of the French column had reached the hedge with their muskets still on their shoulders and, having got through, were crossing the lane when one of the Scots battalions, which had gone forward to line the hedgerow on their side, stood up and fired a volley into them before they could level their own muskets. For a moment the head of the column seemed about to break, but then the French fired an answering volley which was equally as deadly and it was the Scots who were thrown back in disorder. With that, the French came bursting through the hedge *en masse*, yelling in triumph, believing they had captured the crest of the ridge.

Suddenly the cry rang out from the captain in front, to be taken up immediately by the lieutenant and ensigns: 'Up Forty-Fourth! On your feet! Frenchies coming through the smoke! Look lively now! On your feet! On your feet!'

Jem was up in an instant and, making sure those about him rose, too, he hurried forward with the rest of the company as the whole of the 44th, along with the Royal Scots, rushed to re-occupy the abandoned ground. The massed ranks of French were still advancing towards them like a series of steady slow-moving walls ten deep: but Jem and most of his comrades had seen such things before and, as he had been trained to do, he instantly brought his musket up to his shoulder and squinted along the barrel. As the officer's sword flashed down, his company fired their volley into the enmasking smoke. The effect was shattering: the French infantry came to a shuddering halt. A second volley crashed into them, then a third. At that, a great roar went up as the battalion surged forward to close with the enemy, driving them back across the lane, through the hedge and down the slope.

In the furious and protracted struggle which followed, Jem was skewered through the cloth of his sleeve by the bayonet of a Frenchman, who ran madly at him. Somehow, a desperate Jem managed to grab the muzzle of the Frenchman's musket and hold it before he could pull it back and make another attempt: then one-handed, he skewered the Frenchman in the throat with his own bayonet. He did not know or care whether it was a fatal wound for his enemy so long as the man wheeled away.

The desperate fight on the muddy slope continued in a whirl of shouting, explosions, lunging bayonets, the bang of musketry close by, cries of agony and shouts of fury and desperation, some in French, some in English. The corporal fighting alongside Jem suddenly sank down with a groan, wounded in the thigh by a French ball: others about him were also falling, some silently, some crying out, some immediately still

Jem managed to reload his musket three times and fire into any small group of bluecoats that he could see amid the engulfing smoke, unsure whether he hit anyone, but needing to keep them at bay, otherwise it was butt and bayonet work. Soon, it was quite clear that several of those around him were running out of ammunition, for many were calling to their officers about their predicament. Jem himself had only three cartridges left and they were in desperate straits when suddenly Gordon Highlanders came down the slope to their aid. Though only two hundred and fifty strong, they formed up two-men deep and rushed forward at the wall of enemy. At first, the French stood motionless: then, yielding to the wild cries and determination of the Highlanders, they panicked and began to wheel away.

Just at that moment, Ponsonby's heavy cavalry brigade, the Royal Dragoons, the Scots Greys and the Inniskillens, also fell headlong upon the French column, shouting to their comrades to make way and bowling over those who did not as they passed through them and around their flank. The French endeavoured to stand together, but with their front driven in, their centre penetrated and their rear dispersed, it was in vain: many fled, throwing away their arms and anything else that encumbered them. Two thousand or so others were rounded up as prisoners and marched to the rear, leaving the ground behind covered with killed and wounded and strewn so thickly with knapsacks and their contents and arms and accoutrements that it was virtually impossible to avoid stepping on one or the other.

FIVE

IT WAS at this time that the first of two incidents occurred which were to change Jem's fortunes. His battalion were back in the clover field when a young ensign from his company, severely wounded in the leg, limped back over the crest of the hill: blood was pouring from a gaping wound in his thigh where he had been slashed with a sabre and it was clear he needed to go to the rear. As a trustworthy sergeant, Jem was detailed by the lieutenant to help the ensign to where springer carts were picking up the wounded and taking them to a small hospital set up for officers by a surgeon in the Mont-Sainte-Jean farm stables, a half-mile or so behind the lines. Jem was trusted not only not to dawdle but also to return promptly to the line, for several men who had helped comrades to the rear during the cannonading had yet to return to their posts.

Indeed, Jem was in the very act of rejoining the rear rank when, unexpectedly, a solitary steel-plated French cuirassier appeared behind the battalion's line, where he should never have been. He came galloping madly along the reverse slope of the ridge, probably having forced his way across the lane and through the hedge farther to the east and, becoming detached from his own squadron, was charging along, seeking a gap in the extended British line so as to make his escape.

For some reason, perhaps thinking there was no escape unless he forced it, just as he drew level with the rear of Jem's battalion and found his way blocked yet again by the line of British soldiers, all facing to the front, he pulled his sweating mount round, pointed his sabre and, with an unintelligible yell, charged straight at Jem and the men about him, intending to crash through them from behind. For a second or so, as the cuirassier thundered straight towards him, Jem was too surprised to do anything: but, being the only one who had observed him and realising that the lives of several of his unsuspecting comrades depended upon him, he smartly levelled his Brown Bess musket and brought the Frenchman's horse down with a single shot when mount and rider were no more than twenty yards from him.

On the field of battle, it is kill or be killed and the instinct for survival is a vicious spur. Without so much as a thought, Jem ran over to the fallen cuirassier as he lay winded and unable to get up in the mud of the churned-up ground and, with his bayonet already fixed, dispatched him into oblivion with three brutal lunges. A rapid search of the dead man's body revealed a leather purse tied to his belt, which Jem quickly cut free, his own body shielding the act from his comrades, who had turned to watch and to cheer their sergeant: the purse was quickly stuffed inside Jem's jacket.

Jem felt no guilt: it was not uncommon for a soldier on the field of battle to stop and search the clothing of a dead enemy even as they went forward into attack. The purse was a weighty one: later, during a few minutes' lull in their part of the line, Jem loosened the drawstring and tipped its contents into his hand: he could not conceal his delight and let out a whoop of surprise as out tumbled ten gold forty-sous Napoleons.

Alongside him, Will Ponder gave a quick glance down. 'You lucky beggar, sarge!' was all he said as Jem returned the coins to the purse and slipped it quickly into his knapsack.

'I shall be if I survive this,' was Jem's grim reply.

After that, there was no time to think of his good fortune: and such was the nature of the desperate battle that Jem, like thousands of others, expected his life to be extinguished or himself at least to be wounded at any time by an unseen musket ball, an exploding canister shell, hurtling cannonball or sudden lance or bayonet thrust. But come the late afternoon, when Wellington ordered the whole of his army to retire off the crest of the ridge to form square in a desperate attempt to stave off the seemingly victorious French, Jem was still alive, having survived yet more pounding from the French cannon.

When they formed square, four deep with one of the Scots battalions, Jem was kneeling in the front rank as part of the bayonet 'hedge' to deter the hordes of steel-plated French cuirassiers milling all around them. Some rode right up to the square to discharge their carbines or attempted to hack with their swords at the men standing behind, who volley-fired back, aiming low deliberately to bring down horses and impede those coming up behind. Jem and the others forming the bayonet 'hedge,' however, were forced to hold their fire so they could not be overwhelmed while reloading and could only prod their bayonets up into the bellies of the pawing horses to drive them off. One French general who had penetrated their square lay dead within it: no sooner had he been shot from his horse than a dozen British soldiers rushed at him and stripped him of his emblems and were tucking then into their shirt fronts as they returned to their posts.

The grimmest hour of all followed when the French brought up their cannon to within three hundred yards and fired canister shot directly into the squares. Fortunately for Jem and his comrades, their shots were directed mostly at those across the main road and at a nearby square formed by Hanoverians, though Jem's battalion did not escape entirely and they still lost the greater number of their men at that time, even though they lay down again as the shot mostly whistled over them: somehow, though, he survived it all.

Later, the whole of the Ninth were pulled closer to the main road, behind the cross-roads, to strengthen the centre. Though they were still cannonaded, Jem was unscathed still when, in the late evening, the seven battalions of the Imperial Guard advanced up the muddy ground and, turning slightly to their left, made straight towards that part of the ridge to the west of the main road held by Maitland's Brigade of Guards in what was to prove Napoleon's final attempt to win the day before the Prussians, approaching in numbers from the east, joined the battle.

The more forward Dutch troops retired and, to the Imperial Guard, it must have seemed as if the ridge were deserted: but it was not. Lying in the corn before it were two battalions of the First Foot Guards. At the very moment the French thought they saw victory within their grasp, Wellington shouted, 'Now Maitland! Now is your time!' The cry went up, 'Up Guards!' and all at once a long red barrier seemed to spring up from the ground. 'Make ready!' shouted the officers, then, 'Fire! Fire! Fire!' and a series of devastating volleys tore into the shoulder-to-shoulder columns of the French.

At the same time, the 52nd of Foot were brought round to enfilade the left flank of the enemy as they passed across them: the volley from the Peninsular veterans halted the French in their tracks and, seizing their chance, the Foot Guards, many of them firing from the hip, so close was the range, pressed home their attack over the lines of the enemy's dead and dying. The whole of the Imperial Guard was driven back down the hill and began a general retreat to the cry of '*La Garde recule!*' even as the Prussians, under the command of the bewhiskered grandfather, Marshall Blucher, finally fought their way through the village of Plancenoit in force to attack Napoleon's right flank and rear from the east.

At the very moment that the Old Guard wavered, Jem clearly saw the great Duke himself, accompanied by the sole surviving member of his entourage, galloping helter-skelter along the ridge from division to division, waving his hat in the air as a signal for a general advance: for by then it was almost night and everywhere the French were fleeing the field.

The smoke of battle, which had clouded the whole scene ever since the French had fired the opening salvo that morning, was finally clearing as Jem's battalion, in two extended lines, four deep, with bayonets fixed, began its slow, measured descent of the churned and blood-soaked slope to the left of the main road, past La Haye-Sante farm and the hundreds of bodies which surrounded it, through the flattened fields of rye, corn and barley, stepping over the dead and occasionally despatching with the bayonet any wounded Frenchie they came across, then up the slope on to the southern ridge which a half-hour before had been occupied by the French.

The whole line gave a cheer when in the distance they clearly saw the road to Genappes was thronged with the fleeing enemy and the valley and ridge to the left were filled with Prussians. The last of the cannons, which had fired into them from across the valley as they moved down the slope, killing and wounding several even as the battle ended, had at last ceased and the gunners were throwing down their arms and packs and were themselves fleeing.

The French Guard made one last attempt at a stand on the rising ground to the west of La Belle Alliance, forming four squares, but a charge from General Adam's brigade drove them back again and everything fell into Allied hands: guns, baggage tumbrels, ammunition wagons, drivers, in short, the whole materiel of the fleeing French army.

SIX

AS IT HAPPENED, the pavé road south from the battlefield towards Genappes was so choked with the wreckage of baggage wagons, overturned guns, caissons and carriages, some with the horses dead in their traces, and the ground in the fields either side so mired and churned that not even a company, let alone a battalion or a brigade, could march through it without having to heave carriage and caisson aside. Consequently, the 44th of Foot, hungry and weary to death, weighed down by their drenched blankets and greatcoats, which lay upon their shoulders like logs, bivouacked for the night just off the main road at the bottom of the slope in a field of trampled rye just as a large round moon came up to light the scene of so much futile carnage.

Ahead, towards Genappes, shots still rang out: the old marshall had vowed that his Prussians would continue to pursue the fleeing French all night and vengeful Prussians, having had the black flag of 'no quarter' raised against them two days before at Ligny, now were chasing down the enemy and refusing to accept any attempt at their surrender. The British and their other allies, however, were too exhausted after eleven hours of fighting to give chase and most had simply settled into their bivouacs upon the French positions.

From the plateau of Mont Sainte-Jean to the heights of Rossommes farm across the valley, the ground was covered with the dead bodies of men and slain horses: the dead choked the ditches around Hougoumont chateau and lay in piles in the courtyard: they covered almost every square yard in the smoking grass beneath the shattered trees in the orchard of La Haye-Sante farm and lay in sprawled heaps under the walls. Where the Allied regiments had stood and died in their double ranks all along the ridge, they lay in neat lines, like rows of wheat cut down by the reapers' sickle: and where the squares had faced the late desperate onslaught of the massed enemy cavalry, their prone forms lay still in their formations all across the churned ground. Indeed, so great had been the slaughter on both sides that it would take seven days to bury all the dead.

Worst of all for the new and young recruits was that over the whole field of battle, which stretched no more than three miles east to west and two miles north to south, a continuous moan arose from the thousands of wounded still lying there. The younger recruits, who had never seen or heard the like of it before, went white at the sound: the old warriors, who had witnessed it on other fields, simply closed their ears, ate what food they had, drank what rum they could find and went to sleep.

As a precaution against the number of desperate and lost French soldiers still wandering about the countryside, the battalion had set up two guard pickets, one forward of their bivouac on the road and one to the rear. Jem, as a sergeant, Will Ponder and the three other survivors of his platoon, Padraig Cannon, George Herron and Billy Pike, were detailed to the rear picket: they agreed that Will Ponder and Billy Pike would take the first watch for three hours, while Jem, Padraig Cannon and George Herron snatched some sleep.

The fact that some of their own comrades had taken the chance to slip away from the bivouac to go looting was evident from the sound of splintering wood and excited English voices nearby. They were rifling through one of the many carriages overturned in the ditch in the hope of finding a pouch of gold or diamonds, or both, hidden there: for, it was rumoured that French officers who rode in the finer carriages carried boxes of such treasure as *necessaires*. Normally, of course, an officer would have stopped them from leaving the bivouac area, but the battalion had lost four officers and sixty-one other ranks killed and wounded that day and, after so gruelling a battle, the surviving officers were too exhausted to care what their men did so long as they answered muster in the morning. They, like their men, were at that moment either sleeping the sleep of the exhausted in the hope that it would help to dispel the horrors of the day or searching for food and drink themselves.

It was sometime after three o'clock as Jem and the two Irishmen stood the second watch, peering out in the dim, smoke-curtained moonlight at the wreckage of carriages, overturned guns and caissons at the sides of the road and the still visible forms of the hundreds of dead horses and several thousands of men heaped about the field, that Jem suddenly saw the figure of a woman in a thin blue silk dress, with a light shawl pulled over her shoulders, moving quietly amongst the grotesque dead not forty yards from him. Every now and again, she would stoop to look at the face of a fallen soldier, then move on down the hill towards them.

All during the watch, unnervingly out in the darkness, Jem and the others on the picket had been startled by sudden piercing shrieks, always to be followed by the sounds of low moaning and muted sobbing. Scores of women, who two days before had waved a tearful goodbye to their soldier husbands in the Place Royale in Brussels, were beginning to arrive on the field of battle to search by the light of lanterns amongst the clusters and lines of corpses for their menfolk, either to bandage their wounds, if by some good fortune they found them still alive, or to bid a sorrowful farewell to their lifeless corpses.

Other shadowy figures were searching, too, but for different reasons: Germans, Netherlanders and Prussians as well as British soldiers and Walloon peasants had seized the opportunity afforded by night to creep from one scene of carnage to the next, stopping every now and again to turn over a corpse before rifling its pockets and pack. Those who were wounded and unable to move, but who lived to tell the tale, say they feared the Walloon women the most: for, in order to take his purse, they saw some slit the throat of a wounded man as calmly as if they were gutting a rabbit before skinning it: and some were not averse even to cutting the fingers off a living man, badly wounded and unable to help himself, just to steal his wedding ring.

Since the woman was not touching any of the dead, but was merely peering into their faces, it was immediately clear to Jem that she was not a looter, a fact borne out by a procession of three small girls who following silently behind her, pausing when she paused, moving when she moved, none above the age of six or seven. It was evident, too, every time the woman stooped and the way she stood up, one hand on her back, that she was pregnant by several months.

On seeing a British sergeant and two privates standing by the roadside, leaning on their muskets and smoking their 'clays,' the woman crossed to them.

'What regiment are you?' she asked as blithely as if she were meeting them on a country road in England and there was no carnage of battle all around her. Behind her, the three children saw the silhouettes of the three soldiers outlined against the lighter sky and the glint of moonlight on their bayonets and quickly closed up to their mother, clutching at her gown. By the manner of her speech and her slightly imperious demeanour, it was also clear to Jem and the others that she could only be an officer's wife: and that, as she was in her mid-thirties, she most probably was at the very least the wife of a lieutenant or a captain.

'The Forty-Fourth, ma'am,' replied Jem, coming to attention and giving a smart salute, since the question was addressed to him. 'The Fighting Fours. We are bivouacked just ahead to the left of the road.'

'I have come from Brussels. I am looking for my husband,' said the woman, as though it were the most expected thing in the world to be doing at the scene of a great battle. 'He is a captain in the Seventy-Third of Foot, Captain Charles Sloane. I have been told that he was wounded two days ago, but that he may have remained with his regiment. Do you know where the Second, Seventy-Third are?'

All Jem knew of the 73rd of Foot was that they were called Macleod's Highlanders by some, but did not wear tartan and had green facings on their uniform. 'They were with us two days ago at the Quatre-Bras cross-roads,' was all he could tell her, for he had seen them on the march back: but where they had been that day or where they were bivouacked at that moment neither he nor either of his companions knew.

As it happened that day, the 73rd had lost six officers and two hundred and twenty-five men killed and wounded, in addition to their losses of fifty-three killed and wounded at Quatre-Bras. The battalion's casualties, in fact, were the second severest suffered by a line infantry regiment, after the 27th Inniskillings, who had lost four hundred and fifty of seven hundred or more in holding their square and Wellington's line. During the fighting on the ridge, the 73rd had been charged eleven times by French cavalry and had remained in square without breaking and were still fighting right at the finish, helping to drive back Napoleon's until-then invincible Old Guard.

As the disappointment, almost resignation, fell across the woman's face, Jem suddenly remembered: 'If your husband was wounded in the fight at Quatre-Bras, ma'am, he may well be back in Brussels by now. Some of the wounded from two days ago were put on carts only this morning, along with some of ours, before the battle began, several officers among them. There were most likely Seventy-Thirds from two days ago with them, I expect. They were to be taken back to Brussels so they would be out of the way of today's fighting. It is possible, ma'am, that the captain is in a hospital in Brussels right this minute.'

'Thank you, sergeant,' said the woman, thankful that she had met a courteous soldier. Then, pulling the light shawl more closely over her shoulders, she called to the three children: 'Come, girls, we have a long way to walk back to Brussels. The English sergeant says your father may well be there.'

'Would it not be better to wait till daylight, ma'am?' Jem interjected quickly. 'It's eight or nine miles to Brussels. The roads are muddy and choked with wagons all the way through the forest, I hear, and there are dead everywhere.' He was thinking more of the children shivering beside her and the long tramp they would have to make back to the capital, passing again the scenes of carnage they had already walked through: better, surely, to wait till daylight before setting out. 'It would be safer, ma'am. There are deserters out there and there are still Frenchies about as well.'

'If my husband is there, I must get back to him. I must find my husband,' the woman said calmly and firmly: and without further ado, she turned on her heel and went back up the slope, followed by the children.

For a few moments Jem watched her go: as she picked her way around the overturned guns and carriages, a sense of shame came over him: someone, he felt, should at least escort her and the children part of the way back, at least till they were clear of the field as a precaution against whoever might be out there.

'We can't let her and the little ones go like that,' Jem said to Padraig Cannon alongside him. 'She's an officer's wife. It's too dangerous out there for a woman of her kind to be walking about, with three little kiddies in tow. One of us ought to escort her some of the way back, at least as far as the village.'

Padraig Cannon eyed Jem suspiciously, a sly smile on his lips: neither he nor his countryman were overly concerned for an English officer's wife. 'You go if you want to,' Padraig said with a shrug. 'Me, I'm staying here. If an officer comes, I'll say you've gone off for a piddle or something.'

He said it with a sniff of disdain: clearly, he suspected a ruse in Jem's sudden altruism, thinking it more likely he was intent upon going on a scavenging hunt of his own rather than acting as an escort for an officer's wife and her three brats.

'On your head be it, Jem,' declared George Herron with a shrug, not wanting to question his sergeant's motives. 'So long as you're back in time for muster, no one will know the difference.'

As Jem slung his musket and went out into the darkness, the burly Padraig Cannon shouted after him: 'Watch out for that Walloon scum! They'll slit your throat as soon as look at you and there are plenty of them about! We ought to shoot the lot of them!'

Jem quickly caught up with the woman and made his request. 'With respect, ma'am, it ain't safe for you and your young kiddies to be walking alone. There are some queer characters about here tonight – Prussians and Dutch and Belgians and Germans and such. If you would allow me, I'd be happy to walk you and your kiddies at least a couple of miles or so till we are well clear of all this – for your kiddies' sake.'

'My kiddies? Oh, you mean my children! Oh, how quaint! My kiddies!' she answered with a slight smile. 'Yes, you may accompany me, sergeant. I should be grateful for your company. Thank you, you are most kind.'

His fears were borne out in a matter of half a minute. As they negotiated their way up the slope past several overturned gun carriages and other wagons and dead horses by the La Haye-Sante farm, three dark figures suddenly rose up in front of them: they were black-uniformed Prussians and they had just dispatched a groaning Frenchman left behind by his comrades near a sandpit. One of them, a thin, blond youth with bulging eyes, holding a knife, was pocketing a watch, while the other two were sharing out some coins.

Jem, as it happened, was momentarily obscured behind an overturned gun carriage and so was not visible to them: all they saw was a woman and three children, and a youngish woman at that, with a bag, which must contain something, and alone except for the three *kinder*, easy pickings on any dark night and all the more so on a battlefield with so much debris and wreckage lying everywhere and so many shrieks from others to drown any she might make. No one would know whether she was being attacked and robbed or had just found her dead husband. First, though, they had to scare off the *kinder*.

The thin, blond Prussian with the bulging eyes suddenly jumped forwards towards them, raised his arms in a crooked fashion and let out a frightening ogrish roar. Jem had already seen the three girls turn and look round at him and now saw the alarm upon their faces as they let out shrieks and darted behind their mother. For one on the alert for just such a happening, just hearing the excited guttural voices of the Prussians had been enough of a warning for Jem. The next thing the looter with the bulging eyes saw was the barrel of a Brown Bess levelled straight at his face from the shoulder of a British infantryman not a dozen feet from him with a gleaming bayonet attached and a determined look on his face.

'Away with ye, you damned Prussian scum!' Jem shouted, moving forward to position himself in front of the captain's wife and children. 'Away with ye or I'll send you and your friends to kingdom come!'

As he said it, he took another stride foward: the resolve of an experienced British soldier was too much for a half-trained militiaman drawn from the Konisberg gutters and he took several paces back, fear showing on his face.

'Kamerad! Friend! Friend!' cried one of the Prussians behind him, raising one hand to signal that he and his comrades intended nothing more than a jape to scare the children, when clearly they had intended something far worse.

'Friend, Englander, friend,' the youth with the bulging eyes repeated, backing away even further, his hands also raised in surrender. A curt, guttural command from one of the men behind and, in an instant, the three black-uniformed Prussians had melted away into the darkness, though a sudden explosion of laughter as they disappeared convinced Jem that he had been right in his assessment of what they had intended.

'I had better stay with you till we are well clear of all this and you are safe among our own, ma'am,' Jem told the captain's wife, which he did, escorting her and the three girls well beyond the cross-roads and even carrying the youngest child, who was almost asleep on her feet, part of the way.

The road leading through the village of Waterloo itself and through the forest was jammed with wagons and carriages which had been abandoned by their civilian drivers two days before in the rush to escape from the French. In many instances, they had simply cut their animals loose and ridden off, leaving their vehicles to block the way. Now, trying to weave through all these were wagons carrying the wounded back to Brussels, where houses and convents, schoolrooms and churches were being hurriedly opened to receive them. Even then, thousands more would have to wait days for attention, some just sitting on the streets till someone went to help them. Many of the walking wounded did not even get that far, dropping by the wayside, while others had just enough strength to crawl into the forest and sit with their backs against a tree, some never to rise again.

As they walked, not unnaturally, the woman asked several questions of Jem: his name, where he had done his soldiering, of the places he had seen and where his home was in England: and when Jem told her it was a small village named Hamwick Dean and he mentioned the names 'Hamwyte' and 'Melchborough,' she seemed particularly interested.

'I know both Hamwyte and Melchborough very well. I have an aunt and uncle who live near Melchborough, at Nadbury Hall,' she said, naming a village five miles or so to the east of the county town. 'I visited Nadbury and Melchborough many times as a girl. I always liked the fact that it was so convenient for travelling up to London and yet is such a lovely town in pleasant countryside and with good shops. Yes, I have always liked Melchborough. I know it well. I have also been many times to Hamwyte, too, We often went to the spa to take the waters there when I was a young girl.'

After being so long away, it heartened Jem just to hear the names of two towns which he knew spoken of so pleasantly by another and it stirred in him the longing to see the old places again.

Jem would willingly have escorted her and the girls the whole way through the forest, which was at least four miles deep: but it was too far for him to go and be back in time for muster. Finally, he set the sleeping child down and her mother gently prodded her awake. By then the carnage of the battlefield was a long way behind them and there seemed to be more English voices in the darkness and decidedly fewer foreign ones. So from that point onwards, Jem reasoned, they should be relatively safe, or as safe as anyone could be with so many dubious figures flitting about. With luck, she should reach the outskirts of Brussels by early morning and, with luck, too, might well be reunited with her husband come evening, if he were still alive and if she could find him amongst the thousands of wounded in the many makeshift hospitals.

'We thank you for your company, sergeant, you have been most kind,' the woman said, offering him a soft, gloved hand. 'We shall be all right from here and you have to get back to your post. I shall remember your kindness and your bravery. The "kiddies" and I will not forget it.' Jem touched her hand as a matter of courtesy and then saluted her smartly. With a final smile, she and the children disappeared into the darkness.

In the morning, the battalion formed-up on the road and marched in column with the rest of the army through Genappes, where the French had been caught in their flight by the Prussians and where, it was said, Napoleon himself had escaped only by jumping from his carriage on one side and leaping upon a horse as a Prussian dragoon tugged open the carriage door on the other side.

As it turned out, the rumour that the battalion's destination was Paris was correct. French resistance collapsed and, on June the twenty-fifth, they entered that city from the plain of St. Denis, their battalion being by then only some five hundred strong, and bivouacked for three weeks on the Champs-Elysees, within range of the batteries on the Butt de Montmartre.

Napoleon abdicated four days later when the Chamber of Deputies refused to support him further. The wreck of his army had by that time retreated over the Loire and he was seeking to escape to America, but, finding no ship, he surrendered himself to the captain of *HMS Bellerophon* off Rochefort, whence he was taken across to England. The *Bellerophon* anchored in Plymouth Sound on July the twenty-sixth and remained there till August the fourth while the hated French emperor's fate was being decided, though that hate did not stop the curiosity of the people of that region, for every evening at six-thirty, when Napoleon took a turn on deck, the townsfolk and people from miles around would row out to get a glimpse of the man who had caused them so much misery.

Jem, and his comrades-in-arms, meanwhile, spent a bleak November camped in the Bois de Boulogne, before finally moving out to Versailles, pleased to be away from the Prussians, who were acting like vandals in destroying or stealing everything they came across.

Then, in January, the battalion marched to the coast at Calais and went into billets while they awaited transhipment to England. One day they were paraded in a hollow square, handed a medal authorised by the Prince Regent and then disbanded after a speech by their colonel. Not that Jem minded: he had done his duty, he had served his King and Country and he had survived: and in his knapsack still were the ten gold coins and a bounty of ten pounds received on disbandment of his battalion.

Some of it was spent carousing in Dover, but then, anxious to have done with the army, he and Will Ponder had said goodbye to their comrades and taken the coach up to London. By chance, walking past the Red Lion at the Aldwych milestone, they had spoken to the wagonman on the 'fly' and had accepted his offer to take them to Hamwyte for nothing other than their company on the road. For them, it was a more practical request: they could sleep en route: the severity of the frost which plagued them and kept them awake for much of the journey was unexpected.

SEVEN

HAMWICK DEAN then was a village of some five hundred and fifty souls and a hundred or so small and mean cottages, tiled and thatched, rickety and tumbledown, spread along both sides of its three principal thoroughfares, which together formed a rough triangle a mile-and-a-half in circumference. Most cottages lined the threequarter-mile length of The Street, the broadest of its ways, which formed the right slope of the triangle, while others lay along the similarly half-mile length of Heath Lane, forming the left side of the triangle, and the rest were spaced along the half-mile Forge Lane, the base of the triangle.

In area, the whole parish comprised no more than eighteen hundred and thirty-four acres, two roods and twenty-three perches, with its northern boundary lying all along the bottom of the wooded northern slope, while eastward, along the ridge-top itself and only a mile or so from the cross-roads guidepost where Jem had paused at the village's edge, the boundary adjoined that of the neighbouring parish of Lower Rackstead, with a hamlet of a mere forty houses at the centre of its eight hundred and seventy-three acres, twelve roods and twenty perches.

To the south, it was bounded by the nine hundred and fifty acres, ten roods and fifteen perches of the parish of Merchant Staplers, also with a hamlet of thirty-seven houses at its centre astride the unturnpiked road which ran from the small market town of Maydun, three-and-half miles to the southwest, all the way to the walled Roman garrison town of Wivencaster, thirteen miles to the east.

On Hamwick Dean's western side, the slow-flowing Langwater stream, which rose several miles to the north of the village amid the uplands to be found in that part of the county, meandered around the parish's edge to form another boundary, before wending its way to meet the River Melch amid the salt marsh at Tidwolton, where the two flowed as one under the hump of Maydun hill before emptying into the long, bleak, tidal estuary of the Langwater.

The village itself lay at the western end of the flat-topped ridge, which ran east to west for three or so miles amid a gently undulating landscape: on its northern and western slopes, the ridge was thickly wooded and fell away too steeply to be ploughed: but to the south the fall of the land was altogether more gradual and the country more open and arable.

The Wayfarers' Inn, where Jem was lodged, was a Sixteenth Century, low-ceilinged, timber and plaster structure and stood near to the northern end of The Street. At the other end, where five routes converged – or diverged, depending upon which way the traveller was heading – was the Carpenters' Arms, the village's second ale house, a small, ill-ventilated, dirt-floored place and really no more than a beerhouse comprising two cottages opened into one, with half serving as the ale house and other part as the living quarters of the landlord and his wife and their brood of seven children.

From its junction with Forge Lane, Heath Lane, forming the left side of the triangle, became Parsonage Lane, continuing on past the grey, flintstone St. Bartholomew's Church, newly built only three decades before to replace the ancient and by then derelict St. Peter's chapel of ease, which, being sited a mile out of the village proper down a long and narrow winding lane at the foot of the ridge, was considered too small and too inconvenient for the villagers to attend it easily. In truth, the old chapel had been built for the convenience of a Fourteenth Century Bishop of Melchborough and his retainers when staying in a timber-framed, moated manor house nearby rather than for the consideration of the serfs who laboured in the fields which the manor then owned. Now, unwanted and unused, windowless and open to all weathers, weeds and thistles sprouted on the old chapel's path and gorse and bramble straggled amid its gravestones, while bats and birds flew about its rafters.

The hundred-acre manor estate, as it then was, had belonged to the Church since Saxon times and was recorded as such in the Domesday Survey of 1086: it was imparked by one of the succeeding bishops in the Fourteenth Century and a clay wall built around it. In fact, it was so favoured as a retreat by that one bishop that he spent all his Christmases there, well away from the duties of the cathedral church in the county town.

Various subsequent bishops continued to reside there over the next century or so till the turmoil and upheaval during the reigns of the Tudors, both Catholic and Protestant, brought about a change in the fortunes of so many clergy, for the worse in the case of the then Bishop of Melchborough, who favoured the one religion over the other, chose wrongly for his time and was martyred at the stake at Spitalfields. Thereafter, the manor lay abandoned till bought by the first of the ten Darcy-Harpriggs to reside there, who purchased it solely to establish himself as the new lord of the manor and squire of the village, with all the 'appurtenances' or rights of the property attached.

Hamwick Hall, as the old manor house came to be called, one of only five large and fine-standing houses within the environs of the parish, was situated on the lower part of a gently falling slope, overlooking the winding, willow-lined Langwater stream and the open country to the west. It lay more than two miles from the village proper and thus stood in isolated splendour in the extreme southwestern corner of the parish, screened from the gaze of the common villagers at work in the open-fields which lay between by the twelve acres of oak, ash, alder, beech, birch and thickets of thorn which made up the shadowy darkness of Likely wood.

When the manor house was first built for the bishops, brickmaking was a forgotten art in England, so it was constructed in the manner of the time, stout oak framing infilled with wattle and daub. Then, it had consisted of a single large medieval hall, open to the roof, with a central hearth, plastered and whitewashed inside, divided into two parts, one for the humans and the other for the animals and fowls. At one end had stood a kitchen, larder and buttery and at the other an outside wooden staircase leading up to a 'solar' or parlour living quarters above.

Over time, however, additions and modifications by the Darcy-Harpriggs had changed the old manor: three gables had been added along its south-facing frontage in one century, along with a central timbered entrance porch in another, while, internally, the great vaulted hall had been divided into two floors, each further divided, below into a parlour, dining room and study, but with the kitchen, larder and buttery still in place, and above into a number of bedrooms. The earth-floor had been boarded over in dark elm and carpeted by Middle Eastern rugs and the rooms panelled in oak and hung with paintings: and, whereas once the open hearth had served to heat the whole hall, now a large open stone fireplace, resting on columns and bearing the Darcy-Harprigg arms, had been set at one end to warm the parlour and the master bedroom above. In addition, a further stack of chimneys had been added on the north side to heat the other bedrooms, the whole number now reached by an internal cage newel staircase, the doorway to the old outside stairs having been blocked long before and the timbered staircase itself burnt in the great hearth.

A three-sided moat, some twenty or so feet wide, fed by a nearby spring, still enclosed the Hall on three sides, while within its boundary the old outbuildings for the farm servants, the chambers for the bailiff and the grooms and the old bakehouse had over the years become a stable, a dairy and a cattle byre: only the granary and the dovecote had remained in use, the latter lastly housing pigeons, the droppings of which had been spread annually over the Hall's garden and vegetable plot.

Sadly, at the time of Jem's return, the last of the Darcy-Harpriggs had died seven years previously and the old hall lay as if abandoned once more, its windows all shuttered, its doors padlocked, its furniture sheeted over against settling dust: bats flew about the courtyard, owls hooted in the rafters of the barn, swallows' nests accumulated under the eaves of the other outbuildings and thick weed clogged the moat.

During the early years of the war, cattle drovers from the Welsh marches used to bring their cattle all the way across England and herd them into the park and pay the Old Squire a handsome sum for doing so, fattening them there after their long trail over bad roads before driving them all filled out and healthy the thirty-eight miles to the London markets. Now the parkland was overgrown with weeds and thorn bushes: and, though a lawyer living in the village, acting as the land agent for the property while the affairs of the estate were settled by the slow-grinding progress of chancery, paid for two of its meadows to be mown for hay once or twice a year, the greater part of it, comprising some two hundred acres by then, was a forlorn sight, a far cry from when in the middle of the previous century, with the family's prosperity at its height and rich returns from his holdings in two slave-worked sugar plantations in the West Indies, the eighth of that line of lords of the manor, Sir Clarence Darcy-Harprigg, had, as a thank you to God for it all, bequeathed a sum of four thousand pounds in his will for the building of a larger and finer flintstone church just threequarters of a mile from the village's centre.

As is the way of such things, it was started, abandoned for a number of years, restarted and finally completed and consecrated just in time for the outbreak of the war. Not unexpectedly, being the religious focal point of a rural community, it was consecrated to Saint Bartholomew as the son of the furrows, with a sturdy stone tower and octagonal wooden spire atop soaring a hundred and twenty feet from the level to its weathervane, fine arched windows fitted with bright stained glass, a solid stone porch and a nave large enough, it was jested in the Wayfarers', to hold the whole parish and half of those from the neighbouring Merchant Staplers if they all stood and crammed themselves in together.

Unsurprisingly, too, the new church, surrounded by lofty elms and horse chestnuts, was built on spare Church land immediately alongside the old parsonage so that the incumbent rector or parson did not have to walk too far through rain and other inclement weather to be about his daily business. The red-and-blue-brick Jacobean mansion of a dozen bedrooms and eight tall chimneys which was his home had been built by the fifth of the Darcy-Harpriggs for an incumbent brother, who held the ecclesiastical benefice of Hamwick Dean during the last years of the unfortunate Stuarts. The locals deferentially referred to it as 'the Big House,' for it bespoke the rector's status as one who demanded and expected the respect and obedience of his flock.

It stood at a sharp right-angle bend of the lane and was approached by a short driveway leading up to a high-arched porch and solid oak door: from its place on the ridge, it commanded sweeping and pleasing views over the whole of the countryside, all the way to the distant blur of Maydun hill. On three sides, huge mullioned windows looked out over flowerbeds and lawn which a man and a boy from the village dutifully scythed once a month, kept its herbaceous borders straight, flowering and weeded in the spring and summer, kept the topiary trimmed and the half-acre of orchard ever fruitful, for the incumbent rector was a wealthy man and, as well as a part-time gardener and his boy, he employed a live-in parlour maid and a live-in cook, as well as from the village a live-out maid-of-all-work and cook's help and a milkmaid on the Glebe farm, who also worked in its buttery.

Along with the Hamwick Hall estate's own private Likely wood, nine other substantial areas of woodland, lay at varying distances around the village, remnants of the ancient greenwood which once stretched the length and breadth of Old England, from the Channel shores to the very slopes of the Pennine hills. The largest, Chantrey wood, spread itself across fifty or more acres just north of the cross-roads on the northern side of the long hill leading down to Hamwyte. Others, with local-given names such as Mope and Grove and Sparkey, lay to the west on the steep ridge slope, with two further woods, Milepole and Captain's, close by the southern boundary and the smaller Spickett's and Mountain Grove completing the ring up to the top of ridge again, where the last, Shut Heath wood, lay in the northeast part, divided from Chantrey on the circle only by a narrow drovers' way leading to Lower Rackstead and the larger Higher Rackstead, lost amid a maze of back lanes.

On the edge of the village, upon another smaller triangle of land just south of Forge Lane, formed by the intersecting of three back lanes, stood two adjoining low cottages converted into a 'Dame School' by a woman who had been in service as a governess elsewhere in the county in her younger years before marrying and settling in the village. For a modest fee, Old Mother Rae, as the pupils called her, taught the rudiments of the 'three Rs' to those village children whose parents could afford the cost of sixpence a week: and there were not many of them, no more than a dozen in all at any one time of the near two hundred children in the village. They began their lessons at six in the morning, with an hour's break at eight for breakfast, before continuing till one o'clock: often learning to write was simply a matter of copying from Aesop's Fables or from a letters book: those making the fewest errors received praise and the others a caution to do better or receive a rap across their knuckles with a ruler.

The pupils remained at the school till their eleventh birthdays, if able: then boys were deemed fit to begin work on the land and girls either went into service in a big house in another village or town somewhere or stayed at home to help their mothers, often just to raise their younger siblings. Those who could not afford the fee for the Dame School, mainly because their parents had neither regular employ nor money to 'waste on learning,' were taught to read and to write and to count as best they could at a Sunday school held in St. Bartholomew's, taken by one of the parish's two young curates, the Reverend William Waters, who would walk over from Merchant Staplers, where he performed the pastoral duties at the small St. John's church. The lessons were always held in the afternoon from two o'clock till an hour before evensong, the children scratching their letters and numbers on small sand trays with wood styluses: those who went, that is, for not all did. Those who did go at least learned to write in a rudimentary fashion, some to read better than others and some to count well enough to multiply and divide as well as to add and subtract and some by the time they left even managing fractions and long division.

The majority of people in that Hundred, indeed that county and that region then, were, of course, village-dwellers and owed their livelihood to the lan. Of the two hundred or so of Hamwick Dean's men and older youths who worked the land, more than sixty did so as husbandmen, renting from a single furlong to five or six acres, and four even as 'small farmers' in their own right, working half-yardlands of nineteen acres apiece. The greater number of the remainder were employed either as landless day-labourers on five larger farms around the village, occasionally by the husbandmen and the four small farmers, or were in trade some way for themselves or helpers to one of the artisans or apprenticed to one.

For instance, two worked at the blacksmith's forge to shoe the numerous plough horses, wagoners' horses and ponies for the traps which abounded amongst the district's better-off. As well, the village boasted a full-time saddle and harnessmaker with a helper, a basketmaker with a helper, a corn miller with two helpers, a wheelwright, a cordwainer and a bricklayer, each with an apprentice, in two cases their sons, two publicans at the Wayfarers' Inn and the Carpenters' Arms, a rakemaker also with two sons helping, a grocer with two sons helping, likewise two butchers and two bakers with assistants, and a part-time dog-whipper, that is, one who ensured that dogs did not harry the animals on the common.

But, as idyllic a picture as the mind's eye might conjure of a rural community from this, the truth was that, in the two years since the first peace of 1814, the great prosperity of the war years had ended abruptly and the whole country had fallen suddenly into a state of extreme depression.

When, in November, 1806, the megalomaniac emperor across the Channel had issued his Berlin Decree by which all Continental ports would be closed to British ships or others trading with Britain, the country had to produce more food or starve: thus, agriculture, which hitherto had provided only a livelihood for rural communities but without any fortunes attached, became a great capitalist venture. The price of everything rose as a period of great prosperity flourished throughout the land: and, as the price of corn soared, so men had invested wildly in land upon which to grow it, some taking out exorbitant mortgages to rent that land, not caring so much about the fertility of it in the long term so long as they could grow corn upon it in the short term and make a profit from it. Fortunes were amassed by the landowners who leased that land to the farmers and by the tithe-owners, both clergy and impropriator, who collected from it. The farmers, too, benefited and many grew wealthy enough themselves to be able to extend their lands, buy their wives and their daughters and themselves fine clothes, send their sons to fine schools, improve their houses, add lawns with peacocks strutting upon them, even pull down old farmhouses in some cases and build finer ones in their places or rebuild rickety barns and derelict stables and tumbledown milking sheds.

But, at the war's end, a great demobilisation of the armies and navies of England had taken place, as Jem himself had found with the abrupt disbandment of his battalion at Calais. A quarter of a million able and willing men were released from the King's service on to the labour market without the work to occupy them and for most little prospect of any. In that short period, the agricultural industry of England passed suddenly from prosperity to deep depression: and those farmers who had borrowed heavily during the bounty years suddenly found themselves struggling, unable to pay rents which had increased five-fold in some cases.

In some places, farms were being thrown up, notices to quit were pouring in upon those where debts could not be met and large numbers of tenants were simply absconding, leaving large tracts of land untenanted and uncultivated. In consequence, agriculture was stagnating: improvements were at a standstill, livestock was being reduced to a minimum, lime-kilns ceased to burn, less manure was being used on the land and the hiring of labour had been drastically curtailed by surviving farmers to hold down their own costs. In this, the tradesmen, the innkeepers and the shopkeepers of the country towns and villages also suffered heavily through loss of custom: blacksmiths, wheelwrights, collarmakers, harnessmakers, rakemakers and carpenters all now found work hard to come by. Many large and middling farmers were as destitute as the labourers they had once employed and were themselves applicants for the pauper allowance which had been sharply reduced by the fall in the number of payers: those farmers, instead of growing wheat and barley and potatoes to feed the nation and paying their poor rate taxes, now passed their days chipping stones on parish road-building projects simply to obtain the very relief they had once helped to fund.

EIGHT

IT WAS to this England that Jem Stebbings had returned with his plan: for all during his years of service in the heat and dust of Spain, toiling up hills and across dusty plains, marching through driving spring and autumn rains or encamped in freezing snow-bound winter quarters, he had dreamed of returning to the milder climes of England and becoming one of the husbandmen of Hamwick Dean, that is, one who cultivated strips of land under the old system of common landholding which then still prevailed there, as it had since medieval times and as it did still in a hundred other places in that county alone and in a thousand places in other counties throughout the land.

The whole of the gently-falling, south-facing slope of the ridge upon which Hamwick Dean stood was then divided into three great common 'open-fields' for arable farming, running in a wide sweep west to east below the village, each, in turn, divided into long strips. The largest of the arable land, lying to the west, was the hundred and ten-acre First Field, with four hundred and forty strips in total, and was the most fertile: adjoining it directly to the south of the village was the narrower sixty-seven-acre Long Field, with some two hundred and sixty-eight strips, while the Third Field, which comprised fifty-seven acres of a more tenacious loamy soil and so was of a lesser arable worth, had only two hundred and twenty-eight strips and lay to the southeast.

In turn, all three of the great fields were themselves sub-divided into three 'lesser fields,' each possessing a name of its own peculiar to the history or geography of it, such as 'Ash Grove field' forming the top third of First Field, so named because a clump of those trees had once grown at its edge and containing two hundred and thirty of the open-field's total strips. Below that, parallel to the road which ran alongside the boundary wall of the manor estate, lay the hundred and twenty strips of 'Barrow' field, called so because the hump of an ancient tumuli was still visible and high enough to deter any attempt to plough over it: and, thirdly, to the east of Barrow lay the ninety strips of 'Thornbush' field, named from a thicket of blackthorn which had been cleared from it. Each of the three divisions lay adjacent to the next and required no hedge or fence to divide them, just one to surround the whole and separate it from the next great open-field, Long Field, named so simply because its two hundred and sixty-eight strips in total stretched all the way from the village's edge down to Milepole wood lying close to the parish's southern boundary along the Maydun-to-Wivencaster road. This was also sub-divided into 'Snook's' field, named after a former tenant of that part's hundred and thirty-eight strips, the smaller 'Badger's Hole' field of sixty strips with its abandoned set, and 'Partridge' field of seventy strips, which took its name from the partridges which nested there. Adjacent, to the east, lay the two hundred and twenty-eight strips of the irregular-shaped Third Field spreading across both sides of a well-used cattle driftway, with a hundred and eight strips on the northern 'Reeve's Croft,' called because a reeve had once owned it, fifty-five below it on 'Farthing' field, which related to a former tenant's rental, and sixty-five on 'Gravel Pit' field, where the stones and shingle for the road-mending were quarried from a pit at its northern edge.

Generally, each of the strips was a furlong in length and a perch wide, that is, two hundred and twenty yards (or forty perches) from headland to headland, and sixteen-and-a-half feet or five-and-a-half yards (one perch) in width. The medieval perch was derived via the French from the Latin *'pertica'* for a long staff or measuring rod and was the standard land measurement then, though the old English unit of measurement, the rood, equalling forty square 'rods' or 'poles' of the old way of measuring, which translated to a quarter-acre, was also used. Thus, four strips of ridge-and-furrow each a furlong or forty perches long and a perch wide, comprising a rood or quarter acre in area, made up one acre, similarly defined as an area four statute perches wide by forty perches long – hence the importance of the perch: the acre, of course, was the accepted area of land which one ox team could plough in a day.

Some men rented a few of the arable strips, while others farmed many, scattered almost arbitrarily over the fields, it seemed, for it was the nature of the enterprise to divide up the field and give each man a plot at different points so that one man did not get all the best soil and it was shared fairly amongst them all. Thus, a man with eight acres might have three acres of the best soil scattered, say, throughout the Ash Grove, Thornbush and Barrow divisions in First Field, two acres of the medium-growing soil in the three divisions of Long Field and three acres, say, of the poorer soil in Third Field, all as separate strips, neither adjoining nor abutting. In a single lesser field like Ash

Grove, Barrow or Thornbush, there might well be thirty or forty men farming strips amounting to an acre or two down to a mere fifteen perches and the holding of each so divided as to lie in ten or twenty or thirty different places so that to work his land, excluding those which lay fallow for that year, a man might have to trudge past a dozen or two-dozen strips belonging to his neighbours to reach another of his own, sometimes even having to go from one large field to another before he could begin his work. Nor were all strips of a uniform shape or length: some were shorter and irregular in shape, half-strips where the furlong had been divided or where boggy ground and poor drainage precluded full cultivation and thus the husbandman farmed what he could of it. Each strip was separated from those lying parallel to it by either a grass balk or a ploughed furrow, which helped with the drainage, the balk also providing a footpath by which one husbandman might approach his land without crossing that of another.

In some villages, it was the custom for the strips scattered across the open-fields to be redistributed every year by ballot so that, if a man received infertile land or stony land or poor land one year, he might receive better land the following year. In Hamwick Dean, however, as well as the two hamlets, by complacency and by agreement amongst themselves, men held and cultivated the same strips year after year so that each man knew the lie of his own land and the 'goodness' of it and so was more inclined to manure it and cultivate it.

By agreement, all strips were cultivated on a uniform system: each year, one of the three lesser fields of each great open-field was left fallow, while the other two lesser fields of the same open-field were cultivated, one planted with a winter grain of wheat or rye, say, another planted with a spring crop of oats or barley and sometimes with beans or peas or white turnips. Thus, by leaving one of the lesser fields fallow, one-third of the arable of the open-fields was always being allowed to recover its 'goodness' in the time-honoured fashion of the countryside. For example, in one year, Ash Grove on First Field would remain unploughed after a corn harvest, Thornbush fallow the next year after its corn crop had been gathered-in and Barrow unsown after its barley crop, say, in the third year and so on similarly across each part of the three great open-fields. After the grain harvesting was finished, those fields were opened to pasturage for cattle, for the corn stubble was always left a foot high so that cattle could be grazed upon it.

Of the two-hundred and thirty-four acres of arable land making up Hamwick Dean's three open-fields, the Church, through the succeeding Bishops of Melchborough, owned ninety spread throughout the three, plus substantial acreages of the same in Lower Rackstead and Merchant Staplers. A further sixty or so of Hamwick Dean's arable acres lay with the lords of the manor still, even though no one had as yet succeeded to that vacant title, while the dean and chapter of Christ Church College at Oxford University and their lessees possessed upwards of thirty of the village's arable acres, plus a further forty in total in the two hamlets. Except for a very few husbandmen who actually owned the strips they cultivated – no more than a dozen – the rest of the arable land in all three places was owned by a dozen other persons who lived in other places, one a dowager duchess, who held a good third of what was farmed in Lower Rackstead alone, while other acreages were held by various gentlemen of London, merchants, gentry and the like, none of whom had ever set foot in either the village or the two hamlets in all the years of their birth, neither they nor their antecendents. Yet they drew annual rent from their holdings and paid their tithes to the impropriator, the lord of the manor, whoever he might eventually be, and to the rector as the receiver of the great tithes.

Hamwick Dean's common meadowland or pasturage, comprising several hundred acres also, lay mostly to the east and south of the village, extending right to the boundary with both Lower Rackstead and Merchant Staplers, and was so intermingled with the common pasturage of those parishes that few knew exactly where the true boundaries lay or cared so long as they were recorded on maps and leases somewhere, if not in men's minds. Like the arable open-fields, the common pasturage was also divided up, pegged out and distributed amongst the husbandmen and other villagers who had common rights. And so that no one man ever held the best of the grass-growing area and, therefore, the best of the hay, the various hurdle-enclosed plots were still balloted for each year under the medieval system. Great swathes of it were also owned by the Church, the lord of the manor, the Oxford dean and scholars and others: they, too, were thrown open as pasture for cows of the village's common herd after the hay had been mown and harvested.

The rougher common wasteland, which was owned solely by whomever was the lord of the manor, was used as common pasture all year round: it lay mostly to the northwest of the village, where the ground sloped more steeply down towards the Langwater stream and so was boggy and liable to flood. A further area of waste also lay towards the boundary with Merchant Staplers, in part woodland, in part heathland, much of it covered in furze, gorse, bramble and anthills, a legacy of the fact that most of the land rising up from the north bank of the Langwater estuary still contained an excessive spread of flints, for it was said the northern shoreline was the exact point at which twenty thousand years before the Ice Age cliffs had ended their creep southwards: and when, after a further ten thousand years, they had eventually retreated, they left behind all the flints and pebbles and stones collected in that southwards push, or so it seemed to the local inhabitants.

Commoners had six rights over the use of the common waste – pasture, for the grazing of livestock such as cattle, sheep and horses: pannage, for the grazing and rooting of pigs: estovers, the right to take bracken for bedding and fodder and brushwood, furze and gorse for fuel: turbary, the right to take peat for fuel: piscary, the right to the fish in the streams and ponds: and soil, the right to take sand, stone and gravel.

Though in total the arable, pasture and waste of Hamwick Dean encompassed twelve hundred and three acres in total, with a further four hundred and sixty-one acres of the same at Lower Rackstead and four hundred and twenty-eight acres at Merchant Staplers, none of the husbandmen and small farmers in any of the three parishes actually owned the land which they cultivated. The woods, too, which encircled the periphery of the parish, were also privately owned by a number of individuals who lived in other places and extracted their rents from their use for pannage and wood collecting.

Jem knew that he would have to begin as a husbandman in a small way, renting perhaps a half-dozen strips and ploughing and seeding the ground himself. In time, he hoped that he might be able to rent enough strips which adjoined or abutted each other so as to be able to remove the balks in between and consolidate them into a single parcel of several acres as some men did, perhaps as much as a half-yardland or even a full yardland, and that way become a 'small farmer' as well, with all the status that would bring, as opposed to being a mere subsistence husbandman.

Not unnaturally, he also nurtured a further hope that, in time, too, he might find himself a wife for company and cooking: like most men he had no conception who that might be and neither did he dwell upon the thought over much: it was just a wish at the back of his mind that would put the seal on his return and future life. If needs be, she could be a spinster left on the shelf by others or a widow seeking a second marriage perhaps, for he did not expect the eighteen-year-old and nineteen-year-old girls still unmarried, if there were any, would want to take up with a man nearing thirty with a crooked arm and a limp. A woman approaching his own age, maybe, or perhaps one a little older, in her mid-thirties, who would not be too fussy about having a man with such wounds of battle restricting his movements, was, he reasoned, probably the best for which he could hope. Also, if she were found in time and if she were still able to conceive, perhaps he might sire himself a son, or even several sons: for he never doubted his own ability in that field: but first he must become a husbandman and perhaps in time the rest would follow.

NINE

DURING THE WAR years, Hamwick Dean's hundred or so day-labourers, men, 'threequarter men' and 'half-men,' had relied mostly upon three large farms to provide them with regular employment at any one time of the year, and women, too, at harvest time. The largest of these was Goat Lodge, a parcel of a hundred and fifty-two acres, or four yardlands, lying directly to the east of the common meadowland down a lane of the same name, close to the boundary with Lower Rackstead. Next was Smallponds, with three-and-a-half yardlands or a hundred and thirty-three enclosed acres, situated a mile or so to the southeast of the village towards Merchant Staplers, and third was Milepole, comprising three yardlands or a hundred and fourteen enclosed acres, located some two miles from the village along the Maydun-to-Wivencaster road.

Though the tenants of these farms had grown wealthy during the bounty years and had taken up yet more land, they had done so prudently due to their own circumstances and so none had incurred the great debts which had brought despair and ruin to so many other avaricious farmers in other places: but, as it happened, it was upon these three farms that the greatest changes had occurred in the years that Jem had been away.

When the wars against the French had begun with the First Coalition twenty-two years before, the old masters of the three farms – Isaac Peakman at Goat Lodge, Samuel Howie on Smallponds and Ezekiel Godwin at Milepole – had still been prepared to pull on a smock and walk as many miles behind a plough and a harrow as the labourers they hired and would think it nothing to pass the day alongside their men, weeding during the same spring rains, harvesting in the same heat of the August sun and lifting turnips standing in the same November fogs and frosts. They were kindly men, of the old school of masters, affable and considerate to their labourers and always spoken well of in the Wayfarers' Inn and the Carpenters' Arms, as far as any man will speak well of an employer. They were men, too, who would never have thought to reduce a man's wages to save a little money, but would always see to it that he was paid his worth and that he had enough to provide for himself and his family: for, they reasoned, what good was it if a man were half-starved since a half-starved and weakling man did not work as well as a healthy one with a full belly and contentment in his heart? Nor were they begrudging to their labourers, but would allow their men to take straw for a pig if they needed it, turnips and green peas in the summer, too, and they were not above giving a man a piece of field ground to grow potatoes: sometimes they would also let him have a half-sack of wheat at a reasonable price and perhaps give him a five shillings Christmas box and a joint of pork for Boxing Day if they had had a good year and he was a valued worker.

By the time Jem returned, however, Old Isaac Peakman and Old Samuel Howie lay in their graves in St. Bartholomew's churchyard and Old Ezekiel Godwin, in his seventy-fifth year, sat all day in his rocking chair in the farmhouse kitchen at Milepole staring blankly into the space before his eyes and not knowing where he was or who anybody was around him. Within five years of the hostilities being renewed following the short Peace, all three farms had passed into the hands of their eldest sons: Goat Lodge to Amos Peakman four years after the hostilities resumed, Smallponds to Marcus Howie two months later, as the winter took both the fathers, and Milepole to Joshua Godwin a half-year after that, all at a time of momentous happenings.

The sudden elevation to a wealthier life through the folly of the 'Corsican Corporal' introduced the three sons to other expectancies which inevitably follow from the accumulation of such rapid wealth: they had, in their own eyes, become men to be looked up to, as men of wealth expected to be. It was their privilege now to sit with their own families at the very front of the church on a Sunday morning, to have two or three carriages, to be able to employ several servants from amongst the village girls, not in the old way of their fathers, allowing the maids to live with them under the same roof and all sitting at the same table. Now the maidservants were hired simply on a daily basis, as and when needed, so that they had to walk to the farms each day to perform their duties and walk back to their homes again at night.

As men richer than their fathers had ever been, their manner, too, had become haughty and their language domineering: they had become more remote and unsympathetic: there was an aloofness about them unknown in their fathers' time. For instance, they no longer took part in the physical work of the farm and, when they went into a field, it was to order their men and to increase the speed of their labour: they were more calculating, seeming to care more for money and less about the welfare of the labourers whom they employed. Amongst them, the ties of a common heritage, if not entirely severed, had at least been loosened.

As the war neared its end and the great slump in agriculture manifested itself, Amos Peakman, Marcus Howie and Joshua Godwin simply cut the rates of their men's pay as their own profitability shrank and hired only by the day: and during slack times, particularly over the winter, they would lay off most of their labourers and let them collect poor relief. Unhappily, the three large farmers in the two hamlets – Silas Kempen and James Allen, at Lower Rackstead, and Thomas Godbear, in Merchant Staplers – who gave employment to most of the day-labourers in those places, did the same, following the example of the others and all profiting from it. For that way, a labourer's yearly income was made up partly of wage payments and partly of poor relief: and because the labour-hiring farmers paid only part of the cost of poor relief, this option enabled them, in effect, to shift some of their labour costs on to other payers of the poor rate. It meant that those day-labourers in Hamwick Dean who had found temporary work of a week here and two weeks there still had to join the queue at St. Bartholomew's porch door from time to time for a measure of relief to make up their money to subsistence level, while their wives and children queued as usual at the back door of the parsonage for a bowl of porridge or a basin of mutton soup.

It was cause enough for any man to grumble, but, perhaps wisely, most kept their opinions to themselves: when one lived almost wholly on turnip-pies, potatoes, oatmeal porridge and stirabout winter long, one did not complain aloud so that the master or one of his servants might hear, but kept one's silence, touched one's forelock and took the work, even when it was reduced by a further shilling a week during the ploughing and the corn drilling and sixpence a week during the reaping, the gathering, the stack-building and the threshing and winnowing, knowing full well that it might be dropped again the next year.

TEN

IN THEIR OWN estimation, the three sons considered they had risen in status far above the old rural society of their fathers' time thirty years before. As a result, instead of being respected, Amos Peakman, Marcus Howie and Joshua Godwin were heartily disliked and chided for it in the smoky confines of the Wayfarers' bay-windowed parlour and the fug of the Carpenters' Arms' vault, for they had even abandoned the old traditions existing between a master and his labourers. Whereas, in their father's time, a labourer seeking orders during harvesting, say, would have called at the farm's front door and been given a jug of home-brewed ale to quench his thirst while he sat in the cool of the kitchen out of the heat of the day, now he knocked at the back door and was made to stand outside whether rain or shine, hat in hand, abject, waiting for his orders while his master finished his breakfast or his lunch or his tea.

Of the three, Amos Peakman was the most prosperous, possessing not only the largest farm but having inherited the largest sum: so perhaps it was to be expected that, of the three, he would be the most impatient, the most ill-tempered and grasping, the most scornful of everything and everyone, with an imperious, distancing manner about him. He was then thirty-seven years of age, burly and broad-shouldered, with a large jaw, red, round face and thick dark eyebrows, supposedly the better educated of the three since he had been provided with the longest schooling, but which, unhappily, seemed to have added little of value to his character and, at its end, had merely produced yet another arrogant and inconsiderate young man, as so many did, who considered his wealth gave him rights and privileges of speech and action which were not to be challenged on any account.

Indeed, it was always said in the village that Old Isaac's one mistake in his life had been to pay to send young Amos daily to the national school in Maydun till the age of nine and then, in the very year of the revolution across the Channel, to send him on to an expensive boarding school, the Allison Academy for Sons of Gentlemen, housed in a large grange in the middle of a north Anglian county town, where for twenty-five guineas a year, as a 'parlour boarder,' he was taught English and common arithmetic, the kings and queens of England from the Conqueror onward, but ignoring all Anglo-Saxon monarchs before, as if they accounted for nothing. In a lesson commonly called 'geography' and taught by an indifferent master, who was actually a student sent down from his university for misconduct and in need of a living, he had learned, too, all the nations of the world on a globe, the major rivers and mountains, that the produce of France was wine and of Ireland pigs and potatoes and of Wales and Scotland sheep and of the latter also, whisky, a bottle of which was frequently tasted by the same master.

However, young Amos's academic learning had fallen well below the required standard and when his fees were raised to thirty-five guineas a year so that Latin, Greek, French and two further branches of mathematics, algebra and geometry, might be added to his curriculum, Old Isaac had choked at the additional expense. Besides, the war was under way by then and the country needed to grow food, so he had brought his son home on his sixteenth birthday to join him on the farm.

His years away had detached Amos Peakman from the tenor of life in the village in which he had been born and in which he had spent the first nine years of his life. The alteration in his character showed immediately upon his return when, hardly had he been back a day, than he began to address the men in a way Old Isaac never did, irascibly and contemptuously and with no concern for their plight or well-being, like some rich young lord scolding serfs: he earned their enmity from that day forward.

As a result, too, of the company he had kept at school, he had come to harbour ideas above his station, in their view, so it was no surprise when his father died and he inherited the farm at age twenty-seven that he should suppose himself, by virtue of his wealth and education, to be no less of a country gentleman than a true country gentleman. At twenty-one, he had married a young lady from one of the more prosperous families of Hamwyte's minor gentry and so was already divided from the villagers by the tastes to which she introduced him and the company he was obliged to keep on her behalf, also by his own pretensions, his own ambitions and his display as was thought by him to befit a country gentleman, indeed, the whole manner of his life.

For instance, he liked always to ride around in a carriage as he felt one of his station should, he spent liberally on fittings and furniture for his house and regularly drove his wife and their two daughters the thirteen miles to Wivencaster in preference to the smaller Hamwyte, where they went first into the millinery shops and then into the dressmaker's shops and returned to the farm often dressed in their new finery and put their noses in the air when their carriage passed the farm labourers trudging homeward.

As was to be expected, his farmhouse was the grandest of the three sons' places, with a false front modelled on a fashionable Regency design to conceal the older dwelling, incorporating as it did a portico and a panelled front door, three rows of high multi-paned windows, dormer windows in the roof and a high wall built around the garden to divide it from the farm's other buildings and yard to ensure his privacy.

In the last year of the war, he had even sent his wife and two daughters to the spa at Cheltenham for the summer in the hope that the elder, young as she was at fifteen, might catch the eye of some youthful swain from the true gentry with an eye to the future and not much in the way of prospects of his own. But even with a substantial dowry in prospect, they had returned from their three months' sojourn without the poor girl having caught a sniff of interest and, since she was such a freckle-faced and frizzy-haired frump, anyway, no one in the village had expected anything else, though it was said it had cost her father a small fortune in travel, lodgings, food, hirings and entertainments, even if he had done it simply to appease his wife and silence his daughter's caterwauling and gain for himself some relief from all that and a blessed quiet about the house.

Yet that same Amos Peakman was willing enough to tell one of his occasional day-labourers, nineteen-year-old Tom Parrott, when he had asked for a married man's wage, that he could not afford it and, if he were foolish enough to take young Rebecca Hayes as his wife and, in time, have children by her – if indeed they had not started on that business already – then, when he fell out of work in the winter, as he surely would, he had no right to claim the necessary food to keep his and their bodies and souls together or to the relief which was owed to him by the parish: and yet he was expected to stop his work and stand and remove his hat and touch his forelock when his carriage-riding master and his wife and daughters went past and speak only when spoken to, otherwise to hold his tongue and keep his opinions to himself.

Marcus Howie, thirty-three years of age, a bluff, bullish, red-faced, rushabout type, somewhat short of stature and stooped like his father, was also a product of the day school at Maydun and a 'parlour boarding' education up in the next county, though at a different and less exalted school than Amos Peakman, where the fees were much less and the teaching poorer for it, yet he seemed to feel the need to act the same as the older man for no other reason than he believed it was the way a reasonably well-off employer should act.

On his father's death, he had, at twenty-four years of age, become the master of some ninety-six acres, but, by taking up the leases on several acres of common pastureland and two parcels each of a dozen acres abutting his boundary as they had become vacant, he had increased his land to a hundred and thirty-three acres by Jem's return. His farmhouse was a more solid, plain red-brick affair which had replaced a small timber and plaster cottage in which his grandfather had started out. Two wings, with high chimneys, had been attached by his own father as the family's prosperity had grown during the years of the war so that the house comprised a dozen rooms as opposed to the original two of the cottage. Further efforts at gentrification had included the building of a high wall all around it like Amos Peakman and the laying of a lawn where the old muddy yard had once been, with brick pillars and a lantern surmounting an ironwork arch at the entrance to the sand and shingle driveway.

At twenty-four, he had also taken a wife, but she was not gentry: she had been a governess to someone else's children, had one leg which was slightly shorter than the other and so on some days, when it pained her, would walk with a pronounced limp which seemed always to irritate her husband, especially when they arrived at church and he strode up the short path always five paces ahead of her and she seemed always to be hurrying to keep up. As yet, she had not delivered him a son and heir to whom he could pass on his acres, but had given him three pretty young daughters, though she was pregnant for the fourth time in four years and under strict orders this time to 'make it a boy': she would deliver another girl.

He, too, preferred to employ day-labourers from the village only when it suited him, such as gathering-in his harvest or sowing his corn or ploughing his fields or herding his cattle or dibbing his turnips and potatoes or weeding his grain fields and was as unsympathetic as his fellow farmers. The previous year, in laying off old John Jolley in the November and forcing him to go into the village's poorhouse, in effect two ramshackle cottages set aside for the purpose on Forge Lane and maintained by the Vestry, where the old, sick, infirm and abandoned and their dependant children were confined, he had said, in the hearing of others, that when a man grew too old and could no longer do the hard work about the farm, he would be better to 'get out of the way,' that is, to die, and that the only ground he ought to occupy from then on was a few feet of earth in the churchyard rather than being an encumbrance on others.

Joshua Godwin, aged twenty-seven, the youngest of the new bloods, but as pushy and as impatient as the other two, was a lanky, lean-bodied and long-striding man, with blond, almost white, hair, a thin face, high cheekbones and cold grey eyes, whose head when he walked, peculiarly, nodded in step, as if he could not get to a place quickly enough and the motion of his head speeded or lengthened his stride. He was the third of his generation to farm at Milepole: he had been brought up on the farm and had seldom left it, except to go to market with his father, or after he had taken it over, to attend a farmers' association meeting in Maydun or Hamwyte or Melchborough. His schooling had been no better than the lessons he had received from age seven to eleven under Mother Rae at the village's Dame School, so he had no real cause to put on airs, but did so anyway, to keep up with his betters, with whom he considered himself an equal.

His farm comprised about ninety-eight acres of arable, plus twelve acres, two roods and ten perches of pastureland and four acres of woodland. The farmhouse itself was a sturdy, extended, five-roomed, redbrick dwelling, with mullioned windows and twisted chimneys: several outbuildings of brick and timber were grouped around a yard, one of them a small dairy and another a quite substantial timber barn. The greater part of his acreage abutted the Farthing and Gravel Pit parts of Third Field, separated from them only by a straggling hedge and a line of sheep hurdles.

His father, Ezekiel, being a good Christian church man, had always been a benevolent and well-liked master to his day-labourers, especially those who held no land on any of the three open-fields and so relied upon their labour on his and the other farms for their livelihood, as so many of the villagers did and had cause to thank the father for his kindness in paying a living wage when others did not and would not. The same, however, could not be said of the son and, the same as the other two, he also employed his labourers on a daily basis and liked to ride around in a pony and trap and, also like them, to drive his wife to the same fashionable shops at Wivencaster as they went with their wives, though having three sons, none above the age of six, it cost him considerably less than having two adolescent daughters or three young girls with all their wants.

There were two other farms around the village: Redhouse farm and the Glebe farm. Redhouse was still tenanted by old Zeikiel Jaynes, but he was nearing sixty by then and his sole offspring, an idiot son in his early thirties, was unfit for proper work and mostly he relied upon a few hired day-labourers or did the work himself. It was a surprise to Jem that the farm was still worked the way it was, even though there was no squire or lord of the manor resident at the Hall (and had not been for six years or more) to direct him. Ziekiel Jaynes simply kept on working the land from season to season, paid his rental, delivered his tithe dues to the church in kind and, of the rest, what he did not take for himself and his wife and their idiot son, he sold at Hamwyte market each Tuesday or at the county town's market each Friday.

When Jem's father had come to the village as a young man of nineteen from another place to marry Jem's mother, an orphaned village girl working as a servant on Redhouse farm, he had always appreciated the fact that Zeikiel Jaynes, then starting out, had been the first to give him work as a herdsman and a ploughman. Thus, after a year or two, having become a valued worker because of his knowledge of a farm and its workings, Aaron Stebbings had not only been accepted into the village but had also been able to move his wife and baby son into the rented Vine Cottage on the Lower Rackstead road. In time, too, he managed to acquire the rental of a dozen strips of his own on the open-fields and, when he had not been ploughing, seeding or harvesting those, he had worked regularly as a day-labourer, sometimes weekly, other times fortnightly, solely for Zeikiel Jaynes, always ready to answer his call, come harvesting, ploughing or drilling, since he had employed him when others would not.

As he settled and prospered, so there had been money enough to send Jem to the village's Dame School till he was aged eleven so that he would at least be able to read and write and count and say his Lord's Prayer and know his Catechism. It was to be expected that, when Jem left the school on his eleventh birthday, he would begin his working life alongside his father, which he did, joining him on Zeikiel Jaynes's farm on occasions, working as a 'lad' at harvest time, that is, one who had left school as opposed to a 'boy' still at school. Boys helping on farms earned less than the 'lads,' the older youths of thirteen, fourteen and fifteen years who were taken on as 'half-men,' being paid half a man's wage and doing mostly the light jobs during harvest, such as carrying the 'elevenses' and 'fourses' snacks into the fields at eleven in the morning and four in the afternoon, taking the loaded wagons to the stack yard or leading the staid old jobbing horse that had lost all its sprightliness after long years of hard ploughing as it drag-raked the ground: other times they might work as a bird scarer or a gleaner after the harvest or as a cowherd or help with the turnip hoeing.

When a lad reached sixteen or seventeen years of age, he was generally taken on as a 'threequarter man,' getting threequarters of a man's wages, but doing all the jobs a full-man did, except pitching the sheaves of corn up on to the wagon. Jem, however, was still being paid as a 'half-man' when first his father and then his mother died within days of each other: and, since it was not enough to sustain him or to pay his rent, he was quickly turned out: and as an orphan with no permanent home and no relatives in the village with whom he could board, was deemed a surplus mouth for the parish to feed, especially since none of the other farmers was willing to pay him as a day-labouring 'threequarter man.' Then, with the overseer of the poor, Elijah Scoble, not being able either to find a bricklayer or a barrelmaker in need of an apprentice well away from the village or a farmer in another parish in need of a live-in hand, it was decided by the Vestry that it would be cheaper in the long run to give him his two-pounds 'enlistment bonus' and send him off to Melchborough to join the militia, which they duly did.

The smallest of the village's farm was the Glebe farm, comprising just twenty-six acres, sixteen roods and twenty-eight perches only of dairy meadows, lying opposite the church down Mope Lane and straddling the western end of the flat ridge-top and the steep northern slope itself. It was administered not by a tenant but by a bailiff, who lived in the farm's four-roomed cottage and oversaw the milking of the cows and the churning of the butter and cheese, part of which went to the parsonage and the rest was sold at Hamwyte's Tuesday market, all the monies derived from it going to the incumbent parson or rector.

Such by then was the divide between the farmers and the day-labourers in Hamwick Dean that what one man had said at the death of old Isaac Peakman – 'He was a generous and sympathetic man, one of the old school, considerate to his workers, never haughty in his manner, not one to use language, a man I could respect, a good master.' – the same would never be said of his son, or the village's two other large farmers, for that matter.

'Make money at any price and damn the worker!' was the verdict on them from the same day-labourer the previous winter when, like many others, he had been in some distress and on the parish relief. No one who heard it disputed his assertion.

What the day-labourer of Hamwick Dean was learning when touching his forelock to masters as uncaring of his welfare as were Amos Peakman, Marcus Howie and Joshua Godwin was that all that was wanted of him was work: that he was born to labour and, when he could work no longer, what was the use of him?

So the state of England, so also the state of Hamwick Dean on Jem Stebbings's return at the beginning of a depression which was to continue for twenty years.

ELEVEN

SO TIRED was Jem from his journey that he slept for the whole of the day: thus, it was well after seven o'clock in the evening when he awoke to the deep hubbub of men's voices coming from below, pierced now and again by the shrill laughter of women. The Wayfarers' then, more so than the Carpenters' Arms, was the centre of the village's evening life: on the rough wooden benches of its bar parlour and smoke-stained taproom, the men sat and discussed the issues of the day, the progress of their crops, the needs of themselves and their families, the vagaries of the weather, matters which were local to them rather than national to all. For the daily welfare and troubles of their own kind were enough of a source of conversation and concern to occupy a whole evening's talk: and, if they tired of that, then there was a skittles alley in the yard at the rear where they could forget even those troubles for an hour or two.

However, both the large bay-windowed parlour and the taproom were full that night, not only with the husbandmen, shopkeepers and others who always drank there but, unusually, also with many of the village's landless day-labourers, who seldom did, preferring the rougher comforts and cheaper ale of the other hostelry. For between the two, there was a certain resentment stemming from the fact that from time to time a husbandman might have to seek employment on one of the larger farms of the village to supplement his livelihood – being his own master one day of the week and a servant or day-labourer for another master the next. That had always been resented by the landless day-labourers, which was one of the prime reasons why the husbandmen all tended to drink in the Wayfarers' and the day-labourers frequented the Carpenters' Arms, though there was no actual bar to either entering the others' domain.

The landless day-labourers were present that evening for the simple reason that the Wayfarers' Inn, being the larger of the two hostelries, was the only place in the village with room enough to hold a large gathering in reasonable comfort. So when Jem went down just before eight o'clock in the hope of a meal, as he had arranged with Caleb Chapman that morning, and pushed open the door from the stairs, to his surprise, he found the large room filled, with upwards of a hundred and fifty or so, with yet more crowded into the taproom leading off from it. Mostly, they were men and older youths, but with a good number of women amongst them, as well as some younger lads, who, being aged eleven and twelve upwards and working, felt themselves deserving of the right to sit drinking Caleb Chapman's dark home-brewed ale along with their fathers and their elder brothers and probably their mothers, too. Clearly, some form of a celebration was in progress: and so crammed was the place that several of those pressed against the door to the stairs, not knowing who Jem was, were disinclined to allow him to enter and, when he tried to do so, regarded him with barely disguised hostility, the same as they would any stranger attempting to push in amongst them. Indeed, they would have barred him with their backs had not a man's cry from the far end of the parlour made them turn their heads, first to the one who gave the cry and then to the one at whom his remarks were directed and at whom his finger was pointed.

'Gawd Christ! If it en't Jem Stebbings back from the dead!' came a deep, rumbling voice. 'Make way there, lads, make way! He's one of us! Let him through, let him through!'

The speaker – or, more accurately, the shouter, for there was such a babble of voices around him that he needed to shout to be heard above it – was a tall, straw-haired man with the apple-red face of an open-air labourer, the palest of blue eyes, a sharp, thin nose, high cheekbones and a prominent bobbing Adam's apple. On seeing Jem framed in the doorway, he had risen from a table at the far end of the room, his eyes wide with surprise and delight, and now he was standing with a pewter tankard gripped in a large calloused hand, grinning broadly to show yellow, tobacco-stained teeth.

Dick Dollery, one of the village's husbandmen and an occasional day-labourer on other people's farms when it suited him, was the same age as Jem and, indeed, if Jem could call anyone in the village a long-time friend, it was Dick Dollery. As boys, they had often gone bird's nesting together, rabbiting with a pet stoat on the wasteland around the village, fishing in the Langwater stream with a home-made rod and line or shooting sharpened arrows from a willow bow at pigeons and doves nesting in the rafters of the derelict St. Peter's chapel of ease. Together, too, aged eleven and twelve years, they had passed many a day in the three great open-fields, scaring rooks and crows off the growing corn with a wooden rattle apiece or picking stones with other boys and girls and piling them in heaps at the side of the lands: and on two occasions at least, as six-year-olds, even though best friends, they had been made to fight each other with bare fists as part of a wager between their respective fathers till, after Dick had received a bloody nose from Jem's fist, their angry mothers had put a stop to it and their disgruntled fathers had gone off to the Wayfarers' together to drink away the disappointment that their wives did not seem to comprehend the importance of their sons' test of courage. Jem and Dick Dollery had not seen each other since the day Jem had walked out of the village to Hamwyte with the five other 'balloted' militia youths and caught the coach to Melchborough to sign his name in the enlistment book – the only one of them able to do so, for he at least had learned to write during his years of morning lessons at Mother Rae's Dame School.

The packed assembly duly parted at Dick Dollery's bidding and the eyes of all were fixed on Jem as he pushed his way through.

'I don't believe my eyes, truly I don't!' exclaimed Dick Dollery, putting down his tankard and leaning across the table to pump Jem's hand. 'Christ Almighty, Jem Stebbings! Who would have thought it? We all thought thee was dead and gorn to meet thy Maker long agoo, boy. That we did. Gawd Christ! T'is a sight to gladden the heart to know thee are alive and whole and back here with us and no mistake.'

He motioned for three of the men seated on a bench in front of Jem to make room for him at the table. 'Give the man a seat,' he ordered. 'He's a soldier come home from the wars – someone I never expected to see again, that I can say.' He was laughing with the sheer delight of the moment.

'It's good to see you again, Dick, and a relief to be back among old friends,' said Jem, squeezing down on to the bench between the three men seated opposite Dick Dollery, who shifted somewhat reluctantly to make room for him.

'Glad to see thee again, Jem, boy,' said a grinning, lanky, stoop-backed man, with staring blue eyes and bushy sidewhiskers grown to compensate for a receding hairline, reaching across the table to offer Jem his hand. Enos Diddams, a year or two younger than Jem and Dick Dollery, was also a husbandman for most of the year and, like his friend, only became a day-labourer working for others when it suited him, which was not often, except when he needed extra money.

Alongside him sat a smaller, stockier man, with a thick nose, square jaw and a mass of straight, dark hair: John Romble, the village's taciturn, thirty-three-year-old wheelwright, took his clay pipe out of his mouth and blew a cloud of smoke into the air before reaching across in turn to offer his hand. 'Glad you made it back safe, Jem,' he said quietly, with a smile. 'We often wondered what had happened to you. Glad to see you are home and well.'

The man seated at the far end of the bench upon which Jem now sat merely turned to acknowledge him with the slightest of nods, continuing to puff at his clay pipe as he did so. Nathaniel Newman, the village's blacksmith, at thirty-five years of age, was the oldest amongst Dick Dollery's small coterie: heavy-set, with broad shoulders, a barrel chest and muscular arms developed over the years from pounding with a hammer, he was not much given to handshaking or back-slapping or shows of friendship of any kind. Jem had also known him in his youth and acknowledged the greeting, such as it was, with a smile anyway.

Of the other two seated at the table, Jem did not recall either till he was told, for both were several years younger than him and, indeed, would have been only nine or ten years of age when he left the village. Not knowing Jem, they greeted him in the way of their kind with strangers, with a half-smile and a desultory nod and a grunt rather than a handshake and a spoken welcome. Thomas Judd, chubby, cheery-faced, red-haired and red-bearded, was a cordwainer (one who made shoes from cordovan leather) recently out of an apprenticeship and, at twenty-two years of age, still a happy bachelor and, by his talk amongst the other men, not inclined to go marrying till he was good and ready for it, if ever, or so he frequently told everyone. The other, William Stubbs, was a spare, shy, thin-faced harnessmaker of the same age as the former, with dulled grey eyes and a weary look about him, who, not remembering Jem at all, now regarded him with some awe on learning he had been a soldier against Napoleon, and mumbled his perfunctory greeting at the table-top rather than look into the newcomer's face.

'Gawd! Ye give me a shock when thee walked in through that door,' declared Dick Dollery, still beaming, taking a drink from his tankard. 'Thee'll have to tell us where thee has been all this time, boy. We en't heard nought of thee since ye left to go soldiering along with the others – ' He paused remembering and recalling the other five who also had left. ' – God rest'em. It must have bin twelve years agoo, if it's a day. Are ye out of the army now? Ye'll have to tell us all. Why ye've come back, for a start.'

Caleb Chapman had come pushing through the crowd with the promised plate of cold meat, cold potatoes and warm gravy and a tankard of his ale for Jem's supper and now stood by the table. 'He come back this morning,' the landlord interrupted in a gruff, matter-of-fact manner, banging down first the plate, then the mug of ale in front of Jem before dropping the knife and fork alongside.

'Well, ye could have told us, Caleb,' Dick Dollery admonished him, but in a friendly way. 'An old friend comes back after all these years and thee says nothing! What were ye thinking of, man? T'is the best news we have had in this village in a long time.'

All it drew from the landlord, who was known for the dourness of his character, was a scowl. 'I en't had much of a chance to gossip with anyone, not with the likes o'this lot drinking me dry, have I?' he growled, unsure as whether he was being teased or not. 'I've been too busy serving them, en't I?'

The rebuke, however, was lost on the straw-haired labourer: as the landlord retreated, still muttering to himself, Dick Dollery merely laughed, took another drink from his tankard and turned back to Jem. 'I tell thee, Jem, old friend,' he said, as he and the men watched with interest as Jem took his first sip of their favourite brew, 'there were a few times when I thought of thee and wondered how ye was doing, soldiering against they Frenchies, and where ye was. So where hast thee bin on thy wanderings, if thee don't mind telling us?'

Jem did not mind at all: he had expected them to ask: it was the natural curiosity of men who had not been anywhere themselves expressing veneration for one who had. 'I've been at quite a few places,' he told them quietly with a smile, adding somewhat enigmatically: 'A lot of them places I wish I had never been.' Like many of his comrades-in-arms, he often preferred to refer not to a battle by name but simply to say he was 'at such-and-such a place' since it somehow rendered the horrors of the actual battle there less of a traumatic memory.

'Our battalion was with the Duke of Wellington himself – Old Nosey or Old Hooky, as we called him on account of his nose.' he went on, giving a shrug as if the disclosure were a matter of no consequence. 'We were at a number of places in Spain with him for nigh on four years. There were one or two times at one or two places when I thought I might not see the old village again, I can tell you, a fair few times when I thought the Grim Reaper might be about to take me along with all the others he took.'

The men at the table all nodded sympathetically at this, as though they understood the kind of memories he must retain. 'We'll, I'm glad he never got thee,' said Dick Dollery with genuine thankfulness, raising his own tankard as if in a toast.

'Amen to that,' declared Enos Diddams.

'Was thee at the last one then, Jem?' enquired Dick Dollery expectantly, lowering his tankard, having taken another long, satisfying swallow of ale.

'Aye, I was there,' Jem replied with a sigh. 'I've just come from France. We've been camped outside Paris with the Duke's army for the past six months, but now my battalion has been disbanded and we have all been paid off and told to fend for ourselves. So here I am, a free man again. No more soldiering for me. I have other plans.'

They did not ask him what his plans were, for they were more interested in his experiences as a soldier. 'Thee must have some real tales to tell, from all that fighting thee has done, especially where thee has been and what thee has seen, things the likes of us en't never likely to see in our days on this earth?' queried Dick Dollery.

'Aye, I have seen a few things,' Jem acknowledged, but with a slightly regretful sigh to let them know that he did not relish or truly wish at that moment to relate his tales on that matter, 'a few things I wouldn't want to see again either. I'll tell you sometime, lads, but all in good time, all in good time. Not now.'

'Aye, we understand, Jem, we understand,' said his old friend, with a smile, 'we'll leave them tales and the good honest lechering ye no doubt got up to till another time when there en't so many young ears about.' He gave a laugh, knowing that the bachelor, Thomas Judd, never having had a woman, would very much like to hear the stories of Jem's soldiering and most particularly the ones concerning 'foreign women' and what they would do for a man: and the more salacious the tale, the better he would like it.

Instead, the men talked awhile about themselves, as if reintroducing themselves to their old friend, their information, brief as it was, covering the years Jem had been away. Dick Dollery, for instance, reported that he was married and had been since he was nineteen years of age, had five children to his name already, all daughters and then proceeded to name each in turn and give their ages, not one above eight years, as if he expected Jem to remember each. Enos Diddams, too, had been married since he was nineteen and had four children, two sons and two daughters, and would have had another of each, but, sadly, had lost both to the churchyard, which put a more sombre complexion on the proceedings, till it was cheered by a comment from a red-faced John Romble.

'I've managed three myself with my old lady,' said the wheelwright somewhat sheepishly, as if merely to mention the fact would somehow allow the men to conjure in their mind's eye a picture of him and his wife performing the actual act of procreation.

In his turn, Nathaniel Newman grumpily, almost as if defending himself, admitted to having been married at twenty-two, to living still in his father's old cottage beside his forge on Forge Lane, directly opposite the Carpenters' Arms, and to having had six offspring in six years with his overly plump wife.

They quickly passed over the bachelor, Thomas Judd, seated one side of Jem, for there was not much that they could say about him: he had no vulnerable point such as wife and children. Instead, they settled upon teasing the second of the two younger men, William Stubbs, seated upon Jem's other side. 'And Billy boy here, he's newly married. En't been married more than a twelve-month, which accounts for the thin look o' him. She's draining the life out o' him, we reckons. It 'on't be long afore he is wasted away through too much of it, if thee asks me,' said a laughing Dick Dollery, blatantly alluding to the frequency of the newly-wed's nocturnal coupling. It produced only blushes from William Stubbs and a shy smile at their overly optimistic judgment of his prowess.

Of course, being a friend newly returned amongst them, it was not long before Jem found himself being chided for being a bachelor still himself, in the way that men do of other men.

'Thee ought to get wed thyself now thee is home and join us,' suggested Enos Diddams, with a broad grin. 'I don't see why thee should escape it when we has to suffer.'

'Aye, why should he be happy and us miserable?' from a similarly grinning Dick Dollery.

'He 'on't escape for long,' John Romble asserted with mock sourness. 'A good looking chap like him, there'll be some woman out there after thee afore the year is out, mark my words. It comes to us all in time whether we wants it to or not.'

'A man can't live by bread alone. He needs other comforts now and again,' Enos Diddams pointed out in a low grumble.

'No, but he can live by drink!' declared the bachelor Thomas Judd amid laughter, raising his tankard and downing the remainder of his ale in one gurgling swallow.

'A young chap like thee, Tom Judd, should be making the most of it while thee's young enough to enjoy it,' a sullen Nathaniel Newman unexpectedly chimed in, 'because there'll come a time when ye can't and ye'll be in bother then.'

The other men began to snigger: only then did the slow-thinking blacksmith realise that they had mischievously interpreted his remarks as a confession of his own failings and he scowled even more.

'T'is the only thing they en't put a tax on yet,' laughed Enos Diddams.

'Give the Government time and they'll find a way,' interjected John Romble, somewhat seriously, before Dick Dollery brought the matter back to humour.

'Enos here says he does it every night he en't drunk. En't that right, Enos?' The straw-haired husbandman glanced at his friends and gave a sly wink to the others as he added: 'Trouble is he's drunk six nights o' the week and can't do anything when he gits home because of brewer's droop so his missus only gits it once a week if she's lucky!'

Whether it was true or not was lost in the brief bout of joshing which followed, all done in good heart amid much laughter, not only from those at the table but also amongst the other men and youths who had paused in their own talk to listen to the jesting of the six at the table as soon as the subject of nightly coupling was introduced and now threw out derogatory comments of their own because it cheered them all to smile and to laugh.

TWELVE

'IT'S A BIG gathering,' said Jem, indicating the men, youths and women all crowded around them, some seated, but most standing, chattering and drinking their ale.

'Aye, t'is a send-off,' Dick Dollery told him, taking a clay pipe from his pocket and tamping in a pinch of tobacco. 'Four lads is leaving the village tomorrow and we have come to say goodbye to 'em. Those four there – ' He pointed to four youths seated on a bench along one wall, none of whom could have been older than seventeen or eighteen years. They already appeared to be half-drunk, for they were all flushed and grinning inanely and waving their half-emptied pots before them in the manner of the inebriated as well as exchanging remarks with those around them.

'They're making for Liverpool, so they say,' Dick Dollery went on, 'aiming to take a boat to British America now we has stopped fighting the Americans and Johnny French is well and truly put in his place, thanks to the likes of thee and the Old Duke. They are the first from round here since the Peace was signed, but I don't think they'll be the last. They're saying, "To hell with Hamwick Dean! We're off!" and they're a-gooing, though I en't of a mind to goo myself. If we all starts leaving, the country will be empty in no time and the damned Irish will all come rushing in behind us like they're a-doing now. There are enough o' they travelling Irish gangs wandering the countryside as it is, taking other men's work and then scarpering with the money other men used to earn.'

Several women were in the company gathered around the four youths, but, unlike the men and the boys who were all talking cheerfully and laughing together, ribbing each other as men do when they are merry and under the influence of drink, the women seemed to be downcast, particularly two sad-faced girls, who sat beside two of the youths, each clutching at the arm of one of them as if wanting to hold him there for some reason. Unknowingly, Jem had returned to a time of great upheaval throughout the land.

During the years of war, emigration had been curtailed. Though with plenty of work and good wages due to the desperate need for war production, there had been no need for a farm labourer to seek out different lands: but the massive demobilisation of the King's soldiers and sailors over the past year had altered all that. The country was overpopulated for the work that was available, some said: therefore, the Government of landowners and property owners, of knights and lords and dukes, thought it better to rid themselves of the burdensome poor rather than help to raise them up. Low fares were being offered to encourage the unwanted poor of England to populate other lands: from the villages of East Anglia, in particular, a steady stream of impoverished landworkers was beginning to flow through the ports of London, Liverpool, Bristol and Southampton.

Some saved to pay their own fares, others had their fares paid for them by the overseers of the poor in their parishes as vestries sought to reduce the numbers of those for whom it was their duty to care and so reduce the poor rate burden on the landowners, farmers, householders and tradesmen. An advertisement had even appeared several times of late in the *County Weekly* – occasionally taken by Caleb Chapman at the Wayfarers' – advertising 'lands in British America, where there is a good market for grain and other production from the earth.' There was a report, too, that the Government was even prepared to make transports carrying returning troops from Canada available to take on passengers at low rates and ship them back over: the four youths who were emigrating were amongst the first to be taking up that offer. Canada, particularly Upper Canada, and the States of America were seen as the new hopes: the two countries were, in effect, competing with each other for immigrants, for America, too, was promising land grants to any soul brave enough to venture into the uncharted Indian Territories beyond the Appalachians and open up the unknown centre and the West.

Liverpool, where the four youths were headed, was the main embarkation point for North America: all that an emigrant had to do was to pay his passage money on arrival at the dockside. One month fares could be as high as five pounds and the next as low as three pounds and ten shillings, depending on the flow of people leaving, though to a farm labourer either was still the equivalent of several weeks' wages. Supposedly, all had to pass a medical examination before boarding a ship: but passing the medical often meant little more than walking into a room and, if a person were able to stand straight and showed no visible signs of a disease, such as scabs or lesions or was not shivering and shaking or the like, then the authorities happily allowed them to emigrate.

So desperate were some to leave the country of their birth that, if they could not afford the fare, they would stow away, for whatever reason – to escape crippling poverty and destitution, to free themselves of a wife and children they could not keep or debts they could not repay, or perhaps simply to escape the Justices who were seeking them for some crime or other.

A search for stowaways was always made as soon as the ship got under way: passengers would be assembled on deck so that a roll-call could be taken to ensure that everybody had a ticket and everybody had paid the right price. While they were topside, the crew would go through the whole vessel armed with a variety of heavy, blunt or sharp instruments looking for those in hiding. Some might hide in packing-cases, some in barrels, others in rolls of material. Those found in the first search were usually put ashore before the coast of old England had disappeared over the horizon. Any who escaped the first search and who were found only when the vessel was halfway across the Atlantic discovered to their cost that the rest of the journey would not be a pleasant one: they were made to do all the menial and unpleasant tasks which needed to be done aboard a ship, enough to make some wish they had never stowed away.

Travel to Australia, on the other hand, was 'free' to genuine emigrants, paid for by the Government for any who wanted to go: though there were more than a few in the Wayfarers' – Dick Dollery being one and Enos Diddams another – who derided emigration and laughed at those who talked of it. They laughingly pointed out that a man could get 'boated' to New South Wales or Van Diemen's Land easily enough, simply by getting caught with a pigeon or a rabbit or a pheasant in his bag when on someone else's land at night. Even so, it was said by some, who had heard it from others, that experienced agricultural workers were in such great demand in Australia that some landholders there were even willing to pay the fares of an indentured man in exchange for a certain period of labour from him. They preferred single men rather than married men with families, for the simple reason it was cheaper and a single man was more mobile and could go anywhere without the encumbrance of a wife and children.

However, even a married man with children, if he had the courage to spend four months at sea to get there, could readily find work at vastly improved wages compared to England: he could also live off the land – hunting at will, if he wished – which in England would have been classed as poaching and earned him a spell in the nearest House of Correction with hard labour for a first offence and the free journey in chains to the other side of the world for a second. After a while, too, in Australia, a man who went of his own accord, once free of all obligations to his master, could select land of his own and set himself up as a farmer in his own right, so it was said, which he would struggle to do at home: and such was the poverty in rural areas at that time, more and more of the poorer country people were increasingly taking up the offer to leave for good an England with harsh ways, privileged lords and ladies and a Church which seemed to care more for the station and comforts of its own kind than for the welfare of the very people it was supposed to serve.

'I'd goo to Australia myself if it were nearer,' declared Nathaniel Newman, quite seriously, unaware of the incongruity of his statement, frowning as the other men laughed.

'A man can git there right easily enough with the Government's help if he has a mind to,' Dick Dollery reminded him, the tone of his voice leaving no doubt as to the meaning of his words. 'It don't take much – a bit o' thieving and they gives thee a free ticket. There's one or two likely candidates for that which I know of.'

'You 'on't git me going nowhere!' protested Thomas Judd. 'I'm staying here in England. Let them that wants to goo, goo, I say. I don't want to goo anywhere.' It was clear that he had taken Dick Dollery's remark as casting aspersions on himself in particular and certain nocturnal visits he was known to make into the woods around the village, from which he usually emerged come morning with a rabbit or a brace of pheasants to complement his widowed mother's table.

'Me, if I were to goo anywhere, I reckon I'd goo to that New Zealand place,' ventured John Romble, puffing out a cloud of smoke, eager to calm the conversation again. 'They say it is jest like England. If I had to goo anywhere, I'd goo there and never mind they Maori folk being there already and supposed to be all fierce, like. T'wouldn't bother me. Better to goo there than the cold of Canada – they say Canada can be real cold in the winter and has snowdrifts fifteen or twenty-feet deep if they are an inch and polar bears and brown bears that'll kill you with one swipe of their paw. And, of course, they've still got the Frenchies in Quebec.'

Dick Dollery never could understand how anyone could even contemplate leaving the country of their birth to spend the rest of their lives in a foreign land. 'Never mind gooing to bloody America or the Cape or Upper Canada or t'other side of the world to Botany Bay,' he would exclaim whenever the conversation turned towards whoever was thinking of going, banging his great gnarled fist down upon the table. 'I have no desire to goo to any o' those places. None whatsoever. Make things better here for ourselves is what we need to do.'

'Why are the lads leaving?' Jem asked, as one who had just returned to the village, curious as to why four others should be leaving it.

'Same old problem – overcrowding,' Dick Dollery growled in a low voice, shrugging as he did so, for to his mind that one word conjured up a host of explanations which did not need to be stated and the subject was such that there were those who stood and sat not ten feet from them who, had they overheard the word, might have thought he was referring to their circumstances and taken it amiss.

'The cottages round here is all too small by half for the size of the families people has. Most on us has big families round here, as you know – it's nature, like,' he went on, flushing slightly with the embarrassment of one who had five young daughters of his own. 'And when someone has a big family and there are eight or ten in one bedroom – girls as well as boys – well, it stands to reason, don't it, that sooner or later one or t'other will have to goo? There just en't the room, not for young lads with all a young lad's liveliness and that. I could tell you of dozens o' places round here right now where seven or eight lads and girls are all sleeping together in the one bedroom with the beds all pushed up agin one another and no room to hang a blanket between for decency's sake for the girls, because they is more minded about that than a chap is. Most times, the girls have to move in with their mother or the lads have to shift out and find new lodgings elsewhere, especially when they gets to fourteen and fifteen and the old blood starts thickening. Young chaps and girls can't stay cooped up together when they is all near grown-up – it causes no end o' trouble, don't it? There is no harm in it when they are children, all sleeping together in the one bedroom, but when they starts to git into their fifteens, sixteens and seventeens, then it becomes a problem, don't it? A real problem.'

His pipe had not caught and he broke off to strike his tinder box again and fuss with lighting that from a taper, puffing at it to get it going, before resuming, still with his voice low, though in the raucous atmosphere of the large room it was unlikely any would overhear him unless they were straining their ears,.

'We've got a few results of that kind of thing round here right now. People try to keep it dark, but we know. We en't daft, even if some folks think we are. You only has to look at some o' the little'uns in some families to know what a brother and sister got up to one night while their mother and father were snoring away in the next bedroom. You can tell inbreeding jest by looking at 'em. They jest don't look right, though I suspect it's the lads that do the pushing, not the girls. They usually do, lads, don't they? Too much red blood gooing round their bodies. It happens too often in some families, though. That's why the young chaps has to goo when they gits grown-up – either that or they gits theirselves a girl and gits married to stop the pot from boiling over like it do. I've known some on'em to do it on their first harvest wage. Can't wait. Nature's rampaging. That's why all the cottages is taken up – too many of the young lads sent packing by their families and too many young girls getting wed too quick. There used to be cottages empty round here twenty, thirty year agoo, but now there en't none to be had anywhere. That's why these four lads is gooing.'

Dick Dollery again indicated one of the youths who was leaving, a curly-haired and pink-faced fellow of no more than eighteen years, who was being teased by most of those around them, but who was smiling happily at it all, pleased to be the centre of attention.

'I know his mother,' he said, still keeping his voice low lest he be overheard by those around them. 'They has a two-bedroom cottage like mine and like the one I was brought up in. She and her husband sleep in the one room and their three sons – Silas there is the oldest at eighteen – still sleep in the same room as their two girls, Alice and May, thirteen and fourteen. She's a decent, respectable body, the mother. T'is a constant dread to her, them all together at night in the one room. She'd give anything to git a cottage with three bedrooms and keep young Silas from going, but she can't a-cause there en't none to be had. Now he's leaving the village for good most like. She don't want him to goo as she might not see him agin – she knows that – but she's a mother and he's grown and she has to think of her daughters. It fair tears your heart sometimes.'

'The cottages around here are all owned by others,' said John Romble, anger creeping into his voice. 'They is all rented. The Church has twenty on'em, the old squire or whoever buys his land has others, Amos Peakman has a few as well and the rest is all owned by outsiders. I don't know of a man in this village who owns the cottage he lives in, that I don't. If they wants to hold them that's not yet gone and bring back them that has, they has to give 'em better wages and better houses and charge lower rents. A family needs three bedrooms in a cottage if lads and girls is growing together, but the landlords 'on't build'em like that and they don't seem minded to change it either. They finds it cheaper to build 'em small and put a lot on'em together and yet they still charges us the same high rent. It'd be something if some of they pious Christians who goo about spouting their Bible talk knew the half of what we village folk has to suffer, but they just ignores us, like everyone else.'

As they sat there, some of the younger men began to make fun of a youth with a drooling mouth, bulging eyes and a misshapen head, jogging his elbow as he tried to drink his ale, pulling at the back of his smock and knocking his tattered hat forward over his eyes, teasing him so that the poor fellow could hardly take a sip. The youth, nicknamed 'Prickle,' was one of a family of fifteen in the village named Witney, who were considered to be somewhat deficient in sense and awareness: indeed, 'Prickle' Witney was regarded as the epitome of a village idiot, and, as such, was a natural target for the teasing of the other youths of his age and the older men when he went amongst them. None of it was hurtful or vicious: it was just a way for the men to jest at the expense of someone else's discomfort.

Jem knew from his time in the village before he left it that there had always been a measure of imbecility in the place amongst the various generations of the half-gypsy Witneys: the youth 'Prickle' was just the latest progeny of an incestuous liaison between a brother and a sister who were themselves somewhat retarded for the same reason.

'You see there why the women worry so,' said Dick Dollery with a nod in the direction of the unfortunate youth. 'That's what inbreeding gives you and there en't no better way to git inbreeding than to have grown-up lads and grown-up girls sleeping all together in the same room!'

THIRTEEN

IN THOSE DAYS, the very fabric of Hamwick Dean's life revolved around the seasons and the farming year and its festivals: Plough Sunday, Lady Day, Michaelmas, Lammas Day, Rogation Sunday and the three Rogation Days. For instance, Michaelmas, the festival in honour of the Archangel Michael on September the twenty-ninth, was as important a feast day to the old countryman as was Christmas to others, if not more so. It was traditionally the end of harvesting and it was the day upon which the 'stubble' goose, fattened on the stubble left after harvest, was served up, supposedly because Queen Elizabeth was eating goose on the day that she received news of the defeat of the Spanish Armada. It was also a quarter day and it was on quarter days like Michaelmas and Lady Day, the latter on March the twenty-fifth, that farming tenancies were set: and the husbandry of Hamwick Dean was no different in that to any other place.

Lady Day had once been the start of the new year, till the move was made from the Julian Calendar to the Gregorian Calendar sixty-four years before and the first day of January was made the start of the new year, even though not a single shoot was pushing up from the ground, when only a few half-starved birds flew about the sky, when the wisest of animals were still in hibernation and there was not a single leaf upon a single tree or hedgerow. The older folk, born under the old calendar, still lamented the change: and, governed by the seasons rather than by dates, still considered Lady Day as the new year's start.

Lammas, derived from the Old English 'hlaf-maesse,' meaning 'loaf-mass,' was in past times an earlier thanksgiving than the present church service and was held on August the first at the beginning of the harvest season, for which farmers made loaves of bread from the fresh wheat crop and these were then given to the church as the communion bread to be blessed by the parson during a special service thanking God for the harvest. It derived from Anglo-Saxon times when tenants were bound to present freshly harvested wheat to their landlords on or before the first day of August and in the *Anglo-Saxon Chronicle* was called 'the feast of first fruits': in Hamwick Dean, as in other villages, it was invariably marked by a plentiful harvest supper and much drinking in the Wayfarers' and the Carpenters' Arms.

At Rogation, the three days – Rogation Monday, Tuesday and Wednesday – before Ascension Thursday, which itself falls forty days after Easter, the husbandmen had their crops blessed by whoever was the incumbent parson, as was usual during the spring, though in Hamwick Dean of late that duty had fallen more to one or other of the two curates, the Reverend Waters, who usually tended a small flock at St. John's church in Merchant Staplers, and the older Reverend George Snetterton, who performed the same pastoral duties at St. Cuthbert's, Lower Rackstead. It was also the day of 'beating the bounds,' in which a procession of Hamwick Dean's parishioners, again led by one or other of the curates, would proceed around the boundary of the parish and pray for the village's protection in the coming year: it was also, of course, the start of the three weeks till Trinity Sunday when no marriages were allowed to be solemnised, so weddings were often rushed for Easter, particularly if there were a good cause, which invariably there was and which usually presented itself a few months later in the form of a squalling babe.

The husbandry of the open-fields was governed by what the villagers called the 'Little Court,' in effect, a medieval manor court, comprising a steward and twelve jurors, one of whom served as the foreman, which met each month, as it had done since medieval times, though the old prerogatives of the 'manor court' had been defunct in the village since the days of Cromwell and the Republic. The Little Court's sole purpose by then was to regulate the complete management of the common fields and common pastures, determining by an agreed set of byelaws such things as mattered to the husbandmen and which interested and affected them and no others. In effect, no husbandman, however large his holding or however important his social position, was at liberty to cultivate his strips as he pleased: the whole system was settled for him by the jurors of the Little Court.

For instance, the jurors decided each year which seed should be sown in the different lesser fields: they also decreed that no one could mow the wheat until after Lammas and the first loaf had been blessed and all ploughing on the strips was to be done in a clockwise manner rather than anti-clockwise, as might be the custom elsewhere. Peculiar as it was, the effect of this latter law was that lands became raised a foot or so in the centre, while, at the top and bottom of each furlong, where the plough was lifted out as the teams turned, a small amount of earth was always pushed forwards along the direction of the share which over time formed into a substantial mound, called a head or butt. The jury even had a law to deal with those: once the use of the butts or headlands as a turning ground was over, they could also be ploughed, the Little Court decreed: and, since not all strips lay parallel, but some lay at various angles to their neighbour and to others as the lie of the land dictated, the cultivator sowing his seeds, manuring or harvesting had the right to tread two-and-a-half yards on to his neighbour's land in order to do so. However, anyone who carelessly drove a wagon or cart over land belonging to someone else could be fined from sixpence to a pound, depending upon the nature of the trespass and the damage the tread of their horse and the roll of their wagon wheels had caused to the other's growing corn.

The Little Court also determined the date upon which the harvested arable was to be breached or thrown open so that livestock could feed off the stubble, at the same time manuring the field with their droppings for the next crop. It restricted, too, the cutting of weeds on the arable so that this source of feed would be available for livestock when the field was fallowed: and it also routinely enforced regulations for clearing the ploughed ditches and maintaining balks and fences or hedges, as well as dealing with encroachments and enclosures.

It also prevented the overuse of the common by restricting its use to those living in the village and further enforced this by insisting all cows carry the village's mark, branding to be done only on Lady Day, when the sheep were also to be sheared: further, pigs were to be ringed through the nose to stop them from eating down to the bare soil when they were turned out.

Such were some of the rulings and decisions of the Little Court. In previous times, the lord of the manor's steward would have selected the jurors: but they now selected themselves annually from amongst the number of husbandmen as tenants of the strips, taken in a haphazard rotation, in both the village and the two hamlets. In their craftiness, they chose to sit for the greater part of their session in the Wayfarers' Inn rather than in the church Vestry as in former times, simply because it allowed them to drink while they talked and it was also the one place that the present parson, being abstemious, would never seek to attend. To the jurors' way of thinking, transacting their business in the Wayfarers' forestalled any interference from the clergy in a process which had worked well enough for the past two hundred and fifty years and which they saw no reason to change, as had been done in some other places of which they had heard and never any good coming from it. In short, the jurors of the Little Court transacted that business of the land which previously had been carried out by the old manorial court, excepting that for dealing with felonies, which had long since passed to the Justices of the Peace at Hamwyte.

Except for those who rented their land from the Church or who paid their dues to the appointed local agent of the dormant lordship of the manor, many of the other husbandmen of Hamwick Dean did not truly know to whom they actually paid their rent, but paid it year after year each Michaelmas as they had always done and carried on with their farming as they had always done, supposing any transactions which involved change of ownership by purchase or by bequest were recorded somewhere upon some deed which lay somewhere gathering dust upon some lawyer's shelf.

The appointed land agent of the dormant lordship of the manor and also of many of the absent landowners in both the village and the two hamlets was, for convenience's sake, as it turned out, also the steward of Hamwick Dean's Little Court – Peter Able, a somewhat overweight, cherubic-faced lawyer, in his late fifties, with white-hair falling to his shoulders, who dressed always in black and who had a practice in Hamwyte. He lived in a white-painted Georgian mansion, not unnaturally named 'The Whitehouse,' which, being situated in the very centre of the triangle of roads at the village's heart, lay directly opposite the Wayfarers', up a short shrubbery-lined drive leading off The Street, and was perfectly placed for him to carry out that part of his business.

Though he may have had the appearance of a Quaker, and may well have been one for all the villagers knew or cared, he did not have the ways of one, but drank regularly in the old inn with the other men and liked to sit and talk with them as much as they liked to sit and talk with him, for he had a dry wit about him and they admired him for his friendliness and for his good common sense which he dispensed to one and all with or without their permission, especially during arguments when he was often called upon to act as both the judge and the jury: for, being a learned lawyer amongst mostly unschooled and sometimes hot-headed countryfolk, he was more dispassionate in his reasoning.

As the agent collecting the rental for most of the absent landlords, particularly the trust managing the Old Squire's defunct estate, every Michaelmas he seated himself at a table in the Wayfarers' at ten o'clock in the morning and remained there the whole day while the husbandmen trooped in with their cash in advance of the evening of feasting that lay ahead, at the same time slowly drinking the pots of ale which Caleb Chapman regularly placed before him throughout the day, almost without being asked, till finally, with all dues paid and recorded, the feasting off the goose would begin and the drinking, of course, would continue.

A less amiable man of Mr. Able's acknowledged learning might well have shunned the Michaelmas feast in the Wayfarers' as being beneath his dignity, for a hundred and more would attend, all male, of course, including all the area's husbandmen and small farmers and even some of the day-labourers who usually drank in the Carpenters' Arms, if they were friendly enough, gathering mostly in the big bay-windowed parlour, but often overflowing into the taproom and sometimes into the vault which lay to the right of the central door, and was mostly unused except on such occasions.

Mr. Able, however, always attended – indeed he had not missed the Michaelmas goose feast in fifteen years – and would sit happily amongst them all, drinking every pot of ale placed before him, till eventually he had to be helped back, somewhat unsteadily, across the road and up his drive, to be met at the door by the fierce looks of his shrewish wife and the inevitable scolding which followed and which echoed throughout the great, empty, childless house, to the amusement of whoever saw him home as they walked back down the driveway.

The rotund, black-suited lawyer had served as the court's steward, albeit for a small stipend, as far back as the time of the late lamented Squire, having been requested by him to take up the post as a fount not only of good common sense and wisdom but also of calm and fair-mindedness. In between his perpetual snuff-taking and sipping at his ale, Mr. Able meticulously recorded in his leather-bound accounts book, as only a scholarly lawyer could, not only such things as the payments of rents and fines but also the transfers of land and sub-lettings.

So empowered was the Little Court in the village's husbandry matters that, before anyone could claim a tenancy by inheritance, if, say, they were one of the very few husbandman families who had managed to purchase some of the strips they farmed, he as the steward had the powers to summon them to appear before him and the other jurors to prove their succession, by descent or by a will, and then to pay a sum upon taking up that tenancy: and, if any tenant wished to sell, mortgage or sublet holdings, he had to 'surrender' the land to the court, acknowledging the ownership of the land and that land was then granted by the court's discretion to the new tenant, who swore fealty and paid the entry fine.

There was always business for Mr. Able at the Little Court – and drink and company, of course.

FOURTEEN

JEM HAD ALWAYS looked to Lady Day, when the farming tenancies were set, as the likeliest first opportunity when something might come up which would enable him to fulfil his dream of becoming an independent husbandman. It so happened that, just before the quarter-day meeting in late March, he learned that the widow of a tenant, 'Bunny' Hebborne, one of seven older villagers who had succumbed to the cold that bitter winter and now lay under their mounds in the churchyard, was looking to surrender several strips of good arable glebe or Church land, amounting in total to eight acres, ten roods and eighteen perches.

With the death of her husband of fifty years and having outlived her issue, Widow Hebborne had neither the money nor the heart to oversee the work of day-labourers on her late husband's land or even to pay one of the village's two experienced ploughmen, Johnny Thickbroom or Ned Munson, to turn the earth with their heavy horses. What little money she possessed, she needed to keep herself out of the village's poorhouse till the time came a few months hence when, she happily predicted without fear, she expected to join her husband in the churchyard – 'to join his soul in Heaven' was how she worded it – and leave behind the woes of a world that no longer held any happiness or meaning for her.

Glebe land in Hamwick Dean and the two hamlets then was subject to a fine of one year's value upon either the death of the leaseholder or the transfer of the property to another, to be paid by the incumbent tenant: since the old widow could not pay it, she had asked Dick Dollery if he knew of anyone who might take up the arable land as well as an acre of allotted common meadow pasture and all rights it carried. She was willing to surrender it back to the Little Court, as was the custom, if someone would take over the tenancy at the Lady Day meeting rather than wait till Michaelmas and also pay the heavy fine which would be imposed for the transfer.

Though the land was owned by the Church and the rental dues went eventually to the Bishop of Melchborough, the village's white-haired, hook-nosed parson, the Reverend Doctor William Wakefield Petchey, or 'Parson Petchey' as the villagers called him (sometimes 'Squarson Petchey') had no interest himself in who took over glebe on any of the three open-fields or meadow pasture so long as all dues and fines were met and paid on time and so long also as the tenant, whoever they were, was a God-fearing Christian and regularly attended his church – or did thereafter on taking up the tenancy: for if they did not, then they would incur his disfavour! Apart from that, he was content to leave the matters with which the Little Court dealt to the churchwarden, Andrew Norris, who sat as one of the jurors, being an open-field tenant with four acres himself, and so was able to apprise the parson of any matters which appertained to the Church, though some said Parson Petchey was too much of an Oxford man and too immersed in university theologies to concern himself with the more mundane matters of village life as might 'a proper parson,' hence his delegation to his two curates of the crop-blessing and beating the bounds.

The news of Widow Hebborne's intended surrender was passed to Jem by none other than Dick Dollery in the Wayfarers' one blowy evening at the start of March: curiously, the lanky, blond-haired husbandman waited till Jem went to the outhouse in the backyard before following him out.

'There's likely some good arable coming up for surrender at the next court meeting,' he whispered as the two stood side by side at the trough, at the same time looking behind him to ensure that no one had come up behind who might overhear. 'Glebe land, eight or more acres, part sown already with winter wheat, still with eleven years of the lease to run, so I am told. Old "Bunny" Hebborne's widow wants to get shot of it as soon as she can. T'is a boon, Jem boy, eight good acres, so put thy bid in smart like if thee has the money, but don't go blabbing it about. To keep it legal, give Caleb a letter saying thee is interested when it is quiet and he'll pass it on to them as needs to have it, Mr. Able and Pete Sparshott, the foreman. I'll goo round and see the old widow and put her mind at rest a-cause she is fair worried sick that she will have to pay the fine herself. She en't asking to make no profit from it, just to pass the land on to someone who'll settle the fine for her. The court'll asccept it. They won't want it lying fallow. But, for Lord's sake, don't tell anyone what thee is doing. Enos, Nat and the others know about it, but they 'on't say anything. They're not blabbers. We don't want the whole village to know the old widow is giving up her husband's ground. We has our reasons.'

He tapped the side of his nose and gave a sly wink, the way people do when they impart such secrets, before buttoning his front and returning to the bar parlour whistling nonchalantly as if he had never had a conspiratorial thought in his head. Jem did not require any urging: after a near lifetime of receiving orders from others, or so it seemed to him, his sole wish was to be independent of everyone: the eights acres which the widow was surrendering would do thnat.

'T'is enough to keep thee busy year round, I reckon,' Dick Dollery had further informed him. 'I'd take some of the land myself, but I can't afford it. Enos would have taken some, too. It would keep him busy so he don't have to goo looking for day work on Peakman's or Howie's or Godwin's.'

Dick Dollery himself had five acres, fifteen roods and twelve perches, all of which he rented from the Church for a few shillings annually, though like the rest it was located in twenty different places on the three great open-fields: the straw-haired labourer also kept a half-dozen cows with the village herd on the common pasturage and geese on the waste. Likewise. Enos Diddams had four acres and nine roods and eighteen perches, also rented solely from the Church and similarly scattered throughout the three open-fields: he also kept a half-dozen sheep and goats apiece on the common and two pigs in a yard behind his cottage which he sent into the woods each year under a right of pannage to feed on the beechnuts and acorns. As did the other husbandmen, they both spent the whole day going from one scattered strip to another, sometimes walking two or three miles to each in turn in a day.

The widow's holding, however, was more consolidated. In each of the three lesser fields of the hundred-and-ten-acre First Field – Ash Grove, Barrow and Thornbush – it consisted of fifteen of the furlong strips lying unbalked as adjoining parcels of five together, that is, an acre and a quarter, with a dozen other strips likewise consolidated as single acres in the Snook, Badger's Hole and Partridge fields of the narrower Long Field and another half-dozen strips spread randomly across Reeve's, Farthing and Gravel Pit in the poorer land of Third Field, plus a good acre or more on the common meadow, which was already hurdled-off for hay-making. It was more than Jem had ever hoped for to begin: and since two of the parcels lay in Barrow and Thornbush and within a stone's throw of Redhouse farm, he knew from past experience, when his father had worked it, how good the land was in that part.

Jem was even willing to advance the widow the small fee she requested for giving up her rights on the common pasturage and the common waste, which she would no longer require as all her animals, three cows, six sheep and two pigs, had been slaughtered at the beginning of the winter, again as was the custom in the countryside then to avoid the need to provide them with feed and shelter over the long winter months.

Jem did as he was advised and handed his letter to Caleb Chapman the next evening, declaring not only his intention to apply to the Little Court for a change in the lease of the Widow Hebborne's land, both arable and pasture, as Dick Dollery had told him to do and as he was required to do under the court's byelaws, but further that he would be pleased to put in an offer to take over the full thirty-two-and-a-half strips of the widow's arable glebe, and whatever common meadowland rights she also held and was giving up. Further, he was also willing to pay the same rental of a shilling and sixpence per acre, come Michaelmas, with eleven years of the lease of twenty-one years still to run and also to pay the fine that would be imposed upon the old widow at the surrender.

As Jem handed his letter across the bar, he incautiously offered an explanation of its contents to the grumpy innkeeper. 'Caleb, this is my letter for the widow's land. Dick told me to hand it to you – ' he began.

'Hush, man, keep your voice down!' Caleb Chapman hissed in some alarm. 'We don't want everyone to know just yet, especially one person hereabouts. The old widow 'on't take kindly to her business being the talk of everyone. So keep it quiet, for goodness sake!'

Later that evening as Dick Dollery slid on to the bench beside him, Jem informed him quietly: 'I have let Caleb know I am interested in the widow's land and have given him my letter.'

But if he was expecting Dick Dollery to discuss the matter, he was quickly disabused. 'Good,' was all Dick Dollery said, giving the merest nod in acknowledgement, 'but, like I said, don't go blabbing it about.' Again he tapped his nose and gave a conspiratorial smile the same as before.

None of his companions wanted to talk about Jem's good fortune either and, if they thought Jem was about to bring up the subject, they would switch their talk to other matters, which left Jem even more puzzled. It did not help that Caleb Chapman was forever glancing across to where they sat as if trying to discern what they were saying and signalling with his eyes for them to be guarded. Why there should be such secrecy, defeated Jem.

While Jem waited for the quarter-day session of the Little Court, he passed his days by walking around the district, renewing his acquaintance with old sites and sounds, as would any man who had spent twelve years away from a place. On two occasions, he walked to Maydun and on one of them, a mild, spring day, he strolled the whole eleven-mile length of the Langwater estuary's bleak northern shoreline, stopping halfway along the winding seawall for a drink and some luncheon at the old Chessman Inn in Gledlang square, before resuming his long walk to Cobwycke at the estuary's mouth. On three other occasions, he rode into Wivencaster with the village wagoner, Daniel Gate, purely to save money since the old man would not charge him as he was 'glad of the company.'

It was while he was idling away his time that, in the second week of March, Jem decided to walk into Hamwyte to visit his old comrade-in-arms, Will Ponder. Though Jem had twice been into Hamwyte on the Tuesday market days, he had not seen his old friend amid the throng on either occasion. It was time, he thought, to look him up and see how he was faring since his return and, as they had promised to do, to have a drink together in remembrance of old comrades-in-arms who had not returned.

FIFTEEN

BY THEN, Jem had spent almost half of his ten pounds bounty money, not only on his board and lodgings but also on the purchase of two shirts, a pair of second-hand breeches, several pairs of woollen stockings, a waistcoat, a thick dark topcoat and a pair of stout country boots, keeping his faded and patched uniform and other boots as 'spares,' if needed. He had also exchanged the ten gold Napoleons he had taken from the French cuirassier for pounds, shillings and pence at the new bank in Hamwyte High Street, a transaction which the delighted banker was more than pleased to do on learning that Jem had been a soldier at the great battle, albeit at an exchange entirely beneficial to himself.

In view of the nearness of Lady Day and in anticipation of being successful in his application to take over the lease of the widow's land, since no one else had shown any interest, Jem deemed it wise to have his capital to hand in cash so as to be able to pay the widow's fine and also to pay for the hire of a horse and one of the village's two fixed mouldboard ploughs. Further, it would also allow him to pay a couple of half-lads a fortnight's wages to help him draw a drag-rake across the turned furrows and then to purchase some corn seed, broadcast it and cover it with a 'brush' of bound tree branches dragged behind another hired horse, all, of course, supposing he was not rejected, which he did not expect to be.

The remaining capital would be needed to sustain him over the months of that year while his crop grew and he awaited some return on it: but the main benefit in having the money in pounds, shillings and pence was that it meant that, whatever happened during that first year of his venture, whether he made a profit or a loss, he would still be able to meet his first obligation at Michaelmas when the dues for the past year were settled with Mr. Able, and also be in a position to begin again at the start of the second year and have enough money to see himself through that as well.

It would also, of course, allow him to continue in his lodgings at the Wayfarers' till the time, he hoped soon, when he would be able to rent a small cottage of his own, were one to be had in the village. All in all, he was in a confident mood as he walked to Hamwyte that fine March mid-morning, arriving just after noon.

He eventually found his old friend, Will Ponder, after much searching, amongst a small colony of poor, tumbledown, single-storey cottages at the lower or eastern end of the town: not knowing the actual cottage or lane on which his friend lived, he had to ask several people for him by name and they, regarding him suspiciously in his smarter clothes, professed not to know anyone by the name of 'Will Ponder.' It was past one o'clock before he was eventually directed to 'the Widow Allbright's house' in a line of low, sagging-roofed dwellings at the top end of a narrow lane.

A row of washing hung upon a rope line in the sunlight and, when he knocked, the door, which was partly ajar, was pulled sharply back by a woman in her early-thirties, holding a wooden paddle with which she had been turning clothes in a tub, itself balanced somewhat precariously on a low stool just inside the door. The woman's face was reddened and shiny from the heat, her hair had become untied and hung across her face and the upper part of her plain brown dress was dampened from the clouds of steam drifting up. This Jem assumed, must be Will's sister and, as men do, he noted straight away that, though she might be a 'widow,' she still had a slim waist and a shapely figure which clearly had not been spoiled by childbirth, as it usually was in most women of her age. He noted, too, that she stood some five feet two inches in height and that, despite her years, she had retained a certain youthful prettiness with her wavy auburn hair, violet-blue eyes and the unpowdered red cheeks and unrouged mouth of a woman more used to work than idleness.

'Yes?' she demanded, giving Jem a cold stare.

However, before he could state his business, a surprised voice cried out from within: 'Jem, boy! Good God, man, come in, come in! I'm glad to see you, glad indeed.'

On entering, Jem found Will Ponder seated at the table by the sole window, which had been opened to let out more of the steam: he was eating a luncheon of pease porridge, bread and cheese and had a small tankard of ale beside him.

'Mary-Ann, this is my old sergeant, Jem Stebbings,' he declared, rising to pump the hand of a somewhat sheepish Jem. 'He is the one I told you about from Hamwick Dean. We served together in the battalion and messed together for a time when I was in Spain. We were together at the last one, too. Take a seat, Jem, boy, take a seat.' He motioned Jem to a wooden chair and called out to the woman, who, still holding the wet paddle, was regarding Jem curiously and somewhat openly: 'Mary-Ann, have we any ale left in the jug? You'll take a drink of home-brew, won't you, Jem? We'll have that drink we promised ourselves together later – you remember, a drink to honour all the other lads who haven't come home?'

Jem nodded his acquiescence, but in truth he was not paying a great deal of attention to what Will was saying. Instead, his eyes – and his mind – were fixed on Mary-Ann as she moved about the small cottage, going first to a cupboard to take out a cloth-covered china jug and then across to a crude dresser to take out a pewter tankard.

'My sister, Mary-Ann,' said his friend, almost as if it were an afterthought, as she crossed to the table to pour the drink, though only half-filling the tankard, probably in view of her brother's stated determination to go for a 'proper drink' afterwards. 'I'm lodging here for a while, like I said when you and I parted. '

Will's sister acknowledged Jem's 'Thank you' with a barely perceptible nod of her own and a coolness which declared she did not much care for her brother's friends coming into her home. At the same time, towards her smiling brother, she gave that cold, austere look which only a sister can give a brother and by which they acknowledge they will tolerate his presence for the moment, but are actually thinking that the sooner he is gone the better. As a precaution, too, she made a point of returning the china jug to the cupboard and banging the door shut.

The reason Jem stared was that he was sure he had seen the woman before: indeed, as soon as she had opened the door and he first saw the shape of her small oval face, her high cheekbones and her petite figure, he knew that he had seen her before and not in Hamwyte either: but where, he could not immediately recall.

'Mary-Ann's husband died of the fever five years back, soon after I sailed to join you,' went on Will, munching now on a piece of bread and cheese and washing it down with a swallow of ale as Mary-Ann went back to the washtub and began wringing out the clothes. 'He come from your way – Inworth, didn't he, gel? She was working over there as a dairy maid when she met him. Used to stand up at those hiring fairs they had on the heath. Bob Allbright was his name. I don't suppose you would have known him? – '

Jem had not. However, he was interested in what Will had said about his sister: for he now knew where he had seen her before, though he had not spoken to her at the time. It was the mention of the hiring fairs which brought the memories flooding back: of himself as a sorrowful seventeen-year-old, with not a farthing to his name, traipsing behind Elijah Scoble to the hiring fair on Inworth heath. In previous days, workers in the surrounding Hundreds who had no settled employment would stand once a year at the end of September at the Michaelmas hiring fair, especially for farmers wanting good threshing hands, expert with a flail for threshing in a barn over winter. In most places, the practice had died out with the coming of the war because, with so many men and youths away, there was plenty of work. However, it had lingered in certain places through the early part of the war and the Hundred of Hamwyte had been one of them.

Jem had gone willingly enough, for there was always the hope of obtaining better employment than he had had previously: what he did remember particularly was how embarrassed he had felt and how self-conscious he had been having to stand on a platform like some African slave at an auction in one of America's southern States, with a tag around his neck, while a passing parade of farmers and wealthy landowners and tradesmen 'looked over' each man or youth in turn who had 'put himself up' so as to ascertain his strength, his general appearance and his character and then to question each about what work they had done and could do.

By chance, Mary-Ann had been standing that same day on another raised platform opposite with several other girls and single women, being similarly assessed for maid service by farmers and wealthy landowners, especially their wives. The younger girls were always the first to be hired and hustled away to become milkmaids or domestic servants: Mary-Ann, being slightly older than most of the others, had been there sometime before she departed, which is how Jem had come to notice her.

What he recalled was standing forlornly on the men's platform in his tattered smock, with his things bundled up in his father's old shirt, and Mary-Ann mischievously smiling across at him, sensing his embarrassment, giggling with the other women and girls, knowing by the way he blushed that she was most probably the first girl who had ever made eyes at him, which she was, the first girl who had ever looked at him in a way which caused a great hollow in his stomach and brought an almost dizzying rush of blood to his cheeks. So much so that when soon after she went off with her new employer and his wife, with just a backward glance at the youth who had been unable to meet her eyes, he had felt both relieved that she was gone and, perplexingly, sad as well and wondering who she was. To think he had been sharing his mess with her brother ever since he had arrived in the battalion after the battle at Badajoz!

After the hiring fair, Jem had returned to Hamwick Dean with the disappointed Elijah Scoble and, having no accommodation, had lodged with him and his wife, paid for by the parish, of course, till his name had fortuitously been 'drawn out' at the Wayfarers' to serve in the militia at Melchborough.

'I was at a hiring fair at Inworth myself once,' Jem blurted out, 'when I was about seventeen, soon after my mother and father died. I believe I was standing across the way from you that day. You got taken up. I didn't, unfortunately. Soon after that, I joined the militia. I knew I had seen you before, Mrs. Allbright, the moment you opened the door, though I never knew you were Will's sister. That is a surprise.'

Jem's small revelation drew the immediate interest of the brother and he was prevailed upon to tell the brief embarrassing tale of the hiring fair, which, while greeted with chuckles and cries from his friend of 'Well, blow me! Blow me! I would never have thought it! Blow me!' brought no smile at all to Mary-Ann's face: in fact, her gaze hardened and she was almost fierce in her reaction.

'Such a thing was too long a time ago to expect a body to remember it,' she said sharply, a measured iciness in her tone, deliberately throwing some rinsed washing back into the tub with a loud splash. 'I was in service for ten years before I met my husband and I stood at two or three hiring fairs. I don't care to remember those times or to be reminded of them, if you please – being looked up and down and commented upon by some boggle-eyed farmer and his noughty, squint-eyed wife like a horse at a sale! It's a wonder some of them didn't want to count our teeth! I had enough of those kinds of people to last me a lifetime, all put-on airs and graces, and I don't care to remember any of it, thank you very much.'

Jem suddenly felt very ashamed: he had hoped that he and Will's sister could both smile together at the memory, but her acerbic tone and her icy manner told him that there he had made a bad mistake. He had embarrassed her at their first proper meeting: and, for some reason, he felt unexpectedly disconcerted at having done so. He was acutely aware, too, of his own cheeks reddening with embarrassment. 'I am very sorry, Mrs. Allbright,' he stuttered out in apology, 'I perhaps ought not to have spoken so freely.'

Fortunately, Will rescued him: having finished his eating and, sensing his sister's growing displeasure, he rose quickly from his seat, took a final swig from his tankard, banged it back on the table and, after a loud burp, cried heartily: 'Come on, Jem, we'll go to the George. We'll have that drink together like we said we would, for all the friends we knew – ' With a laugh, he added: 'And a few we did not!'

Then to Mary-Ann, who had turned her back on them both and was looking somewhat peeved and flustered as she continued to stir the steaming washtub, he called out with a smile as though nothing had been said to upset her: 'Don't expect me back before bedtime, Sis. I mean to get good and drunk with my old mess mate here. No doubt there'll be a few of the benefit club chaps there as well so I expect there'll be plenty of drinking going on.'

'You do what you like, you always have,' was Mary-Ann's waspish retort, to which she added equally as sharply, without bothering to turn round: 'And don't go spouting out your Government nonsense either. That tongue of yours will get you into trouble with the constables and the Justices before long the way you go on about things that don't concern you. Lot of silliness! Remember, there's other folks that has to live here, too.'

Will explained his sister's remark as they walked along the High Street. 'She means that I say things which others do not like to hear,' he confessed, 'but, I tell you, Jem, what I say is the truth and no more than that. It is just that people do not like to hear it. We have formed a benefit club in Hamwyte, just fifty or sixty of us. We all put a little bit into it each week, tuppence or threppence or sixpence, whatever we can afford, and that way, over time, we build up a fair sum which helps to keep the wolf from the door for the worst off when we ain't in work – ' The slight smile he gave told Jem that he meant himself. ' – The Vestry here are a bunch of skinflints. They'll put you to work on road-mending or ditch-digging soon enough for a measly two and sixpence a week, but they won't give you a shilling extra unless you are near to death's door, that they won't.'

Jem knew well enough from experience that his friend had always been outspoken and opinionated: he was a fierce arguer by nature, almost as if his small size made him even more belligerent towards his taller fellows, for he sometimes seemed to pick an argument where no argument existed in other men's minds. On occasion, he seemed to carry the weight of the world on his squat shoulders and several times surprised Jem and the others in the platoon not only by the vehemence of his arguing but also by the sense and conviction of it.

Now, as if thinking about something which troubled him, he fell silent for a while, leaving Jem to fill in the silence with his tale of what he had been doing since his return: indeed, his friend did not speak again until they entered the George Inn, which, as they walked towards the centre of the town, lay on the right side of the High Street, almost opposite the turn-off to Hamwick Dean and a short way from the larger Black Bear across the road from it.

'This is the place, Jem. We'll have a good old drink, you and I,' said Will Ponder, pushing open the parlour door and seeming to have regained his cheerfulness at the prospect of drinking. 'If you stay till evening, you'll meet a few of my friends. They haven't seen what we have seen, but they are good old boys, nevertheless.'

As it happened, after only their third tankard, Will somewhat sheepishly confessed that he had no more money: he had bought his sole round on coin given him by his sister and had none left, which meant that Jem would have to buy the ale for the rest of the session: not that he minded: he had more than enough to spare and it was not the first time he had stood an evening's drinking with his friend. The last of Will Ponder's bounty money had been used up two weeks before and Jem suspected that the greater part of it had been spent on too frequent visits to the very inn in which they sat, though, like Jem, he had had to replace his old frayed uniform and worn out boots with civilian clothes.

Jem, Will and the other demobilised soldiers of the 44th should have been issued with civilian clothing at Dover, paid for from the regiment's funds, but somehow no one in his company had been and everyone suspected that the quartermaster sergeant had either sold the clothing or it had been diverted to another regiment. Or, more likely, the clothing had never been purchased in the first place, which is why they had had to travel home wearing the same old and faded uniforms they had worn on their campaigns and which both had been pleased to discard.

SIXTEEN

WILL PONDER, Jem also learned, had been unable to find regular work since his return, neither as an agricultural labourer, of whom there were many in the town, nor as a bricklayer or a barrel-maker or a woodsman or even a yard man at any of the town's five inns, though he had tried for all. Indeed, such was the level of unemployment everywhere since the war had ended that almost threequarters of the labouring population of Hamwyte were receiving relief from the poor rate and going to the overseer of the poor for a weekly dole of two shillings and sixpence was not unusual for a labourer in the town.

In good times, the majority of the men and youths would have worked on the many farms surrounding the place: for even the villages which still had open-fields also had three, four or five larger farms within their parishes, tenanted by yeomen farmers like those at Hamwick Dean, to which the men and youths would willingly walk two or three miles each morning, glad of the work and the pay. The great slump had ended all that and now they were as badly off as their country cousins, if not more so, for being landless and more numerous, they found that their own lesser gentry were more uncaring than a privileged squire or a sanctimonious parson were ever likely to be simply because there were, as the gentry repeatedly said, 'too many of them.'

However, unlike most of them, Will Ponder had fought for his King and his Country: and, being unable to find work on his return, that fact alone had made him more embittered than most of those whom he joined in the queue which formed at the Moot Hall's side door each Tuesday market day when the relief was paid out.

As the afternoon wore into the early evening and their drinking in the George continued, Will Ponder's speech began to slur, for, by that time, it was seven o'clock and the two of them were on their eighth or ninth tankard, mostly paid for by Jem, though, out of deference to their fallen comrades-in-arms, he had not counted the cost of it all and to deny Will a refill when he called for one would have been churlish

'T'is not the England that you and I fought Boney for,' declared his friend solemnly as they sat amid the early evening gathering. 'In this town, they regard the common man with contempt and make no effort to conceal it. When we go for our weekly relief, all two hundred and more of us is kept standing out in the rain and the hail and anything else the good Lord sees fit to throw at us, while they sit in the dry and tell us to wait and to have patience. T'is as though they are the lords of long ago and we are still their serfs and the centuries have never passed at all. T'is those same lords and the wealthy landowners who hold all the high offices and, by their positions and their greed, take all the wealth for themselves while we poor folk are kept in want. They sit in Parliament in their fine robes and make laws which protect them and their kind and their interests alone at the expense of ours and yet they are the very same people who are the magistrates and the judges and the lawyers who prosecute us if we break those same laws – laws which protect mostly them.

'You tell me, Jem, why should a lord and lady live in a fine big house surrounded by a hundred acres of land, with all their peacocks and their rose bushes and their fancy hedges to be cut into fancy shapes and their high-walls to keep out the likes of us – why should they live so while we, the poor, have to live in hovels?' He realised what he had said, reddened and quickly corrected himself. 'Oh, I don't mean my sister's place. She keeps a tidy house. I mean all the close, cramped cottages round about us, with hardly room to swing a cat, all jumbled higgledypiggledy with no room to pass between. It ain't the way for a man to bring up a family, that it ain't. We ought to have better by law – by law.'

His remarks echoed exactly those of Dick Dollery and Enos Diddams in the Wayfarers': it was not something Jem had ever thought about, having lived solely with his mother and father in the one small cottage till their sudden deaths from the sweating sickness had orphaned him. That had begun very suddenly, with his father complaining first of violent cold shivers, giddiness and severe pains in his neck, shoulders and limbs and thinking he had a 'bad air' malaise: the next day his mother had succumbed, too, so that both lay abed shivering. The day following they were sweating even more yet without any obvious cause: both complained of splitting headaches and intense thirst, followed by sharp pains in their chests and after that delirium which kept them prostrated till their demise. A further sadness for Jem was that, had the Fates been kinder, he would have had two siblings with whom to share the mourning, but both his younger brothers had died in infancy when he was still toddling himself: it had broken his mother's heart and it had hardened his father.

The recall of it came briefly back to him, but he quickly dismissed it: that was a long way in the past. Will Ponder's pessimism was the problem for the present – that and the fact that his voice had risen steadily, almost to a shout, and he repeatedly banged his fist down on the table to emphasise his points, spattering even wider the pools of dripped ale lying on its top, so that several times Jem had to wipe his forehead or cheek.

Alarmed by the passion as much as the loudness with which his friend was speaking, Jem found himself constantly turning towards the door, half-expecting to find the town's two parish constables entering, for he knew that they patrolled the streets in the early evening and also that they were not averse to slipping unnoticed into an inn and standing quietly in a passageway while they listened to the conversation of the men in the snug or the vault or the bar parlour, just to ensure that there was no seditious talk coming from them or plans for a revolution – not that there ever would be in Hamwyte, of course. Fortunately for Will and Jem, the two stalwart upholders of the King's Peace were not abroad that evening, though others in the bar parlour, where the two comrades sat opposite each other in a corner, had paused in their own drinking to look across at them, some smiling knowingly, some even nodding and murmuring their agreement, willing Will Ponder on, in their hearts applauding what he said even though they dared not say it aloud themselves.

'Keep it quiet, Will,' Jem warned, remembering his friend's sister's edict: but Will Ponder was not to be deterred and dismissed his friend's warning with a wave of the hand.

'The time is coming, Jem, when the common people will unite in a common cause – all of us together – you and me and all my friends here,' he cried and, unexpectedly, a cheer went up, though an ironic one, from several of those who were listening.

'We need reform, Jem, the whole of England needs to be reformed. The common man has no voice in anything. We must sweep away these "penny packet pocket boroughs," like Hamwyte and Melchborough and Maydun and Wivencaster, where no more than fifty hold the vote amongst three thousand and yet that fifty elects our Members to sit in Parliament. T'is those same people who have all the law-making power in the Commons and the Lords together. T'is them who divides up the highest of the Church offices between themselves, who become all the high judges and the high admirals and the high generals and make sure that only their own kind follows them. What name can you give to that kind of government, Jem? Some people calls it a democracy. To my way of thinking, it is no democracy. T'is a band of great nobles, who, by sham elections and bribery and corruption, have obtained sway in this country. That's the nature of the government which rules you and me, Jem, the government we fought for and too many lads died for. If I had my way, I would burn down Parliament, for it does us, the common people, no good. It is just a talking shop made up of landowners and the gentry, who are one and the same when it comes to protecting themselves. This is no longer the England that you and I fought for, Jem – t'is not what I fought against Boney for, anyway.'

Yet again the cheers rose from those around them: men were smiling and commenting themselves now: they had heard such things before, much it from from Will Ponder, but did not mind hearing them again. Worried as Jem was about any sudden appearance of the town's two constables, for he did not wish to be arrested for sedition, he managed to force a smile: though he knew his friend was in deadly earnest, he felt that he had to make light of it all in view of the nature of the subject and those who were listening.

'I don't know what I fought for, in truth, Will,' he said with a shrug. 'I suppose I fought to stay alive mostly and for a bowl of stirabout at the next mess and perhaps a drink of rum or wine to go with it – and a roll on a bed with some town moxie now and again to put myself at ease with myself. I never fought for no Parliament of landlords and gentry. That was the least of the things I fought for. Maybe for the King. I took his coin so I suppose I fought for him. But I think I fought mostly because they told me to and I could do no other and because Johnny French was doing his damndest to kill me and had to be stopped before we could all come home again. That is what I fought for. The rest is of no note to me. I hope to be a husbandman soon. That is all I am interested in now. I leave politics to others. I have put in a bid and hope to take over the lease of some land in Hamwick Dean. That will be my future from now on. That is all I wish for, to be a plain husbandman. I'll be content with that.'

Will Ponder was not to be put off by his friend's feigned indifference or his honesty. 'Too many of us in this town are destitute, Jem,' he went on. 'Too many of the people in this town, the labouring classes, hardly have the money to feed themselves let alone a whole family. We are trod down by a system that is against us all from birth to the grave. It is not for the want of looking that I have not been able to find work since I came back. I have looked and asked in a dozen places, but there is nothing to be had. And those who are fortunate enough to find a day or two's work as day-labourers are paid a beggarly seven shillings a week for it, A man alone can barely survive on that wage, let alone a man with a family. Prices are rising everywhere – the price of bread is soaring. My sister is always on about it. Paying a few shillings to a labourer who is out of work or a pauper needing to feed his family and pay the rent on his cottage is not my idea of a home-coming, Jem. There is something rotten when so few vote and the seat for Parliament is owned by one person or one family only and they alone choose who shall sit for it in Parliament without so much as a flick for the rest of us. It ain't right when privilege is upheld against the wishes of those whose labour creates the wealth of this country, the working man. T'is a people's charter of rights we need, Jem, a people's charter to give us, the common people, what ought to be ours, what should be ours – by right!'

At this, several of the listeners jumped to their feet and began to applaud openly, shouting their agreement. In Jem's view, however, a great deal of it was mocking in its tone: they agreed with everything Will Ponder said, but then he was known as a firebrand. It was not the first time he had spoken out so voluably and so violently in the George: and he had red hair, so it was to be expected that he would tend to become excitable about things, especially politics. He was short and stocky, too, all the attributes of one who, being small, was prepared to take on things that were greater than himself, a David against a host of Goliaths: so they cheered him all the more.

When eventually the two friends left the George, Jem, who had drunk less than his friend, saw him safely home, helping him down the High Street and along the narrow lane to his sister's cottage: an oil lamp was still burning, even though it was long past ten o'clock. However, having brought Will Ponder home as near to being legless as a man can be and still stagger, Jem had not the courage to face his friend's sister a second time: so he propped his old comrade up against the doorpost, knocked loudly upon the door and fled quickly into the shadows across the lane.

Standing in the darkness, he saw the door open and heard Mary-Ann's scolding remarks to her brother as she helped him inside, for he was incapable of doing even that himself: 'Drunk again, are you? Get inside, you drunken sot! Get inside! If this is what happens when you go out with that friend of yours, then he had better keep away in future!'

Will Ponder must have retched at that moment, for a cry of disgust went up from his sister and the scolding grew louder. 'Where did you get the money to get yourself into this state?' she demanded, then answered her own question: 'From him, I suppose, because you didn't have any except what I gave you. Yours is all spent...'

Will must have mumbled a reply of sorts, probably confirming that his old friend Jem had paid for most of the ale: for just before she closed the door, Mary-Ann glanced out towards where Jem was standing hidden in the shadows and, almost as if she suspected he was there, declared loudly, enough to ensure that he heard: 'Then more fool him, I say, more fool him!'

With that, she banged the door shut and concentrated.upon scolding her brother even more.

SEVENTEEN

JUST BEFORE seven o'clock on a cold March evening, on the quarter day of the twenty-fifth, Lady Day, with the rain beating against the window panes, Jem squeezed himself into a seat in the bay-windowed parlour of the Wayfarers': that evening, the old inn was crowded with upwards of a hundred or more villagers, primarily male, for all were allowed to attend the monthly Little Court, if they so wished, especially if a lively session was in prospect. Barely had Jem taken his seat and swallowed a first sip of his ale than the procession of jurors came stamping in, shaking the rain off their hats and coats and complaining bitterly of the weather being 'fit only for ducks!' As courtesy and custom dictated, they had as usual opened their meeting in the Vestry of St. Bartholomew's and said the opening prayer and then, again as was their custom, adjourned and walked through the driving rain to reconvene in the Wayfarers' larger and warmer parlour, led by the foreman of the jury, Peter Sparshott, a lanky, dour-faced, slow-talking bachelor, one of the four small farmers of the village, part-leasing and part-owning three parcels amounting to nineteen acres all told and working them the year round, but still beholden to the husbandman system.

Now, seated at a two long tables placed together at the far end of the room, with the fire in the grate at their backs, they waited patiently while Caleb Chapman placed a tankard of ale in front of each, including one for himself: and as soon as each had his drink, they stood together and toasted 'The King,' as was their custom also. Then they got down to their deliberations, which were marshalled as usual by the steward, Mr. Able, who had already begun his drinking since he did not go to the church to take part in the prayers, feeling it a waste of time, but not discouraging others from the old custom.

It was one of the rules of Hamwick Dean's Little Court that a husbandman taking over from another still needed to obtain the sanction of two-thirds of the other stripholders: thus, ever since his return, Jem had made no secret of his wish that something would turn up eventually and most of the husbandmen with whom he drank in the Wayfarers' seemed only too willing to give their acceptance of him.

He also required the twelve court jurors to vote in his favour: so to enhance his application, he had not stinted on providing his share of the ale of an evening, though never taking success for granted, even though there might be no other bidders.

Of course, it helped that amongst the jurors also were four of those same drinking companions, namely Dick Dollery, Enos Diddams, Nathaniel Newman and John Romble, and the man who served them nightly, Caleb Chapman himself, who held two acres and nine roods on the open-fields and so was as eligible as the rest. With them sat also the old cordwainer Matthew Cobbe, who had apprenticed Thomas Judd, as well as one of the village's two butchers, William Hoskins, and also Andrew Norris, the baker, and Ephraim Simms, the grocer, for they, too, all held several strips on the open-fields and kept either cows or goats or sheep or geese on the pasture or waste. The presence of a wheelwright, a blacksmith, a butcher, a cordwainer and a baker amongst the jurors was not so strange as it might seem: for it was not uncommon for the small band of husbandmen who undertook the decision-making to be supplemented by co-opted men from other professions so long as they also held a strip or two here and there. Thus, as husbandmen of good standing (though that was debatable in Dick Dollery's case), they were all eligible to serve.

A smile and a wink from Dick Dollery as he passed gave Jem some reassurance as to how the evening's proceedings might go. However, before the matter of the transfer of the widow's land could be voted upon, the jurors of the Little Court, being men who had lived all their lives in the village and so had the knowledge to judge matters which concerned them and were familiar with local custom, were that evening called upon to rule on several matters, two of which were outstanding from meetings several months back.

Usually the Little Court did not begin its business till eight o'clock and, indeed, that had been the time announced when the notice proclaiming the meeting had been fixed to the door of St. Bartholomew's a week previously. However, the previous afternoon, in view of the number and complexity of the matters due to come before them that evening, Mr. Able, as steward, Josiah Bright, as the clerk, and the jury foreman, Peter Sparshott, had agreed between themselves that they should begin one hour earlier, at seven o'clock, so that as much business as could be got out of the way would be got out of the way and they would, at the close of it, have a decent hour or two for drinking, as was their custom also. This had then been communicated in the usual way to those who mattered – Josiah Bright went around the village to tell them – and since all assented, the notice was duly corrected by the foreman that same evening and tacked to the church door again.

The customary rules which regulated the culture of the strips in the open-fields were such that they could not be broken without the likelihood of one husbandman or another sustaining a loss of some kind and tenants of the fields were expected to keep exact time in the operation of their agriculture, otherwise their neighbours' rights of way and pasturage might well damage, or even ruin, their corn. It was this common happening, the spoiling of one man's corn by his neighbour, which was the first matter of four upon which the jurors had to rule that evening before they could hear Jem's plea.

The previous autumn, an argument had broken out between two of the husbandmen over the claim of one that his neighbour had driven his cattle across a part of his land, thereby doing damage to it to his detriment, and he was suing for compensation for his loss. Trivial as it might seem to some, this matter took up a good twenty minutes before one much chagrined husbandman went stamping out into the rain, face red with anger and disbelief at the fine imposed: 'Twenty-five shillings.' And, while the miscreant went off down The Street to drink at the Carpenters' Arms for the rest of that evening rather than have to sit and see the smirking face of his accuser, the second, buoyed by the prospect of compensation to come, seated himself at a table amid the others, smiling happily to himself, content that justice had prevailed.

Once the explosion of chatter which followed this verdict had been subdued by the loud rapping of the steward's gavel on the table-top, the second matter was dealt with. It also concerned two husbandmen who had come to the court also after exchanging words and near blows when one, a good manager of his land, had sown his corn the previous year and had found, when it had come up, that he was left with a large bare patch where his careless neighbour, who held two strips at right angles to the former, had gone well beyond the dividing headland or half-balk and had turned his plough upon his neighbour's ground and cut up a sizeable part of it so that nothing had grown in the churned area. The first was seeking compensation for his loss, as much to spite the second as in any hope of obtaining overmuch redress for a bushel or two of grain lost: but since the case had been brought and the charge made, the jury would have to rule upon it one way or the other. 'Five shillings,' was the fine handed down, which satisfied neither, one because it was too small, in his opinion, the other because it was too much, in his opinion, with the result that neither remained to drink in the bar parlour either, but, to the chagrin of poor Caleb Chapman, both pushed their way impatiently through the smoky haze which filled the room by then and disappeared into the night.

The third main disagreement for the jurors to decide that evening was a simmering dispute between, on the one side, several of the husbandmen and, on the other, several of the drinkers from the Carpenters' Arms, the landless cottagers, who only ever worked as day-labourers, that is, when they were able to get work. It had broken out in the Reeve's Croft part of Third Field following the previous harvest and there had been a violent quarrel between several of them, the rumblings from which had continued all winter long. For the sake of village peace, the matter needed to be resolved once and for all before the same situation blew up again: so important was it to all that the Carpenters' Arms drinkers were prepared to quit their own hostelry that night and enter the lions' den, so to speak.

The dispute had arisen because every husbandmen had the right to put a horse and ten sheep as well as a cow into the harvested fields to eat off the stubble-eddish as soon as the corn was all brought in without paying a fee: now several of the landless cottagers, whose cattle had been let loose to provoke the argument the previous autumn, were claiming the same right by ancient custom, declaring that their fathers and their fathers' fathers had all done it so they ought to be allowed to do it, too. The husbandmen, however, argued that, prior to the dispute breaking out, no day-labourers had exercised any such right in any of the fields in sixty years of anyone's memory, if they had ever done it at all, so any right was deemed to have lapsed. Clearly, some form of compromise which would be agreeable to both sides, and workable, too, of course, was required and the legal skill and affability of Mr. Able came to the rescue as the two parties, husbandmen and jurors on the one side and day-labourers and, therefore, non-husbandmen and non-jurors on the other, argued their points back and forth: the whole argument lasted for upwards of forty minutes.

Fortunately, in an attempt to resolve the matter, the rotund, black-suited lawyer had searched back through several decades of musty, leather-bound account books kept by the previous Little Court stewards and, in the end, his wisdom prevailed: it was decided and voted upon by a majority of the jurors, including Dick Dollery, Enos Diddams and John Romble, but not, strangely, by the grumpy

Nathaniel Newman, who did not like anyone being given an advantage over him, that, though the landless cottagers had no actual right to turn their cattle on to the stubble, as a compromise and to restore and maintain the peace, the husbandmen should put their cattle to graze off the stubble-eddish, 'overhushing,' as it was called, for two hours a day for two days once the harvest had all been gathered-in, after which the cattle of both husbandmen and day-labourers could be put to the stubble-eddish in common till winter.

The decision brought smiles to the faces of the day-labourers, who immediately left Caleb Chapman's establishment, despite the heavy rain outside, to run down to the Carpenters' Arms to drink with the rest of their fellows there, thinking they had won a victory, not realising that, if the husbandmen were to put enough of their animals on to the stubble-eddish during those first two days, they would take the best of it and leave only pickings for the other animals.

The only other recourse, as Mr. Able had pointed out to the husbandmen in his judgment, was to hedge-in the disputed part of the common field at their own expense in order to prevent trespass, which considering the considerable expense that would entail did not go down at all well amongst most who were bound up in the dispute and there was much grumbling and complaining, which, of course, amused those not a part of it. To them, the Little Court was an entertainment as much as anything and its decisions were always subject to long and serious discussion afterwards, sometimes over days and sometimes over weeks if they were more contentious than expected.

No sooner had the dispute with the day-labourers been dealt with than two other men, who had been sitting gloomily in different corners of the bay-windowed parlour, glaring at each other, stood up and made their way forward to stand before their peers.

'We present Thomas Clarke for ploughing away a balk between Thomas Pitchley and himself,' intoned the clerk, Josiah Bright. In this case, the miscreant claimed ignorance of a law which stated that it was forbidden to plough the balks specifically where they occurred between neighbours. But when he began to argue his case, he was politely cut short by Mr. Able: and, since his excuse had been ignorance, he was reminded of the rules, *That every one of the inhabitants that have ploughed up any of the balks in the fields between theirs and their neighbour's lands, that before the feast day of St. John the Baptist next coming, they and everyone of them so offending shall lay the same down again and so suffer the same to lie as formerly.'*

More because the transgressor tried to argue his case, the fine was set at five shillings, which was double the expected two shillings and sixpence and a rude shock to him and he, too, stalked out in high dudgeon without so much as a nod or a 'Good evening' to anyone: he, too, was heading for the Carpenters' Arms, where he could drown his sorrows along with the others.

The thought of the takings he was losing seemed to upset Caleb Chapman, for from his seat he gave his wife a worried look as they watched yet another customer depart, though, of course, neither could say anything, but had to accept it and hope that in future the fines would be less severe and men would stay and drink whatever the verdict against them. Such were the powers of the Little Court in settling its disputes: it was a salutary lesson to Jem and to anyone else who was present.

The business of these four cases had taken up a good hour and a half: so it was not till eight-thirty that Josiah Bright finally held up the letter which the aged Widow Hebborne had scrawled in a spidery hand, of her wish to surrender the said number of acres in the said places, she being so unused to putting pen to paper that the writing almost sloped off the bottom corner of it. Mr. Able, meanwhile, shuffled amongst his own papers to pull out the late 'Bunny' Hebborne's tithe map, which he and Peter Sparshott had drawn up several years before and now perused with much murmured comment: only then was Jem called forward to stand before the table, trying to ignore the broad grins of Dick Dollery and Enos Diddams, which, in effect, were really smiles of welcome, though he did not know it.

Jem's letter to Caleb Chapman declaring his willingness to pay the widow's fines was also produced and, though it was 'unusual' for someone to pay the fines of an incumbent tenant who was not a relative, none could see it as an actual obstacle since they had not come across it before. 'What do it matter so long as the fines are paid?' was Dick Dollery's express opinion.

Even if the court procedure had been more or less cut and dried before Jem had even appeared, the jurors of the Little Court were still required to show some diligence, if only to satisfy the onlookers. First, the clerk passed Jem's letter and the widow's letter to Mr. Able seated beside him for his confirmation of their legality, as well as their retention amongst his papers: after reading the two, the cherub-faced lawyer gave a nod of assent and passed them to the foreman,

Peter Sparshott. He, in turn, declared things 'all in accordance, as far as I can see,' without explaining with what it was necessary to be 'in accordance,' it being a phrase he had heard Mr. Able use one time and, liking the sound of it for the legal expertise it suggested, he used it on almost every occasion that he considered warranted it. Curiously, he did the same with the word 'equilibrium,' which he had also heard Mr. Able use at some time and, though not knowing the meaning of it, still dropped it into conversations whenever he thought it appropriate, especially in the presence of the men in the Wayfarers'.

Not unexpectedly, others had picked up his 'in accordance' habit and, as the letters were passed from hand to hand around the table for all to read, each glanced at them for a second or so with a furrowed brow and then declared in turn that each was 'in accordance,' till finally they were given to Enos Diddams, who repeated the phrase to much silent sniggering, for all knew he could hardly read at all.

'You have seen what we have to rule on and you still wish to take up poor old "Bunny's" land and join the ranks of men who will never grow rich and who must, by necessity, always be content with their lot?' enquired Peter Sparshott, with a sigh, supposedly in jest, but sounding more in frustration.

Next, the regulations by which the court abided were read out to him, as they were to all newcomers, whether they knew them or not or had read them or not. That all took time, which necessitated the replenishment of several of the jurors' tankards, at Jem's expense, of course, which was called for by a laughing Dick Dollery and happily seconded by a smiling Enos Diddams, while Josiah Bright droned on from his written list with an explanation of the other business of the court, such as the enforcement of village bylaws and regulations through the presentment and amercing of offenders, which enabled the open-field system to operate effectively and discouraged breaches of the peace such as had been dealt with that evening.

In particular, they were empowered to counsel in disputes between individuals on such matters as debt, trespass, detention or breach of agreement: and, if Jem became involved in such a case, he was required to bring it before the court as a plaintiff and both the plaintiff and defendant would have to produce named pledges to stand surety for them so as not to waste the court's time. In default, it was further slowly explained to him, a defendant was allowed three summonses, that is, three *distraints* for failing to appear, and three *essoins,* or excused absences, before being required to defend a case should one be made against him. The trouble with that, of course, which the clerk did not explain, was that a case could be pending for months before the jury finally decided the outcome. Many times, too, cases were agreed out of court before the final stage was reached, though there was still a fee to be paid for licence to agree.

'If Brother Stebbings is willing to abide by all the byelaws of the Little Court, I do not think this business need occupy us any longer,' Peter Sparshott said finally.

'I am, brother foreman,' was Jem's simple reply.

It was then time for the vote. 'If none of you has any objection, I propose we accept Brother Stebbings to the lease of the widow's land at a shilling and sixpence per acre, subject to the fines for the changeover being paid by him and the acceptance of his paying the remainder of the year's rent till Michaelmas,' declared the foreman, looking about him. 'All in favour, say "Aye".'

A chorus of sombre, deep-throated 'Ayes' went round the table as hands were raised in agreement: the deal was done, the changeover was approved, the fines duly set and paid there and then and the whole proceeding duly minuted by Josiah Bright, in accordance with the usual way of doing things. Handshakes of welcome were exchanged all round and, there being no other business that need keep them, they drained their tankards as one and once more, as was the supposed custom, Jem was prevailed upon again, now as 'a new member of the brotherhood,' to order refills for all at the table.

Not that he need have worried about succeeding: for not only were Dick Dollery, Enos Diddams, John Romble and Nathaniel Newman jurors but they and Thomas Judd and William Stubbs were all a part of the same 'tithing,' that is, a nominal group of ten men forming a body of collective guarantors for the good conduct of each member, which is why they drank together: and the chief man of their tithing – 'the tithing-man' – was none other than Caleb Chapman, former churchwarden, former parish constable, former assistant overseer and now landlord of the Wayfarers' Inn, which is why Dick Dollery was always given credit there and why he stayed drinking there. Jem had now joined his group: and so the company settled down to drinking for the rest of the evening, even 'persuading' Mr. Able to stay and join them, which he did without hesitation since the company of men, even if agricultural labourers and village artisans, was more preferable to returning to a cold and unwelcoming house and a cold and unwelcoming wife.

EIGHTEEN

HARDLY had they begun their drinking than there was an unexpected rumble of wheels into the yard.

'Someone in a pony and trap,' said one of the men on the bay-window seat itself, parting the curtain to peer out. 'Gawd Christ, it's Joshua Jaikes!' he exclaimed, letting out a groan, which was immediately echoed by several others.

'The bailiff of the Glebe farm,' Dick Dollery informed Jem, 'our new churchwarden.' Such was the contempt in his tone, none could doubt his utter dislike of the new arrival.

Jem had yet to meet Joshua Jaikes: all he knew of him was what he had heard from the other men in the Wayfarers', that he was an incomer from Lincolnshire four years since, mean-spirited and sour-speaking, who, being the bailiff of the Glebe farm, was 'well in with the parson' – 'too well in' for the liking of most of the villagers.

It was true in one respect: that soon after his arrival, Joshua Jaikes had got himself elected as the verger and Vestry clerk, for he was a reasonably educated man living amongst villagers many of whom were barely educated or totally uneducated. It meant that he headed the procession down the aisle carrying the gold cross at the start of every service and led the singing and the responses. He had even volunteered his childless wife to sweep the church, polish the brasses and put out the vases of flowers for the Sunday services. Then at the last Easter Vestry, he had managed to become the parson's appointment as one of the two churchwardens, which was an irritation, if not a surprise, to everyone: to their way of thinking, Jaikes had gone out of his way to ingratiate himself with the parson in a way none of them would ever have done.

'The parson's boot-licker,' was how Enos Diddams had described him. 'Thinks hisself grander than us. Has ideas above his station, if you ask me. Always running after the parson, he is, doing his bidding, him and his wife. Never out of the damned church, she en't, polishing and sweeping.'

'He don't have enough to do on the Glebe farm, that's his trouble,' was the verdict of Dick Dollery: and then in the manner of one puzzled by it: 'Shouldn't have took it on if it weren't enough to keep him busy...'

What was apparent was the men's general dislike of the bailiff, for no sooner had his arrival been announced than, as if by an unseen signal, several of the village men retreated into the taproom, some even hurrying into the vault, which meant they had to cross the small central space hurriedly to reach it before the inn's front door was pushed open and Joshua Jaikes came stamping in, shaking the rain from his cape and his wide-brimmed black hat, one hand gripping the stock of a coiled silver-knobbed whip. Even to a casual observer, it would have been noticeable how most of those who remained standing in the bay-windowed parlour turned their backs on him the moment he entered, as if not wanting to catch his eye.

Anger was showing clearly on the face of Joshua Jaikes as he pushed his way through them and stood glowering down at the table where Mr. Able, Peter Sparshott, Dick Dollery, Enos Diddams, Nathaniel Newman and John Romble sat. Jem, was also seated there, for Dick Dollery, never one to let a good opportunity pass, had again made those on one of the benches squeeze closer together so as to accommodate his friend and their new brother husbandman at one end, especially as he was buying.

Jaikes was a tall, stooping, narrow-shouldered, long-striding man, some six feet in height, lean bodied and long legged, then aged forty, with dark straight hair and dark sidewhiskers: his eyes were sullen and deep-set, his nose long and angular above a thin mouth and a prominent jaw. To most in the village, he seemed to have a perpetual scowl on his face, as if he trusted no one and looked down upon everyone and did not care whether they knew it.

'The court, it is not over yet, is it?' he demanded gruffly, in the manner of one who, simply by asking, expected that they would say it was not.

'It is, Mr. Jaikes. We finished ten minutes agoo,' Peter Sparshott informed him politely in his slow-speaking way, frowning at the question. 'The business of the court is all done with for this evening.'

'The Widow Hebborne's land, is it still up for surrender?' demanded Jaikes, running his eye along the line of jurors seated at the table, as if he were suspicious of something and so was fixing their faces in his memory for future reference.

The lanky, lean-faced foreman's frown deepened. 'No, I am sorry, Mr. Jaikes, but all the widow's land has been taken up,' he replied, taking his clay pipe from his mouth and, in his surprise, forgetting to close it.

Dick Dollery looked across at Jem, seated with his back to the newcomer: the moment the Glebe farm bailiff had entered the room, he had known exactly why he had come. For it so happened that one of the acre-and-a-quarter 'lands' located on the lesser Ash Grove field lay alongside an acre of glebe land leased by Joshua Jaikes for his own husbandry and, by taking up the widow's parcel there, he would have more than doubled his holding in that part of First Field where the best soil lay. He knew, too, that Joshua Jaikes harboured a wish to increase his total holding on all three open-fields, but particularly on First Field.

'You can't have finished the meeting yet,' protested Jaikes, pulling a large fob watch on a brass chain from an inside pocket of his surcoat. 'It is only just gone nine. I wanted to make an offer to take on the widow's land, particularly the piece alongside mine on Ash Grove. You can't have finished the meeting so soon. You have no right!'

'I assure you they have every right, sir, every right,' Mr. Able informed him calmly, yet politely, with the faintest of smiles, as some speakers do when they wish to show that they do not seek to be antagonistic, but feel themselves duty bound to inform a person of the facts of a matter.

'I don't want your damned assurances, lawyer,' snapped Jaikes. 'I want the meeting opened again so I can put in my bid. I've driven through driving rain all the way from Melchborough to get here to put in my offer for that land.'

'Whether you require my assurance or not, you have it, nevertheless, sir,' Mr. Able continued, unwaveringly meeting Joshua Jaikes's gaze, totally unfazed by the bailiff's brusqueness of tone and injecting a discernible sharpness to his own, for he had no liking for the incomer either. 'You are too late, as Mr. Sparshott says. All the land has been taken up. The surrender was offered, the fines were paid, a bid was tendered, it was put to the vote and accepted, as is the norm, and it was recorded in the minute book by Mr. Bright here, all in accordance with the rules of the court. The whole matter was conducted legally, sir, I assure you, whether you wish it or not. In view of that, there can be no change made.' He paused for a moment as if thinking and then added with the preciseness of a lawyer correcting himself: 'Certainly no change can be made tonight. Any change, if done at all, would have to be done at Michaelmas, at the next quarter day, and not before. Those are the rules of the court, sir, and we must abide by them.'

Peter Sparshott, somewhat flustered to have the lanky figure of an angry Joshua Jaikes standing over him, slapping the black stock of a whip hard into the palm of his hand as he listened to Mr. Able's comments, did at least manage a faint smile at the lawyer's use of his favourite phrase, 'in accordance.'

'The court has never finished before ten o'clock before,' Jaikes tried in protest: he glowered across at the grandfather clock ticking away in one corner, forcing those standing before it to part quickly so as not to obstruct his view. 'It is only a quarter past nine now. I have been in Melchborough all day on a farm matter. I would have been here earlier but for the damned roads and the rain. I intended to be here at the start to put in my bid, but I was held up. You must have begun the meeting early to have finished it so soon.'

His mention of 'a farm matter in Melchborough' produced several curled lips amongst several of the men, Dick Dollery and friends included, for they all knew what Joshua Jaikes's 'farm matter in Melchborough' had been about that day.

'The time was stated on the notice which was posted on the church door, Mr. Jaikes,' Peter Sparshott announced, somewhat timorously, almost as if making an apology. 'The time of starting was changed yesterday afternoon to seven o'clock rather than eight o'clock because we had several matters to discuss. Mr. Dollery brought it to our attention that we had more items than was usual to debate so Mr. Able, myself and Mr. Bright conferred on the matter and we all agreed it. Is that not so, Mr. Able? – ' The cheery-faced lawyer nodded, but only the once as if not actually bothered by any of it. ' – It is true that we started earlier than we normally do, but the time was announced as per usual and we began at the time stated and not a minute before, Mr. Jaikes, I assure you of that.'

Emboldened by Mr. Able's calm manner, Dick Dollery thought it a good time to chip in with a comment of his own in support, on the basis that three voices speaking against one might deter Joshua Jaikes from causing more of a fuss and continuing with his demand that they reconvene, which the straw-haired juror was really in no shape to do, being on his fifth tankard by then. 'If thee had read the notice, thee would have known what time the court was due to sit as well as us,' he growled with a sarcastic sniff. 'We all knew the time of the meeting was changed. So did Mr. Waters and Mr. Jacks because they was both in the church when we all assembled in the Vestry for the seven o'clock prayers afore we come here and they locked up after us. Everyone knew, it seems, except thee. We weren't to know thee wanted to attend to make an offer tonight, were we?'

For a moment it seemed as if Joshua Jaikes was steeling himself to lash out at the lanky husbandman: his face reddened, his jaw tightened and just for an instance the stock of his whip began to rise before his arm fell back to his side. Clearly, the situation needed to be defused.

'We do not see you at our meetings very often, Mr. Jaikes,' said Mr. Able, again in the politest of voices. 'May I ask, did you communicate your wish to make an offer to anyone? The Widow Hebborne perhaps? Or Mr. Sparshott or Mr. Bright here? By letter perhaps as is required or you?'

'No, I did not,' snapped Joshua Jaikes, angrily, 'I had no time.' The question alone irritated him, for the fact was he had not known till that very morning that the matter of the widow surrendering her late husband's land was to come before the Little Court that evening, so devious had Dick Dollery been in the two weeks since he had first mentioned it to Jem, and thus he could not have written a letter had he wanted to do so.

'Everyone knows that land on Ash Grove lies next to my land,' went on Jaikes. 'It stands to reason I would be interested in the old widow giving up the lease. You should have known I would be putting in an offer for it once it came up for surrender and held the court open till I got here. Had I been here, I would have put in my bid as fairly as any other, as is my right. I can't see why you can't reconvene the court so that I can do it now like I intended.'

'We cannot reopen the court's proceedings. They are done with, sir. Whether you wanted the land or not, you are too late,' Mr. Able retorted, becoming irritated himself that Jaikes was still expecting them to do as he demanded. 'The court is over. The land has been taken up. You are too tardy by half, sir, too tardy by half. You will have to wait another day if you wish to take up more land.'

'I insist you take my bid. I won't be thwarted by a bunch of ignorant yokels,' Joshua Jaikes shouted.

'Have a care what you call me!' snapped Mr. Able, for an 'ignorant yokel' he was not. It was now the lawyer's turn to reveal his anger: his nostrils flared, he puffed out his cheeks and waved the leather-bound minute book at Jaikes. 'This, sir, is a record of the transaction. It is legal and binding. It cannot be undone and will not be undone simply because you desire it. So there!'

The determination of the lawyer not to allow himself to be browbeaten angered the Glebe farm bailiff even more. At any other time, he might have carried his case had he been dealing only with the other jurors, but here he was up against a man who was used to argument, indeed who revelled in it. He had been made to look foolish in the eyes of the others: to all those who sat and stood watching and listening, he had been exposed as the blusterer he was.

While all this had been going on, Jem had risen discreetly from the table, unheeded by Joshua Jaikes, and had made his way through the listening throng to the polished plank bar to collect the next round of refills, which he had called for at Dick Dollery's behest and which Caleb Chapman had been in the act of drawing from a barrel on the back wall. Jaikes's unexpected entry had forestalled him to the point that, having filled four of the tankards, the nervous landlord was holding the fifth under the tap and, as if frozen, was making no attempt to fill it. Calmly, Jem motioned for him to continue.

A grinning Enos Diddams, meanwhile, pleased to see Joshua Jaikes so disconcerted by the lawyer's calm defiance of him, decided that he would add to the bailiff's discomfort with a humorous interjection of his own, as his friend, Dick Dollery had done. 'I don't know why thee is making all this fuss,' he declared with a laugh. 'There en't never been a special time set for finishing, has there? We finishes when we finishes. Always have. No one has ever grumbled afore that we finished too early. Thee are the first there. Most times my wife grumbles that we finish too late and that, if we didn't take so long with our business, we wouldn't drink as much as we do. Of course, she don't know we do most of our drinking after the court meeting, do she?'

Several of the men around him began to laugh, for his meaning was clear: as far as those who attended the Little Court were concerned, the 'proceedings' of the court lasted as long as Caleb Chapman and his wife would continue to serve ale or as long as they had the money to pay for it: and, in the case of one or two, like Dick Dollery and Enos Diddams, as long as they were capable of consuming it. Joshua Jaikes, however, did not see the humour of the remarks and gave the balding husbandman a withering glance: then, looking first at the lawyer and then at those about him, he demanded: 'Who has the land now?'

Mr. Able waved his hand in a vague gesture towards the bar. 'The gentlemen there has taken on the widow's land,' he said with a weary sigh.

Almost as if at a signal, the crowd between the table and the bar shuffled back to reveal Jem standing with his back to them all. 'And who the devil is he?' demanded Joshua Jaikes, staring hard at Jem, not having seen him before.

'Jem Stebbings is the name,' Jem replied, turning to face the bailiff and return his cold stare with one of his own. As one who had been used to replying to the snaps and snarls of officers and sergeants for twelve or more years, the aggression of a mere farm bailiff was not going to daunt him overmuch.

'I have never seen you before,' said Joshua Jaikes in a grudging manner, before turning back to the lawyer to ask: 'A squatter, is he?'

'No, sir, he is no squatter!' Peter Sparshott answered sharply. 'He was born in this village and has as much right to be in it as have you and I.'

'He has been away fighting for King and Country,' a grinning Enos Diddams added boldly, testing his luck again, having not been verbally rebuked earlier as he had expected he might. 'He only come back a few weeks agoo.'

'Widow Hebborne's land on Ash Grove,' Jaikes declared bluntly, without so much as a preliminary nod of acknowledgement to Jem. 'I'll take it off your hands. You can keep the rest of it, on Barrow and Thornbush and Long Field and Third Field. You'll still have a fair holding. I just want the land next to mine on Ash Grove. If you have already paid the rent on it, I'll give you a shilling more than you paid for it. All you have to do is tell these gentlemen you are prepared to accept my offer – ' The word 'gentlemen' was said in a scoffing manner. ' – It'll be between you and me and no one else. So, what do you say, friend? I can't say fairer than that, can I? A shilling on top?' Again, as was his way, he said it in the manner of one who expected Jem to accede to his request there and then, for, at the same time as he was speaking, he was pulling a small purse from his pocket and tipping some coins into his hand.

'No, thank you, friend,' Jem replied politely and firmly, his use of the word 'friend' as icy and as meaningless as had been Joshua Jaikes's use of it. 'I have no wish to let any of the land go now that I have taken it up. I have put my name to the deed and I intend to work all of it, including that on Ash Grove. It is good land there – I know the value of it.'

It was not what Joshua Jaikes wanted to hear and he was as taken aback by Jem's quiet, almost disinterested refusal, as he had been by Mr. Able's calm defiance: his face reddened, he seemed unable to speak for a second or so. Finally, he blurted out: 'I am offering you more than you paid for it before you have even set a plough upon it or turned over one furrow. Come now, it is a good offer for anyone. In time, you will be able to rent a piece of land elsewhere to replace it.' Again he proffered the money and an expectant silence fell on the company.

'I do not need your money, my friend. I have enough of my own,' Jem coolly replied again, taking up the six tankards Caleb Chapman had drawn, three in each hand, and crossing back to the table to rejoin the others. 'I do not intend to give up any of the land, not today, not tomorrow, not next Michaelmas or next Lady Day, not to anyone, and certainly not to a man who thinks he can make me change my mind by jingling a few paltry coins in his hand.' And, having seated himself and distributed the tankards amongst the others, he stared calmly back up at the bailiff as if unconcerned by his presence, which only infuriated the Glebe farm bailiff all the more.

'You'll hear more of this,' Joshua Jaikes blustered, almost choking with rage. 'Everyone knows I wanted that land. It is mine by right – '

'On what grounds?' Jem interrupted him. 'You had the same chance as I to make an offer. Simply because you wanted it does not give you a right to it anymore than anyone else. The court has approved the changeover. I have taken it on fair and square and all legally, as Mr. Able says.'

All Joshua Jaikes could do was to let out an oath, turn on his heel and storm out of the inn: the men watched from the window as he remounted his pony and trap, wheeled it around in the yard, flicked his long whip out across the pony's ears and rattled off into the darkness and the teeming rain.

Behind him, the fact that he had been thwarted in acquiring 'Old Bunny's' land was the source of great amusement and much laughter for some time afterwards: however, one or two were a little more reticent.

'You have made a bad enemy there,' warned Peter Sparshott, grimly. 'You have made a fool of him before this company. I do not think he will forget your refusal too soon. Mr. Jaikes will not take kindly to having his wishes thrown back at him. He is a man who likes to get his way.'

'I fear he may be right,' the red-cheeked Mr. Able added solemnly, then brightening as if to dispel the gloomy prediction, he raised his glass and said, smiling: 'I raise my glass to you. I wish you well in your enterprise and hope it turns out well.'

'Aye, good luck, Jem, good luck,' chorused Dick Dollery, Enos Diddams, Nathaniel Newman, John Romble and others, including several who had crept back into the main bar parlour, as much in hope that Jem might extend his largesse to include them as the fact that Joshua Jaikes had gone.

NINETEEN

WHATEVER the villagers thought of him, Joshua Jaikes cared only for the fact that he had been made to look a fool in front of a hundred others: and a fool he was not! He had seen them sniggering as he left: they would have known he would want the land on Ash Grove alongside of his: he could not prove it, but he suspected there had been skulduggery somewhere.

What rankled with him was that he had anticipated that old 'Bunny' Hebborne's land would be up for surrender at the Little Court sooner or later. Indeed, as long ago as four months, on hearing that the old man, then in his seventy-eighth year, was becoming enfeebled and more than likely to succumb to the winter weather, as several of the village's elderly did each year, and that his widow, if she did not go with him or soon after him, would most probably want to end her obligation, he had cast his eye especially over the acre-and-a-quarter parcel next to his strips on Ash Grove field.

He could envisage it with the foot-high balks removed so that there was no divide between it and his own land and imagine, too, how the whole two or more acres would look ploughed, sowed and covered by waving corn – his waving corn. In his mind's eye, he imagined an even greater acreage one day, perhaps a 'close,' say, of fifteen acres, or even a half yardland of nineteen acres in that part of First Field, all parcelled as one holding, with a hedge planted around it to keep out the weeds which invariably spread from the holdings of the more slovenly of the other husbandmen. Then he would be a man of more substance than a mere bailiff of a small glebe dairy farm, someone else's servant, a position for which he did not particularly care, but one with which he was prepared to continue. To his own way of thinking, he had not come all the way from Lincolnshire to remain a farm bailiff for the rest of his life, which was what that pious fool of a parson seemed to think. Whoever this Jem Stebbings fellow was, he would regret turning down his offer: he would see to that.

The fact was he had not expected that the widow would seek to surrender the land so soon: in truth, when no one had ploughed the rest of her acreage on First Field after the winter corn sowing, or on

Long Field and Third Field, he had anticipated it was more likely she intended to leave it fallow and surrender it at the Michaelmas quarter day in the September when not only would it gain from being left but she would avoid the heavier fines which an earlier surrender would incur. In fact, so sure had he been that he had been prepared to wait, impatiently, as was his way, but to wait nevertheless. Out of curiosity, he had inspected the widow's other parcels in the Barrow and Thornbush lesser fields, and on Long Field and Third Field, but the land on Ash Grove was what he wanted first and foremost. What puzzled him was how the old widow had found the money to pay the fines. The old man must have salted some away, was all he could think.

Jaikes, in fact, had learned purely by chance that morning that the widow was surrendering the land at the Little Court that very evening. On his way out of the village in his pony and trap to deal with the 'farm matter in Melchborough,' he had stopped at the cottage of Lemuel Ring, a middle-aged bachelor, not well liked by the other men of the village, whom he employed more frequently than any other on the Glebe farm, mostly as a herdsman for its dairy cows so that they were always kept separate from the village herd and also as a general labourer. The bailiff's intention was to remonstrate with him about some fence work which had not been done to his satisfaction, but the crafty labourer, simply as a way of diverting the other's ire from himself, had enquired midway through his scolding, as a matter of interest, whether the bailiff intended to make an offer for 'Bunny' Hebborne's land as he had heard from gossip in the Carpenters' Arms that it was being surrendered that very day.

It mattered to Lemuel Ring only in as much as, though Joshua Jaikes was the tenant of the various strips on the lesser parts of First Field and further strips on the lesser Snook's, Badger's Hole and Partridge fields of Long Field, he did not work them himself, but delegated all that needed to be done, the ploughing, the harrowing, the sowing, the weeding and even the harvesting, too, to Lemuel Ring, paying him to work them almost full-time since he himself was busy with the business of the Glebe farm, or so he told the parson. What annoyed Joshua Jaikes more than anything was that Lemuel Ring had known that the widow's surrender was to be discussed at the Little Court and had failed to inform him: despite all Dick Dollery's precautions, no secret was ever truly safe in a small village.

All he could do was to curse the man for his foolishness: there was no time for him to turn back to discover anything further, such as whether any other was intending to make a bid, which, in those straitened times, he did not consider at all conceivable since, save for a few, the whole village was impoverished and it was unlikely anyone would have the money to take on extra land or want to do so. He would still be able to go to Melchborough in his pony and trap to deal with the 'farm matter' at hand there and to return in good time for the start of the Little Court's session. If anything, he cursed himself for the fact that he did not attend more of their meetings, but then he knew he was not overly liked by the villagers and to join a bunch of 'southern yokels' in their drinking sessions did not appeal to him: he preferred to do his drinking alone elsewhere.

As it happened, the 'farm matter' which so concerned him in the county town that day was at the Quarter Sessions, where he was to give evidence against 'two brats from the lower end of Hamwyte,' both twelve-year-old girls, whom he had caught the previous week gathering dead twigs from the ditch alongside one the hedgerows which bounded Mope Lane and which they hoped to sell for kindling. The hedgerow and the ditch were both the property of the Glebe farm and picking up the twigs was a clear case of theft, even if they were dead twigs which had fallen from the trees the previous autumn. Jaikes had spied the girls and had followed them all the way back to the town, managing to get ahead of them in his pony and trap to alert the town's two parish constables so that they were waiting on the road to apprehend the girls as soon as they entered the High Street with their sack: and, since the girls had already appeared before the magistrates at Hamwyte for an identical felony elsewhere the previous year, they had been sent for trial to the Quarter Sessions at Melchborough, where the punishment was certain to be more severe for such a repeated infraction.

Jaikes and one of the Hamwyte constables were the main witnesses for the prosecution, but, unhappily for him, with so many cases to be dealt with that day, his case had not been called till nearly seven o'clock in the evening, forcing him to kick his heels for some nine hours, which had not improved his temper, especially in view of his need to get back quickly to Hamwick Dean. That the girls were found guilty in the ten-minute trial and sentenced to three months in the women's House of Correction at Melchborough, which lay then by the river, had been of some consolation for his long wait: justice had been done and the guilty deservedly punished. But his return had been delayed for far longer than he had anticipated, the consequence of which was his non-appearance at Hamwick Dean's Little Court when it had reconvened in the Wayfarers' bay-windowed parlour after the usual walk from the vestry.

That absence, as well as his failure to communicate his wishes to acquire any of the old widow's land had surprised Mr. Able when he had first sat down with the others: he had confidently expected that the bailiff would appear and make a bid to take up the tenancy of at least that part of the widow's land adjoining his own and, knowing Jaikes, come Michaelmas when the rent was due to be settled up as usual, he would more than likely, as a man of steady means, be able to make a bid for a good part of the rest of it. However, without any communication from him, there was little that he, as the steward, or the jurors could do when Jem Stebbings had applied instead to take over the lease of the whole acreage, except, that is, to proceed in the usual fashion and accept the request of the only interested party since it was approved unanimously by the jurors.

He was not to know that Dick Dollery and certain others had connived to deny Joshua Jaikes the land he so coveted simply because, in the words of Dick Dollery, they considered the bailiff of the Glebe farm to be a 'blustering, bullying, mouthy, uppity Northerner': nor was he to know that two of the jurors, Dick Dollery and Enos Diddams, had visited the widow to ease her worries with the promise that there was a trustworthy man of whom they knew who, even in those straitened times, was willing to take up the land and would not only settle the matter of the outstanding rent but had the money also to pay the fines incurred by her early surrender and so there was no need for her to hang on to the land till the Michaelmas quarter day.

Neither did Mr. Able know that, when they had taken the letter from her, they had given it for safe keeping till the night of the court sitting not to Josiah Bright, the clerk, but to the innkeeper, Caleb Chapman, the chief of their small tithing group, blithely reminding him of that and of the many years they had favoured his establishment with their custom and also of the many years of custom still to come, 'God and their constitutions willing.'

Nor did Mr. Able know that Caleb Chapman had handed the letter to the clerk only the day before the court was due to sit, which was the prime reason for the requested earlier starting time, suggested as it was by Dick Dollery, who was standing with him at the time. All were facts of which Mr. Able was totally unaware and would have considered as most definitely not conforming to the patterns of conduct usually accepted or established as consistent with the principles of any personal and social ethics to which he aspired: in short, he would have considered them downright immoral, if not downright illegal. But then he did not know anything of it. Not for sure, not with proof, but he could read faces and smiles and sly looks as well as any lawyer who ever examined a witness in a court and knew full well that some skulduggery was afoot: in short, he guessed it all and continued smiling.

Even then, Joshua Jaikes might have made it back – would have made it back – to be at the Little Court in good time had not one of the wheels of an iron-wheeled 'fly,' the very same which had brought Jem and Will Ponder from London almost two months before, sunk into one of the many deep ruts on the unturnpiked section of the old Roman road between Melchborough and Hamwyte. The continual rain of that month had made a bad stretch of the high road between the county town and the market town, which never was the best, even worse: and the rightside wheel of the heavily laden 'fly' had become so deeply embedded in the rut that all hope the old wagoner might have had of pulling it out with his own team had been given up. No attempt would or could be made till twenty horses had been assembled from nearby farms and villages, for that was the number, harnessed together, which he estimated would be required to drag out so heavy and cumbersome a vehicle, even when unladen. One nearby cottager had volunteered to ride off to collect them, but it would still be an hour or even two hours before they could all be assembled, for that might entail having to go to more than one village to achieve it.

The ways in that region then were never properly maintained: though the high road from the City of London was turnpiked to Melchborough, that is repaired and made firm by the various parish surveyors of the places en route, it was done only for a short distance beyond the county town and again only on its final approach to Hamwyte and for a short distance beyond and again only for the last few miles into Wivencaster, from which point, rough and ungravelled, it wound its way further eastwards, now climbing and dipping over higher rolling hills and into steeper valleys, past more isolated villages, until it came eventually to the river port of Witchley, some twenty miles across the county boundary.

By bad luck, the blockage had occurred at a point at the top of a rise where the road narrowed to only a few feet in width so as to present only a single passage as it ran between two high banks. By the time Joshua Jaikes came trotting up, huddled on his trap, cursing the wind and the driving rain and the discomfort of his journey, a queue of a half-dozen other vehicles had formed on his side of the 'fly', which was half-tipped on its side, so deep was the rut: as well as farm wagons, they included the returning *'Old Blue'* from Mundham in the next county and the returning *'New Wivencaster'* from the garrison town thirteen miles beyond Hamwyte with passengers bound for there and beyond.

The wagonmaster of the 'fly' seemed unbothered by it all or by the number who were gathered around him, pleading with him as much as they cursed him, especially as he had unharnessed his team and had walked them fifty yards farther on down the other side of the hill where he had tethered all eight and put on their feed bags as nonchalantly as one would in a stable or the yard of a coaching inn.

'The whole thing is stuck too deep for my team to pull it out. If you wants to get on, you'll all have to goo round as best you can,' was his unsympathetic advice to the exasperated drivers of the blocked traffic.

Unfortunately for them, there was no immediate way to go round: they could not get past the 'fly' as the lean of the vehicle blocked the whole of the narrow road and the high bank prevented them from attempting to squeeze past anyway: and they could not go via the fields either side because a stream flowing under a hump-back bridge at the foot of the hill, swollen by the rains, had overflowed on both sides of the road, flooding the land a foot deep for a half-mile or more on either side. Consequently, any who wished to go forward on their journeys was required to make a diversion, which for the Hamwyte-bound and Wivencaster-bound traffic was a good two miles back along the way they had come.

Joshua Jaikes, being at the back of the queue on the Melchborough side of the hold-up, was amongst the first to wheel his pony and trap round and head back. Eventually, he came to a lane branching off to the left which at first looked promising, but, as it turned out, it wound around so much and twisted and turned so repeatedly that he had gone no more than a mile-and-a-half along it when he found himself faced again with the same lake of floodwater. Forced to retrace his route and, not being familiar with that area of the countryside, he attempted to go in a wider circle, but missed his way in the darkness and the rain and so added a further half-hour to his normal journey time, which accounted for his late arrival at the Wayfarers' and the black mood he was in when he finally stamped into the bay-windowed parlour to find the court had ended and someone whom he did not know had acquired the parcel of the widow's land which he hoped would be his:

some stranger, who had then refused a reasonable offer to give it up and seemed determined to hang on to it.

TWENTY

A GOOD husbandman, Jem well knew, having worked upon the land as a boy, was fully aware of the importance of keeping the soil in 'good heart,' as the husbandmen referred to it. Though knowing nothing then of the chemistry of nitrogen, phosphates, potassium and other nutrients, they at least understood that, whenever anything was taken off the land year by year, they were draining the soil of its 'goodness,' its humus, its fertility, as surely as water drained from it into a ploughed furrow or a ditch: and the best way to make good this loss of fertility and return 'the heart' to the soil was by adding his own dung and his animals' dung or through leaving one of the three lesser fields unsown or in 'bare fallow,' thus providing a resting and restorative period in the rotation of the crops.

The husbandman believed that the land, in the same way as his animals, needed periods of rest: though, in reality, land left fallow was soon covered with all manner of plants, thistles, docks, sorrel, burdocks, wild grasses and a host of other weeds as well as stubble from the previous harvest and grain plants growing from seeds missed by harvesters and gleaners. Some of the livestock was kept on the common meadowland and some on the common waste, but many animals, especially sheep, were put on to the fallow to eat the weeds, grain and stubble: at the same time, they fertilised the land ready for the next crop of grain: so the land was worked in a self-sustaining cycle of arable and livestock production.

Jem knew, too, the manner of a husbandman's way of working, the cycle of his year. During the frosts of January and February, when the ground was iron-hard, the husbandmen would spend their days making and mending tools for the coming year, such as shaping the teeth for rakes and harrows from ash or willow, fire-hardening them and inserting them into a wooden frame: they would also cut out the wooden shovels for casting corn during winnowing, fashion yokes and bows, forks, racks and rack-staves, twist willow into scythe-cradles or into traces and other harness gear. Meanwhile, the women would plait straw or reeds for neck-collars, stitch and stuff sheepskin bags for cart saddles, peel rushes for wicks and make candles from goose fat and the like. Those who kept sheep on the common pasture also had their days further taken up by the late February lambing.

For the husbandmen of Hamwick Dean and the two hamlets, the new year really began in earnest on Lady Day, March the twenty-fifth, when the ploughmen went out to prepare the strips for the spring sowing of the oats, peas and beans. Hamwick Dean's two ploughmen, Johnny Thickbroom and Ned Munson, could both plough several acres a day with their horse teams and vied with each other to turn other men's land: their work often continued well into April and consequently they were the two best-employed men in the village, especially as they were also practised in numerous other country skills, such as stacking, thatching, hedging, ditching and looking after horses.

The ability to draw or plough a straight furrow and lay a level stretch was the one skill above all others which drew the highest acclaim in the countryside. Indeed, so great was the interest in ploughing a well-finished stretch with straight furrows and so keen was the rivalry between the two that one drank in the Wayfarers' and the other in the Carpenters' Arms and each would think nothing of spending the whole of an evening 'ploughing the land once again' in their talk and disparaging each other's work to anyone who would listen.

Under Hamwick Dean's three-field system, a lesser field would always be sown with a single crop, the oats being broadcast by each man on his strips in 'the dust of March' and the peas and beans then 'dibbed' on the strips of another lesser field by hand with a sharpened stick used to make a hole for the seed, the planting often continuing into May. The strips were then harrowed to cover the seeds, some by the old way of tying bundles of weighted blackthorn brush behind a horse and dragging them across the ground, others using the sturdier harrow made during the winter to cover their seed more efficiently. Even so, it still needed children with slings and rattles to walk the fields from dawn till dusk to scare off marauding crows and other birds: only the protected doves were sacrosanct: killing one of them brought a heavy fine from the magistrates.

June was the time for shearing the sheep and hay-making, the latter a great communal effort when the husbandman moved down his patch of meadow with a long-handled scythe to cut the grass close to the ground, while the women and children followed spreading the cut hay and turning it to ensure it dried evenly before it was gathered into stacks.

July was 'the hungry month': then the grain stores were at their emptiest, awaiting replenishment from the coming harvest, and the husbandmen in need eked out his diet as best he could, some by foraging for nettles and other edible plants, others by mixing wheat and rye flour for their bread since it took longer to digest during their labour: pottage and pease pudding were the staple diets – pease pudding hot, pease pudding cold and more often than not more than nine days old.

Between the hectic days of haymaking and the summer harvest the loathsome work of weeding the crop-bearing fields was the most important task. Many a cautious husbandman in Hamwick Dean abided by the old maxim, 'He who weeds in May throws all away,' which was why the men did not begin weeding their strips till St. John's Day on the twenty-fourth of June, for that was the earliest date set for cleaning the land: tradition held that thistles cut down before St John's Day would multiply threefold before the main harvest. Weeding called for special tools, the most common being a pair of long-handled sticks, one with a Y-fork at the end and the other with a small sickle blade which were used together to cut the weed as close to the ground as possible.

Naturally, August, the harvest month, was the busiest time: then the women and children would join the men and youths in the fields and they would work from the time that the early morning dew was off the corn till the last glow of the setting sun, back-bending work with sickle and scythe, when men actually prayed in earnest daily for a warm or a hot sun and for God to send no rain. 'Harvest weather' was what they pleaded for, since at that time of the year, when the corn was ripe and ready for cutting, a single lashing downpour of a half-hour or so the day before they were to begin work with the scythe and the sickle could flatten a whole crop and ruin a whole year of a man's labour.

The winter-sown crops of wheat and rye ripened first and so were harvested first, followed by the spring grains of barley and oats. If the weather were against them, harvesting might well continue well into September, though, by tradition, it had to be completed before Michaelmas, September the twenty-ninth.

A third and final ploughing of the fallow field might also be undertaken prior to the sowing of the next winter crops of wheat and rye: after that, as the November rains and fogs came and the cold closed in under skies grey for day after day, they would flail their corn in the several small barns about the village where their grain was stored before being taken to market or ground into flour for themselves. There was one other important event then: that was the time when animals were killed, for there was often not enough feed to carry them over the winter.

In December, what work could be done was done: all the outdoor work was complete, animals were cared for, dung from the barns was stockpiled to be mixed with marl and spread over the fields, though there was never enough to fertilise more than the closest strips. After that, men would return to making and mending tools again, so completing the year's cycle.

Jem's holding was everything he wished: the greater part of it was good arable land and it was spread well enough about the nine lesser fields so that there would always be a majority of it to be worked to keep him busy when other parts lay fallow every third year. The area of it, too, was sufficient to keep him occupied for much of the year, he anticipated, so he would not really be overly dependent on going day-labouring, while the money he still possessed would be more than sufficient to see him comfortably through the first year and perhaps even through the second year – the good Lord granting him a good harvest in both – and might even extend into a third year before he needed to rely on any hoped-for profit for his capital.

One thing Jem did realise was that, without the bounty of the French cuirassier's purse, he would never have been able to set out on that path: and, of all the friends who sat together in the Wayfarers' Inn, his holding was the largest and the least scattered, particularly in comparison to Dick Dollery's five acres fifteen roods and twelve perches, which lay in twenty different locations. Thus, for his friend, the expense of reaping and carting his corn or barley was increased in proportion, especially as the horse and the wagon had to be brought from a distance to gather it. On the common pasture, too, Dick Dollery's hay also lay in so many little parcels in balks and lodes and at such a distance from each other that again it cost him almost as much to gather it as it was worth: Jem's being all together, he was at least spared that.

Jem's first task, of course, was to obtain his seed from Hamwyte market, which the village carter, Daniel Gate, brought back for him the following Tuesday and stored in one of the small barns on Forge Lane. The Ash Grove field having been already sown with winter wheat, Jem paid Johnny Thickbroom to plough the other strips on Thornbush, where barley was to be sown, leaving Barrow fallow in common with the others, then to turn the earth on Badger's Hole and

Snook's on Long Field, where spring wheat and peas and beans combined were designated by the Little Court, leaving Partridge fallow, and finally to plough Reeve's Croft and Farthing in Third Field, where more spring wheat was to be sown along with white turnips, with Gravel Pit left fallow.

Thus, he was able to begin sowing his barley on the Thornbush acre-and-a-quarter at the same time as the majority of the other husbandmen began their work, walking up and down his strips the same as the others walked theirs, broadcasting or 'fleeting' the seed on to the ground by hand from a small seed-bowl secured on his chest by a leather band around his neck. The method was that, with every stride he took as he moved down the field, he would pinch a small amount of seed between his finger and thumb and sow it in step: that is, as his left foot came up, his left hand dipped into the seed bowl and scattered the seed. It was a skilled job to sow with both hands and to keep in step, as the rhythm could easily be broken: then, the sower would have to stop and start again as a break in the rhythm meant a blank patch in the field. Also, few men, could judge the amount of seed to sow at each pinch of the thumb and forefinger: turnip seed was sown at the rate of half a pint an acre and, if the sower dug too deeply into his bowl with his thumb and forefinger, he would not make his seed last.

Not more than one or two men amongst them could sow at the necessary rate with two hands: most men were able to sow only with one, which was necessarily slower, but the sower who used one hand only was able to carry a seed-hod, which is a bigger container, on one side of his body: the seed then was sown by a broader casting, that is, covering half a strip on one side in one direction and the other half of the strip on the return journey. After that, he dibbed his peas and sowed his white turnips, as mindful as everyone that if he sowed too little seed the weeds would choke the growing crops and if he sowed too much seed the crops would choke themselves.

The leasing of the widow's land also brought Jem other rights, such as the right to depasture any stock he purchased on the meadows: so a month on, using more of his windfall from the dead cuirassier's purse, he bought three milk cows, a sow in season and six sheep and a ram, all of which he grazed on the pasture to the east of the village, which had also been divided into strips. The hope was that, in the cycle of things, as well as depasturing them, he would feed them from the crops he grew on his arable and they, in turn, would provide meat he could sell at market and milk for making butter and cheese, as well as wool and hides and tallow, which he could also sell. Further, they would provide him with the manure without which the soil of the arable would eventually become exhausted: even the straw left after harvest, he hoped to be able to sell for roofing or for fuel.

Soon after obtaining his strips, Jem left the Wayfarers', much to the chagrin of Caleb Chapman – since, to him, it was a considerable loss of business – and went to lodge more cheaply with an aged widow, Sally Wenden, in a tiny cottage on Arbour Lane, a short run of road which cut across the main triangle of the village from midway along The Street to Forge Lane and formed a smaller corner triangle of its own. Widow Wenden, being troubled for the past half-dozen years by an irregular beating of her heart, preferred always to sleep upright in an old chair by the hearth rather than lie in the darkness of a bedroom alone, for she had a dread of her heart stopping if she lay down.

Thus, she had no need of the single bedroom in her tiny cottage and she had let it be known she would rent it out for a small sum each week, which would at least keep her out of the village's poorhouse and give her company of a kind at night should the rhythm of her heart begin its irregular beat, which it frequently did: so frequently, in fact, that in his first month there Jem was awakened at least a half-dozen times by the poor old woman clutching at her breast and crying in a pitiful voice: 'My heart! My heart! I can hear it beating, I can hear it beating. I'm going, I'm going.' She did not 'go,' of course, and, glad as he was to find lodgings there, Jem was still glad to escape into the fields each morning.

However, there was always a cooked supper provided for him when he returned in the evening, though, as a part of the deal, he had agreed to perform certain tasks about the cottage for her, such as emptying the privy bucket, fetching her two pails of water each evening from the old pump by the fiveways junction outside the Carpenters' Arms, chopping wood and on occasions even escorting her to church, which, since she rented the property from Parson Petchey as one of the twenty cottages which the Church, through the Bishop of Melchborough, owned in the village, she and the other tenants were expected to do.

Indeed, everyone in the village then was expected to attend church at some time or other, especially those who leased land or a cottage or both from the parson, except, of course, the very old who could not walk there, the sickly and the smallest babes who could not crawl there and women either in confinement or still within the three months of giving birth and not yet 'churched' who were banned from attending. Just as the old widow went, so did Jem himself, as a tenant on glebe land, he, too, was expected to attend, which he did, albeit grudgingly, having been too long a soldier to be overly religious, but having no wish to fall foul of the parson either.

In the evenings, when the sun had set and Jem had eaten his meal and performed whatever chores there were to be performed, he would wander up The Street to the Wayfarers' to join his old friends, Dick Dollery, Enos Diddams *et al*: since his return, he had gained something of a reputation as a man who could tell a tale or two of the happenings in Spain, both the brutal and the salacious, most particularly about the brothels and the camp followers he had known, but, most of all, his part in the defeat of 'Johnny Frenchie' at Waterloo with 'Old Hooky' himself, almost as if the men who sat there believed that Jem and the Duke were on greeting terms with each other.

It was during one of these evenings that Jem finally learned the full facts about the death of the old squire, Sir Evelyn Darcy-Harprigg, the last in that line, so it seemed, since the ancient Hall had been empty and abandoned since his death seven years before.

'He never were the same man since the mutiny on Inworth heath,' John Romble blurted out unexpectedly one evening without stating exactly what he meant by it: and suddenly everyone in the bay-windowed parlour was looking across at Dick Dollery and Enos Diddams and they were looking decidedly ill at ease.

TWENTY-ONE

JEM'S memory of the late Squire was of a genial old man, with a grey moustache and beard, dressed in a white waistcoat, dark coat and white breeches and a tricorn hat, riding about the narrow lanes and byways on a great, grey hunter as if he were some feudal Norman baron, minus his armour, come from his castle to inspect his surrounding domain and his Saxon serfs after the Conquest seven hundred or so years before.

However, unlike the Norman barons of old, when the Old Squire, reined in his horse alongside a tenant husbandman, he would greet them in a polite and interested way, respecting them and their families and showing true concern for whatever problems they reported to him. For he was not only the lord of the manor but also a Justice of the Peace and sat regularly with the other Justices on the bench at Hamwyte and also at the Melchborough Quarter Sessions: and, though he punished those who broke the law according to the law, he was never overly harsh with them: a fine of five shillings for this demeanour or that demeanour, for stealing some apples from an orchard, say, or for taking an item of someone else's linen from a hedgerow, or for vagrancy or drunkenness perhaps, nothing ever serious. Yet the same man, if a villager lost a cow by sickness or old age or a couple of sheep through rot and went to the Hall to inform him, as they were expected to do, he would be most sympathetic and hand him a sovereign in recompense without it even being expected.

Jem's father had even been one of his tenants on the open-fields, renting all four of his strips on the First Field and five on Long Field from him, and considered himself fortunate to be so, as did many of the other husbandmen, who were following all the others who had rented their lands from the Old Squire's antecedents over the previous two hundred and fifty years, all the way back to the doomed boy king, Edward the Sixth. Jem recalled, too, that his father always spoke respectfully of the Old Squire and expected him to do the same and, in truth, he had never heard a bad word said against him that he remembered.

That the old man became somewhat peculiar after the death of his wife right at the start of the war was confirmed by the fact that his housekeeper, a woman from Inworth, whom he took on at the Hall after he became a widower, was never paid a single penny in wages in all the years she was there, but was kept in food and lodging and clothing and, every now and again, the Old Squire would simply hand her a bag of gold coins and ask her if it were enough, which it always was, more than enough, in fact. For, by that means, she was able to accrue quite a small fortune, in comparative terms, for one who had been an impoverished widow when she took up the position. It was she who found the Old Squire when he committed suicide: suffice it to say, he rode home one day from an exercise of the local Volunteers on Inworth heath, poured himself a port, sat himself in his favourite chair in his parlour, drank his port and then put a pistol into his mouth and squeezed the trigger.

The villagers would willingly have collected for a memorial tablet to him to be put up in St. Bartholomew's, but the Bishop of Melchborough and the new rector, Parson Petchey himself, had refused them permission since he was 'a suicide.' Yet mention of the Old Squire's ancestors in the village was to be found in the parish's records dating back to mid-Tudor times and marble memorial plaques to three of his lineage were fixed to the walls of the nave in the new church, one a mottled white marble plaque on the south wall commemorating the death at sea of an ancestral ship's captain while pirating for Elizabeth against the Spanish off Cadiz, the second a scrolled Grecian tablet on the north wall recording the death of a Lieutenant-General Darcy-Harprigg, the Old Squire's grandfather, while leading a Regiment of Foot under Marlborough against the French at the Battle of Blenheim, both transplanted from the abandoned St. Peter's chapel, and the third, a newer and plainer plaque, mounted to the left of the main door remembering the Old Squire's only issue, his son, James Dawlish Darcy-Harprigg, born in the Hall, schooled as a 'parlour boarder' up in the next county and dead at the age of twenty-six while serving as a lieutenant aboard the *Temeraire* off Cadiz at the Battle of Trafalgar.

The gallant *Temeraire,* students of history will know, went to the aid of Admiral Horatio Nelson's flagship *Victory* when the French admiral's *Redoubtable,* with its portside gun ports shut, had sought to close with the *Victory* and board it: but as the *Temeraire* came alongside, the French ship's bowsprit had fallen across the *Temeraire's* gangway and the British sailors quickly lashed it to their own rigging and then fired into the captive enemy with all their starboard guns at a distance of a few yards till the enemy ship struck its colours. Sir Darcy's son was one of the forty-seven British sailors and marines killed in that engagement simply because he had sought a place on the ship alongside its captain, Sir Eliab Harvey, who was a friend of his father and from that same county.

The opinion of some was that the death of his son broke the widowed old man's heart and that it was that which turned his mind and drove him to commit that final dreadful act: but others said the cause was 'much nearer home,' meaning within the village, and pointed to the fact that, even after his son's death, the Old Squire had soldiered on for a further four years as the Colonel of the Hamwyte Volunteer Corps, which he had led since it was first raised in 1795 and then reformed in 1803 at the resumption of hostilities after the first Peace, almost as if to occupy himself with a means to escape all thought of his loss. All agreed, he had thrown his energies into the colonelcy of the Volunteers, designing the uniform of the reformed first company, seeing to its cut at the tailor's in Hamwyte, dealing with the day-to-day running of the voluntary militia, forming a second company, dealing with all requisitions for ball and powder and bayonets, planning the exercises, attending every parade, chivvying up the men on the march, overseeing their drills: always energetic, always dedicated, always keen so long as Napoleon threatened.

No, they said, it was the shame and ignominy of the 'mutiny' on the heath and the despair of that rather than the death of his son which provoked his suicide: that he did it because he could not face the disgrace amongst his peers over what happened that day. It was noticeable, the gossips said, that neither Dick Dollery nor Enos Diddams, who had both served under him in the Hamwyte Volunteers, were standing with the rest of the villagers on the day of the funeral when they lined the roadside three deep for a hundred yards and more to the new church to pay their last respects to the old man: and nor were they part of the guard-of-honour formed by the rest of the Hamwyte Volunteers, lined up along the church path with their muskets reversed when the Old Squire's polished oak coffin was carried out and taken the last mile down the long and winding hill to his final resting in the abandoned St. Peter's churchyard, where his wife and all his other ancestors lay.

Not only were Dick Dollery and Enos Diddams missing on that day, but, whenever the matter was talked about in the Wayfarers', both, were overly quick to deny any culpability: they would give each other a sly look, almost one of embarrassment – some said it was guilt – and shrug their shoulders as if to say, 'Yes, we were there, but you cannot blame us for what the Old Squire did … '

The actual story of his friends' so-called 'war service' in the Hamwyte Volunteers and why it was such a great source of amusement to the other men in the bay-windowed parlour Jem learned the night John Romble blurted out his comment after Jem had told a tale or two of his doings in Spain, especially at one particular town.

Spurred on by the men's demands to 'Tell us your story, Dick,' or more to the point, roused up by their jibes of 'You were in the Old Buffers, weren't you, Dick?' the lanky straw-haired husbandman had pulled a face, emitted his customary low growl of disapproval and had then begun the calamitous tale of his and Enos Diddams's service in the cause of their King, accompanied by much sniggering and even outright laughter at times.

Dick Dollery's demeanour, however, suggested that he was not overly happy with what had been his lot or at being forced to recount a tale of his past for the pleasure of his fellows, who had heard it all before anyway, but who wanted to hear it all again: already around him men were beginning to smile.

'At least thee was in a proper army,' he growled to Jem, seated alongside him, 'not the clackity lot we were in. Gawd help us if the French had ever come! If they had landed along the coast here, they'd have walked to bloody London because there weren't nothing to stop 'em save two hundred dragoons in the camp at Melchborough and a half-dozen militias like the Hamwyte Volunteers – the "Hamwyte Buffs," as they got called. If the Frenchies had come, there wouldn't have been a man left to face 'em for miles, in my opinion. The whole damned lot on'em would have buggered off westward at the first sight of them to get as far out of their way as they could goo.' Clearly, Dick Dollery had had no faith in the Hamwyte Volunteers, even as one of them: indeed, he grimaced at the mere mention of their name.

TWENTY-TWO

THE STORY of the Hamwyte Volunteers was not a proud one. Jem was just five years of age when, on the first of December, 1792, the Government, foreseeing that trouble was brewing on the Continent following the French Revolution, took the initial steps to reconstitute the dormant militias, requiring the Lords Lieutenant of the various counties to comply with the Militia Act. In the February of 1793, with an invasion expected daily, the militias were called out nationally and almost one in five able-bodied men enlisted in some form of military organisation, militia or volunteers or yeoman cavalry. For the first time, the war against the French had become a national endeavour: though, in that region of the county, the rush to arms was confined mostly to the inhabitants of the larger towns, such as Melchborough and Wivencaster.

In Hamwyte, the mayor and the Justices did call a hurried meeting of the Court Leet and, after three hours of debate as to what they could and should do, undertook finally to provide eighty 'pioneers' – that is, eighty paid labourers from the town, under the direction of a 'captain' – who, in the event of a landing, would rush out and break up the roads of the district leading in from the coast with pickaxes and shovels. That, they hoped, would be enough to hinder any French march inland with wagons and cannon till the soldiers from the entrenched camp at Melchborough and the garrison at Wivencaster and any local militias they could assemble and coordinate – if they turned up, that is – could march up and drive them back into the sea.

To their credit, the loyal and patriotic inhabitants of Hamwyte did also further volunteer to provide twenty-one of the parish's carts and wagons and their drivers to assist with any evacuation of the populace westward which might be deemed necessary to clear the way for fighting by others and also to help with the movement of the army itself by conveying soldiers and arms from other places to the sites of any battle, as and when required, as well as offering the services of all the Hundred's millers and bakers to contribute to the commissariat's supply.

Various young bloods of the Hundred, like the Old Squire's son, were, however, more keen to contribute to the defence of their country and a dozen or so braver souls from each of the various towns did join the Colours of various regiments, determined to prove their valour and their manhood on the field of battle, while others were impressed into the Navy, though there was no great rush amongst the remaining populace of the town to form a volunteer company of their own as in other places.

Not till the first full invasion scare two years later, in 1795, when it was fully expected that the French would actually make a landing on their coast, did the inhabitants of Hamwyte agree to provide by the December of that year a complement of forty-eight armed privates and three officers to form their rather grandly named First Hamwyte Volunteer Corps, along with two guides, all drawn from the town, comprising mostly the younger men under thirty years of age from the gentry, the professional classes and the more well-to-do traders only, both captains being the town's two lawyers, whereas in the ranks were the sons of the town's surgeon, the mayor and its two main brewers and several prominent landowners.

For their colonel, even though the Corps was not the size even of a company, there was but one choice, Hamwick Dean's own Squire, Sir Evelyn Darcy-Harprigg, who lived but three miles away and was the most experienced soldier in the area at that time, having purchased himself a captaincy in a Regiment of Foot and served briefly, for six weeks all told, during the final part of the War of Independence against the rebel American colonists: the Darcy-Harpriggs were also, of course, a family of long standing in the Hundred and the most prominent of its yeoman gentry.

Units such as the Militias, Volunteers and Fencibles – the latter from 'defencible' army regiments raised in the United Kingdom which had no liability for overseas service – provided an acceptable alternative to the army and allowed the provincial gentry and the middle-classes of small market towns like Hamwyte and Maydun and Shallford to channel their military enthusiasm into opposing the French without actually having to take the field against them.

Unfortunately, the parades of the First Hamwyte Volunteer Corps were marked by a degree of unexpected levity due to the fact that the volunteers, being mostly young gentlemen and having had some years of schooling and some even education at university, found themselves being addressed and lectured like so many children by an illiterate retired former regular sergeant from the 'lower orders' returned to the ranks in order to drill them in the profession of arms. They found it difficult to stifle their laughter because the sergeant could never quite get over the fact that he had so many adult 'young gentlemen' under his command and was far too deferential, prefacing his commands with, 'If you young gentlemen would not mind…' or 'Would you be so kind, sirs… ' or 'I would be obliged, sirs, if you would…' which did not seem at all militaristic to them.

The basis of their training was drill, moving in close, synchronised order, which usually took place in a field to the north of the town, though, in wet weather or during periods of extreme cold, they drilled in the old spa assembly room at the Moot Hall. As young gentlemen, of course, they underwent sword training and by the August had even moved on to practising street firing with powder and firing with ball at a target in a gravel pit: and on one occasion they had marched all the way to Melchborough to practice skirmishing in the fields outside the county town with other volunteers and yeomen cavalry from other parts of the county, marching home again with the feeling that they were at last proper soldiers and as fine a body as had ever marched up and down Hamwyte High Street and, thus, were ready to meet any French revolutionaries who landed anywhere along their coastline.

The gentlemanly spirit and schooldays' camaraderie of this small and exclusive force was to be short-lived, however: for that same year the Government brought in the Supplementary Militia Act, calling for the embodiment of a further sixty-four thousand men who could be stationed anywhere in Britain. Foolishly, however, it decided to exempt anyone belonging to a volunteer force, such as that at Hamwyte, whose duties were strictly local. Perhaps unremarkably, there was a sudden surge in the numbers of the Hamwyte patriots and the First Hamwyte Volunteers grew to a hundred and eighty within a short period of time, many of them men aged thirty and above, with fifty new men being enrolled at just one parade, which rather changed the demeanour of the unit.

With so many volunteering to defend King and Country, the Hamwyte Volunteers were divided into two companies, one of a hundred and ten of the younger men under thirty, the other of seventy of the older men who could not march as fast or as neatly and that was the cause of the first serious dissension of what had hitherto been a unified company, or Corps, of the young bloods, along with a sprinkling of still-fit husbands and fathers able to march a half-dozen miles of a Sunday without gasping for breath.

The first problem this sudden increase in numbers created concerned the promotion of one of the lawyer officers, who, having already served for over a year, considered himself more eligible for a senior rank of a major in the expanded force than a proposed newcomer, who happened to be a friend of the Old Squire. The lawyer officer felt himself slighted when the promotion went to the latecomer, whom he had to admit was of a more superior status and of greater wealth in the town than himself, being the son of a marquis. Letters were exchanged with the Lord Lieutenant and, at one point, that particular company was threatened with disbandment till the matter was settled by a secret duel with epees in a wood clearing north of the town one September morning, the loser being 'pierced in the upper thigh,' as it was discreetly described to the ladies, from which he bled profusely and thus took no further active part in any military matters and for days afterwards was able only to ride in a carriage about the town with his 'war wound.'

Yet it was not that spat which caused the greatest test of camaraderie within the ranks of the Hamwyte Volunteers: it was their different choice of dress, which for most of them was the sole reason for volunteering anyway, since a young man in uniform walking around the town, attending church parades and even wearing it to go to the theatre was a sure way of attracting the attention of Hamwyte's young ladies. Nationally, the various Corps then were allowed to design their own uniform and, since they were paying for it themselves, the young bloods of the First Hamwyte Volunteers wanted to display themselves in colourful outfits: the uniform they adopted was of a royal blue jacket, white waistcoat and pantaloons, red half gaiters and a round black hat with a black feather.

The older members of Hamwyte's society – that is, the seventy above thirty years of age in their own company – considered the outfit worn by the 'young bloods' as beyond the bounds of what was 'proper,' and adopted for themselves a more sober blue double-breasted coat faced with buff, two rows of silver buttons stamped with the town's arms, a buff woollen waistcoat and buff breeches, half-gaiters and a cocked military hat. It had immediately earned them the colloquialism of the 'Old Buffers' and was scarcely less conspicuous since the silver buttons glittered at two hundred yards on a sunny day and would have presented an easy target to any half-observant enemy. Nevertheless, to show their patriotism, they paraded happily and marched to church every Sunday with a certain amount of pride, if with a certain shuffling of feet in the ranks, for there were always some who could not quite march in the step with the rest.

However, hardly had they got their uniform tailored to the satisfaction of them all than they were disbanded in the December of 1801 following the Peace of Amiens, though, by that time, as the threat of invasion had faded, the number of the 'Old Buffers' turning out for their weekly parade had declined from seventy in the first year to a mere twenty-two, the prime cause being colds, other illnesses, refusals by the wives to let them go for some, eventual disinterest for others, but mostly the pressure of business elsewhere, which translated to apathy since they had achieved their primary object of not being posted away from the town into some other militia – and, of course, of resisting the French.

Like Jem, Dick Dollery and Enos Diddams were just lads at the time and played no part in these early happenings, though it had been a source of much pain ever since for one Hamwick Dean thirteen-year-old of that time, who, on learning of the Peace and that the French were not coming after all, foolishly remarked within the hearing of the then parish constable, 'I wish the bloody French had invaded and hung our bloody King along with those two other rogues and thieves, the Archbishop of Canterbury and the Archbishop of York, and all the other bloody lords and ladies as well!'

Fortunately, the newly elected parish constable of the time, Isaac Hicken, a saddler, took young Richard Dollery by the ear, after cuffing it, of course, and delivered him back to his horrified mother, who promptly gave him a severe cutting across his calves with a stick for his 'traitorous' remark about 'Good King George and their High Graces': for several days thereafter, Dick Dollery had walked about the village with a painful limp and, friends being friends, he had not been allowed to forget it.

TWENTY-THREE

EVEN at the time of the signing of the Peace of Amiens, the Government knew that it was no more than a breathing space, an armistice before a resumption of the war: and, in preparation for that resumption sooner or later, they had despatched three forms of 'schedules' to parish constables requiring certain information. Schedule one required the total of males between the ages of fifteen and sixty, those infirm or incapable of active service, those serving in volunteer corps or armed associations, aliens, Quakers, persons who from age, infancy, infirmity or other cause would probably be incapable of removing themselves. Schedule two required the number of stock, oxen, cows, young cattle and colts, sheep and goats, pigs, horses, wagons and carts, corn mills and the quantity of corn they could mill in twenty-four hours, number of ovens and the quantity of bread they could bake in twenty-four hours, the average amounts of dead stock – wheat, oats, barley, beans and peas, hay, straw, potatoes and quantities of flour and meal. Schedule three listed the number of persons between the ages of fifteen and sixty willing to serve and in what capacity – on horseback or on foot, how armed (swords or pistols for cavalry, firelocks or pikes for foot soldiers), also the number of persons between the ages of sixteen and sixty willing to act as pioneers or labourers, what implements they could bring – that is, felling axes, pickaxes, spades, shovels, bill hooks, saws et cetera – as well as the number of persons between the ages of fifteen and sixty willing to act as cattle drovers or as guides and servants with teams of animals. At the same time, all the men and youths of the parish between the ages of seventeen and fifty-five were divided first into the able-bodied and the infirm, and then again into four broad categories according to age and marital status, which was how Jem had come to be 'balloted.'

The Government, having called out the militias in the April, declared war on France again in the May: the Hamwyte Volunteers Corps was immediately reformed, with Sir Evelyn again being nominated by the Lord Lieutenant as its commanding officer, since he was at least a knight of the realm, the chief magistrate on the

Hamwyte and Melchborough benches, possessed an estate worth more than four hundred pounds a year, had held the rank of full captain in the Lord Lieutenant's old regiment, albeit twenty-four years before in America, so he at least knew what was what, and was an old friend. This time, however, his role in the reformed Volunteers was more of an honorary one since he was near to sixty years of age by then and really not fit enough to go riding about in all weathers at the head of his men, especially during the bitter snowy winter which followed.

This time, too, there was a far broader intake to the reformed Corps, many of the new recruits coming from the dozen or so villages around the town as well as from the ranks of gentry and traders within it, which created its own problems when some of the more affluent of Hamwyte's 'Old Buffers' resented having to stand alongside 'swedes' and 'clod-hoppers' from the countryside when they drilled on the town's High Street or on the cowpat-covered field north of it. The recruitment of the 'lower classes,' they declared, had most decidedly resulted in a lowering of disciplinary standards.

Hamwick Dean 'did its bit' for King and Country, of course: as soon as the Volunteer Corps was reformed, a gathering of all male parishioners was called in the Wayfarers,' first to ballot six 'unwanted mouths' – one of which was Jem – into the Melchborough Militia to avoid paying the forty pounds fine decreed by the Government and, second, to draw up a list of those willing to put themselves forward as recruits for the Hamwyte 'Buffers' for the next five years, which was what Dick Dollery and Enos Diddams and three-dozen others happily did after Jem had gone and that way, if lucky, escape being inducted into the regular army. In fact, the village provided enough volunteers to form their own sizeable 'platoon,' though, to the chagrin of most, they found themselves placed under the command of a man who was a stranger to them all, a houseowner from Higher Rackstead, who was appointed an acting-lieutenant, because he claimed an estate of a hundred pounds a year and was given six months to prove it and supposedly had had some experience of militia duty at a place of which they had never heard. The Old Squire even trotted up to the inn from the Hall on his grey hunter to administer the oath as a Justice and formally enlist the men, as proud and delighted as anyone could be that his village had formed a platoon three-dozen strong, the one drawback to this being that, with seventeen of them husbandmen, the summer's exercises had to be geared around harvesting and haymaking.

Not unexpectedly, for the ensuing months, the Wayfarers' became the platoon's twice-weekly meeting place and the sizeable front yard their drill square, which made it all a lucrative business for Caleb Chapman, having all proceedings at his hostelry, for one monthly accounts entry recorded an amount of two pounds seven shillings and sixpence for beer served to volunteers after drilling – 'during it, more like,' declared the churlish landlord of the Carpenters' Arms, Jack Tickle, because in the same period he had to be content with takings of a mere seventeen shillings and tuppence ha'penny.

Over the months, the Hamwyte Volunteers grew steadily till more than four hundred, divided into three and then into four companies, paraded on the market town's High Street every Sunday morning. Though several other volunteer militias around the kingdom were ordered upon actual duty, either as part of a detached corps or brigaded with regulars and sent to various counties other than their own, the nearest the four Hamwyte companies came to being moved out of the town was at the end of the critical year of 1805, the closest Britain came to being invaded.

The summer had been a time of particular tension in the country: on the other side of the Channel, the 'Little Corporal,' now the self-crowned Emperor of the French, had spent two years slowly building up a substantial invasion fleet – the same sailboats and rowing barges which had threatened Jem's battalion on Guernsey. In the November, the Hamwyte Volunteers were placed on notice to march to the coast in the event of the expected invasion forces making a landing: yet when it was proposed that they should go on permanent duty for two or three weeks, it was met with general disagreement and the few who did agree to it did so reluctantly and only on condition they did not have to leave the town.

There was trouble almost from the first month of the reformation. 'It was a bloody farce from the start,' was Dick Dollery's blunt judgment. 'They still couldn't decide on which uniform to wear. Old Sir Evelyn tried – he wanted to get rid of the fancy outfits, which only the gentleman soldiers could afford, and give us all a simpler dress, more practical like, one that we could all wear. Caused a bit of a stir did that. We privates was offered a cloth uniform, the same as the sergeants, free, of course, but when the Old Squire tried to persuade the battalion officers to accept the ordinary clothes of the privates, giving them a greatcoat as a sweetener, they come over all high and mighty and said they was having none of it and they all threatened to resign, the whole lot on'em. It was a real stand-off, with handbills abusing the poor old Colonel appearing all around the town, pasted up everywhere.

'Of course, we privates got the short straw every time,' he went on, with a resigned shrug, as if one could expect nothing else. 'After a while, a couple of years or so, people in the platoon got fed up attending company parades and nothing happening. It weren't fun n'more. I know I got fed up, having to walk all the way to Hamwyte every Sunday morning for the full parade as well as drilling here twice a week with the platoon, but the so-called lieutenant made us goo over to Hamwyte and said he'd fine us if we didn't. I did miss a few of the big ones for one reason or another and got fined a shilling, which I couldn't afford, and they kept increasing it, which was a bit rich as half the time only five out of the fourteen officers we had ever bothered to turn out for the parades and they weren't fined, to my knowledge. Too busy elsewhere, they said. Discipline were always a problem, as well, because no one took much notice of old Sir Evelyn by then. He weren't the same man after his son were killed. He'd been a stickler before, but he didn't seem to bother so much after it. And the fuss about the uniforms, well, that was just a bunch of uppity types not wanting to parade with the likes of us. Most times, we was under a captain who weren't there half the time so at reviews and inspections our company was always thin in number because, if he didn't bother, then we weren't going to bother either.

'We had one large inspection assembly of the whole Corps, all four companies, with both regular and volunteer forces over at Melchborough when the General come to inspect us and he weren't best pleased with what he saw. Our drill was a shambles, with some turning the wrong way and most of us out of step from the start because the sergeant put us off on the wrong foot. He was off "By the left, quick march!" afore half of us at the rear had heard the command and we spent the next thirty yards all shuffling to get back in step. When you has a half-dozen who don't know their left foot from their right and who turns the wrong way to the rest on us, well, it do spoil the effect of the whole, don't it? The other Volunteer companies from all over the county were real military, like, and they put us to shame with their drill. It weren't any wonder the General didn't give us a "Well done" and why we was eventually disbanded.'

'Tell him about your medal,' a laughing John Romble cried. 'Dick won a medal for shooting, didn't you, Dick?'

'Aye,' the lanky, straw-haired husbandman acknowledged. 'It was the only thing I enjoyed was the shooting. They gave me a silver medal because I put in most balls out o' our company firing at a target in a competition they had to find the best shot. It was the only time we did any real shooting, excepting for when we was called on to fire a volley up into the air on the King or Queen's birthday and also, of course, when we celebrated our victories, Cape St. Vincent and Trafalgar, by the navy, otherwise it were a complete waste of time. I had signed the enlistment form and Enos had made his mark so we had to stick it out because we couldn't get out of it. I wish I had never bloody volunteered, I can tell'ee. Played havoc with my work, it did.'

TWENTY-FOUR

'WHAT about the alarm?' shouted another voice from across the smoky room.

There was an immediate ironic cheer from the rest of the company and a discernible reddening of both Dick Dollery's and Enos Diddams's cheeks: both shifted uneasily on their benches: across the room, several men who already knew the story and knew what was to come were wiping at tears before Dick Dollery had even begun.

It so happened that, from the eastern part of the ridge-top, especially by the junction of Goat Lodge Lane and the ridge-top road, a panoramic view was offered over the flat, marshy coastal plain and the silver ribbon of the Langwater estuary four or five miles distant running eastward to the sea: it was there eight hundred years before that the Tenth Century Saxon king, Edmund, had built a watchtower and a beacon to warn of the approach of the despised, geld-seeking Danes up the Langwater in their longboats to demand tribute from the earldoman at Maydun, whom they defeated in a bloody battle, celebrated still in an epic poem.

The beacon had been built a second time two hundred years before, when Phillip of Spain had sent his Armada up the Channel against Elizabeth and they had anchored off Calais and Dunkirk till the English fireships were sent in amongst them and they cut their anchors free in panic. The parish constable and the watch of Hamwick Dean were said to have stood by their beacon for three days and nights in case any of the fleeing galleons sailed up the Langwater: but they never did and, instead, were all blown northwards, most to their doom on the rocky coasts of Scotland and the west of Ireland. The remains of the third beacon, prepared when yet another foreign tyrant, the unlamented Emperor of the French, eyed Britain's shores, still littered the slope of the hill.

'The alarm were the biggest farce of all,' Dick Dollery growled in a low, unhappy voice. 'T'weren't my fault, it were all the fault of old Billy Dann – he's dead now, thank Gawd. He was coming back along the ridge road from the Compasses at Greater Tottle one night, drunk out of his skull, when he reckons he can see a beacon fire burning near the coast at Cobwycke, which was always a likely landing place. We'd made a beacon of our own in case they did land, just like in the Armada days. Anyway, Billy reckons he has seen the Cobwycke beacon lit and staggers up to the parish constable's house, old Isaac Hicken's place then, bangs on his door and shouts up, "The Frenchies has landed! They've lit a beacon fire at Cobwycke. I've seen it from the ridge!" Remember it was near twelve o'clock at night by this time – aye, at least twelve o'clock – and old Isaac has been roused from his bed, which didn't please his missus much. Perhaps old Isaac was on the nest at the time or just getting started – who knows? Well, when he hears what Billy has seen, he gets all excited, saddles up his donkey and rides off to the Hall to knock up the Old Squire, who comes galloping up into the village demanding to know what the hell is going on and was it all true? Old Billy had raised half the village by this time, going into the church himself and ringing the bell so most people was either up or gitting up. "See for theeself," says Old Billy and takes the Squire along the ridge-top road a bit. Sure enough, there's the beacon fire over Cobwycke way. Five minutes later the Squire comes galloping back. "Tis the French, lads," he says. "The blighters have made a surprise landing at Cobwycke! It's up to us to do what we can and warn the rest." It were like a madhouse by this time, people rushing about everywhere, women weeping and wailing, kids all crying and the people all running back to their homes to pack what they could and take to the woods to hide. "Someone will have to goo to Hamwyte damned quick and rouse the Volunteers there," the Squire says. "Who's got the fastest pony?" He writes out this message, like, saying the Frenchies has landed and we've been invaded and gives it poor old Caleb there because he's got a fast pony and trap – '

Behind the bar, where he was distracting himself knocking a bung into a barrel in order to listen and ensure that he was not maligned, Caleb Chapman grimaced at the memory as much the others were laughing at it.

' – Caleb has to ride over to Hamwyte to alert the magistrates and the rest on'em there. He en't even got time to dress properly. Well, he does that – takes him about half-an-hour – and, o' course, they all panic in Hamwyte and rings the church bells there and that raises the whole of bloody Hamwyte and half the places around and remember it's still the middle of the night, about two o'clock by this time, eh, Caleb?'

'Three o'clock in the morning,' was the grumpy answer from the bar.

'Well, eventually the Corps, or what they can round up of it, all forms up and set outs to march here,' continued Dick Dollery, wetting his throat with a swallow of ale. 'Meanwhile, o' course, they has lit their beacon at Hamwyte and, consequently, a whole string o' them now gets lit all the way from Maydun hill to Melchborough and beyond to warn the troopers at the camp there and all the way to Wivencaster, too, to alert the garrison there just like it was two hundred or more years afore when they feared the Spanish Armada was coming up the Langwater.

'In the meantime, Enos and me and the other lads, Tom Dunne, "Tutter" Jordan, Job Birkin, "Moot" Johnson, Eli Easter and that, are standing in the middle of The Street with our muskets, which we en't fired more'n a dozen times, two-dozen of us supposedly blocking the way o' the whole French army with just fifty rounds of ball and powder between us and the Old Squire astride his horse behind us, dressed in his uniform, with two pistols stuck in his belt and his sabre over one shoulder – and behind us half the village packing their things and getting ready to run in the opposite direction. Enos and me and a few o' the others pushed a couple of carts across the road at the junction by the Carpenters' Arms in the hope that that might stop them for a bit till the rest of the Corps gits here from Hamwyte, which they did eventually, about five in the morning. Then, for some reason, the Old Squire decides to march the lot of us the five miles to Salter to intercept the enemy there, delay 'em a bit, like.

'It were light by then and we could see this great column of smoke burning over Salter way. "Dang me if they en't set fire to the village!" someone says. We all thought they had, too, because there was a great column of smoke spiralling up into the sky just like you'd expect to see from a burning village. Well, as you know, there are three ways to Salter from here and we don't know which way the Frenchies are going to come, so we divides ourselves up into three smaller companies and each takes one of the roads, which means there's about forty-five of us in each likely to come across forty thousand or fifty thousand Frenchmen all armed to the teeth so all of us is hoping it will be one of the other lots that meets 'em and give us warning so we can follow the rest of the villagers in making a run for it.

'We didn't find any Frenchies, o' course, because there weren't none – we did manage to disturb three bullocks in the pinfold at Budwick. Someone suggested we let them out and drive them ahead of us in case we do meet the French on the road and that would give them a real nasty shock – being charged down by some good old English beef which they en't expecting. The farmer who come to get 'em back the following morning weren't best pleased when he found they was gone, I don't suppose.

'The alarm, it turned out, weren't an alarm at all. It were all an accident – there weren't no beacon fire. It was just some farmer who had heaped up his oil-seed rape in his close and had tried to set it alight. It wouldn't burn so he left it. Then somehow the wind got up in the evening and it all flared up – nothing more than that. It had probably been smouldering all that time. That was what Old Billy Dann mistook for the warning beacon, burning rape stalks. The oily smoke it give off was what we mistook for Salter burning. Of course, it were too late by then as half the county was roused up. As soon as we knew the alarm were false, we was all ordered back.

'News must have spread about our gallant foray against the enemy that never came because – danged me! – on the way back we was hailed as heroes all the way. People come out of their cottages and stood by the side of the road all a-cheering us and hallooing us and we stopped at five ale houses, to my reckoning, for free drinks, toasting the King's health, like, and "Damn the French!" Didn't goo down too well with the other militias when they all come marching up from Melchborough and Wivencaster and we told 'em, "Sorry, it was a false alarm." Still, we did our best. At least we turned out, which is more'n some did. They hot-footed it. Took two days for some on'em to come back.'

There was a general murmur of approval for their valour: they had indeed done their duty that night and set off to face the enemy, but in reality everyone was laughing at the Hamwyte Volunteers: the whole place was jolly with laughter and they called for more of the happenings of the Second Hamwyte Volunteers to help them to pass a pleasant night since Dick Dollery's droll way of telling it only added to their amusement – that and their own memory of it all.

'The uniforms, the uniforms,' someone prompted him.

'Ah, yes,' Dick Dollery acknowledged, 'the uniforms.'

The tale of the uniforms came about because, eventually, the Government came to the conclusion that the Army of Reserve and the succeeding Permanent Additional Force were unsatisfactory. The experiments to provide a form of national training, begun with the Levee-en-Masse Act of 1803 and continued under the Training Act of 1806, achieved its final form in the Local Militia Acts, by which those volunteers who were less fit, less capable and less likely to want to bother with all the route marching and weekly drill imposed were given the option of resigning. A hundred and twenty-three of the Hamwyte Volunteers, including a sizeable number from Hamwick Dean, took up the offer, leaving two hundred and sixty-four privates to continue with their weekly drills and occasional nightly patrols, amongst them still Dick Dollery and Enos Diddams as two of the ten remaining military men from the village.

Another sup of ale was taken before Dick Dollery continued: 'We was all to get new uniforms in the July of '08, after they had weeded out all the slackers and the dodgers,' he went on in his same droll way. 'We gets these new uniforms sent down from London which we is supposed to wear so that we'd all look the same as the rest of the Volunteers in this area for this big exercise in skirmishing on Inworth heath, with the Lord Lieutenant himself taking the salute afterwards. Well, we didn't get these uniforms till the very morning we was to march from Hamwyte to Inworth and when we puts on what they has sent us, blow me, if the majority on'em en't too big for most on us. Hardly one fitted a man proper.

'Our lot must have been made for six-footers, Foot Guardsman, most like, because they was outsize for us. Well, we tried exchanging jackets and hats and the like, but it weren't no use. You couldn't match anything up proper. There weren't no time to tailor'em and make'em fit. We just had to put them on, fall in and march off to Inworth as best we could, sleeves all a-flapping something awful. I had to roll mine up a good four inches. On some on'em, the jackets was falling off their shoulders even when buttoned and most on us had trousers so big we couldn't march proper in'em. We had to hold our muskets over our shoulders with one hand and keep the other hand on our belts so we could hitch up our trousers as we went, which don't do for a military-like sight, do it? And you durst not present arms with both hands for fear your trousers'd fall down around your ankles!

'Well, when we got to the heath after an eight-mile march, instead of falling in with the rest of the Corps at the roll of the drum, three on us, Enos, myself and another chap from Hamwyte, well, we just quit the ranks – told the Old Squire that we weren't going to goo marching about the countryside on any more fool's errands to suit him and his kind, not in uniforms like we had, and we all headed off back towards Hamwick Dean. I'd had more than enough by then – so had Enos – the uniforms were the final straw – everyone in the other companies was laughing at us – I was going home. So I went. There weren't no pride in it anymore, y'see. The upshot was, of course, the Old Squire sent a sergeant and three file of men to fetch us back and we was arrested and ordered to be taken back to the town as prisoners under guard. Old Sir Evelyn, he was fuming near to bursting, purple-faced he was. As a punishment, he wouldn't let any of our company take part in the skirmishing exercise and ordered the whole lot of us to march back to Hamwyte, with me and Enos and the other chap still under arrest.

'On the way back, we got to talking about it all, even though we weren't supposed to be talking in the ranks, but no one cared by then. It weren't just Enos and me, it were most everybody in the company. What with all the fuss over the uniforms, there was near-mutiny in the air. When we was marching past the Compasses at Greater Tottle, some of the men decided they was going to go inside as it was hot and have a sup of ale and "Hang old Harprigg!" who was riding on his horse, anyway, so he was all right. He ordered us to keep on gooing, but no one took any notice, the men was all thirsty and we all piled into the ale house, disorderly like, just quitting the ranks and piling through the door, everyone, before the officers could stop us. We formed up again afterwards, of course, about a half-hour later after we had had a drink, and marched back to Hamwyte like regular soldiers, but it were too late by then.

'Old Evelyn had gone off himself. When we took no notice on'im, he just rode off in a high state and that same day he wrote out his resignation to the general and sent it off to Melchborough. We weren't to know that he'd take one of his pistols and shoot himself, were we? T'weren't our doing. T'weren't mine. He didn't have to shoot hisself. We reckon it were more over his son than what we did that day. It was the loss o' him more than his loss o' face. Made a right mess of hisself, he did – blood everywhere in the big parlour, they said, all splashed up the wall and that. That was something we hadn't seen coming, I have to admit, but it weren't our fault, it was they clowns in London who sent us the wrong uniforms who was to blame, in my opinion. But for that, we'd have been all right, I reckon. It just tipped things over the edge.

'The Corps was under the command of the major after that. At least he had risen up from a lieutenant over the years and he weren't a bad chap. Seeing what he had seen, though, he was reluctant to goo on and take command and he called a meeting of all the other officers at his house in Hamwyte, including five who was absent that day at

Inworth, it should be said. The upshot was that they all decided they would give up their commissions – resign them, like – because it weren't worth gooing on the way things was. No one was bothered n'more. Several on'em took back their resignations the next day, o' course, but the damage had been done and the General over at Melchborough, he disbanded us at the end of the year, though the newer recruits who wanted to complete their twenty-four days o' training to avoid call-up to the county militia was allowed to go on. I got a five-shilling fine for our poor discipline, which was lucky because it was damned near a mutiny. Everyone got fined for breaking ranks at the ale house so we weren't the only ones. So that's where I did my service, in the bloody Hamwyte Volunteers and a sorrier bunch o' soldiers you never saw this side of Christendom and that's a fact!'

The Old Squire was five years in his grave in the old St. Peter's churchyard when the Treaty of Paris was signed on May the thirtieth, 1814, between a defeated France and the seven victorious allies – Britain, Russia, Austria, Prussia, Sweden, Portugal and Spain – and so was spared an example of the futility of war, a war in which he had lost his beloved son and only heir. For the treaty proved to be a lenient one: France was allowed to retain all the territory it held in Europe as of 1792 and was not required to pay an indemnity. Britain even returned to France all its colonies, except Tobago, Saint Lucia, and Mauritius: instead the Congress of Vienna was called to thrash out the resettlement of territories that had been taken by Napoleon.

The nations were still arguing – or, more diplomatically, the conference was still under way – when Napoleon returned to France on March the first, 1815, in an attempt to regain power, and Jem stood against him and his army at Waterloo: the 'Little Corporal' abdicated a second time and a new peace treaty, actually a treaty of alliance, was signed in Paris on November the twentieth, 1815, by Britain, Austria, Russia, and Prussia. This time, the boundaries of France were reduced to those of 1790 and she was made to pay seven hundred million francs in war damages and to finance an allied army of occupation for a maximum of five years. The Treaty of 1814, except for provisions not revoked by the Treaty of 1815, was to continue as binding, as were the territorial arrangements of the Congress of Vienna – not that Jem or any of the others sitting in the bar parlour of the Wayfarers' laughing along with Dick Dollery and Enos Diddams would have cared about any of it.

'Ah, the futility of war, the futility of war,' was Mr. Able's comment upon the subject, delivered with a deep sigh from his usual place near to the fire, slowly sipping his ale and looking about him at the chattering, pipe-smoking regulars who filled the room, while outside a wind howled and rain beat upon the window panes. Damned queer weather they were having, he mused to himself: not a proper summer at all really.

TWENTY-FIVE

THE REVEREND Doctor Petchey had never been a man of the world in the way other men had been men of the world: except for a brief and unsuccessful foray into the world of teaching, he had spent the greater part of his life since youth cloistered amid the quadrangles and colleges of Oxford's 'dreaming spires.' Ever since he had obtained his doctorate in theology, his life had predominantly been one of study and contemplation. He much preferred discussing Christian perfection or the holiness of heart and life, or sitting with his peers in the great hall of Christ Church, the same hall in which Charles the First had held his Parliament at the beginning of the Civil War, and happily discussing the nature of divinity, mortality and mankind. Or, while taking quiet walks along the banks of the Cherwell and the Isis, or ambling across the Meadows, or walking around the Tom Quad and perhaps pausing deep in thought under Wren's splendid bell tower, contemplating whether the Christian could in this life come to a state where the love of God, or perfect love, reigned supreme in his heart.

In the Romanesque cathedral, he had happily attended the daily services, lifting his voice in praise of the Almighty on High as if He were personally waiting above to hear his, and only his, act of devotion: he was, in fact, so immersed in God and religion, it was almost to the exclusion of all other life, till one day the thought came to him that he had spent so much time considering the theory of Christian spirituality that he had never so much as saved a single soul, rescued a single sinner, brought a single lamb back to the fold or directed a single lost traveller on the right road to the Kingdom of Heaven.

In his fiftieth year, almost in desperation, as if it were something he must do if he were ever to be allowed into the higher precincts of Heaven – that there were higher precincts for men of his station and depth of devotion, he never doubted – he had left the quadrangles and halls and 'dreaming spires' bent upon taking up the living of a rural parish, where the real poor dwelled, where few cared about his Church as did he, going amongst the heathen poor whose souls he must save for their own sakes, whom he must turn from the paths of wickedness to the paths of righteousness.

So, seeking out his old friend, the Bishop of Melchborough, who had studied theology at Christ Church at the same time, he had asked him if he knew of a respectable living in his diocese which he could take up, no matter how humble, no matter how small, perhaps one where the incumbent was too old or too infirm to continue. What he had received was a more than comfortable living in a village of five hundred and fifty souls where the incumbent, sadly, had recently died, one with a substantial yearly living of several hundred pounds, derived from the rectorial great tithes and a Glebe farm of twenty-six acres, sixteen roods and twenty-eight perches of dairy meadow, managed by a bailiff, plus a large, red-and-blue-brick, Jacobean parsonage with seven bedrooms and eight chimneys, a spacious church itself built only three decades before and, therefore, not in need of any repairs and capable of holding comfortably a congregation of four hundred or more.

Further, he had also received the oversee of two curacies in two adjoining hamlets, Lower Rackstead and Merchant Staplers, each with their own small churches, St. Cuthbert's at Lower Rackstead and St. John's at Merchant Staplers, but with a joint Vestry, which, as in other places, dealt with matters appertaining to the administration of the three parishes and the upkeep of the churches in each. It also dealt with the Poor Law, maintained the parish pumps, repaired the roads, except turnpikes, controlled vermin and had also maintained the parish cage till the latter fell into disuse during the war. All in all, his old friend, the Bishop, had been exceedingly benevolent.

That was how the white-haired, hook-nosed parson had arrived in the village, three years after Jem Stebbings had left it, inducted to the historical living as rector at a time when church-going in most places was not popular, but determined to save the souls of everyone there before he himself was called to his eternal rest and an eternity in Heaven as his undoubted reward, which he considered was no more than his due and of which he was unquestionably assured, since he had spent a lifetime in the service of the Lord. Yet he knew nothing of the place to which he came or its people or its way of life, simply arriving with his wife one June day in his little pony and trap, seduced by the tranquil picture it gave high upon the ridge-top, with a blue sky above and a profusion of dog roses hanging upon its hedgerows.

The Reverend Doctor had always considered himself a benevolent man, who believed passionately in the righteousness and truth of the

Gospels, that God ruled above all others, that prayer, the Scriptures, meditation and holy communion were the means by which God transformed the believer: that he, as God's representative on earth, must, therefore, rule over the common people of his three united parishes, to be both a father and a shepherd to them all and to ensure that they did not stray from the straight and narrow pathway to Heaven. Unfortunately, what he discovered was that there were those amongst the labourers who sat in the Wayfarers' and the Carpenters' Arms on a Saturday night who regarded that path as being broad enough to allow an occasional diversion from it by way of a night-time foray into one of the many woods surrounding the village and easy enough to be found again with a muttered prayer come the Sunday morning, particularly if there were a rabbit or a pheasant hanging from a nail in the scullery.

Hamwick Dean and its two hamlets were far from the idyll for which the good Doctor had hoped: quite inadvertently, he had come upon another side of England of which he had never dreamed existed, one of hardship, of despair, of oppression and pauperism, where there seemed to be a loss of hope everywhere, an absence of morals amongst many and a loss of faith amongst the same, people who seemed to be almost ignorant of God and His Glory.

The inhabitants, or at least a good two-thirds of them, seemed to suffer from an air of malaise, decrepitude and a despair which he could not comprehend: instead of a village of cream-walled cottages with thatched roofs and trellised roses around the front doors, as he had expected, he had found a village of ramshackle dwellings lining all three of its three principal thoroughfares, twenty of which the Church alone was responsible. And along some of the back lanes branching off from the other ways were other so-called 'cottages,' more beggarly and wretched still, some so small and haphazardly built that they appeared to have been thrown up overnight and all inhabited by people who seemed quite prepared to rely upon a vagabond existence and willing to resort to pilfering of every kind, of anything which came to hand.

He had changed all that: Parson Petchey, the villagers had quickly discovered, was a man of a different kind to the jovial old Reverend Burlingham: indeed, his first act after his induction had been to bring the solemnity back to the communion and evensong services by banning the monthly visits of the Rackstead Players, a band of roving musicians who assisted the congregation 'in raising their voices in holy melody,' as the late Reverend Burlingham used to say. The

Players were simple men with simple ideas: one was a hurdle-maker and rail-mender, another a candlemaker, a third a wagoner, another a shopkeeper, a fifth a shoemaker, all from Lower and Higher Rackstead, one playing a clarinet, another a bass-viol, a third a French horn, the next a cornopean or cornet and the last an ophicleide, a conical serpent-like instrument bent double which made deep, resounding sounds that made the children laugh.

Sitting in the newly built church with his parents as a boy, listening to the Rackstead musicians playing once a month, with the old reverend tapping his hand on his knee to their music, was one of Jem's happier memories: their coming always filled the church: it was one of the highlights of church-going: other times the place was half empty.

They were noted for the good music they played and received requests for sacred performances from churches all over the Hundred: indeed, the Reverend Burlingham had been so pleased with their playing one Sunday evening when they had filled his church for him that he thanked them in the middle of the service, declaring: 'Both myself and my congregation feel greatly indebted to you for the admirable way you have assisted the musical side of our devotions.' As a 'thank you,' he told them all to go to the Wayfarers' and order a gallon of best ale in his name, which they did, and half the congregation joined them and they continued playing there for the rest of the evening, though, it being a Sunday, they finished before midnight.

Their music, however, was not reverential enough to God for the new parson's liking: one could not praise Him with a French horn, a clarinet, a cornet and an ophicleide: so he banned them, simply by taking down the notice on the church door of their next arrival and screwing it up in his palm before solemnly intoning from the pulpit in conducting his first communion: 'There will be no more of that vulgar music in God's House.'

'The damned fool of a parson said it weren't proper religious music. Said it was vulgar, profane or summat! What would an old fool like him know about church music?' a young and bitter Enos Diddams complained in the Wayfarers' at the time: for he, like the three hundred and more others who had gone to church that first Sunday out of curiosity about the new parson, liked to tap a foot to the Players' music while his mind dwelt upon other things, most particularly young Emma Challis, who sat just across the aisle and was continually giving him the eye.

However, not content with that, 'the new parson' – as he was and would always remain, never to be truly accepted – had next put a stop to the Vestry's ancient tradition of 'bounty' payments to control the village's vermin when he had sat for the very first time with the chief overseer of the poor and his assistant and the two churchwardens of that time in the church's nave to watch the distribution of relief to the queue of 'impotent poor' waiting in the porch outside.

That morning, two boys, Thomas Thickbroom, the ploughman's son, and Daniel Brady, the shoemaker's son, neither above ten years of age, had entered first, carrying a small sack apiece, the contents of which they cheerfully proceeded to tip on to the table in front of the new parson, smiling as they did so: from the sack tumbled the tiny heads of five moles, so tiny that the Reverend Doctor had to ask what they were, never having seen such creatures before. The boys, thinking he was interested, obligingly informed him what they were and explained how they had smoked them out, dug them up and bludgeoned them to death as per usual. When the second sack was emptied, out came the remains of eight sparrows which the boys had also killed with a net and their sticks.

It had long been a custom of the Vestry to pay a penny for every mole head and dead sparrow brought to them: but for the new parson it was so horrible a sight, such a terrible shock to him that such barbarism could still exist, that he could barely control his rage. He almost felt like taking his cane to the young savages who stood before him as he had had to do many times to the dullard students whom he had once briefly taught Latin and Greek, before deciding that he was not fitted for the life of a schoolmaster and had returned gratefully to the more peaceful, contemplative and academic existence of Oxford. What irritated him further was that the overseer and his assistant and the two churchwardens seemed quite pleased with the boys, congratulating them on their 'bag': they had even begun counting out the money till he had swept the whole lot off the table and ordered the two boys to leave the church.

Now, nine years on and with no new lord of the manor resident at the Hall, since the unforgivable suicide of the Old Squire two years after his arrival, and the whole matter of the estate and lordship of the manor lost in the chancery courts of London, the good Doctor sat at the top of the hierarchy of the village: and by the time of Jem's return, his authority was unquestioned, his passion undiminished – indeed, if anything, it was even greater, for he could look into the churchyard at any time of passing and note with satisfaction the low mounds of at least forty saved souls gone to their eternal rest since it had been consecrated. At last, his life had a purpose: the Lord's mission was being fulfilled.

TWENTY-SIX

ALL THROUGH the morning, one after another, the line of pathetic recipients for poor relief had shuffled into St. Bartholomew's vestry, all expecting to receive that for which they asked and for which they believed themselves entitled simply because it had always been given or was paid to others and, therefore, it was their right to be given the same. None was refused: to have denied them would have been un-Christian, though unusually that morning, the Friday after Dick Dollery had given his account of the Old Squire's unhappy demise and for the first time in over a year, Parson Petchey himself was again seated in the vestry along with the chief overseer and his assistant: the Reverend Doctor felt that some of the recipients were making too much of their plight and, in consequence, were receiving more than they ought.

The chief overseer of the poor for the three parishes at that time was a retired revenuer by the name of William Hurrell, who had occupied the post for nine years and had performed the duties diligently enough: while in some places the overseer was not much liked by the day-labourers or the husbandmen, it was generally acknowledged in both the village and the two hamlets that old William Hurrell had done his duty fairly and honestly. His latest assistant, elected reluctantly two Easters previously, was the butcher William Hoskins, who begrudged having to undertake the task as much as anyone else who did it and who had been elected simply because it was his turn and because, like Caleb Chapman in his time and Andrew Norris in his time and Ephraim Simms in his time, he had an outbuilding behind his butcher's shop, which was ideal for use as a store for the various articles which the overseer was required to hand out to the deserving poor.

Neither was overly happy to be seated with the parson: for, though everything given and to whom it was given, whether money or kind, was assiduously written down by the chief overseer in a large book, signed by him as a true record and countersigned by his assistant before the book was put away in the parish chest, Parson Petchey had decided he wanted to see for himself if the recipients were truly as much in need as they said they were.

Seated with them that day as usual was the people's churchwarden, Andrew Norris, and also the newly-elected incumbent's churchwarden, Joshua Jaikes, who had suggested the Reverend Doctor might like to take a look at what was going on and how the poor rate money was being dispensed. In consequence, Parson Petchey now wished to add his signature to ensure that the overseer was being diligent in his duties, just as the week before he and the new churchwarden had perused the annual listing of all the parish's ratepayers and how much they paid to ensure that every pound, shilling, penny, halfpenny and farthing of the poor rate was accounted for accurately.

Two types of relief were available then to those who required it – outdoor relief, which was the norm, under which those who needed it were left in their own dwellings and given either a 'dole' of money on which to live or were given relief in kind, such as clothes, bed linen and food: or, alternatively, there was indoor relief, under the terms of which those who required it, if they were ill or orphans, would be taken into the village's poorhouse.

Before the Reformation, it had been considered a religious duty for all Christians to undertake the seven corporal works of mercy, that is, deeds aimed at relieving bodily distress. In accordance with the teaching of Jesus, the people were to feed the hungry, give drink to the thirsty, welcome the stranger, clothe the naked, visit the sick, visit the prisoner and bury the dead.

Then, in 1563, the poor of England had been put into different categories according to their state: that is, those who would work but could not were labelled the 'able-bodied or deserving poor' and, as such, were to be given help either through outdoor relief or by being given work in return for a wage. Second were those who could work but would not: they were the 'idle poor' and they were to be whipped through the streets until they learned the error of their ways. Third, were those too old, too ill or too young to work: they were the 'impotent or deserving poor' and were to be looked after in almshouses, hospitals, orphanages or poorhouses. Orphans and children of the poor were to be given a trade apprenticeship so that they would have a means of livelihood to pursue when they grew up and the first compulsory local Poor Law tax was imposed, making the alleviation of poverty a local responsibility.

During the last years of Elizabeth's reign, in 1601, in an attempt to remove vagrants and beggars from the streets and roads, an Act of Relief of the Poor had consolidated all the previous legislation: each parish was made responsible for its poor by law and a compulsory poor rate was to be levied on property owners in every parish. It was further decreed that each Vestry should appoint a chief overseer of the poor and an assistant from the ranks of its churchwardens, which restricted it somewhat in Hamwick Dean's case since one of the requisites for office was that the overseer be a 'substantial householder,' which William Hurrell was, living by himself in his own house along the ridge-top road.

Under the Old Squire, the position of chief overseer had fallen mostly to the larger farmers of the three parishes such as old Isaac Peakman, Samuel Howie and Ezekiel Godwin, each being the required 'substantial householders,' elected at the Easter Vestry meeting to serve at least a three-year term. As yet, their sons had still to serve and the feeling amongst most was that it was best for the paupers of the three parishes if none of them did: the ageing William Hurrell was at least fair and scrupulous, even if sometimes a little forgetful. The assistants had always come from the ranks of the shopkeepers and tradesmen, of late William Hoskins, Ephraim Simms, Andrew Norris and Francis Clutter, the other butcher, and even Caleb Chapman the one time, all being eligible as payers of the poor rate and members of the joint Vestry.

The duties of the overseer and his assistant were to collect the poor rate, which would then be spent 'for setting to work the children of all such whose parents shall not be thought able to maintain them… for setting to work all such persons, married or unmarried, having no means to maintain them and who use no ordinary or daily trade of life to get their living by,' otherwise called the able-bodied pauper… 'for providing a convenient stock of flax, hemp, wood, thread, iron, and other ware, and stuff to set the poor on work' and 'for the necessary relief of the lame, impotent, old, blind and such others amongst them being poor and not able to work,' in effect, the 'impotent poor.'

Both the 'able-bodied poor' and the 'impotent poor' were queuing in St. Bartholomew's porch that Friday morning, some simply to get a handout of money, two shillings or two shillings and sixpence, if they could get it, some to use it to buy food, others wanting money for their rent, some having their rent paid every six months, others being 'weekly pensioners,' receiving regular weekly payments. Relief was not only given in casual cash doles, but sometimes as loans, by grants of clothing, shoes, bed linen, cloth, fuel, flour, meat, soap, and, occasionally, tools for work: rents, rates, fees for burial, fees for nursing care: doles for widows, doles for children, doles for the sick and the aged, for the latter were always amongst recipients of poor relief, especially in times of high unemployment as then. In such times, too, able-bodied men also received relief for their families, simply to be able to feed them, but also for a variety of other reasons, for medicine, for a surgeon's bill sometimes if the Vestry agreed a surgeon were needed, for funeral costs if he could do nothing for the stricken sufferer.

Charles Mole, for instance, had walked yet again from Lower Rackstead to stand, hat in hand, head bowed as he did every week, repeating the same depressing tale that his family had no food in their cottage and there was no wood or coal either to lay a fire and could he please have two shillings, if they could spare it: yet he had been seen going into the Green Man at seven o'clock two evenings previously and was unlikely to have left before midnight, since he never had done so before.

A glance back through that parish's records told a sorry tale of his life as a debaucher. Twenty-five years before, as a young man of twenty, he had fathered two children out of wedlock, the first to girl named Rebecca Willis, the second to a girl named Mary Garner, and had been ordered to pay maintenance of a shilling a week for each. In fact, he was still paying for both the children when he had married his present wife and had gone on to father a further nine children in the ten years since with her. He was already in that parish's employ for road-mending, verge-cutting, hedge-trimming, digging drains, lopping tree branches and the like and, as such, a monthly allowance was being provided to the family to keep them alive since the work he did was infrequent. But there he was, back again, asking not only for the two shillings but for a further five shillings to buy a shroud for his three-year-old son, named Charles like him, who, it was true, had just died of a fever. Yet, having been granted five shillings for that by the overseer and his assistant, after a brief conversation, he had then presumed upon their good nature by asking if they could spare a further shilling for the grave digger's fee and, oh yes, another shilling for the church's bell to be tolled 'to see the boy to his grave, like.' The list of what these people thought to claim was, to the good Reverend Doctor, never ending.

Next in line was one Patience Sayer, a slip of a girl, in the parson's view, aged just nineteen, from Hamwick Dean, whose twenty-year-old husband was another occasional day-labourer, which meant that for much of the time he was not in work, but was reliant upon the parish: both he and his wife were illiterate and, like so many who had married at the church, both had been able only to mark the register. She, too, had become a regular, waiting at the church door of a Friday, sent by her husband to plead for 'a shilling or two,' in the hope that the Vestry would look more sympathetically upon a woman than a man, especially if she were young and pretty.

Her good looks had got her into trouble in the first place. The marriage two years before had been as hurried as many others: and five months after it, she had given birth to a son, though he had died at just one month and a small amount of relief had been granted for a shroud and a coffin to bury him in the churchyard, where, Parson Petchey hoped, it would be 'of some consolation to her to know that his innocent soul would at least have gone straight to Heaven.' Now she had given birth to a second son and he was as sickly as the first

Her husband had found some day-labouring of late, but it was not well paid, only a shilling and sixpence a day, she said, and she was asking the parish please to allow her two shillings a week relief to 'make up' his wage since she could not go to work herself because she had to remain at home to care for the sick child. She was granted one shilling and sixpence.

Henry Brickell, of Merchant Staplers, was a regular, too: he was somewhat simple-minded and, in consequence, had not found a woman to marry till he was in his twenty-eighth year, which was late for a man. He had eventually gone to the altar with a woman three years older than himself called Mary Kray, who was herself regarded as somewhat backward: depressingly, they, too, had been able only to mark the marriage register.

Within four months, the wife had also given birth and, in the years since, had managed to add a further five children to the crowded two-bedroom cottage: and, since the husband, because of his simple-mindedness, found even occasional day-labouring difficult to come by, the family had been placed on an employment chart and were provided with regular amounts of poor relief which would 'make up' for the lack of income during his underemployment. This time, he professed to be suffering yet another bout of illness – his third in the past year – which, he claimed, meant he could not work: also, his wife and his eldest son had fallen ill, something to do with some stagnant water near their cottage, he said.

Now he stood before them with a dirty rag in one hand to mop his sweating brow, the other hand up to his mouth to prevent his cough from spraying everywhere: indeed, at one point, it seemed he had been about to retch so that Parson Petchey had quickly asked the others to grant him his two shillings and sixpence just to get him out of the vestry.

Fourth, but far from the last that morning, was eighteen-year-old Rachel Jenkins, also of Hamwick Dean, who, according to the parish records, was an illegitimate child born to a forty-year-old-widow: a shilling-a-week bastardy order had been placed upon her father, a labourer from another parish, but the good reverend was happy to see that she had been baptised, though her parents had never married and so she had been brought up on a combination of her mother's wages as an occasional servant at Amos Peakman's farmhouse, bastardy maintenance irregularly paid by the father, and continual parish relief. Now, 'like mother like daughter,' she, too, had given birth to an illegitimate child and the Vestry was having to provide her with a monthly allowance, while the overseer and the parish constable were seeking a bastardy order against that father. She was given two shillings and, from the parson, a stern lecture on immorality.

And so it went on, some asking for money, some for coal for their fires, some for cloth to make a blouse, or for a few bundles of wood to keep their fire going, the details of each carefully written down by William Hurrell, watched by the parson's eagle eye: '...to Eleanor Crabb, a poor woman of the parish, the overseer to provides two flannel shifts and a blanket at a reasonable price for her use... to Mary Stock, the overseer to provide four measures of potatoes and four bundles of wood for the fire... to Hannah Church, ordered one tobstand of wool... to Thomas Townsend, husbandman, as relief, a bushel of rye for seed and two bushels of barley for bread... to Elizabeth Male, as relief, five shillings to buy herrings for salting at Maydun... '

In addition to those who sought a supplement for their low wages, or for their rent, there were other monthly payments to those on the 'bastardy list.' It was an appalling fact, upon which the good Mrs. Petchey commented repeatedly, that, in the past year, the names of five girls from Hamwick Dean and two others from the hamlets had been added to that list, the awards made being always dependent upon the mother naming the father of her child at the moment of birth – as she was always likely to do – or soon after so that a bastardy warrant could be served on the culprit: 'Sarah Edwards, child by Thomas

Bateman... Elizabeth Coffey, child by Peter Brewster... Lucie Pound, child by John Stocker... Mary Sharpe, child by Richard Thacker... Hannah Heath, child by Thomas Downs... Mary-Jane Heath, child by John Gilbert... Elizabeth-Ann Jobb, child by Henry Cobbe... ' and not one of them above eighteen.

It was not an unusual sight, the Reverend Doctor had observed from the start of his ministry, to walk around the village and see eight or nine women all in various stages of pregnancy and some of them merely young girls and clearly unmarried: once it had been a rare thing for a girl to be with child before she was wed: now it was as rare that she was not. It happened no matter how often and how vigorously he railed against it from the pulpit, human nature being what it was: he had lost count of the number of times he had spoken out against the 'sins of the flesh' since his arrival. Indeed, twice the previous year the Vestry had had to raise the poor rate tax after it was set and the way things were going those charged would have to keep paying more and more. A dozen bastard babies seemed to be born each year and some girls would not even name the father and so received no relief whatsoever, nor asked for any, but lived at home with their parents and passed their time helping their mothers in looking after their younger siblings and milking the family's cow, that was, supposing they had one.

There were other girls, again most seeming to be no older than seventeen or eighteen years, who, when they went up the aisle, were 'almost at the point of dropping the child,' as his wife was want to put it scornfully, though, never having been blessed with children of his own, he did not care to dwell upon thoughts of women swollen by pregnancy or the manner in which they delivered themselves from that condition: the very thought of it made him shudder. He could not help but shake his head in sadness and disbelief that, almost without fail, the parties to the union standing before him, being so poor, were compelled to throw the expense of the wedding on the parish, which duly paid for the sake of the unborn child and the face-saving of the girl, who too often was the innocent in what had happened, or so all the women he knew would have him believe, for they always blamed the animal instincts of the predatory male.

There was, the Reverend Doctor had long ago detected, a palpable immorality amongst certain villagers, who seemed to him too intent upon carnality and less upon their Saviour: they bred far too quickly for his liking, especially since a man earning a shilling and sixpence a day might have six or seven or eight children: too many of the children were dying before they reached their seventh or eighth birthdays – of scarlet fever, of diphtheria or other infections. The old graveyard at the abandoned St. Peter's chapel of ease was dotted by small overgrown and forgotten mounds and the new one, which had been open only since the new church was built, already contained a dozen or more. Yet the numbers of children seemed to grow greater every year and had become a drain upon the parish.

A walk through the village by a keen-eyed observer would have been all that was needed to note a certain weak-mindedness had manifested itself amongst the children of certain families. On Forge Lane, for instance, at least two of the grimy-faced urchins of no more than four or five or six years of age who played by one particular laneside cottage displayed all the signs of it: one drooling from the mouth, another possessing bulging eyes, and the manner of both that of the totally retarded: and, while some might attribute their afflictions solely to the conditions under which they lived, others more in the know knew that it was due to a more shameful cause.

The villagers' ignorance upon matters of their health appalled him also. Once when walking along a back lane in the heat of summer, where a half-dozen tumbledown cottages stood, he had had to hold a handkerchief to his face or be violently sick by the roadside just to get past them, such was the foul stench emanating from the ditch running the length of the lane which, in effect, was nothing more than a stagnant and stinking cesspit. The cottagers, having little ground at the rear, had built their privies right up against the mud walls of their homes, which meant in time the wall became saturated and the foul stench of it could not help but penetrate inside. These same privies drained into the ditch, yet children played by the laneside as if inured to it all.

Indeed, so many of the children around the village, who should have been strong and healthy, raised as they were in wholesome country air, were, in fact, stunted and malnourished, went about day-long with their faces unwashed, wore rags, were barefooted and had rickety legs that at first he had attributed it to the smallness of the cottages in which they lived and the insufficient air in them rather than the careless manner in which they disposed of their night waste and their ignorance of the sicknesses it brought.

It was only through the munificence of one of the past squires that the villagers had a supply of water at all for their needs, other than rain caught in a barrel: their sole supply then was obtained from a solitary pump by the Carpenters' Arms which had been bored sixty feet into the earth a hundred years before. All water had to be carried from it by hand and, therefore, was precious, as he had learned the day after his arrival.

At the time, he was walking on the outskirts of the village down one of the narrow lanes, inspecting his parish and hoping to find inspiration from God's creation to assist him in writing his very first sermon for the Sunday: it was a hot day and he had stopped at one of the cottages which the church owned and had asked an old woman sweeping the path if she would be so kind as to give him a cup of water from her pail.

Not knowing that he was the new parson, the woman had angrily rebuked him. 'I en't giving you any of my water!' she had cried. 'We has to goo too far to fetch it, over a half-mile and uphill all the way. If it weren't for my son-in-law gooing every other evening and fetching me a couple of pails, I should have to goo without! If you want a drink, take it from the rain tub. You can have that – t'is only used for washing clothes. T'other water is too precious to be giving it away to just any passer-by.'

It was such a shock to him that one of his own 'flock' should refuse him a drink of something which was sent by God upon at least a hundred days of the year that he felt duty bound to put the old woman right as to who he was and the fact that her cottage was owned by the Church and, therefore, him. Thereafter, till the day she died, she attended Holy Communion every Sunday, come hail, rain, snow or shine and, in his presence, walked always with her head bowed as if paying a penance for some moral misdemeanour.

What disturbed the parson more upon his arrival, though, had been the baseness of two families who had erected their own so-called 'cottages' down one of the back lanes: he had never expected to find such idle and dissolute amongst the rural poor: to him, they seemed both to be dens of the most wretched and worthless of types, accustomed to a vagabond subsistence and all too ready to resort to pilfering if needs be. They were the lowest of the 'lower order': poachers, deer-stealers, sheep-stealers, thieves, the perpetrators of offences of almost every description, people who were a terror to all quiet and well-disposed persons: Melchborough's old gaol would have been an empty shell were it not for their kind. His second act upon taking up his incumbency was to have the overseer of the poor and the parish constable escort both families back to their parishes of origin since they had no true reason to dwell in Hamwick Dean and never attended church anyway.

TWENTY-SEVEN

WHETHER the Old Squire had died or not, in the tight, small world of Hamwick Dean's hierarchy, by the mere fact that he was a theologian and had spent so long amid the halls and quadrangles of Oxford, the Reverend Doctor naturally assumed himself to be morally and intellectually the superior of any other in the place. The villagers, he had soon discovered, were 'common working types,' as he had been forewarned – uneducated, for the most part, the greater number illiterate and irreligious, little better than the peasants of France had been before the Revolution. Admittedly, courtesy decreed he give a nod in the direction of the portly lawyer, Mr. Able, but he was the only one: and what was he to make of a lawyer who liked to spend his evenings drinking with those self-same villagers in that den of iniquity, the Wayfarers' Inn, and who, in the nine years he had been there, had never deigned to set foot across the church's threshold to attend even one of his services? Not even a funeral or a wedding had tempted him.

Right from the start of his incumbency, the Reverend Doctor had made it his holy duty to draw in each and every one of the sinners of the village and especially to ensure an increase in the total number of communicants. In the nine years since that very first communion, when curiosity alone had drawn the villagers to 'see what the new man was like,' he had succeeded in filling St. Bartholomew's almost every Sunday with upwards of three hundred and fifty of his parishioners, sometimes four hundred or more, excluding the very young and the sick, a five-fold increase since the time of the previous incumbent, the late Reverend Burlingham, well liked as he had been.

Not surprisingly, the good Doctor put his success in 'returning so great a number to the fold' down to the power of his sermons: in so doing, he appeared to be totally oblivious of the fact that the sudden upsurge in religious fervour amongst the populace of Hamwick Dean in particular after his arrival had more to do with the fact that the Church's local representative, who drew rent from its twenty cottages as well as its acres of glebe in the three great open-fields and on the meadow pasture, was a very different proposition to the late Reverend

Burlingham. He had frequently been absent from his duties due to acute abdominal pain and gas distress, leaving most of the work to his two curates: having no medical knowledge, he did not know it was caused by his poor eating habits, such as eating too much of the cabbage he was given in tithe and too many onions and too many beans.

Almost every husbandman rented at least one or two and some a dozen or more of his strips from the Church: thus, it was not unexpected that a man who relied upon the Church to provide a roof over his head or for a good part or all of his livelihood, and who required, too, the approval of that self-same representative for his outside relief, particularly when times were hard, as they were then – it was not unexpected that he should come to the conclusion that life would be easier if he, his wife, his daughters, and even his sons if he could coax them there, spent an hour or so of their Sunday rest at one or other of the services, 'Hosannahing in the Highest' or 'Amen-ing' in unison at the end of prayers even if they did not fully understand why they did either.

At least from time to time the Church did sanction maintenance of a kind upon its cottages, a broken tile replaced, say, a gutter repaired, a window pane reglazed, a rotting door fixed, which was more than could be said for the absent landlords of the others, like the trustees of the defunct lordship of the manor, who held the rental on twenty also and employed a small, thin man from Hamwyte by the name of Hendry to collect their rents monthly and, consequently, he never sanctioned the repair of so much as a rotted door or a worm-eaten window frame, as neither did the dean and chapter in Oxford, who held the rent of a further fifteen. The rest were held for the most part by her ladyship, Lady Amelia Blight, who lived somewhere unknown to those who rented her ten cottages, twelve by the Dowager Marchioness of Thrapstone, living in a palatial house in London somewhere, and six each by two city gentlemen similarly unknown to the villagers as well as one or two others.

Thus it was by the leverage of his rents for home and field and his say upon the giving of the parish relief that Parson Petchey now filled his church each Sunday like a shepherd penning his sheep, as if only by their prayer and supplication before the good Lord could his flock be counted and 'cleansed' of its week of 'sinning.' What it also did, of course, was to allow his two churchwardens to note who amongst his sheep might be missing from a Sunday communion or evensong and, if missing more than twice, to pay them a visit, in a pastoral way, to ensure they did not miss again. For, having filled his church, the one thing above all others that Parson Petchey feared was that his parishioners might begin to desert him and join a growing group of Dissenters, who had set themselves up in a chapel in Hamwyte on the very road to Hamwick Dean not three miles away and were supposedly attracting more and more of the faithful of that town to their new sure, passionate and evangelical form of religion.

In fact, so much of a good shepherd to his flock did the Reverend Doctor wish to be that, before morning communion, he would send his two churchwardens around the village's triangle of roads and along the backroads, even as the bell was tolling, just to ensure that all of his sheep were safely gathered into the fold and none was lost or straying at other pursuits. Or, to put it another way, that no man was intending to creep away and go rabbiting or shooting partridges or pigeons in the many woods: that no woman was delaying her arrival at the House of the Lord and defiling the Sabbath by hanging her ragged washing on a hedgerow to dry when she should be at prayer: and that the boys of the village, being disinclined to spend half their sole day of rest inside a church, anyway, were not gathering as they often did on the triangle of green by the cross-roads guidepost to smoke and talk and play ha'penny up.

One jerk of the thumb from either of Parson Petchey's two emissaries and the mere mention of his name was enough to send them slinking the threequarters of a mile along the road to the church, grumbling as they went, but going nevertheless, with the churchwardens following close behind to ensure that they got there and praised their Maker and saved their souls for at least another week. For such were the times then that, in some places, a warden himself might be imprisoned for not going to church. It helped, too, that Caleb Chapman and Jack Tickle both closed their premises during divine service and attended themselves so that none could while away their praying time in either place, though it was noticeable that there was always a lesser number at evensong when the Wayfarers' and the Carpenters' Arms were open.

Not that Parson Petchey allowed his religious duties to compromise his secular comfort as befitted a doctor of divinity, a gentleman and a reverend: a tour of the rectory would have found in the 'best bedroom,' for instance, a mahogany four-post bedstead with a feather bolster and two pillows, straw mattress, four blankets, two sheets and a counterpane: also a mahogany chest of drawers, mahogany dressing table with swing glass, a painted cupboard and closet, mahogany bidet, three padded chairs and an embroidered footstool, four work boxes belonging to his wife, three baskets, a carpet covering the boards, a tender and fire irons in the hearth, two deal boxes and bonnet basket, Wedgwood foot tub, basin and ewer. And, in one corner also, a stump bedstead, that is, one without posts which the rector sometimes used when returning to the bedroom in the small hours of the morning after composing his sermons so as not to disturb his wife, though the servants whispered it was used for another reason, particularly when there was chill in the house's air: the rector's wife, they said, could be quite shrewish and shrill at times

As well as the 'best bedroom,' there were also four other main bedrooms similarly well furnished and a dressing room, a nursery unneeded and unused, two attic bedrooms for the two servants who 'lived in,' a drawing room complete with a square-pianoforte, nine music books and a music table, an entrance hall, dining room, study, schoolroom with a grand pianoforte, kitchen, butler's pantry, linen cupboard, cellar with fifteen casks, four hogsheads of ale and four of cider, six dozen bottles or port wine and twelve bottles of brandy, larder, servants' hall, stable with two horses which his Glebe farm bailiff supervised, coach house for trap and hackney carriages, yard, garden and orchard.

In his study overlooking the churchyard, he sat at his secretaire and composed his 'hell and damnation' sermons by the light of his flickering candles and in his bedroom prayed each night upon his knees with such an intensity and earnestness that his wife had often fallen asleep before he had finished and it became necessary to wake her again if he were to be 'eased' and set comfortable for sleep. A browse along the shelves in his study would have gained a measure of the man from the very titles of the books there and from which he drew the subject matter for his sermons, pious, insightful tomes such as *'Precious Remedies Against Satan's Devices,' 'Practical Observations Upon Our Saviour's Miracles,' 'Saints' Memorials,'* and, most thumbed of all, *'Smith's Pious Breathings.'* The sermons he composed from these he delivered at morning communion and evensong alike with an almost messianic fervour: for it was a fact, which the villagers would not dispute, that Parson Petchey ruled over the moral and social well-being of the villagers with the same zeal as any Mohammedan imam, Jewish rabbi, Catholic priest or Scottish Presbyterian minister ruled in any other place: his opinions, his wishes, his decrees and his prejudices were law: at the sight of him approaching along the road, the fainter-hearted trembled.

Perhaps because of his sincerity and piousness, the villagers of Hamwick Dean were always ready to smile and smirk behind their hands when they sat listening to his preachings, an example of which had occurred on Plough Sunday, the Sunday after Epiphany, just before Jem had returned, when the parish's two ploughs, bedecked with ribbons, were dragged into the church before the communion service to be blessed as the ploughing season began. It was one of the few old customs in which Parson Petchey, rather than one of his curates, took part since it was a direct plea to Heaven for God's special attention to his domain and also did not involve him having to traipse over the muddy wastes in wind and rain looking for weed-smothered boundary markers or walking across the acres of the open-fields blessing each crop in turn. Such things as that were best left to his curates. That Plough Sunday, however, the talkers in the Wayfarers' and the Carpenters' Arms all agreed, with smiles, Parson Petchey had been at his evangelical best and his most laughable.

The custom was, after the blessing on the Sunday, on the next day, Plough Monday, teams of youths would drag the ploughs around the village, seeking contributions for 'ale' and a night of revelling at the village's two inns – and woe betide the cottager who failed to stump up something, no matter how small: all manner of mischief was caused to them. Of course, on the Plough Tuesday, heads would be aching and more often than not time would be spent in recovering before the work could begin in earnest on the Wednesday.

In his church on the Sunday, however, standing in the pulpit, with his eyes screwed tight shut, his face raised to Heaven, the palms of his hands pressed hard together, Parson Petchey had pleaded so fervently for his flock that the ardour of the moment had made him visibly shake, 'like a man with the palsy,' some said.

'Almighty God,' he pleaded, 'bestow upon all who till the ground wisdom to understand your laws and to co-operate with your wise ordering of the world and grant that the bountiful fruits of the earth may not be hoarded by the selfish or squandered by the foolish, but that all who work may share abundantly in the harvest of the soil. O Holy Spirit, you fill the earth with your riches for the use of your children. On all who are in authority bestow your gifts of wisdom and goodwill, that, being lifted above self-regard, they may establish a new order, wherein the needs of all men shall be supplied, through Jesus Christ, our Lord.'

'God speed the plough,' intoned the congregation on the nodded signal from the churchwardens.

Even as the rumble of their voices died away, Parson Petchey was beseeching the rafters yet again: 'O Lord Jesus Christ, you warned your disciples, having put their hand to the plough, not to look back – bless this plough and the skill of the ploughman for the service of mankind.'

'God speed the plough,' intoned the villagers a second time.

'God speed the plough and the ploughman, the farm and the farmer. God speed the plough, on hillside and in valley,' went on the fevered parson. 'God speed the plough on land which is rich and on land which is poor, in countries beyond the seas and in our fields.'

'God speed the plough,' intoned the villagers solemnly once more in the pause.

'God speed the plough, in fair weather and in foul, in success and disappointment, in rain and wind, in frost and sunshine,' cried Parson Petchey, his voice again soaring to the rafters of the vaulted ceiling. 'May the ploughman's hope be fulfilled in a plentiful harvest, through Jesus Christ our Lord. Amen.'

'God speed the plough,' the villagers intoned dully for a final time.

After that, when the service ended, they had gone home through the January sleet to their cold, poorly heated cottages to sit at a bare table for a pottage of mashed turnip and carrot and chopped onion and dried bread soaked in acorn 'tea,' while the Reverend Doctor and his skinny, bespectacled shrew of a wife returned to a table of roast beef, potatoes, cabbage, carrots, parsnips and gravy, followed by individual apple pies, each seated at one end of a table, with a silver candelabra in the centre, unlit, of course, a jug of claret at the parson's elbow and the two maids standing nearby to clear after them before they could eat their own dinner from the leftovers.

TWENTY- EIGHT

A HAILSTORM in May was not unusual in England: but the fall of hail soon after Jem had sowed his first corn seed was altogether different. Hailstones the size of large pebbles fell on seven consecutive days, a freezing chill pervaded the air for the whole of that time and violent flashes of lightning and loud cannon-like crashes of thunder directly over the ridge-top sent everyone darting for cover on three of those days: the violence of it was almost Biblical, according to some, like the weather would be at the ending of the world. Old memories were stirred, but none could recall weather so extreme.

Jem, the other husbandmen and small farmers about the village and the two hamlets, as well as the middling and larger farmers of that Hundred, that county and that region, were experiencing the same freakishness of the weather as extended right across England, Wales, Scotland and Ireland. Each morning, as they looked up to the sky to try to gauge the coming day and knelt each Sunday in the church under the reproachful eye of Parson Petchey, to pray for the sun or a milder rain, as was required at a particular time, they were not to know that a violent volcanic eruption on the island of Sumbawa ten thousand miles away in the Dutch East Indies in the April twelve months before had thrown enormous amounts of dust into the stratosphere, which spread around the globe. The fallout from the explosion of Mount Tambora in the April of 1815, drifting across the northern hemisphere even before the battle of Waterloo was fought, shut out the sunlight, caused the heavy rains and floods throughout Europe that year and was still distorting the weather a year later when Jem began his enterprise. In fact, the very year in which Jem took up the Widow Hebborne's land is forever recorded as 'the year without a summer': and the ten years from 1810 to 1819 inclusive were to be the coldest in England for more than a hundred years.

The spring in that region had been peculiar for a start: snow had fallen all day on Easter Sunday in the April, blanketing the open-fields even as Jem was 'fleeting' the seed: and, though spring and early summer snowfalls are not unknown in England, the men still stood and scratched their heads over it, for there was a definite red or brown tinge to the settling flakes which they could not comprehend. The peculiarity and the wonder of it was much discussed and commented upon in the Wayfarers' and the Carpenters' Arms, as it was in a thousand other hostelries in that region.

Then, in the May, from the twelfth onwards, had come the first heavy deluge of hail: worse, continuous rain began to fall soon after, lasting well into mid-June and from then onwards there was a long spell of cold and dull weather so that at the time the grain should have been ripening under a warm sun, it had hardly sprouted at all, while both Jem's pea and beans crops in the late July were poor, the pods of both flat and undersized. The cheerless weather continued into the autumn: the whole country was affected by it: there was a poor harvest everywhere and it was not until late August that Jem and the other husbandmen and small farmers were finally able to go on to their lands to attempt to bring in what they could of their failed crop. What they found was ice on the puddles in the furrows in the early mornings and blackened ears of corn where an overnight frost had nibbled at them.

In Hamwick Dean then, the traditional method of harvesting the grain crop was by hand, using a sickle or a scythe, and requiring as many hands as could be gathered in the one place to do the work. In that respect, the husbandmen and day-labourers would forget their differences and band together to harvest each of the lesser fields one at a time, sometimes two at a time if there were enough to do it and the corn was ready in both: and, if the weather were threatening or being fickle, the whole village would turn out to gather-in the harvest as speedily as possible. Even the likes of Caleb Chapman and Jack Tickle, the innkeepers, the two butchers, the two bakers, the wheelwright, the blacksmith, the cordwainer, the rakemaker and the ratcatcher would shut up shop to go into the fields to wield a sickle or a scythe to ensure their plots were included in the great gathering-in and leave the business of their shops or inns to their wives.

A first line of men would mow the wheat and lay it evenly behind them with scythes fitted with cradles made of iron rods: each was followed by two women, the 'gavellers,' paid a shilling a day to rake the mown corn into gavels or rows ready for tying into sheaves, or for carting. Both boys and girls were employed, too, as 'bind-pullers,' working with a 'tier-upper,' the man or the woman who came after the reapers and gavellers and tied the corn into sheaves. When the tier-upper took a bunch of corn into his arms, the boy or girl acting as his bind-puller would be ready with three or four ears of corn pulled from a bunch lying nearby to hand them to the tier-upper when he was ready to make his knot.

Behind the gavellers and the tier-upper usually came eight teamsmen to 'shock up' the sheaves, placing ten in a shock or stook so that the cool late summer breezes and hoped-for autumn sun would dry them: that way, two hundred or more acres of wheat could be cut in seven or eight days, with carting taking a further eight or ten days so that, generally, twenty days were needed to complete the harvest on the open-fields – weather permitting, which that August it was not.

As it happened, such was the anxiety of getting in that summer's harvest as the few dry days during the rainy weather allowed, Amos Peakman at Goat Lodge, Marcus Howie on Smallponds and Joshua Godwin at Milepole – the three large farms – went around the village, knocking on cottage doors in a desperate bid to recruit as many men and youths and women as possible, for they were in the same predicament as the husbandmen on the open-fields and needed to gather in their harvests equally as quickly.

The three large farmers in the two hamlets – Silas Kempen and James Allen, at Lower Rackstead, and Thomas Godbear, in Merchant Staplers, did the same – and, since they were all offering better money and beyond that the prospect for a good number of them of work all winter threshing the grain by hand and winnowing it, perhaps even till Lady Day came around again, it was an offer which Jem and the other husbandmen could not match. Consequently, the best of the day-labourers, plus the 'threequarter men' and even the 'half-men' opted to go on one or the other of the larger farms, as many as fifty together at Amos Peakman's place, forty at Marcus Howie's and a slightly lesser number at Joshua Godwin's, the others willingly traipsed the short distance to Lower Rackstead and Merchant Staplers to take work there.

So the husbandmen and the small farmers of eighteen or twenty acres or so, like Peter Sparshott, Jonas Bunting, Reuben Frost and Peter Hull, in Hamwick Dean, had to recruit their extra labour as best they could, from their own wives, sons and daughters and from the more aged and less energetic day-labourers and the younger boys and girls. All told the number of men, women and children who congregated in the one place, sharpening scythes and sickles to begin harvesting the winter wheat crop of the lesser Ash Grove field on First Field was less than half what it should have been: but then the day-labourers were wanted for once, so none could blame them for going where the money and the longer employment lay.

Fortunately, though the weather that first day remained cold and cloudy, a wind was blowing enough to dry the corn to cut and that needed to be done as quickly as possible, for there was no guarantee that the days of rain had come to an end. For Jem, it was to be the first of several hurried harvestings.

Fate can play unexpected hands and it dealt one the very next morning: at exactly eight o'clock, as Jem was standing at the guidepost by the Carpenters' Arms, waiting for Dick Dollery and Enos Diddams to appear and so continue with the harvesting of Ash Grove, a cart came rumbling down The Street from the direction of Hamwyte, loaded with the possessions of some poor soul who had been evicted from their home. Such sights were common then: the furniture amounted to no more than a single iron bedstead, a straw mattress, two chairs, a kitchen table, washtub and a stool and a small food cupboard, along with some linen bundles containing clothes and the like, as well as an assortment of pots and pans and buckets and other utensils which women accumulate for cooking and cleaning purposes. The solitary figure of a shawled woman sat up front beside the carrier and it appeared to Jem, when he briefly turned to look back on hearing the rumbling of the cart's wheels, that the woman leaned inwards when she saw him, as if she were hoping to hide herself behind the driver's back, and that she pulled the shawl across her face so as not to be recognised: it was only as the cart drew abreast of him and he looked up again that Jem recognised the woman's form: it was Mary-Ann, Will Ponder's sister.

The cart would have rumbled on down the long, gently sloping hill towards Merchant Staplers had not Jem surprised himself by stepping out into the road. 'Good gracious, Mrs. Allbright! Wherever are you off to?' he cried, raising one hand to signal the carrier to haul back on his reins. 'Where is Will?'

A red-faced Mary-Ann emerged from behind the driver's back and stared shamefacedly down at him, her cheeks blushing crimson. 'Will is in the House of Correction at Steadleigh,' she said with a sigh of exasperation. 'That fool of a brother of mine – ' There was sudden anger in her words. ' – that fool of a brother of mine stole a chicken from a farmer. He is such a hothead. He thought he would not be caught. He thinks only of himself. He is not the only one who is suffering. Other people are in the same boat as he is, yet they do not steal. He is just too quick with his ways and his temper, that's always been his trouble.'

Jem knew full well Will possessed a quick temper: he had seen him grow angry and flare up often enough. When they were drinking in Dover on their return from Calais, he had become involved in an argument with some youths in a tavern and would have taken them all on by himself had not Jem and Padraig Cannon bundled him out of the place.

Jem could see from Mary-Ann's flushed appearance that she felt she had to explain her present situation: the wagon carrier was in no hurry and sat leisurely with one foot set on the board and the reins resting on the lead horse's withers. He had heard many such tales as Mary-Ann told while carting people's household goods on his wagon half across the county, the lucky ones, that is, who could afford to pay him to do so. Others just closed their cottage doors and vanished, like the father of eight from Salter the week before who had absconded, leaving his whole family to go on the parish and not a child above nine years of age and his wife weeping and wailing one minute and cursing him for the man that he was the next: and no one knowing where he had gone, though most suspected it was north to one of the mill towns, traipsing the streets there in the hope of finding work.

A month back, in the July, Mary-Ann explained, Will had gone to the parish constable and had obtained a magistrate's 'certificate of leave' so that he could go to a parish of Rivershall five miles to the north of Hamwyte, where he had heard from a carrier that a farmer was looking for men to dig drainage ditches along the edge of his land to run off the water from fields which lay close to the rise of the Guith, a tributary of the Langwater stream, and which were still flooded as a result of the days of continual rain.

There were four of them working together in the hope, too, they might get harvest work afterwards: the promised pay was not much, but, with Will's bounty money all drunk away at the George, it was something at least, better than the relief he was receiving: and with the washing Mary-Ann was occasionally able to take in, they would at least be able to make ends meet – just. After a couple of days, the farmer had taken on two more men and had then declared that, as there were now six of them, they would have to accept reduced pay: the same money as he would have paid the four now would have to be shared between six. Will had argued with the farmer, tempers had flared and Will had been dismissed: worse, the farmer refused to pay him what he was owed: things were so bad that the parish constable had to be fetched to escort Will off the farm and to the parish boundary. The following morning, the farmer noticed that his best egg-laying hen was missing: he reported it to the parish constable and they suspected that Will must have sneaked back to the farm during the night, entered the chicken run, rung the neck of his best layer, put it in a sack and set off back to Hamwyte. When the matter was reported to the two parish constables at Hamwyte, they had found Will drinking in the George and, though there was not a trace of evidence that he had taken the chicken, he had still been arrested and put in the bridewell.

The trouble was Will had not gone peacefully: he had compounded the felony by struggling and knocking off one constable's hat and stamping on it and so had had to be put in handcuffs and leg irons. The magistrates had taken that as clear evidence of his guilt 'or why else would an innocent man have struggled so violently to free himself except to avoid an appearance before us? If he were an innocent, he would have had nothing to fear,' they had declared on finding him guilty and sentencing him to nine months in the House of Correction at Steadleigh, three weeks of which were to be spent on the tread-wheel.

As Mary-Ann told the tale of Will's misfortune, a slight tremor came into her voice and tears glistened at the corners of her eyes. 'We were in arrears with the rent, as it was and the parish would not help us,' she said, her face flushed. 'He spent every last farthing of his bounty money in the George, as you well know, and he was borrowing off me from what little I had. He took it all in the end. Because of him, I no longer had money to pay my rent so I am evicted. I am on my way to see a friend at Inworth – we were in service together – she will give me a room for a while. She has always said I could stay with her if there was ever a need. I have no other kith and kin. Will and I are the only ones. I have nowhere else to go. I have spent my last penny paying for the carrier.'

Saddened to hear her tale and unsure of himself, Jem stepped back: the wagoner flicked out his whip and the cart rolled forwards: it would have trundled off to Inworth and out of sight had Jem not suddenly realised that there was no reason why Mary-Ann could not work in the fields alongside the other women and girls: on his strips, for instance.

'There is no need to go on to Inworth,' he suddenly found himself shouting. 'There is field work a-plenty here if you wish, as a gaveller. There is a rush to get the harvest in because the weather has been so bad. We need all the hands we can get. I have a month's work at least on my own land, cutting, stooking and carting and more during winnowing, and you would be earning money – a shilling and thruppence a day, if that is all right with you?'

As he said it, Jem convinced himself that he did it solely because Mary-Ann was the sister of an old friend and for no other reason: he could hardly let her go without making an offer, especially as she was in need. She knew him if she knew no one else in the village so she would not be a total stranger: and had not his mother worked in the open-fields alongside his father and were not other women working in the fields that very day?

Mary-Ann smiled her thanks: her relief was obvious. 'I have a certificate-of-leave from the magistrate in Hamwyte so I can stay in the parish as long as the work needs to be done,' she explained. 'I was hoping to find work at Inworth somewhere. You will find I am a good worker. If there is hard work to be done, I will do it. However, I shall need to find lodgings of some kind in the village so that I can stay till it is all done and not be a burden on anyone. But what can I do with my furniture? It is all I have.'

It was the carrier who offered the solution: he had sat there waiting patiently while Jem and Mary-Ann discussed their plan: he was used to people suddenly changing their minds. With a wearying sigh, he declared: 'Caleb Chapman back there at the Wayfarers' will store it for thee, lady. He has stored things for me afore. His outbuildings at the back of the Wayfarers' are mostly empty, except for his malting shed. There is room enough to take this load and more. He's an old skinflint and he won't do it for nothing, but he'll store your furniture there for a while, I'm sure, if you paid him a price.'

Without waiting for an agreement, he tugged the two horses round and trundled his wagon back up The Street and into the Wayfarers' yard: so once more Jem found himself knocking loudly on the inn's front door to rouse the still-sleeping Caleb, this time with a request that he open up one of his three outbuildings and store Mary-Ann's goods in it while she helped with the harvest on the open-fields. Jem was too good a customer for Caleb to refuse and, though he groused yet again at being awakened from a sound slumber, he agreed: for a rented building was better than an unrented one. His only proviso was that, as Jem had no money in his pocket at the time and Mary-Ann, as she said, had spent the last of her money on hiring the carrier, Jem must pay the first fortnight's rental by that evening or, he threatened in his usual grumbling manner, though probably not meaning it, 'the whole lot'll be out in the yard, rain or no rain!'

Surprisingly, the lodgings were not a problem either. Jem and Mary-Ann were directed by the first villager they asked to the Widow Jessop, a half-mile along the ridge-top road, and within the half-hour he was knocking on her door to ask if she could put up Mary-Ann, which she readily agreed to do, setting only a modest fee as Mary-Ann was female. Several of the older widows would not have a man in their cottage at any price, whereas they were always willing to take in a woman because she would be company for them: a man and his habits could cause ructions, especially with his drinking and his 'other needs' and old widows often worried about those other needs.

Thus it was soon after that Mary-Ann Allbright walked to the First Field with Jem Stebbings, where Dick Dollery and Enos Diddams and the others were already at work, all helping each other in the rush to gather-in the crop. Since Dick Dollery had not seen Mary-Ann before, he raised a surprised eyebrow and gave his friend a questioning look at being so late, while Enos Diddams, Nathaniel Newman, John Romble and the other men all gave a knowing smirk at the sight of their friend entering the field with a good-looking woman as company.

Just as she said she would be, Mary-Ann proved herself to be an able worker: while the men mowed the corn with their scythes, laying it behind them, she joined the other women following behind as a 'gaveller,' even showing a boy from the village school, hired at sixpence a day, how to gather up the corn which she had raked into piles and how to bind it into small sheaves with lengths of straw before placing them in stooks of eight.

Of course, Jem had to answer his friends' queries about her, which, as they worked, were many and all suspicious, particularly when he explained who she was and that he had met her only once before: when they heard she was a widow, they sniggered all the more. For his part, for some reason Jem could not fathom, he found himself continually looking back at the figure of Mary-Ann working behind him.

Dick Dollery noticed it straight away and was not slow to comment in his usual jesting way. 'Thee've not taken a liking to her already, hast thee, Jem?' he asked and then, with a malicious chuckle, added in that peculiar dread way which men adopt when they speak of such things: 'If she gets hold of thee, boy, she'll draw all the sap out of thee and leave thee hollow as a stalk of this here corn, will a woman like that. Thee'll not get an hour of sleep if thee takes her on. Come the morning, thee'll not have strength to stand upright, especially if she en't had a man since her own died.' His remark was spoken as an aside between the two of them, but was loud enough to make Enos Diddams, John Romble and Nathaniel Newman, working alongside, chuckle and cause Jem to redden with embarrassment.

Thus did Jem Stebbings begin to bring in his first meagre harvest as a husbandman.

TWENTY- NINE

IT TOOK the combined efforts of the husbandmen, their families and those they had hired of the old day-labourers, women, boys and girls of the village the full twenty days to complete the final cutting of the three open-fields and the consensus was that less than half the harvest had been saved. It led to some gloomy evenings for the husbandmen in the Wayfarers', while there were broad smiles amongst the day-labourers down at the Carpenters' Arms, who had been well paid for their efforts by the larger farmers. Indeed, Jack Tickle's takings for those weeks were to be treble those of Caleb Chapman and the day-labourers would continue smiling till their money ran out and they were forced back on to parish relief, as many of them would be over the coming months.

All the time that Jem and Mary-Ann worked together, which, in countrymen's parlance, was from 'morn till night,' his interest in her grew, even if he did not know it himself: but, as far as Dick Dollery and Enos Diddams were concerned, he was as good as courting her from that first day. Whenever they were working in the same 'field' together, the two casually noted the number of sly glances their friend would steal back to where she was working: they noted, too, that, if she were the only woman working with them as they helped each other and if she were sitting alone at lunchtime, invariably he would make a point of going across to and offering her a drink of the ale which one of Dick Dollery's daughters always brought to the field for them to drink: also, that she always welcomed him with a smile.

Later, with the cutting of the fields all done and the sheaves all tied, Mary-Ann helped Jem gather them in, standing atop the wagon which he had hired and piling up the sheaves all around her as he and one of the older village men pitched them up to her before the horse was led to the next stand of stooks. It took five loads from his acres on each of the lesser fields before his three corn stacks were built. Indeed, so much had he and Mary-Ann been in each other's company that it was a surprise to no one, least of all to his drinking friends, when she stayed on during the October to help with the hand-threshing of the ears and the winnowing of the grain: he even added threepence a day to the wage he paid her so that she would have a little more to spend upon herself over and above her rent and board at the Widow Jessop's.

As was the custom amongst husbandmen, Jem built his stacks alongside one of the several small barns dotted about the village in which he had hired space from one of the four small farmers so that, after the flail-threshing and winnowing, he could store his sacked grain to dry, keeping it in grain form rather than having it milled because flour did not keep as well as grain and was always a target for rats and mice. Over the coming months, he would either cart it to Abel Tedder to grind into flour at his black-tarred, brick-towered windmill along the Merchant Staplers road or to take it to Hamwyte corn market to sell, though the quality of the grain was poor, ruined by the weather the same as everyone else's.

Mary-Ann was still helping him when they lifted the turnip crop on the Badger's Hole third of Long Field in the November, which again was a struggle due to the mud and the flooded fields. All he ever got from his friends in the Wayfarers' were snide remarks, sniggering laughter and the occasional blunt, 'Has thee had a goo at Mary-Ann yet then, Jem?'

As a bachelor soldier in his twenties, Jem had gone into brothels with his comrades-in-arms in Spain and Portugal and the Lowlands of Flanders, paid-for fornications with foreign women whose use of English was limited solely to one or two crude phrases which they had learned in order to ply their trade. Mary-Ann, however, was English and the sister of a good friend and it was for that very reason that he held back from making any move upon her. Also because she was a widow and, despite what Dick Dollery kept urging him to do, he respected her widowhood and did not wish to transgress upon some imagined sensibilities or impose himself, so to speak, between her and her memories of a dead husband or interrupt her mourning for him.

Like many men, when greeted by a smiling woman, he did not realise that the smile she gave him each morning was a display of affection and not just a way of saying 'Hullo': neither did he interpret the brightness showing in her eyes when he joined her as anything other than the same. For her part, Mary-Ann looked forward to their meeting each day and, particularly, the walk back in the evening to the Widow Jessop's cottage, hoping that he might show some interest in her other than just talking to her about his work or the village, take her hand in his perhaps, even ask her for a goodnight kiss: but the shy

Jem did none of those things. He always stopped ten feet short of the widow's gate, allowing her to walk on to it alone. Then, with a wave of the hand and a smile, he would turn and walk back the way he had come, night after night, leaving Mary-Ann sighing with all the frustration of a woman who knows she has met a good, kind, honest and hard-working man and yet is unable to get him to recognise what she feels.

It would have to change, she decided: and it did one moonlit evening when they were walking back along the ridge-top road. Unexpectedly, Mary-Ann seized his hand and, in the way of a woman frustratedly waiting for the man, told him bluntly before he could break the grip, 'Come with me, Jem,' and had then pulled him into the deeper darkness of a small roadside coppice.

A bemused Jem had meekly allowed himself to be led till they were screened from the road by the trees, unsure even at that point what she was about: indeed, his first thought was that perhaps she wished to show him a couple of rabbit traps which someone had set in their runs, which is what he would have done in such a place, though he would not have gone to fetch them in the darkness like she was in case he trod on one and the thin cord looped itself around his own foot. No, he would have waited till the morning.

In fact, so concerned was Jem in looking about him for the snare in which he supposed she might have seen a rabbit and, at the same time, seeking to avoid tripping over a fallen branch, that he did not notice that, ahead of him, Mary-Ann, while leading him by one hand, was unfastening her blouse with the other: so that when eventually she let go of his hand and turned to face him, the cleavage of her breasts was fully exposed.

'I'm tired of waiting, Jem,' she said calmly. 'If you won't start it, then I shall have to!' And, unexpectedly, despite the cold evening air, she pulled him down beside her on to the damp, leaf-strewn ground. 'Goodness gracious, man, you and I have been looking at each other for the past three months. I've waited for you to ask me, but you haven't so much as tried to kiss me even. I'm a widow and I haven't lain with a man since my poor husband died and that was five years ago. Well, my mourning days are over. A woman can only wait so long for a man to make a move. I'm nigh on four years older than you and not getting any younger. I can't wait for ever. I've tried hard enough to tell you. I've realised that, if I don't do something, you never will!'

Lying back and smiling up into his bemused face, cold as it was, she pulled her skirt above her waist and pushed her drawers down to her ankles before wriggling them over her boots. Then with a great sigh of hope as much as relief, she took his hand a second time, lay back with a sigh, pulled his face to hers, kissed him hard and then gently began to unfasten his trouser front.

After that night, as well as working together, they were to be seen everywhere together, walking hand-in-hand about the lanes and often disappearing together into dark and lonely places: indeed, some noticed that, when working together in the barn, there were also unexplained absences, from which he would return with straw on his jacket and she with a dust patch on the back of her skirt.

As the days drifted into late December, she also began to return to the Widow Wenden's cottage with him of an evening and even to cook for him and the old widow: so it was only a matter of time before she upped sticks from Widow Jessop's cottage and joined Jem nightly in his bed at Widow Wenden's, who, being aged and not caring, was quite amenable to allow it. That they were unmarried did not worry the old woman in the least: it brought another woman into her home, small as it was, and it comforted her that she would be there to look after her and to tend her if she fell ill, even to wash her on occasions, which she could not expect of a man, as well as to cook and to clean and be company in the evenings beside the fire when he went off to the Wayfarers' to sit with his friends.

The neighbours gossiped, as they will, though it was not so unusual a thing for a man and a woman who did not have the money to pay for a wedding in a church to set up together and live 'over the brush' like the slaves on the Southern plantations of America. Widow Wenden was seventy-two years of age and knew her heart would give out soon enough: she was not long for this life and so regarded her neighbours' tittle-tattling with a sniff of disdain. Not so the interest of Parson Petchey: he was not to be dismissed so easily, as Jem and Mary-Ann discovered one Sunday morning.

The Widow Wenden had always been a church-goer and, the closer she got to meeting her Maker, the more she wished to go. In Mary-Ann, she had found a church-going soul-mate, for she, too, had regularly attended services in the old medieval parish church on the hill above Hamwyte while she had lived there and had also been a regular church-goer during her time in service at Inworth.

Like Mary-Ann, most of the wives and daughters in the village went willingly, too: a great many of the men, however, went grudgingly, solely to appease the parson rather than in expectation of eternal redemption, reasoning, perhaps wisely, that an hour given up to praise the Lord was no great hardship when not to go at all might mean a visit from one of his churchwardens. Worse was the fact that all three of the larger farmers of the village were God-fearing enough to go regularly themselves, so a man's continued absence might well be noted by them and count against him when he stood at the farm gate with others, hoping to be hired as a day-labourer.

The old widow quickly prevailed upon Mary-Ann to accompany her, leaning on her arm for the threequarters-of-a-mile walk from where her cottage stood: as old people will, she wished to make her peace with God before she was called to His presence – to put herself 'in His favour and make certain of my place above,' was how she put it. So come a Sunday morning, if the weather were not too cold or too rainy or too blowy, she and Mary-Ann would walk slowly together along Forge Lane into Parsonage Lane to the church, with Jem following and looking smart in his clean smock, which Mary-Ann had washed and hung overnight in front of the fire to dry.

There was one other reason why so many attended – and that was for the loaf of bread given to each of the needy who attended: it was one of the few old customs which Parson Petchey had not yet curtailed: but then he could not since it stemmed from the legacy of a former clergyman of the parish himself, the Reverend Abraham Thurston, a hundred years before, who had left a hundred pounds to be laid out on land, the rental from it to pay for the provision of bread for those who attended church and were most in need. As they left, each was given a slip by the two churchwardens standing in the porch and, come the Monday, they would be standing outside one or other of the two baker's shops clutching their slips for one quartern loaf, each person having their own preference as to which baker they went. Some cynics in the Wayfarers' said it was the only reason Andrew Norris had got himself elected a churchwarden – for the business it brought him!

Though Jem had never spoken so much as a single word to the parson in the short time he had been in the village, one Sunday morning in the January he found himself seated alongside Mary-Ann, listening red-faced to Parson Petchey's sermon, conscious that the eyes of all others were upon him, some even turning their heads to look back, and Dick Dollery and his wife, Lizzie, seated with them, and Enos Diddams and his wife, Emma, John Romble and his wife, Martha, and Nathaniel Newman and his plump wife, Ann, and their families, seated in the pews behind, smirking fit to burst as they tried to control their laughter. For that morning, Parson Petchey was giving another of his morality sermons, laying down the law on 'couples living in sin.'

'Just as Satan disobeyed God out of his corrupt will and heart, so did Adam and Eve,' exclaimed Parson Petchey, his beady, bespectacled eyes moving along the rows of upturned faces before halting, focused exactly upon the pew in which Jem and Mary-Ann sat. 'God did not create Satan to sin, nor did he create Adam and Eve to sin. They chose to set themselves against God by their own free will. Eve ate of the fruit of the tree of life because the serpent tempted her. And Adam ate of the fruit because Eve tempted him. Adam became a slave to that pleasure, a mortal cast out of the Garden, and the end of those enslaved to sin is death! And such a "death" is a separation from God. Living in sin separates us from God and dying in sin will separate us from Him for eternity. God is Holy: He is separate from sin and evil. He is different than everything He has created. He is perfect, separate and sinless. No flaw is in God because He is Holy. He cannot tolerate sin in His presence. Thus, He is a God of wrath and justice. All sin must be punished. Adam sinned and the wages of sin is death!'

If it had not been clear to everyone in the congregation before about whom he was preaching, it was after that: an unknowing person needed only to follow the line of sight of the many eyes to fix upon the two 'sinners,' seated side by side, which almost everyone did.

'You seemed to have stirred the old fool up,' smirked Dick Dollery as a mortified Jem walked back up Parsonage Lane with him, Enos Diddams and the other men, with the whole village streaming past and everyone seeming to turn and look back and smile knowingly, the way people do, just to let him know that they all knew who the parson had been addressing, while a contrite and embarrassed Mary-Ann walked slowly behind with the old widow and the other wives, knowing that she would be the subject of gossip till the next nine-day wonder presented itself.

'There is one way we can settle the matter,' Jem said with a half smile when later he and Mary-Ann were walking alone together. 'We could get married and make it all legal. That would stop the tongues from wagging.'

'If that is what you want, Jem, I'd be more than minded to say yes,' replied Mary-Ann, squeezing his arm and taking a tighter grip upon it as if to say, 'I am just as willing as you for the banns to be read.'

'Then a wedding it will be,' declared Jem, patting her arm in return, and, with a kiss, they sealed the bargain and walked on smiling happily.

To obtain a license, one of the parties, normally the intended bridegroom, had to make a formal sworn statement, called an 'allegation,' which Jem did one evening later that week in the presence of the Merchant Staplers curate, Reverend Waters, acting for the absent Parson Petchey, and making an oath that he was of the parish of St. Bartholomew's in that county, 'now aged thirty years and a bachelor and alleged that he intended to intermarry with Mary-Ann Allbright, of the parish of Hamwick Dean, formerly of Hamwyte, in the same county, aged upwards of thirty-four years and a natural and known widow, and further alleged that she hath resided in the said parish of Hamwick Dean for upwards of fourteen weeks last past January and that he, Jem Stebbings, not knowing or believing any impediment by reason of any pre-contract, consanguinity, affinity or any other cause whatsoever to hinder the said intended marriage, and he prayed a licence for them to be married in the parish church of Hamwick Dean aforesaid.'

The banns were posted the following Sunday and read by Parson Petchey on the following three Sundays: for their betrothal, almost as if she were a girl again, Mary-Ann one day fashioned a ring from a lock of her hair and presented it to Jem as a tentative token of her commitment, it being an old custom in those parts, she said. However, according to the marriage laws of the Church of England, a proper metal ring was required, though it did not matter from what metal it was made: in short, it did not need to be gold or silver. So Nathaniel Newman offered to make the actual wedding rings for them both, heating a piece of iron rod and drawing it out till it was thin enough, then hammering it flat and rounding both the rings to fit, before polishing them on the stone till they glinted as good as silver anyway.

The wedding ceremony in the February was held before noon as was the custom then: there were still some who said it was a rushed ceremony and gossiped that Parson Petchey had left it to his curate to make the arrangements for the marriage service and to coach the couple in their vows rather than speak to them himself because his wife had presumed upon him not to associate himself with an actual couple 'living in sin' till they were actually committed towards achieving a state of grace. He did conduct the marriage service, however, though it was all done in a perfunctory way, with a flat tone throughout: it was all over in ten minutes and he was gone from the church the moment the couple had walked out into the porch, exiting by another door without so much as a backward glance even as they went out on to the road. Mary-Ann's only sadness was that her brother, Will, was still in the House of Correction at Steadleigh and was not due to be released till the May.

Since Jem had no close family, Dick Dollery and his wife acted as the main witnesses, with Enos Diddams's wife, Nathaniel Newman's wife and John Romble's wife showering them with home-made paper petals in the porch before they all walked back up Parsonage Lane in a light snowfall to the Wayfarers', where Caleb Chapman had laid on a small wedding breakfast, paid for, of course. There, the friends remained drinking till well into the evening before an impatient Mary-Ann took a somewhat unsteady, though unresisting Jem by the arm and led him out of the inn by the rear door and back to the widow's cottage, while Dick Dollery, Enos Diddams and the others saw to it that the drinking and merry-making continued within.

They managed to tiptoe past the old Widow Wenden asleep in her chair without disturbing her and quietly closed the bedroom door behind them. That night, they lay together, trying desperately not to make too much noise with a creaking bed under them lest they wake her and she cried out about her failing heart: it caused them much amusement before they fell asleep. The old widow did wake to the creaking and the cries which came from the bedroom, but she just smiled and adjusted her position as she always had done when it had happened before and went back to sleep: after all, it reminded her of her own younger days when her husband had been young and virile – and alive.

To be truthful, she welcomed Mary-Ann's arrival, not just as a cook and a cleaner, but more as one to whom she could talk of her women's problems, especially as Mary-Ann was sympathetic to her ailments, whereas Jem, as a man, just brushed off her panic attacks as the imagination of a silly old woman. Mary-Ann, on the other hand, would put an arm about her and stroke her hair and sit and talk with her, reassuring her till she relaxed and forgot all about the palpitations in her chest.

Then one morning in the mid-April, two months after she had become a wife again, Mary-Ann rose from her bed at first cock crow to deal with the problems which pregnancy causes a woman only to find the poor widow seemingly still asleep in the chair by the hearth. As she approached, however, it became evident that she was not asleep: her eyes were closed, but her mouth was hanging open and spittle was drooling down her chin: she had passed away in her sleep even as the dawn came up: it had happened just as she had predicted it would.

As so happens with old folk, not many of the villagers turned out for the funeral as most of her contemporaries had passed away already and the young, not knowing her, could not be bothered. Jem and Mary-Ann, as her lodgers, led the few that did: and afterwards, being in the cottage, he immediately approached Andrew Norris, as a churchwarden, to ask if he would ask the parson if he and Mary-Ann, now that they were married, no longer 'living in sin' and regular church-goers, could take over the tenancy of the widow's place since they were already living there. The baker 'ummed' and 'aarghed' over the matter, as was his way, but it was done eventually and so, come Lady Day, Jem duly paid his first cottage rent to Parson Petchey through the churchwarden, and, ultimately, into the coffers of the Church and the Bishop of Melchborough.

THIRTY

AT THE VERY TIME that Jem and Mary-Ann and the other villagers were burying the Widow Wenden, coming along the Hamwyte road from Melchborough was a man of some twenty-five years of age, tall and lean, with the pinched look of one who did not eat too regularly and a peculiarly yellowed skin. As he trudged along, he seemed oblivious to the fact that the road was, for a mid-April day, unexpectedly covered by an inch or more of snow which had fallen overnight or that the passage of wagons had turned much of it to slush. Indeed, he seemed unconcerned by his lot, even though he had been walking since early morning, when he had left the shelter of the straw stack in which he had passed the night.

Had anyone asked, he would cheerily have told them that he had been three days on the road from London, a fact they might have deduced for themselves since his worn and patched clothing carried the residue of one barn and one ditch as well as the straw stack. From one shoulder on a rope tie hung a canvas roll which served as his groundsheet and bedding: and, though it was light for a man with his muscular arms, it was cumbersome enough to slow any striding progress. So his pace was unhurried, almost an amble: and, since it was one of those spring days when the pale blue dome of the sky was devoid of all clouds, when there was a refreshing coolness and clarity to the air and a pristine beauty to the snow-carpeted landscape, he would pause every now and again to marvel at the gloriousness of it all. Above all, he was pleased to be breathing the clean air of the countryside, content to progress at his own pace, a man who knew where he was going, even if he did not know how far it was to get there.

Joly Cobbold was his name and he was an unemployed brushmaker on 'the tramp': that is, he was walking from pan shop to pan shop in different towns where there was a brushmaking yard in search of work as a proud member of a group of artisans who had banded together to form what was, in effect, an illegal trade union, though it could not be called that. For such was the intense hostility towards trades unionism from the authorities, that is, the law-making and law-enforcing classes of the gentry and well-to-do in general, that they regarded the combining of men into trades unions to better their wages and conditions as tantamount to sedition against King and Country.

The skilled craft of brushmaking dated back to Roman and Greek times and beyond, for women have always swept their houses and their paths. The men and youths who worked in the trade were proud of their ancient craft and seventy years before had first banded together in Manchester to protect themselves and to better their lot. Since then, similar societies had been formed in other cities, such as Bristol, Birmingham, Sheffield and London, which was the one to which Joly Cobbold belonged. Societies had also been formed in secrecy in smaller towns where there were brushmaking yards, like Hamwyte: and over the decades, the various societies had become a trade alliance, the United Society of Journeymen Brushmakers.

For them, the pan shop of the brush yard rather than the mill, the mine or the foundry was their workplace: they were paid by a piecework rate. Consequently, brushmaking was a precarious employ and the brushmaker could find himself out of work at any time: hence 'the tramp' and the reason Joly Cobbold was on the road. As a fair means of ensuring employment, if work became scarce in one place and a person out of work were able bodied, he could follow a designated route set by the society from one pan shop to the next around the country to look for work amongst his brother brushmakers. Hamwyte, thirty-eight miles from the capital, was Joly Cobbold's first call on the list of possible workplaces which he had been given when he had set out: he had also been given the name of the particular inn in the town which served as the local society's 'clubhouse,' as the United Society's members called it, where they met to conduct the secret ballots they held and to discuss the problems of their kind.

That inn was the Black Bear, where Jem and Will Ponder had dismounted from the 'fly' on their return and which stood not fifty yards from the entrance to the brushmaker's yard on the same side of the high road. Such was the organisation of the United Society that all branches were in contact with each other and Joly knew, as he walked through the arch soon after four o'clock and introduced himself to the landlord, that he could safely ask him to send a message to the pan shop for the secretary of the local society to meet him that evening.

In his roll, Joly carried the certificate of his journeyman status, given by the society in London to say that he possessed the skills of pan-working, hair-sorting and drawing: equally as vital, he also carried his 'Blank,' that is, a blank official book which he had to produce for signature by each branch secretary on his tramp. The secretary was the one who would help to provide him with work if there were work to be had: if there were no employment locally, his blank book would be annotated, he would be given a meal and board for the night, and sent on to the next branch with a small sum to help him on the journey – a shilling and sixpence for every ten miles he would have to walk to his next destination. In this event, it was the river port town of Witchley in the next county, thirty-two miles distant, where he would go to the Wagon and Horses Inn and again make himself known to the landlord: and if no work were available there, as was common in the aftermath of the end of the war, he would walk up into the next county and perhaps the next after that and the next after that on what was in reality a circular route round England, taking in more than forty towns, going up the east coast as far north as Newcastle-upon-Tyne, then across the Pennines into Lancashire and down the west side of England, returning to London via Exeter, Poole, Salisbury, Southampton and Reading – a distance on the tramp of twelve hundred and more miles.

Evening found Joly Cobbold sitting opposite a thin-faced man, whose whole being, face, hands, bare arms, were even more yellowed than his own, the result of a lifetime working day after day amid smoking pitch: even his clothes and the bibbed leather apron he wore were blackened by the stains of pitch. There was, too, a distinct smell of coal oil about him and the fingers which clutched the handle of his tankard bore the scarred tissue of burning caused by hot pitch. William Mann was the secretary of the Hamwyte branch of the society to whom one of the inn's yard boys had delivered the message.

'My name is Joly Cobbold,' said the newcomer. 'I have come from London on the tramp. I am told there may be work here. I have been given your name as a legal shop.'

'Aye, there might be work here –' replied the other man, with obvious suspicion, pausing momentarily before adding: ' – if you are one of us.'

'I am, brother, I am,' said Joly Cobbold, without taking offence. 'I have my certificate of indenture here.' He reached into the canvas roll lying on the bench beside him and, pulling out a long leather pouch, carefully extracted from it a piece of embossed paper rolled into a tight cylinder and tied with string.

'My certificate,' he said, unfastening the string. 'I have been out of my apprenticeship for four years and I am in good standing. My weekly dues are paid up to date.'

The secretary took the paper and, producing a similar pouch from inside his own jacket, unrolled it and read down a list of names. 'Joly Cobbold, you say?'

'Aye,' answered Joly, not at all surprised by the man's caution: indeed expecting it. A list of the 'legal' members of each society was circulated amongst the branches, giving the dates and place of the commencement of each man's indentured apprenticeship and its completion. Thus, there was strict control over entry to the trade, with lists of 'legal' journeymen and apprentices employed by 'legal' masters in 'legal' workshops held at each branch. The name of Joly Cobbold of Shoreditch was on the list.

William Mann carefully re-rolled his own list and put it away in the pouch before slipping it back inside his coat: Joly Cobbold did the same with his own certificate: both knew that it did not pay to flaunt such seditious documents where prying eyes might see them and information be passed to those who sought to find out such things.

'Can you whistle the tune?' the local man asked quietly.

'Aye, I can do that,' said Joly, and duly whistled a five-note secret signal, known only to brushmakers, devised and used so that one member of a society branch might know a bona fide member from another: it had been taught to Joly four years before, on the very night he had come out of his seven-year apprenticeship and had received his certificate of indenture, which showed that he had served his master and was a true tradesman.

'Welcome, brother, welcome,' said the local man, relaxing and smiling broadly as he reached out to shake Joly Cobbold's hand. Now that his suspicions were allayed, he could take a greater interest in the newcomer. 'There is work here for a month or two. We are in need of a good pan hand. There will be no problem with our master. He does not worry himself with what we do so long as his work is done and he will pay the agreed rate. I am sorry it cannot be longer, but times are as hard here as anywhere, amongst us anyway, though the poor agricultural labourers do have it worse at the present. At least we have food on our tables and a fire in our hearths which they poor beggars do not. Talking of food, you must be hungry after your tramp. We will pay for your lodging here at the Black Bear and your meals for the first week till you get your money.'

In this way, Joly Cobbold began his work at the Hamwyte brush yard, presenting himself at the pan shop, located in a long, narrow, two-storey building, at seven o'clock the next morning, as instructed, joining four pan hands working around a pan frame, that is, a strong table with a central hole in which stood a charcoal stove. On this stood a pan of hot – though never boiling – pitch: each man wore a bibbed leather apron and from the cauldron there was a constant heat. The four pan men and the apprentices accepted him readily as one of their own, knowing that, if ever they were to fall out of work, they, too, might be forced on the tramp, a situation dreaded by men with families, for often wives and children would have to follow them and none wanted that: so there was a certain sympathy for their brother from London.

Nearby, lay a pile of brush and broom stocks ready to receive their bristles, each drilled on a hand lathe worked by treadle, with every hole at a slightly different angle: the men and the apprentices, keen to see if there were any difference in the techniques he had been taught to their own, watched with interest as he took up a stock and laid it on the pan frame. The work was basically the same as he had done in London: he selected a small bundle of the right-sized bristles, carefully parting them to prevent any natural curvature bending them too much in one direction, then dipped the root end into the pitch and quickly tied it with twine. The knot, as the bundle was known, was then dipped again and inserted quickly into the stock, for the pan man had only a second or so while the pitch was still hot to position it correctly. A good broom would have ninety knots and each had to be inserted by the pan hand to keep the natural bend of the bristles running the right way at each different part of the broom head – 'getting the bend,' as it was known: and when a good brushmaker had finished a broom, it was said the pile of the bristles would have a feel like velvet.

Brushmakers then were paid a piecework rate based on the number of knots they tied at one penny for twenty and fourpence halfpenny a broom: there were twelve sizes of broom down to the poorest quality, or 'sixpenny' brooms, which would have only thirty-six knots: but for a craftsmen with pride in his work, they were not popular, more work for an apprentice than a time-served artisan.

Watching the young apprentices, still no older than seventeen or eighteen, Joly Cobbold remembered his own first day when he had been seated at a bench and given a bunch of thrums, or strings, to insert into his apron cord: there he had sat all day, practising tying bunches of bristles to insert into holes in brush heads. After several weeks of that, he had been allowed to train alongside the other brushmakers and, to the amusement of the men, had burned his fingers that first day and many a time afterwards with the scalding pitch so that over time he, too, had developed the hard skin and calluses common to his type.

Often as they worked, the men and the apprentices would talk and argue, over all manner of things, their piecework rates, for instance, their lives in general, the politics of the day and the King, politics and the Church, politics and the gentry: it was from these older workers, while still a young apprentice, that Joly Cobbold first developed his own political allegiances.

His indenture in the Shoreditch brush yard, like all others, had been long simply because, amongst brushmakers, the training of apprentices was given great importance: on the night he came out of his indenture, he had been taken to the nearby inn which served as that particular branch's 'clubhouse,' and there had received his certificate before the drinking began. On that night, too, he had become a fully fledged member of the society and, under the rules and articles of association, had paid his entrance fee of a pound, which was high for a youth earning only a few shillings a day.

He had continued to pay his weekly shilling ever since and, as a member of the society, had continued to exercise his vote in the secret ballots that were held from time to time. For, if nothing else, the society was democratic: any issue which was of concern to its members would be voted upon by the practice known as 'taking the voices,' though, because the society was an illegal organisation, any voting had to be carried out without the employer's knowledge. It might be just a choice of whether a neighbouring branch should be lent a certain sum, say, five pounds and ten shillings, or nothing at all: or it could be that a sick member had requested relief of ten shillings: or a master had wronged an employee, or vice versa, and the members were being asked what action did they consider necessary to remedy the wrong?

Any item requiring a vote was written out and placed in a 'tin box,' which was sent by hand to all local shops to be read and voted upon: if the ballot were extended to neighbouring branches, the messages might be sent via the mail coach, a somewhat dangerous practice since secret voting was illegal and several brushmakers at one yard had been imprisoned after a 'tin-box' sent on one mail coach was intercepted by the authorities. For this reason, society documents did not give addresses of members: hence the five-note whistled signal revealing one member to another ensured the box was always entrusted to a bona fide brother and passed to another recognised brother with the minimum of delay, for fines were imposed for delays in circulating the box or interference with its contents.

Being a member of a society which the powers-that-be regarded with hostility and downright suspicion did not bother Joly Cobbold. Indeed, he relished his status as a radical: he was single, twenty-five years of age and an independent thinker: and he liked to believe that, had he been in Paris when the citizens had stormed the Bastille, he would have been amongst them, perhaps even leading them.

Since the very first day of his apprenticeship, when the rights of the society were explained to him, he had been a fierce advocate of the need for all artisans and labourers to band together for protection against exploitive employers: if he had his way, the monarchy would have been abolished, the 'mad King' and his womanising, drunken, gambling-mad son, the Prince Regent, executed along with the rest of the 'useless aristocracy' and Britain declared a republic.

To him, the King was simply the leader of the rich and powerful who oppressed the general population and had instituted inequality by trickery. Men should stand up for their rights as human beings and not allow themselves to be exploited or cowed by the draconian laws of a landowners' Parliament. Britain, he believed, needed a revolution, just as France had had a Revolution. Republicanism was the sole rational means of government: the power of the mob should be used to take control just as the Jacobins had done in Paris from the Girondins at the National Convention, even to forming a similar Committee of Public Safety and ruthlessly eliminating all those considered enemies of the people.

Joly Cobbold wished other brothers could have the same benefits which he and the members of the United Society enjoyed: it pained him to see men and women and youths and girls so cowed by their employers that they took off their hats and stood immobile when some slave-driving mill owner or great landowner swept past in his fine carriage with a liveried footman up front driving and two others standing behind ready to jump down and open the door for their powerful master and his lady. Now, here he was, going amongst the downtrodden and impoverished rural classes: if he got the chance, he would spread the word amongst them and that word was 'revolt.' Revolution!

THIRTY-ONE

DURING THE WAR, the rate of wages paid to an ordinary day-labourer on a farm had risen from ten shillings and sixpence a week at the turn of the century to a high of fifteen shillings as the final years of the war approached. A year or so after the war ended, however, they had been shamelessly reduced by unscrupulous landowners and employers, to nine shillings, to eight shillings and, in some places, to as little as seven shillings in the knowledge that the parish would make up any difference to at least a subsistence level for the labourers and their families. The result, inevitably, was that an intolerable strain had been placed upon the uneven and often inadequate parish relief funded from the poor rate taxes.

At that time, a third of the working population were out of work, a situation exacerbated by the recent introduction of machinery in the mills and factories, the widespread use of child and female labour, plus an influx of Irish, who were prepared to work for as little as fourpence a day, whereas even a hard-pressed English labourer might demand a minimum of ninepence or a shilling.

The attention of Parliament, however, was drawn more to the distress of the landed interests, who were suffering enormous losses, than to its starving poor. None knew it then, but the labouring classes of England were entering upon their darkest decade: one of destitution, violent and bloody riot, agitation, insurrection, arson, strikes, machine-breaking, turmoil and change, all set against a background of hunger and oppression, of mass migration from the land to the towns or emigration to the British North American colonies – Newfoundland, the Maritimes, Upper Canada – or to the United States itself, to New South Wales, Van Dieman's Land, the Cape and New Zealand.

As the war had neared its end, England's farmers realised that the protection of goods within the British Isles would cease: trade would be resumed in earnest and they would have to face competition from outside, most particularly the renewed import of foreign corn, which would reduce the price of their own grain – a fear justified as the domestic price of corn halved in a few short years, falling from a hundred and twenty-six shillings and sixpence a quarter ton or four hundred and eighty pounds weight at its height to just sixty-five shillings and sevenpence by the time the hostilities finally ended in 1815.

Parliament then was unreformed. To sit in Parliament, all Members had to be landowners themselves: thus, Parliament represented the interests of the wealthy landowning classes and, reluctant to lose that wealth and with it the status it gave them, they demanded the Government take speedy action to protect the profits of themselves and their tenant farmers or the agricultural interest of the nation might be ruined entirely. The table of the House was covered by petitions: everywhere there were pamphlets and letters from farmers and landowners demanding higher prices for agricultural produce. Not unnaturally, the Parliament of the same landowners responded by passing legislation which favoured a minority of their own to the detriment of the many: the import of foreign wheat was to be severely restricted: only when the domestic price reached eighty shillings per quarter ton would foreign grain be allowed in free of duty.

However, these 'Corn Laws,' as they have come to be called, rather than solving the problem of high prices, resulted instead in violent fluctuations in food prices at high levels, which in turn encouraged the hoarding of grain: inevitably, the high price of wheat led to sharp rises in the cost of food, particularly bread. More and more, the urban working poor had to spend the greater part of their earnings on meal and bread just to survive and, consequently, they had none to spare to buy manufactured goods from the new factories in the North. As a result, the manufacturers suffered and laid off their worker, causing great distress amongst the working classes in those towns as they, in turn, unable to grow their own food, had to pay the higher prices just to stay alive.

The Corn Laws were almost universally opposed by the populace in general, particularly the poorer classes, such as the rural poor in the Southern and Eastern Counties and the factory workers living in the fast-growing Midlands and Northern industrial towns: during the passing of the Act, the Houses of Parliament had to be defended by armed troops against a large and angry mob. In short, the Corn Laws were imposed upon the country to preserve the high profits of the Napoleonic war-years and to safeguard landowners and large farmers from the consequences of their wartime euphoria, when farms had changed hands at the fanciest of prices and loans and mortgages had been accepted on impossible terms.

There was, of course, an immediate demand throughout the country for the repeal of the Corn Laws: but, since the right to vote was not universal, but depended on land and property ownership, the Members of Parliament had no interest in repealing them. They and the other landholders, the nobility and the gentry, benefited, for they owned the majority of profitable farmland: thus, they had a vested interest in seeing the Corn Laws remain in force.

As bread prices rose rapidly, so unrest, strikes and food riots broke out all over the country, especially in the industrial towns. In Huddersfield in Yorkshire, mill workers broke their machines and rioted in protest at the soaring prices: in the Black Country of the West Midlands, near-to-starving colliers and ironworkers, in their despair, manually hauled to London and Liverpool wagons fully loaded with coal they had hewn and weighing two or more tons to publicise their plight: and when the authorities responded to the breaking of bobbin-net machines at a factory at Loughborough by hanging one rioter, three thousand turned out at his funeral to show their defiance.

All throughout the latter months of Jem's first year as a husbandman, even as he courted Mary-Ann, news had drifted down via the travellers on the various coaches which stopped at the several inns in Hamwyte of food riots in several towns and villages in the counties to the north. The one which was most discussed in the George and other hostelries in Hamwyte was a riot by fifteen hundred farm labourers in a small market town very like their own up in the flat Fenlands, where the labourers had demanded a reduction in the price of bread and meat and had even fixed a maximum price for both themselves above which they declared they ought not to pay a single farthing more.

The mob, it was said, had burned down the house of a wealthy butcher who they said was callously profiting from their misery: then, armed with long, heavy clubs studded at the ends with iron spikes, they had marched on various other towns and villages, carrying a banner inscribed with the words 'Bread or Blood,' and demanding the same wages and bread and meat prices for all. They had even threatened to march on London till the local yeomanry, made up of landowners, farmers and traders, along with a troop of dragoons and the county's militia, had dispersed them with the flats of their sabres.

Now in first months of the following year, as Jem and Mary-Ann began their married life together, disturbances had broken out amongst the ironworkers of South Wales and, in the February, there had been food riots in two other Welsh towns, Amlwch and Tremadoc. March saw food riots at Maryport, strikes and food riots at Radstock and yet more disturbances in other places. But even the threat of the militias could not prevent a hunger-march of cotton spinners and weavers from Manchester heading for London on March the tenth. Though the magistrates would read the Riot Act and arrest twenty-nine men, including two of the leaders, at an open-air meeting of ten thousand on St. Peter's Fields, an area near the centre of the cotton town, between six hundred and seven hundred men still set out in drizzling rain for London, marching in groups of ten, each man with a blanket on his back – hence the name by which they became known, the 'Blanketeers' – and with a petition to the Prince Regent fastened to his arm, requesting that the Prince take measures to remedy the wretched state of the city's cotton trade.

They were followed by the King's Dragoon Guards and one group was attacked a mile from the city, the worst violence taking place at Stockport, six miles from Manchester, where several received sabre wounds and one man was shot dead. Around four hundred or five hundred pressed on and got as far as Macclesfield and Ashbourne before they were turned back at the Hanging Bridge over the River Dove as they were about to enter Derbyshire: in the end, only one man reached London.

While history recorded dramatic events elsewhere, it did not record that at that time the families of many of the 'casual poor' of the small market town of Hamwyte in the Hundred of the same name were as near to starving as anyone could be and still be breathing.

THIRTY-TWO

AT THAT TIME, Hamwyte-with-Wulversford, to give the old market town its proper name, incorporated a number of farms within the three thousand and six hundred acres of its parish boundary, mostly tenanted holdings of thirty or forty acres, but also a half-dozen larger ones of two hundred or so acres: in addition, several small villages and hamlets with their landed estates lay within an hour's steady walk of the town's lower end where the poorer labourers lived.

Thus, when its principal industry, the manufacture of baize, already in decline, ceased altogether during the war against Napoleon after its main market in Spain was cut off, the fortunes of agriculture came to have a distinct influence upon the life and well-being of the town. The greater number of its poor had to rely upon casual day-labouring on the middling and larger farms within the parish and on the estates to the north, east and west of the town. So when the slump brought the same cuts in their wages, the same underemployment and unemployment and the same rising prices, the greater number of them had only the same insufficient relief as the day-labourers of Hamwick Dean and the two hamlets to keep them alive throughout that second winter of the Peace.

A peculiarity of the town was that its actual beginnings lay a half-mile to the northeast of the high road, on the crown of Cannium Hill, a steady rise of ground atop of which the mounded, dual concentric rings of an Iron Age fort were still visible. When the Romans garrisoned Wivencaster, the Iron Age settlement became a way station along the road to Londinium: from it in the Tenth Century, Edward the Elder conducted his campaign against the Danes, then camped at Wivencaster and marauding up and down the coastal estuaries in their longships. In early medieval times, wool merchants, who had grown prosperous on the great flocks of sheep which roamed that and adjoining Hundreds, built several fine weather-boarded and plaster-fronted houses around a triangle of green, which they called Wulversford: and, upon the foundations of a Tenth Century Saxon church, they erected a flintstone parish church, dedicated to St.

Nicholas, with a lofty tower, a sturdy porch, a long arched nave and a fine chancel.

However, from Tudor times, the church was somewhat neglected for the simple reason that, during Bloody Mary's reign, the inhabitants of Wulversford found it more sensible to move closer to the old Roman road at the bottom of the long hill so as to provide for travellers along the way. Thus, by the end of the Sixteenth Century, new buildings were being erected along both sides of the ancient route to form the 'newer town' of Hamwyte and its High Street.

When, in the middle of the Eighteenth Century, a local surgeon discovered a mineral spring near a row of lime trees in a meadow threequarters of a mile to the west of Hamwyte's centre, the town briefly acquired some celebrity as a chalybeate spa. To encourage London merchants and their families, in particular, to visit in order to avail themselves of the spring water's medicinal properties, the surgeon somewhat craftily declared in his leaflets that 'the mineral water, whose virtues and efficacy render it exceedingly beneficial in many chronic diseases incident on mankind, is so exceeding volatile that it cannot be safely transported, even if the bottles are carefully corked and cemented...'

The ploy worked and for three decades or so, in the summer season from June to September, the town was much visited by genteel families out of London 'taking the waters,' for, being only thirty-eight miles from the Aldgate milestone, it was close enough to the capital for the purposes of business and yet far enough from it for the fresh air and country living it afforded. There was even a hope that Hamwyte would someday rival the fashionable West Country spas of Bath and Cheltenham: and, upon the hope of the town continuing to prosper, many fine Georgian houses were built along the High Street to add to the three hundred or four hundred houses constituting the whole town at that time. Those who could not afford to build their own summer places simply purchased the old timber-framed houses and had false Georgian facades added, which, while they enhanced the look and line of the street, hiding away many a ramshackle edifice, they were sniggered at as 'shams' by the older townsfolk, since, by the addition of a new brick front, mere cottages were being made to look like mansions: yet behind the false façade, they were as low-ceilinged and as dark and as dingy as they had ever been.

In the short space of four or five years, the appearance of the High Street changed dramatically. Soon it extended for more than a mile, divided into the upper town and the lower town, with three butcher's shops, two greengrocer's, four baker's, two drapers, a general ironmonger's and various other establishments along its length, as well as five coaching inns, the Black Bear, the George, the Angel, the White Hart and the Old Sun: and, rather than have all the newcomers walk uphill to the old church every Sunday, the wealthier residents subscribed to the construction of another church, erected on a plot of land at the top end of the High Street, the wealthier part, dedicated to all the saints and built in the Early English style of dressed black flint and white brick quoins, with pews for seven hundred, of which four hundred were free. In the height of the season, the seven hundred seats were regularly filled and, at the same time, the local inns were encouraged not only to accommodate visitors but also to entertain them: the White Hart and the Old Sun held assembly balls, concerts, dinners and card games, while at the Black Bear and the Angel aristocratic gentlemen visitors could wager on cock fights and occasional bare-knuckle fighting.

Yet more fine mansions were built in rural settings by other respectable and wealthier gentry able to afford sizeable land purchases, particularly to the north of the town, where the land was more undulating and more pleasant. These country estates added to the genteel aura of the whole place as rich merchants and their families sought to escape the miasmas of London's fetid alleys, drawing their water from fresh wells sunk into the red-brown clay of the region rather than the polluted boreholes of London. It was in one of these mansions just outside the town that George the Second had stayed on his progress to and from his Hanoverian dominions and it was in one of these same grand mansions, too, that Queen Charlotte, consort of George the Third, was received upon her arrival in England.

The London merchants who came to 'take the waters' brought their business ways with them to the advantage of the town, which for a time was known for the gentility of its townsfolk and, over the years, resulting from their wealth and from the large estates they owned, a certain spirit of independence manifested itself, which, in time, led to the building of Congregational, Baptist and Wesleyan Methodist chapels and a Society of Friends' meeting-house.

However, its heyday as an affluent spa town declined after three decades or so and Hamwyte lapsed once again into a sleepy market town, barely disturbed by the setbacks and victories of the war against Napoleon. The only time of real concern for its citizens in the first fifteen years of that century had been the arrival of a regiment of Irish infantry, en route to Wivencaster, in the very month when the fighting against Napoleon first resumed after the Peace. The High Street was markedly deserted for three days while they were encamped around the grove of oaks in the large meadow behind Seaborne's farm, which lay just off the main way. Even the Tuesday market, which till then had thrived, did not tempt the citizens out, though when the soldiers eventually decamped and marched off to Wivencaster, they appeared once more so that by the following Tuesday all was as it should be, with the people of the parishes all around coming in to purchase their cheeses, vegetables, cloths, brushes and other goods and the farmers and husbandmen selling their produce.

It was from the yard of the White Hart that a small cannon was dragged on to the top end of the High Street and fired to signal the news from London that Napoleon had been defeated at Waterloo and that the Allies were marching on Paris: the inhabitants celebrated the French tyrant's final downfall as happily as everyone else throughout the land. Thanksgiving services were held in the new church, with not a seat to be had, and public feasts, processions, sports, fetes and fireworks were hurriedly arranged as the good citizens joyously decorated and beautified their streets and their homes with flags, banners and bunting.

Every few yards at the top end of the High Street to the midway point at the Black Bear triumphal arches were erected, each high enough to allow coaches and mails to pass easily underneath and wide enough to stretch garlands and banners across. Where the mails and coaches entered from London, the first arch was adorned with the single word 'Hope' in large letters in the centre and on each side an anchor surmounted by the words 'Peace.'

Below the Black Bear, on both sides of the street for nearly two hundred yards, plank tables were arranged, where nearly two thousand of the poor and needy, which was everyone at the 'lower end,' men, women and children, Mary-Ann amongst them, sat down to a dinner of ale, pork, bacon, roast beef, mutton, turnips and more ale, all at the expense of the five hundred and more well-to-do of the top of the town. They, of course, were dining with the mayor and the Justices outside the Moot Hall, where a bonfire had been lit and the aldermen and gentry and their families feasted off an ox turned on a spit, while above them was another triumphal arch festooned with more flags and proclaiming 'Europe Free – England Firm' and 'Peace And Plenty For All.'

On one side of the road, one resident had even constructed a Temple of Peace in her garden, with an entrance into a grove between painted marble columns which carried the banner inscribed with such sayings as 'Europe saved by the exertions of England' and 'Wellington, England's Saviour' as well as 'Glory to God' and several others. On the opposite side, ranged along the street were several paintings on canvases stretched between poles, one of which was the figure of an African slave, as large as life, chained and in a supplicating, posture with the motto 'Am I not a man and a brother?' which drew particular sympathy.

The town's maypole was adorned with laurel wreaths and everywhere at the top of the town there were elegant garlands, with flags on each side and further mottos, such as 'Peace At Last' and on the sides of one arch, which bore the names of Wellington and Blucher and which was hung with a homemade Union Flag, were the words 'May peace and plenty on our nation smile and trade forever bless the British Isle.'

Much amusement and scorn was expressed by those who stood around a painting of Britannia pointing to the heavens, from which descended the dove of peace with an olive branch, while below the hated Bonaparte was depicted pressed under her foot, with the slogan, 'The reward of ambition.' Last, over the gate and arch leading to the dean's home, was a laurel wreath, under which were inscribed the words, 'Glory to God in the highest and on earth peace and goodwill towards all men.'

The celebrations went on for three days: children from the town's three schools – one for the sons of the gentry, one for the daughters of the gentry and the other the 'ragged' school – were dressed up in ribbons and suitable paper hats and paraded along the High Street, in proper order, of course, with the ragged school last. Two sons of the gentry were happily dressed as Wellington and Blucher in a tableaux of the heroes of the hour, but no one wanted to be the third member of the tableaux, the hated Napoleon, so one of the 'lower order' children was 'volunteered' and was hissed and reviled and had things thrown at him till, in the end, he ran off crying and refused to return.

'Peace and Plenty' was the hope at that time: but in the twenty-three months since those heady days of celebration, that pious hope had been replaced by anger and despair amongst the landless day-labourers of Hamwyte, despair at the lack of work, despair at the lack of food and anger at the indifference of the Government in London and the local worthies of the town as their plight grew ever more desperate.

In past times, when the number of the unemployed had been less, there had always been the prospect of outdoor relief from the parish to fall back on: money, say, for rent if they could not pay it, for clothing for their children, for a surgeon's fee if they needed one, for food if they were so destitute as not to be able to provide for themselves and their broods: that way surviving as best they could. Now, however, with so many claiming relief, a mood of irritation had overtaken those of the town who paid the bulk of the poor rate: and, as more and more underemployed and unemployed went begging at the Moot Hall door, a mood of intolerance had asserted itself amongst the members of the Vestry. A proposed increase in the poor rate to fund them was vehemently opposed: the pressure on the payers of the poor rate was too great already, they said: payments to the poor needed to be reduced, which they were, drastically, and in some cases denied altogether.

Where the main triumphal arches at each end of the High Street had once proclaimed 'Peace and Plenty' and 'Hope,' notices now were posted warning off any approaching vagrant, roaming the highways and byways of Eastern England, looking for farm work and some, particularly the Irish, they said, looking, for what they could steal: and where squatters or incomers were found, removal inquisitions had already been conducted and the paupers forced to return to their parishes of origin.

The plight of the poor, of course, had been further aggravated by the rapid increase in the national population. By then the populace of these islands stood at eleven million, having almost doubled in a single century. Even in Hamwyte, in the twenty-three years between the start and the end of the hostilities, the number of its inhabitants had increased from fifteen hundred to two thousand and five hundred, which placed a great burden on the relief provided through the poor rate at a time when food prices were rising: as the population swelled so did the numbers of unemployed.

By then almost all the men and youths of the town were without work and without hope. As the hunger and despair of the day-labourers and their families grew, an extra-ordinary meeting of the Hamwyte Benefit Society was called for the first Wednesday in June by men who felt that they could hold out no longer – men who were at the end of their tether, men who that very spring had taken three of their own children to the graveyard. Matters were becoming too desperate to ignore.

So Hamwyte in the second year after the Peace.

THIRTY-THREE

THOUGH THE PRICE of wheat at market had doubled following the introduction of the Corn Laws, from fifty-two shillings a quarter ton at the start of Jem's first year to a hundred and three shillings by the following winter, the incessant rain and the lateness with which much of the grain went to market at Hamwyte meant most of the husbandmen and small farmers of the village and the two hamlets made only a small profit on that harvest, if they made a profit at all. Jem's final tally was well short of what he had hoped to make back in the March when he had taken up the acreage: for others, however, the rising prices promised only hunger, even for the labouring classes in the countryside who harvested the grain.

It was this growing hardship which, over that winter, induced the husbandmen and day-labourers of the village to follow the good example of the Hamwyte poor and band together to form a sick benefit fund of their own, each husbandmen donating sixpence a week and the day-labourers tuppence or threepence. Its purpose was to provide on request a small amount, a mere two or three shillings, say, for the relief of any of their number who fell on hard times through illness or who might otherwise be denied parish relief or receive insufficient for his family's needs. They called it the 'Hamwick Dean Teapot Fund,' in a jesting allusion to the fact that some of the gentry of Hamwyte and the Hundred, who were the only ones who drank proper tea anyway, willingly paid more for their tea from China than they would ever think to pay a labourer for a week of work and also because some were known to keep their money locked away in a safe place with their precious tea.

Unsurprisingly, Amos Peakman, Marcus Howie and Joshua Godwin acted immediately to put it down, fearing it was more than just a sick benefit club and that it might well become a means by which the men would withdraw their labour and make wage demands upon them. They quietly let it be known that any future work for those day-labourers who were a part of it and those husbandmen who occasionally supplemented their income by working for them as day-labourers would be put in jeopardy if they continued to belong to 'that damned Teapot Fund': they also went to Parson Petchey and asked him to speak against it from the pulpit, which the Reverend Doctor duly did the very next Sunday.

'I am much disturbed,' he told his flock, 'to hear that, much against my wishes and against good common sense, a number of you have been so led astray by the ideas of others in this village, over which I have a God-given duty of pastoral care, as to form in this parish what I understand is called a "Teapot Fund," the purposes of which are obscure and might well be construed by the authorities to be used by those with nefarious designs as an intimidation against the good farmers of this district in the matter of wages and working hours. Such a club is unlikely to be treated kindly by the authorities should they come to hear of it, which undoubtedly in time they will. The law quite clearly states that any who makes or enters into a contract or covenant with others to manipulate wage rises, or for other purposes against their employers, shall, upon conviction, be confined in the common gaol at Melchborough for up to three months or sent to the House of Correction at Steadleigh to do hard labour for two months.'

He paused to allow the words to sink in. 'In the name of good common sense, brethren, hear my plea. While it is a man's Christian duty to look after and to assist another when he has fallen on hard times, as did the Good Samaritan when the traveller going down from Jericho to Jerusalem fell amongst thieves, I for one cannot believe that such a club is simply for the payment of benefit to the sick, for that is already the duty of the overseer of the poor, the good Mr. Hurrell, through the pastoral benefice of the Vestry. I, therefore, call upon you, my brethren, to cease and desist from this foolhardy enterprise out of which no good will ever come. I do not know who has led you into this, but I shall expect one of you to name him. There can be no secrets between you and God.'

Those who had devised the scheme were little better than 'combinationists,' he declared, referring to the two Combinations Acts, passed some fifteen or so years before to prevent unlawful combinations of working men, to prohibit trade unions and collective bargaining as a response to Jacobin activity and the fear that workers would rise up and strike during a conflict to force the Government to accede to their demands. His final decree was that none must pay into it or take out from it or the Lord would punish them for their wickedness.

The true fact was that the Teapot Fund was a matter over which he had no control, unlike all other happenings in the village in which he could intervene, deflect, divert, prevent or allow as was his God-taken right: that is, the assumed right of his high position in the hierarchy of the place. Perhaps he feared that the labourer's wife would not be so ready to creep up to the backdoor of the parsonage and queue for milk and bread and a bowl of porridge for her children, humbly begging for help. Worse still, she and the children might slip away from church attendance altogether, if they were no longer beholden to him and his wife for charity.

As it was, not even the parson's sermonising could deter the majority of the husbandmen who met in the Wayfarers' from their aims: it was true that, after the first excitement, the number of those paying their weekly dues did begin to dwindle, particularly from amongst the day-labourers paying tuppence or threepence a week. Some of the more cringing kind who frequented the Carpenters' Arms bowed to the warning of the three farmers, spread their hands as if to say, 'What can we do?' and pocketed the money they had paid in: after all, they said, day-labourers could not afford to fall out with the three main employers of the village.

In the two hamlets, attempts to form similar benefit societies – the Lower Rackstead Friendly Society and the Merchant Staplers Benefit Club – were stifled at birth by the two curates, on the instructions of Parson Petchey, of course.

However, a staunch group of forty husbandmen, all of the village's four small farmers and a few stalwarts from the second hostelry, the whole led by Jem, Dick Dollery and Enos Diddams and including John Romble and Nathaniel Newman, even the wagoner, Daniel Gate, refused to accede to the parson's plea, much as they might have bowed to his will on other matters in the past. They felt the aims of the Teapot Fund were too important for them to be swayed, even by his rantings: further, they were not as dependent upon their good relations with the three larger farmers as the day-labourers and agreed that, if they all stood together, then the parson's ire would be diluted.

On the last Friday of May, the wagoner, Daniel Gate, carried a message to the officers of the Hamwick Dean Teapot Club, namely Jem, as the honorary secretary, Dick Dollery, as the honorary treasurer, and Enos Diddams, as their general helper, inviting them and any other members to join the desperate brothers of the Hamwyte society at their extra-ordinary meeting on the following Wednesday for an evening of convivial drinking and an opportunity for them all to talk over their problems, in effect, a gathering of the oppressed. There would be sixty or so of their own members there, the message said, plus a large deputation from the village of Dark Leyton, seven miles to the north of the town.

The previous Monday, May the twenty-sixth, there had been a disturbance at Dark Leyton's Whitsun fair at which the Riot Act had been read and five youths had been arrested. The week before the fair, a well-to-do landowner had laid off all of his men for a second time in a month, saying that there was no work for them and that he would re-employ them only as and when they were needed. Wages in that region were low already and the larger farmers and landowners for whom the labourers toiled eight to ten hours a day had brought them down even below the level at which a man and his family could reasonably live.

Small wonder that the two hundred or so men and youths who gathered on the village green on the Whit Monday were seething. As the drinking began and continued, so threats began to be made to set fire to the landowner's hayricks in retaliation. Somehow word reached the landowner and he, the parish constable and a local magistrate had ridden over to the green to read the Riot Act and to issue a stern warning to the men and youths that, if anything were to occur such as was being talked about, there would be serious consequences. Nothing did happen, but the five youths were arrested for making the threats and were tried before the Bench the following day: one was acquitted, one was sentenced to two months in the bridewell and the other three were each given six months with hard labour in the common gaol at Melchborough.

In consequence, the Dark Leyton men had been invited to the Hamwyte meeting to talk over mutual grievances and to reaffirm their solidarity with their brothers in the town: there was even a suggestion by one of the Hamwyte men that they might all get up a petition concerning the plight of the poor, asking that flour per stone be fixed at a more reasonable rate and millers and bakers forced to adhere to that price instead of fixing their own prices. Perhaps it could be passed on to one of the town's two Members of Parliament, someone had suggested, and perhaps he might pass it on somehow to the Prince Regent, as the King, George the Third, was in dispose again at that time, so they had heard.

In Hamwick Dean, a general call was put out for as many to attend as possible: and, while Dick Dollery and Enos Diddams relished the prospect of a good drinking session as much as an airing of their grievances, Jem had agreed to go reluctantly: that reluctance stemmed mostly from the fact that Mary-Ann was six months gone with her pregnancy and was still falling sick repeatedly and he did not want to leave her, even for an evening. It also meant a three-mile walk there and a three-mile walk back late at night or in the early hours – and uphill at that for the last part – when probably he and most of the others would be the worse for drink. But, as news had come of Will Ponder's release at last from the Steadleigh House of Correction a week earlier, and expecting most likely that Will would be there, Jem agreed to go, if only to show solidarity with the Hamwyte and Dark Leyton labourers and also to find out, for Mary-Ann's sake, how her brother was and where he was living since he had not contacted them since his release, almost as if he were brooding upon something.

THIRTY-FOUR

RELIEF OF THE POOR in Hamwyte, as it was in Hamwick Dean and other villages in the Hundred, was administered according to the 'Speenhamland System,' based upon the price of bread and the number of children a man had. This system of poor relief had been devised by a meeting of magistrates at an inn in the small Berkshire village of Speen twenty-two years before in 1795. England had been at war with France for only two years, but a series of bad harvests meant that wheat was in short supply: consequently, the price of bread had risen sharply.

The winter of 1794 to 1795 had been one of the severest in memory, with hard frosts and snow from December to March and on some northern hills the snow lay till May: the long winter meant that, by the March, many people had largely used up their winter supply of fuel, gathered in November and December: thus, the population was cold and, because grain could not be imported from Europe due to the war, it was near to starving as well. Not unexpectedly, food riots broke out all over England and the fear amongst the ruling classes was that it was a precursor to revolution, just like the French had had.

As women took a conspicuous part in these riots, some called it 'the year of the housewives.' However, the women did not rob: they fixed prices and, rather than plundering the shops and making off with the goods to their own homes, they organised their distribution instead, selling the food they seized at what they considered were fair rates and handing over the proceeds to the owners. For example, at one place a mob consisting chiefly of women seized all of the wheat that came to market and compelled the farmers to whom it belonged to accept the prices which they, the women, thought proper.

At another place, a band of women accompanied by boys paraded the streets and, in spite of the remonstrations of a magistrate, entered various houses and shops, seized all the grain, deposited it in the public hall and then formed a committee to regulate the price at which it should be sold. At yet a third place, there was a riot over the price of butter: a woman named Sarah Rogers, in company with other women, seized the butter from the shopkeepers and forced them to sell it at a reduced price: though the Assize judge was not so understanding or so benevolent when she appeared before him and sentenced her to three months in gaol with hard labour.

At Bath, a body of women actually boarded a vessel laden with wheat and flour, which was lying in the river, and refused to let it sail: and when the Riot Act was read, they retorted that they were not rioting, but were resisting the sending of corn abroad and sang 'God Save the King.' Ultimately, soldiers were called and the corn was re-landed and put into a warehouse.

In some places, the soldiers themselves helped the populace in their work of fixing prices: at Seaford, Sussex, for example, they seized and sold meat and flour in the churchyard and at Guildford, Surrey, they were the ringleaders in a movement to lower the price of meat to fourpence a pound, and were sent out of the town by the magistrates in consequence.

Prior to the meeting of the Speen magistrates, the Act of Relief of the Poor, passed in 1601 during the reign of Elizabeth, had served as the basis of Poor Law administration: further Acts were passed over the next two centuries to extend the administration or to prevent abuse of the system, such as the Settlement Act of 1662, which made each parish responsible for its own poor, especially if they had resettled elsewhere. By it, parishes were permitted to send paupers back to their own parish to receive relief if they became a burden.

In Medieval and Renaissance England, bread had commonly been sold as the gallon loaf or the half-peck loaf, which weighed eight pounds and eleven ounces. Later, it was nearly always sold as the quartern loaf, which was made with exactly three-and-a half pounds (or a quarter of a stone) of wheaten flour, the finished weight being approximately four-and-a-third pounds: thus, two quartern loaves of finished bread weighed the same as the older and larger gallon loaf.

Under the Speenhamland system, a labourer would have his income supplemented to subsistence level by the parish according to an allowance scale. For instance, if a gallon loaf cost a shilling, an unmarried labourer was to have a weekly income of three shillings for himself: if the loaf cost a shilling and fivepence, his income was made up to four shillings. Similarly, a husband and wife with two children received seven shillings and sixpence if a loaf cost a shilling: and for each penny that the price of the loaf rose, their income was made up from the relief by a further sixpence, till at one and fivepence a loaf the formula shortened and their income was made up only to nine shillings and nine pence and at one and six per loaf to ten shillings and threepence. For an agricultural labourer doing ten hours of vigorous work a day, it provided just above the bare means of subsistence.

The magistrates meeting at Speen felt that the old Elizabethan Poor Law did not give enough assistance and decided to subsidise the low wages of their labourers from the poor rates, in effect, introducing a 'bread and children' scale which, though never law, was quickly adopted by other parishes.

Though 'Speenhamland' was devised with the best of intentions, the magistrates had unwittingly initiated a system which was to produce almost the opposite effect to that desired: for, by choosing to supplement existing low wages from the parish fund up to the intended figure, they had inadvertently reduced all labourers to the same subsistence level, no matter how much or how little work they performed. The distinction between worker and pauper had been obliterated: labourers could now receive a minimum wage for doing nothing. At the same time, it relieved farmers of the necessity of paying a living wage to their workers and, almost as if by custom, they seized the opportunity to drive down what wages they did pay since they knew that the parish would make up the difference to a subsistence level at least – to six or seven shillings a week, say, for a married man with four or five children when really thirteen shillings was needed by him to sustain himself and his family, and to as little as three or four shillings for a single man.

Before the war, in grain-producing areas, where the demand for labour varied greatly over the year, it had been common for farmers wanting to keep the men and youths in a village as a pool of labour to pay them enough over a year to stop them drifting to nearby large towns: even those who employed local labourers only when needed would still pay peak season rates that were high enough to sustain a man and his family for the whole of a year. Then, too, an unemployed man might have gone to a 'freeing day fair' at Salter or on Inworth heath, as Jem had done when he had first set eyes on Mary-Ann.

Now, with 'hiring fairs' seldom held and men being employed only on a daily or weekly basis, with no pay on wet days, the landworker was at the mercy of his employer, who could reduce his wage whenever prices for farm products dropped or lay him off entirely if he wished to save his costs. Generally, the parish would find work for the able-bodied unemployed, such as repairing roads, ditching or coppicing: or in an enlightened parish, the Vestry might reach an agreement with a sympathetic farmer to take on one or more of their paupers at a certain cost, paying out of parish funds the difference between that price and the allowance which the 'bread and children' scale, allowed. A billet or ticket, signed by the overseer of the poor, was handed to the farmer as a warrant for him to employ them and afterwards was taken back to the overseer, signed by the farmer, as a proof that the labourer had fulfilled the conditions of relief. It was considered less menial than the system adopted in some places, where unemployed men were simply put up for auction as roundsmen, sometimes monthly, sometimes just weekly, at prices which varied according to the time of year, with the old and the infirm selling for far less than the able-bodied.

Farmers, of course, contributed to the parish poor rate by way of taxes, sharing the load with all the other property-owning parishioners, though it did not stop the other ratepayers from complaining that their part of the tax was subsidising the farmers' labour. One way round this, used by some unscrupulous farmers, was to hire labourers from neighbouring parishes because then they could lay them off without warning without having to pay them any relief from the poor rates in the parish where he worked.

In addition to the poor rate, farmers also had the burden of the church tithe: originally, this had been the church's right to ten per cent of the parish's harvest: however, the earlier collection of goods in kind had been replaced in many places by a cash levy which was payable to the parson, and which went towards his often considerable living. The cash levy was generally rigorously enforced, whether the resident was a church member or not, and the sum demanded was often far higher than a poor person could afford: small wonder then that there was a continuing frequent grumbling from the farmers.

THIRTY-FIVE

JOLY COBBOLD'S presence on the road to Hamwyte that spring day had been no coincidence: he was fleeing London in fear of arrest. For, some weeks earlier, at the beginning of March, the Prime Minister, Lord Liverpool, and his Government had suspended, initially for four months, the Habeas Corpus Act, which declares all have the right not to be imprisoned without trial. Meetings of more than fifty people were banned and magistrates were instructed to arrest everyone suspected of spreading seditious libel. Troops were also ordered on to the streets and byways to put down meetings and marches, in some cases firing upon the populace marching for their rights with banners held aloft, or riding into crowds with sabres drawn to break up peaceful mass protests, which, in turn, led to violent riot, acts of vandalism, sedition and arson, the very things which they had hoped to deter.

The end of the wars had not ushered in a period of peace and contentment after all. Instead, there was a sense of panic amongst the ruling classes, the same as there had been during the food riots of the early war years, the latter now occurring amid ever-growing demands for political reform. Joly Cobbold feared he might be one whom the authorities would seek to arrest. To his mind, they had good cause.

That January, on the twenty-eighth, he had been amongst the crowd lining the route from Horse Guards to the Palace of Westminster as the fat Prince Regent, George, made his way by coach to the House of Lords for the State Opening of Parliament. Indeed, Joly Cobbold had been one of the seventy or eighty men and youths who had run all the way along both pavements to keep up with the royal coach, hurling abuse and shouting slogans of 'Down with George!' and 'Down with the monarchy!' That day, for the very first time, he had felt himself to be a true radical, who was taking action at last against the bloated monarchy and the avaricious nobility.

Many others in the crowd were also booing and hissing the Regent, though some loyalist souls were managing to cheer and to wave their Union Flags behind the protective line of soldiers. Even so, stones were flying about everywhere and, just as the coach was crossing

Bridge Street, opposite a bow-windowed house by the Ordnance Office, prior to entering the Palace Yard, something struck the carriage door with such force that it made a small round hole in the glass panelling. Joly Cobbold was level with the carriage at the time, which was in the centre of the road, and saw the Prince look down, startled. Whatever had been thrown or 'fired' left a clearly visible 'star' of fractured glass: but what it was he did not know, though he supposed it to be either a bullet, a hard, round pebble or a marble fired from an air gun perhaps, as he had heard no actual report of a gun firing.

Almost before he realised it, Joly Cobbold had given a shout of joy that someone braver than himself had had the courage to 'fire' on the licentious Prince: and while the Regent was in the House of Lords, performing his State duty, Joly Cobbold had waited with the others who had run with him, all discussing in whispers who had 'shot at' the coach and all markedly cheered by it.

When the Prince finally emerged, Joly Cobbold had been one of those who had followed him back up Whitehall, running along the pavement again behind the line of Guards, hooting and hissing, till, unexpectedly, he had been seized around the neck by a Bow Street constable and thrown against the wall of one of the buildings.

'You're one of those bastard radicals,' the constable had cried. 'Well, we know who you all are. We know who the lot of ye are, you and your friends. We shall come after you all in good time, my fine friend, all in good time, my word on it, and you and your friends will find yourself on a boat bound for the other side of the world.' With that, he had punched him hard in the stomach, winding him so greatly that he had been unable to continue following the coach.

After that, Joly Cobbold had begun to look over his shoulder to see if he were really being followed whereas before he would not have cared: he had also begun to look into dark shadows to ensure he was not being watched by the army of spies which everyone in the movement knew the Government employed. In the end, as others he knew were arrested, he had taken to the road, fearing that his activities truly might have made him a marked man, particularly as three months before the stoning of the Regent's coach he had been amongst the multitude at Spa Fields in Islington in the December, cheering and waving his hat in the air as the great orator, Henry Hunt, had addressed them from the window of a public house.

'Orator' Hunt was a gentleman farmer from Upavon, in Wiltshire, who had become a radical and an orator for reform after being sentenced to six weeks' imprisonment following an argument with a colonel in the Wiltshire Yeomanry over the killing of some pheasants: he was one of Joly Cobbold's heroes, along with the radical journalist William Cobbett and the late lamented Thomas Spence, the unofficial leader of the radicals, who had advocated revolution, but who had died two years earlier.

The object of the Spa Fields meeting had been to sign a petition embodying a call for universal suffrage for all men, annual general elections and all voting to be by secret ballot. From the public house window, Hunt, wearing a white top hat as a symbol of radicalism and the 'purity of his cause,' with the proud Tricolour and Cap of Liberty prominently displayed behind him, had spoken on the evils of high prices and over-taxation, as well as the need for parliamentary reform and the greed of the so-called 'boroughmongers,' that, is those who bought and sold the parliamentary seats of boroughs, and also the 'sinecurists,' who held ecclesiastical benefices without requiring the cure of souls.

Those who resisted the just demands of the people were the real friends of confusion and bloodshed, Hunt had shouted: and, he had assured them, if the fatal day should ever come, if he knew anything of himself, he would not be found concealed behind a counter or sheltering himself in the rear. They had all cheered him for that and thrown their hats into the air.

Over the following two weeks, Hunt had made two futile attempts to present the petition to the Prince Regent, but had been twice refused admission to his presence. So when a second meeting was held on the second of December at Spa Fields, to protest at the treatment which Hunt had received, Joly Cobbold had again been amongst a crowd of several thousand, listening as one speaker, standing with several others on a wagon decorated with banners, had harangued them with the same cafe-table exhortation as had been made to the patriots of Paris before they stormed the Bastille.

'If they will not give us what we want, shall we not take it?' the speaker had cried and been greeted with cries of 'Yes, yes.'

'Are you willing to take it?' he had demanded next. 'Will you go and take it? If I jump down amongst you, will you come and take it with me?'

'Yes, yes,' they had cried again.

Curiously, the speaker's words were ones which Joly Cobbold had heard repeated many times by his father in one form or another: they had first been spoken in revolutionary Paris years before by one

Camille Desmoulin, an impoverished lawyer and pamphleteer, who had climbed on to a table outside one of the cafés in the garden of the Palais Royal and had called upon the crowd to 'take up arms' in the struggle for their liberty and had then drawn a pistol from under his coat and declared that he would not fall alive into the hands of the watching police. It was following his call that the mob procured arms by force and on July 14 stormed the Bastille. From the first time that Joly Cobbold had heard this story as a fourteen-year-old, he was to adopt the 'take it' philosophy as his mantra: quick to 'take' anything which by rights he thought ought to be his, like an apple off a market stall, a jacket from a shop or a pair of shoes from a cobbler's, especially while he was a poorly paid apprentice.

That December day on Spa Fields, 'Orator' Hunt had been delayed and so was not standing on the wagon when the speaker did jump down, picked up a Tricolour and, to the cheers of some demobilised sailors and other members of the crowd, announced they were marching on the Tower of London, as if it were 'England's Bastille,' and that they intended to establish a Committee of Public Safety, just as the French revolutionaries had done.

On the way to the Tower, the sailors broke down the door of a gunsmith's to rob it of weapons and a passer-by, who remonstrated with them, was killed: but when they reached the Royal Exchange, they were met by an alderman and seven constables formed in line across the road and, seeing they no longer carried arms, the alderman-cum-magistrate had three of the leaders arrested. Joly Cobbold, fortunately, was trailing at a cautious distance and so was able to slip down a passageway and disappear into the murky labyrinths of that area: by nightfall, order had been restored.

As a youth, having begun his apprenticeship as a brushmaker and having at least learned to read and to write during his five years of schooling, he had regularly bought the *Political Register*, Cobbett's radical newspaper, seeking it out on the Saturday of its publication and happy to put his two pennies down to read the scathing and forthright writings of its founder.

The facts of William Cobbett's life were unknown to Joly Cobbold – that the founder, editor and writer of the *Register*, then fifty-four years of age, was the son of an innkeeper and small-time farmer from Farnham in Surrey who had worked on the land before jumping aboard a passing stagecoach one day and heading for London. There, he worked as a barrister's clerk before enlisting at the age of nineteen in the 54th Regiment of Foot at Chatham, where the colonel, finding an enlisted a man who could write a fair hand, had made him his secretary. When the regiment was sent to Nova Scotia, in Canada, in 1785, Cobbett was made its clerk at Fort Howe: consequently, the whole business of the regiment fell into his hands, which became a problem when he saw that the officers were dishonest and that army provisions were being siphoned off for the benefit of those in charge.

When the regiment returned to England in 1791 and Cobbett received his discharge, as an honest man, he turned over his evidence to the authorities and prepared a petition addressed to the Secretary of War, accusing four officers of various acts of misconduct. However, though a court-martial was summoned for the March of that year, no one showed up to prosecute: further, Cobbett discovered that his evidence had been tampered with to implicate some of his innocent friends so he decided he could not give evidence and fled to France with his new wife, Nancy.

The French Revolution broke out soon after they arrived in Paris and, in mid-August, 1792, he and Nancy found passage at Le Havre on a sloop bound for America, where they settled in Wilmington, Delaware: it was there that he first began his journalistic writings in the *Political Register*. He returned to England in 1800, living first in London and then Botley in Hampshire, five miles east of Southampton and the *Political Register* was launched in England in the January of 1802.

At first, it had a distinct Tory slant, but by 1804 Cobbett had changed its politics to out-and-out radicalism: in his view, the political system was totally corrupt and it was the Members of Parliament themselves who were at fault. Everything about Parliament, he declared, was governed by bribery, blackmail and the general abuse of power, an opinion with which Joly Cobbold readily agreed when he first bought the *Register* as a fifteen-year-old. In its pages, he found, what were to him, excellent pieces of practical argument and some marvellously fine writing of the kind he wished he could emulate. Indeed, he would often copy out sections of it in an attempt to commit to memory some of the more emotive phrases and expressions so that he could call them up for his own use in discussion, or more often argument, with his fellow workers and other tavern drinkers.

Politics and discussion had been his passion from an early age and he had sorely missed them since leaving London: but then he could do little else since the Government considered the Spa Fields meetings part of a 'traitorous conspiracy' for 'the purpose of overthrowing the established government by means of a general insurrection... and of effecting a general plunder and division of property,' the whole thing got up by forty 'disciples' of Spence, who had formed themselves into the Society of Spencean Philanthropists in his memory.

The late Thomas Spence, a schoolteacher from Newcastle-upon-Tyne, had arrived in London in the December of 1792 and had been arrested for selling Thomas Paine's book, *Rights of Man,* in which he defended the French Revolution against a scathing attack by the Anglo-Irish Whig philosopher and political theorist, Edmund Burke, in his book, *Reflections on the Revolution in France.* In his book, Paine had proposed the reform of the Government, a written constitution created by a national assembly and modelled along the lines of the American constitution, elimination of all aristocratic titles, a democracy which would exclude primogeniture and an alliance with France and America and the eventual doing away with war and military expenses. Tax-cuts for the poor and subsidies for their education were also proposed, along with a method of 'progressive taxation' under which more wealthy estates would be taxed more heavily to prevent the emergence of the hereditary aristocracy.

Joly Cobbold agreed with every part of it, just as he did when Spence, in one of the pamphlets his father had bought, had written: 'If all the land in Britain was shared out equally, there would be enough to give every man, woman and child seven acres each.' By then, however, Spence was a broken man: he had spent various periods in prison for selling radical books, pamphlets, newspapers and broadsheets and had been reduced to selling his pamphlets from a barrow, from which he also sold a hot drink which he called 'saloop.' Cobbold senior had once purchased a cup for his son and a pamphlet for himself: father and son had read it together and both had accepted it as Gospel. The ailing Spence used to creep out at night to chalk slogans on walls like 'Spence's Plan and Full Bellies' and 'The Land is the People's Farm.' Joly Cobbold had seen them and had even added his own: 'Revolution.'

All these things were in the distant past as he sat in the small dining room of the Black Bear Inn that early June evening, eating his supper of cold mutton, potatoes, peas and warm gravy and listening to hailstones of all things rattling against the window panes and bouncing off the roof tiles, the night of the extraordinary meeting of the Hamwyte Benefit Society.

THIRTY-SIX

A FEW DAYS before the extraordinary meeting of the Hamwyte Benefit Society, during the Whitsun week, two of its unemployed members had walked through drenching rain to another parish four miles to the north of the town. They had obtained a certificate of leave from the magistrates, as they were required to do, and, upon reaching their destination, had gone on to a farm to ask if the farmer had any employment he could give them: when told there was none to be had, they went away without protest, intending to go to another farm to ask the same question.

However, the farmer and his son did not like the look of the two and rode into the village to tell the parish constable and the assistant overseer of the poor: the outcome was that, instead of finding work, the two Hamwyte men found themselves being escorted to the parish boundary by the two village officials and being vilified all the way by the farmer and his son with such comments as, 'We don't want ruffians like you here!' and 'Get back to Hamwyte!' and 'We know your kind, thieves, the lot o' ye!'

Name calling had begun and, once they were across the parish boundary, the two labourers had turned and yelled their own insults back at the farmer and his son and had picked up some large flints and thrown them, one of which had struck the farmer's horse. The fracas had ended with the farmer riding across the parish boundary and striking at the two men with a riding crop, while his son did the same with a steel-tipped whip. The two labourers, being unarmed, had only one recourse, to break through a hedge and run: both now smarted from bruises to their backs and shoulder and lacerations to their faces. Suffice it to say, that the outcome might well have been worse had not the parish constable and the assistant overseer gone after the farmer and his son, calling upon them to return to their senses, for by that time they were so incensed they were quite prepared to chase the two fleeing men all the way back to Hamwyte if need be. Suffice it to say, too, that one of those running men was Will Ponder, newly released from the House of Correction at Steadleigh.

He was still nursing his sore shoulders caused by the blows from the farmer's riding crop and the cuts upon his face made by the steel tip of the son's whip when he joined the sixty or so other labourers of Hamwyte for the meeting of the benefit society, held not in the George, their usual place, but in the larger Black Bear Inn across the way, the same hostelry in which the United Society of Journeymen Brushmakers had its 'clubhouse' and where Joly Cobbold lodged and where he was sitting eating his supper on the evening of the meeting. The reason for the change was simply that the George did not have an upstairs room considered large enough to hold the eighty to a hundred expected to turn up that night. However, the upstairs assembly room of the Black Bear was large enough and, conveniently, located just across the way and the landlord was sympathetic to the working man's cause.

As it turned out, neither of the two deputations from Dark Leyton or Hamwick Dean were to turn up. The Hamwick Dean men had arranged to meet in the Wayfarers' yard prior to starting out. However, peculiarly, that morning the air over the village had turned sharply, almost freakishly, icy, making them shiver all day as they worked in the fields: not June weather at all, more like January and February. So bitterly cold was it, in fact, that it made a man wonder what was to come for the rest of the summer.

Then, in the early evening, just as Jem was making his way to the Wayfarers' to meet the others, a violent hailstorm engulfed the ridge-top and hailstones as big as oak apples bounced off the road: so violent was it, he had to run for the cover of the inn's porch and bang upon the door for Caleb to let him in as it was latched. Sheet lightning flashes lit up the sky with scarce a second's pause between each: the black clouds seemed to have sunk down to no more than a hundred feet above the rooftops and the explosions of thunder bursting directly overhead seemed to Jem as if the French artillery were cannonading the village. When he finally entered the bay-windowed parlour, brushing the residue of the icy hailstones from his shoulders and tipping it off his hat brim, he found only Dick Dollery and Enos Diddams waiting there.

Unaware that the dust of the Tambora explosion remained in the atmosphere, Jem and thousands of husbandmen and farmers in England simply put the freakish nature of everything down to the vagaries of the English climate: that year was turning out to be no better than the previous one.

'They 'on't be expecting us to goo in this weather, will they?' was Dick Dollery's glum reflection as he stared ruefully out of the parlour's bay-window at the white sheet of hailstones covering the inn's front yard. 'They are sure to put the meeting off and call another later. We'll goo to that one instead.'

Jem and Enos Diddams were not inclined to disagree since, in the hour they waited, no others turned up. So, eventually, while Dick Dollery and Enos Diddams settled down to an evening of slow drinking by themselves in front of the inn's blazing fire rather than making the long trudge to Hamwyte, with the risk of being caught on the road by another violent hailstorm and no shelter other than in a ditch once they had reached the bottom of the hill, Jem waited for a break in the storm and then hurried back to his cottage, where he found Mary-Ann retching yet again, but, curiously, smiling as well. Their son – as she was being so sick, it could only be a boy, she said – would be her first and for 'his' birth she was prepared to accept every suffering of pregnancy.

The twenty-man deputation from Dark Leyton did set out, but got no farther than the inn in the next village of Blanc Leyton: hail began to fall before they had gone two miles so they made for the Cross Keys and remained there for the rest of the evening, till turned out by the landlord. The Hamwyte meeting, however, had been called and, despite the weather, a good number from the town had turned up: so they decided to go ahead with it anyway.

Their object that evening was as simple as it was necessary: to decide which of them were most in need of assistance that week. All were in need, it was in true, but some were more in need than others, so they accepted that they could not all be helped. There was not enough money in the kitty for that, only for the most deserving – or, to put it another way, those whose families were nearest actually to starving. And such was the need of many that they willingly trudged through the hail, the thunder and the lightning from the lower end of the town to gather around the hearth in the large upstairs assembly room to warm themselves, knowing that they had left their wives and families in the hovel cottages they inhabited without the means of even lighting a fire to warm themselves.

At one end of the room a table had been pushed forward and three men sat at it: they were the committee which each of the claimants was to address. At the end of the evening, they would retire to another room to discuss each case in turn and judge each claim upon its merits: ten would be able to receive immediate benefit for that week, but after that, well, no one knew.

The first to make his case was a dark-haired fellow still in his early twenties. Whereas once he had been large-bodied, broad-shouldered and muscular, with large hands and a once large round face, all was now reduced by hunger: his cheeks were sunken and his eyes were ringed dark in their sockets and his smock, which had once fitted more tightly, now hung upon him as if overly large. 'I have had no work for seven months,' he began, 'not since the last harvest ended when I was working for a farmer over Blanc Leyton way. I have tried all winter and spring to get work, especially since my wife is expecting again and she has another infant at her knee and another is feeding off her still. I have offered myself in all directions, but without success. If I go any distance at all, I am told to go back to my own parish – '

There was a loud chorus of agreement from several of the men, for many of them had had the same experience at some time or other. 'Aye, I have had the same happen to me,' interrupted Will Ponder, who was sitting on a chair opposite, at the same time touching the lacerations upon his own cheek. 'I was with Jack here – ' He indicated a companion seated alongside him. ' – I was with Jack here when we went looking for work only a week ago and all we have for our pains are these scars and bruises. That is all we can expect now from the farmers and landowners. Though we only asked for work, the both of us were told where to go. "Back to where you come from! There is no work for you here." There is no work anywhere, my friends, not for anyone wanting it. Even the best workmen cannot find employment. The large farmer is reduced to a small farmer, the small farmer is becoming a labourer and the labourer is becoming a pauper and all the time the bloody Irish are swarming in everywhere taking what work there is at any wage they cares to pay'em!'

The other men in the room chorused their agreement with that sentiment: the man standing before the table waited till the murmurings had subsided before resuming.

'Three times I had to goo to the overseer afore I was granted relief. When I was given it, all I was allowed was three shillings a week for all of my family, two shillings for myself and shilling for the wife and children. For that I am expected to work on the roads from light till dark and to pay three guineas a year for the hovel which shelters me and mine – three shillings is not enough to allow for the support of myself, my babes and my wife. We are approaching starvation. We need food and clothing – '

From amongst the listeners, another interrupted, shouting his protest: 'I am the same. I asked the overseer, "What am I to do to feed my family and myself? I can't survive a whole year on relief alone." He told me to go to the town poorhouse or the Vestry and ask them for relief and then shut the door in my face. Yet when I goes to the town poorhouse, they takes me and mine in well enough, but turns us out agin after three days and gives me two days' work gravel-pecking, and then says they has no more for me. I was that sore pinched, I laid a-bed at my brother's all day just to keep warm. Then next Vestry day when I goos to'em, they gives me one day more of work – and that to last us another whole week till the next Vestry day. Because of that, my missus, me and my boys has to go back into the poorhouse again for another three days till I gets sent out again.'

When he stepped back, his place was taken by a thin-faced, white-bearded fellow. 'I am within a twelve-month of sixty years,' he said in a low voice quavering with emotion. 'I en't never owned no land. I have been a labourer all my life. For nigh on forty years, I have worked mostly on the one farm just outside the town, first for the father, who treated me well, and now since he died for the son, excepting for a few times when I was out o' work and on the parish and so was put up by the overseer as a roundsman to different farms to work. Straight after the last harvest and despite all the work I and others have done for his father when he were alive, the son comes to me and tells me and eight others he has no more work for us. We are not wanted. All he keeps on over the winter are two of the younger men to do the odd jobs about the farm. Never mind the rest of us! We are on the heap! I have spent the winter drawing from the parish. Two shilling and sixpence is all they allows me. It en't enough for a dog to live on, let alone a man and his wife. We have struggled all winter long to keep body and soul together. We was so hungry some days I doubted we would see the snowdrops come up, let alone the bluebells. Yet when I goos to the son to start again on Lady Day, he says to me, "Why are you here? There en't n'work here for you no more. You are too old." Now I has nothing but parish relief to rely on and that en't enough to keep body and soul together, not by a long chalk. T'en't right, I tell you. T'en't right. A man ought not to be treated so. They don't care whether we live or die. Work is all we're good for in their eyes and, when we can't work n'longer, what is the use of us. That is what they're a-thinking and there's some as will tell you to your face.

Why should a man have to stand for that? I have worked hard all my life. I am a loyal man, loyal to my King and my country. I have worked hard all my life, yet I am a pauper still and will die a pauper. I tell you this so's you young'uns'll know what will happen to you. If you do nothing now, it will happen to you as sure as I'm standing here. Well, I ain't about to curl up and die, not to please nobody, though I don't know what I shall do if I don't get something this evening, I don't, I just don't – '

His voice fell away: tears came to his eyes: he began to tremble again and was unable to make his case further. The men around him lowered their eyes and stared at their feet: that way they would not have to look into his brimming eyes and he would not be able to read the sympathy showing in theirs, for he would have been embarrassed by it: he was trembling still as he went back in amongst them.

The bleakness of the scene outside only added to the grimness of the men's thoughts as they listened to each desperate case in turn: for, as the meeting progressed, it became abundantly clear that every man in the room was in need of help of some kind for himself and his family. With so little in the pot, the anger boiled over – anger at the authorities, anger at the rich merchants from London whose homes lined the High Street, anger the landowners whose large estates and farms surrounded the town and were dotted throughout that Hundred, anger also at the clergymen who were also the magistrates of the town and seemed to give a poor man caught poaching to feed his family no more sympathy than they would give a heretic. Anger at the mayor himself, who owned a farm just off the High Street and who, as a wealthy man, was rumoured to think nothing of spending more on a single braided evening coat than he paid three of his labourers in weekly wages, yet at the start of the winter had laid off seven of them.

As the talk grew louder so that anger mounted and the greater became their desperation. They were not ignorant of events: tales of happenings elsewhere had been brought to them by coach travellers and, on occasions, by accounts in the newspapers from London – the riot at Spa Fields in the December, the riots in Wales, in Huddersfield, in Manchester, the riding down by dragoons and yeomanry of land workers in counties to the north of them and the sabre-ing of those in a northern industrial town on a peaceable march to London. All were mentioned, all were commented upon. Small wonder then that, as the drink flowed, for they had all paid tuppence into the pot, there were amongst them some who became roused up enough to declare their belief in 'the justice and right of oppressed people to take up arms in their own defence' against the gentry and the Government which oppressed them, while others suggested it would be a good idea to steal lead from the roofs of churches to make ball shot for their pistols, those that had them, anyway, while yet more called for action to support their aims since it was no good sending a petition to 'the bloody Prince,' who spent more on a single dinner for himself and other bigwigs than the whole room of them earned in a six-month.

'We ought to burn out the lot of them,' exclaimed a newly married young labourer of nineteen, whose seventeen-year-old wife was heavily pregnant with their first child. 'Hanging's the only thing good for them.' He was referring, of course, to the town's gentry and was so fired up that he blithely ignored the fact that even amongst the grumblers and the half-starving in that room there might well be more abject fellows only too ready to report him to those who made it their business to know of such utterances.

'We ought to be like they Frenchies and build us a guillotine,' suggested another, an eigtheen-year-old bachelor, unemployed like them and on relief like them.

'Aye, and first up would be the bloody mayor and all he magistrates,' growled a third.

'And next up'd be all the rest o' they gentryfolk,' declared a fourth, 'every damned one of 'em!'

It was at this point that Joly Cobbold pushed his way forward. When the company had begun to assemble, traipsing past him up the stairs, he had just finished eating his supper in the small dining room. Curious, almost as if sensing trouble, he had followed them: and, since some there were unknown to others in the society and everyone was not known to everyone else, none had questioned his right to be there and had even made room for him just inside the door. As the men made their pleas, he had been standing at the back, listening, and had been much moved by what they said. What these men needed, he decided, was someone to put some fire into their bellies, some fight into their hearts and he had long practised that art, having learned it from others in London.

'Brothers, brothers,' he began, 'I lodge at this inn. I am a Londoner by birth – ' Which was evident to them by his accent. ' – but I work in this town. The innkeeper will vouch for me. I have always pleaded the cause of the working people. You say you are starving, that your families are in want from hunger and that relief is denied you or so reduced as to be of no value. I say to you, a man in want has a right to whatever relief he needs to keep him and his own properly fed and housed and warmed. People should not be allowed to starve for the want of a shilling or two. And it is no man's duty to lie down and die with hunger. No Government has a right to demand that of any man.'

The men were all staring at the newcomer. When he had first pushed his way into the middle of the floor, some, not knowing who he was, had regarded him with suspicion and turned to others to ask if they knew him. Some said they had seen him about the town and knew only that he lodged at the Black Bear.

Joly Cobbold let the mutterings subside and nodded as the secretary, seated in the middle of the three at the table, motioned for him to continue: the committee at least was intrigued by the stranger.

'The laws of Nature, the laws of God, and the laws of England,' Joly Cobbold went on, now with an added passion, 'do they not say that no man shall starve while there is food in the land? In countries on the Continent, where there are no poor rates, it is not theft to take food if it be necessary to preserve life, whether of a man's self, his wife or his children. People are held to have a right to preserve life by taking food belonging to others, unless there be an overseer of the poor or a magistrate or somebody to give sufficient relief to that person who is in danger of perishing of hunger. It is the duty of the overseers of the poor to see that no man shall suffer from want. And it is the bounden duty, too, of the magistrates to hear the complaints of the poor if those officers do not do their set duty, just as it is their duty to command and to compel those same officers to carry out those duties without exception or prejudice.

'Are not those same officers authorised by the laws of the land to extract from the rich of the parish by means of the poor rate as much money as is wanted for that purpose, without any limit as to the amount? And if for whatever excuse – that it be too much or that they are too strapped themselves – they will not do it and society be in such a state that men cannot provide for themselves by their own labour, then I say, according to the laws of Nature and the laws of God, and civil law and the laws of England, too – according to all those, I say it is not theft for the destitute, the cold and the starving to take without payment and without leave what a man and his family requires to keep themselves alive. Even if it be the property of other people, I say a man still may take it, according to the laws of all these, provided he does not take more than is needed to relieve himself and his family and provided also he does not, by taking it, leave those from whom it is taken in want. The right to take is founded on the laws of Nature and it is a saying as old as the hills, a saying in every language in the world, that self-preservation is the first law of Nature. The laws of Nature teach every creature to prefer the preservation of its own life to all other things. According to the laws of Nature, there is no private property. All things belong to all men. By the laws of Nature, my loaf is as much your loaf and, if you want it more than I do, it is more yours than it is mine.'

A fortnight before, Joly Cobbold had obtained from a coachman a pamphlet which labourers of two counties to the north had printed and had handed to their magistrates. News of severe disturbances in those two counties and the despair of the men there had been talked of in the inns and taverns of Hamwyte as much as anywhere else, perhaps more so since they received news of the happenings first-hand and immediate from the self-same coach drivers and wagoners who came down from those very counties. Even some of the passengers were shocked by what they had seen and heard and had added to those tales.

Now, pulling the pamphlet from inside his jacket and briefly waving it in the air, Joly Cobbold informed the members of the Hamwyte Benefit Society of what it was. 'This is the voice of the multitude and we are a part of that multitude,' he declared, his voice rising even more, 'the multitude of the oppressed and the downtrodden. This is what our brothers to the north of us wrote to their magistrates!'

And he began to read in a clear strong voice: *'When our liberties are opposed, shall we not resist those attacks? When we are deprived of our rights, shall we not seize to regain them? When we are oppressed, shall we not complain? We, the voice of the multitude, ask that our wants and conditions be laid before Parliament. We, the brethren of this parish, ask that they be informed that we do not carry our zeal and loyalty so far as to rest silently and submissively under the present seat of corruption. We the loyal subjects of the King command attention. Except by the printing of this pamphlet, we ask how else shall we make known our complaints? We conceive this is a duty which appertains to your office as magistrates and, therefore, we do entrust you will maturely consider this important subject and use your utmost power and influence in forwarding our views. It is with eagerness and anxiety we await the result of this, our third application for the redress of our wants and sufferings. – Signed, The voice of the multitude!'*

Will Ponder emptied the last of his ale even as the stranger lowered the piece of paper and, banging his empty pot hard down upon the table to attract the attention of them all, he jumped to his feet and declared in a loud voice: 'If they blockheads two counties up can have an affray and get something out of it, why can't we have an affray here in Hamwyte? Give the nobs something to be getting on with – show 'em we won't be put down for their convenience. As I see it, it is a question of starvation or fighting for our rights. I was at Waterloo, I ain't afraid of no shilling-a-day specials. As our friends from Dark Leyton and Hamwick Dean have not come, I say we ought to help ourselves. We are Englishmen. We'll fight first. What say you, lads? An affray? An affray to teach the nobs of this town a lesson they won't forget in a hurry?'

'Aye,' shouted another man, 'we ought to be out there fighting for our causes, not sitting here on our rear ends bemoaning things because of the way they are – ' He flung out his arm to point at the window where the earlier savagery of the weather had abated. ' – We ought to be telling they magistrates and gentry out there we ain't going to be treated this way no more. Show 'em they can't go on cheating and robbing us like they do.'

'Aye, we ought to be out there taking what is ours by right,' cried another. 'If they won't give it to us, then we should just take it, I say! Take it and be damned to them all!'

'Damn the King, damn the Parliament and damn all the dukes and lords, barons and earls in it!' shouted Will Ponder, now jumping up on to a chair. 'And damn the bloody magistrates, too! This ain't the life I fought for. Come on, lads, who is with me? Who is for showing them what we are made of? Who is for a riot?'

Such was the mood of the men of the Hamwyte Benefit Society in the Black Bear by then that their response was a roar of approval: men laughed at the thought of it and slapped each other upon the back. But the words had been spoken and could not be unspoken: a feeling had been roused in the minds of some which would not recede till it had been appeased.

Already men and youths were making for the door, shouting as they went.

THIRTY-SEVEN

WITH THEIR COURAGE and boldness fuelled by drink, all sixty or so of the Hamwyte men poured out of the Black Bear on to the High Street, despite the still freezing air and the hail slush underfoot, all shouting aloud their threats against the gentry and other well-to-do of the town, like the mayor, the vicar, the aldermen, indeed anyone who possessed more wealth than they did, which was everyone at the top end of the town. Because of the drink, too, they did not stop to consider what might happen if they infringed the law: instead they armed themselves with whatever weapons they could find from the stables and outbuildings at the back of the Black Bear – clubs, pitchforks, cleavers and one even went into the innkeeper's private parlour and fetched out two pistols which he knew to be kept there, one of which he gave to Will Ponder, unloaded though it was and without ball or powder. Then they set out to cause an affray, serious in their intention to cause mischief, but half-laughing to themselves at their own boldness, not knowing what they would do or what was to come.

The few citizens abroad on the street, hurrying to their warm homes, were stopped and surrounded and, with outstretched hands and gruff demands, were intimidated into handing over what was in their purses or their pockets, a half-crown here, a guinea there, a sovereign from another. The windows of a tailor and haberdasher, who had been a parish constable some years before, were the first to be stoned: as the glass shattered and the tailor poked his head out of an upstairs window, they hurled stones up at him and taunts, too. The door was forced and all the bales of cloth inside were pitched out into the street, rolled about in the mud and slush, danced upon in a crazy jig by the youngest of their number, who were really still youths in their early teen years, but who had become excited by the sudden surge of power and violence which they felt within themselves.

Next the mob broke into a milliner's for no other reason than it was patronised by 'the fancy ladies,' the wives of the wealthier gentry, and, similarly, they tossed the shopkeeper's wares out into the street, where others again trampled them under foot and some even put the silliest of the hats on their own heads and gleefully pranced and paraded up and down till they realised how others regarded them: then they threw them down into the mud and kicked at them.

On up the High Street they surged, to the multi-windowed frontage of a large house owned by a retired landowner, who had once been a magistrate of the town and had, at one time or other, sentenced at least a dozen of them to the House of Correction at Steadleigh and a spell of tortuous and futile labour on the tread-wheel there for minor misdemeanours, whereas a sounder Christian forgiving man would have shown compassion. When he came unsuspecting to the door to answer their loud rattling on his knocker, he found himself facing sixty grinning and cat-calling men and youths, some already masking their faces with kerchiefs and scarves and all slightly the worse for drink, who shouted out: 'Pay us a pound and we will go away!'

The foolish man, thinking himself secure from assault by virtue of his own former self-importance, refused them in an off-hand manner. 'Be off with you! I will have none of your truck here. Be off or I shall call the constable!'

Their answer was to push him aside and charge into his house, where they smashed his mirrors, hurled his vases across the room at his paintings, kicked and stamped and jumped upon his tables till the legs broke and raised his chairs up high and swung them hard against walls and doorposts till they splintered into a half-dozen pieces. What other furniture they could not break, they overturned and kicked and jumped upon or hurled through windows into the street amid shattering glass: and, for good measure, they stole anything that was worth stealing.

The few people who came out to see what the noise was all about quickly scurried back inside in alarm and bolted their doors, some even dousing the oil lamps and closing their curtains. Meanwhile, at the top end of the High Street, the Reverend Tobias Greene, the parish vicar, who was still a local and a county magistrate, on hearing of the sound of shattering glass in the milliner's shop went out of his front door and, seeing the cause of it, hurried to his stables and, with the help of his manservant, quickly harnessed his pony into the shafts of his trap. Then, with his wife for company – she taking the reins – he drove up the street to where the shouts of the rampaging mob were still to be heard outside the landowner's house: he would read the Riot Act to this marauding pack of ruffians and stop them in their tracks, or so he thought.

Unfortunately, by then, the men were in no mood to listen to a foppish clergyman who spent his Sundays spouting about the 'Holy Spirit' and 'Heaven and Hell' to a wealthy congregation and who was seldom if ever seen at the lower end of town: to them, he was as much a member of the uncaring gentry as the rest of them.

As the Reverend Greene drove up, Will Ponder just happened to emerge from the retired landowner's house, pleased with the destruction which had been wreaked inside. 'Bugger off, parson!' he ordered the clergyman, fingering the empty pistol in his belt. 'We'll get to you all in good time. We will visit you when we have done with the others.'

It drew a laugh from the other men and youths, but bravely, perhaps foolishly, the parish vicar stood up in his trap, unrolled the scroll upon which the words of the Act were written and began to read in a loud and steady voice: *'Our Sovereign Lord the King chargeth and commandeth all persons, being assembled, immediately to disperse themselves, and peaceably to depart...'* He got no further than that: for the men quickly surrounded the trap and rocked it so violently that he was unable to continue, but had to grab the side of the vehicle to prevent himself from being pitched from it, while his wife, seated beside him, began to utter hysterical cries as if she were in danger of being tipped out also.

Will Ponder ended their sport: placing one foot on a spoke of the wheel, he reached up and snatched the scroll from the Reverend Greene's hands and sent it flying away into the mud and slush of the road, where it was booted and stamped upon by others.

'Now you can't read a damn thing to us, can you, parson?' he shouted, jumping down amid jubilant cheers, a silver tankard which he had taken from the former magistrate's house almost slipping from inside his jacket. In the end, all the poor vicar could do was to take up the reins from his petrified and whimpering wife, wheel the trap round in the road and retreat to his vicarage, which the men helped him to do by slapping hard at the pony's flanks as it went round so that it threw its head in the air and stepped out a little faster than normal with its eyes bulging.

When eventually the rioters all left the former magistrate's house, they took with them more than a hundred guineas in gold, though not all knew it had been taken: those who did just pocketed what they had found, said nothing and slipped away. Even so, there were still fifty or so of them, leaving a trail of footprints through the hail slush as they tramped up the now deserted High Street, for everyone else had fled inside.

Their next target was the large and impressive home of a bedridden ninety-year-old, who had been the mayor of the town some thirty years before. His housekeeper, an aged crone of some seventy years herself, with no teeth and a wrinkled mouth, opened the door and was roughly pushed aside the same as before, so roughly that her mob cap fell off to reveal her nearly bald pate, which brought more laughter from the men. The same as before, they smashed all the furniture, tables, chairs, sideboards, bureaux, desks and heaved them through the windows and the open door into the street, for no other reason than they were polished and shining and expensive-looking, whereas their own pieces were crude, worm-eaten and really little better than nailed firewood. Once again, too, framed paintings, porcelain vases, decorative plates, ornaments, glass, pitchers, jugs and bowls followed, with those outside cheering as each object came sailing out: and what did not break of its own accord when it hit the stony ground was quickly kicked, pulverised, crushed, fractured, fragmented and mangled by them till the whole street outside was again covered with glinting shards of glass and pottery and strewn with pieces of splintered furniture.

When Will Ponder pulled a painting off the wall and held it up for his comrades to see with the remark, 'Who is this ugly bugger?' the aged housekeeper rushed at him. 'No, no, no!' she cried, trying to snatch the painting from him, for it was a portrait of the old man abed upstairs, dressed in his mayoral robes, painted by a man from the next county who was said to be one of England's finest artists.

'Get off, you old crone!' snarled Will Ponder and such was his mood that he snatched a meat cleaver off another man and might well have struck her had she persisted. Wisely, the old woman retreated into the back of the house, her clenched hands held up before her weeping face as the painting hurtled out of the shattered window to join the rest of the household's goods outside and the sounds of breaking pottery, shattering glass and splintering wood went on.

When they were done there, they continued up the street, going from house to house, banging loudly upon each door in turn till it was answered and any number from ten to twenty were to be found standing on the step: and the demand was always the same from whoever did open the door, house owner or servant. 'Give us a pound or else...' If refused, as some foolishly tried to do, they barged past them and began breaking ornaments and furniture: and if the door was not answered and those within remained silent as if the house were empty, they simply kicked in the door.

Twenty houses were ransacked and ruined in this manner in a half-hour before, eventually, they came to the vicarage, which was considered one of the finest Georgian buildings in the town, to the very house to which the Reverend Greene and his wife had retreated earlier. The vicar had now armed himself with a pistol and, as the mob approached, he boldly came out on to the step, raised the pistol and threatened: 'I'll blow the brains out of the first man to step across my threshold.'

The men looked at each other ruefully, as if disbelieving that a man of the cloth would ever do such a thing as to blow out another man's brains. 'Thou shalt not kill!' What kind of a clergyman was he who would break his own Commandments?

'A threat like that ain't the kind of thing a parson ought to be saying,' said Will Ponder, eyeing him cautiously, taking his hand off the pistol in his own belt, just in case.

'Nevertheless, I will do it, I swear. As God is my witness, I will do it,' the vicar began. But the men had noticed his shaking arm and his trembling cheeks and, while he concentrated his gaze on Will Ponder in the gateway, believing him to be the leader, two others slipped through a gap in the hedge at the corner of the garden, crept along by the house wall and rushed at the vicar from the side, knocking the pistol out of his hand before he could fire it.

Upwards of thirty then surged past him into the vicarage, whooping with delight as they did so, and proceeded once more to wreak their havoc, now with even greater viciousness because the vicar's show of defiance had annoyed them even more. Again, what was there to be stolen was stolen. The vicar, his wife, his two daughters and his three maids and the cook, meanwhile, fled out the back door and through the gate at the bottom of the garden, then made their way across a field into a neighbour's back garden for safety.

There were more shops at the top end of the High Street, finer shops where the men and women from the lower end of town never ventured, for they would not have been well received and, besides, what was the point of going there if they had not the money to buy anything anyway? However, they could loot them and ruin their contents, which some did, while others continued to knock on the doors of other fine homes to demand money and threaten dire consequences for those who were hesitant about giving it.

When the carriage of a well-to-do inhabitant, returning to the town and so unaware of what was happening, inadvertently trotted through, they surrounded him and, with a meat cleaver held over his head, relieved him and his companion of fourteen shillings in silver before allowing them continue on their journey.

By then the two parish constables had been roused from their shops by a posse of concerned citizens, creeping via a back way to reach them, and, though it had taken a half-hour to persuade them to do their duty, they eventually agreed to approach the mob in the hope that placatory words rather than deeds – such as trying to arrest anyone – would persuade the men to go quietly back to the Black Bear or whatever place in which they had been drinking and end the riot, as it would do no one any good to continue the way they were.

Of course, the appearance of the two portly shopkeepers masquerading as constables only drew a laugh. Since Tudor times, the Hamwyte parish constables had been elected with great ceremony at the annual Court Leet from amongst the tradesmen of the town and thus had been eligible to wear the chain of office and carry the ceremonial mace on market days, fair days and high holidays. One year, say, it might be the owner of the tailoring and haberdashery shop in conjunction with the butcher, the next year one of the bakers and one of the town's two cobblers.

As was to be expected of the parsimonious tradesmen who elected them, the positions of the parish constables, like the overseer's post, were unpaid: they drew only what expenses they incurred and then only to amounts that a begrudging Court Leet would sanction. So, unsurprisingly, when it came to apprehending more ruthless felons, the parish constables preferred just to visit their dismayed victims and to record their losses and their injuries in their way books so that they could charge for their expenses of travel and time.

As they nervously approached the figures milling about the High Street, they were spotted and a shout, half laughter, laced with derision and a measure of glee, went up. Slush and mud were quickly scooped off the road and off the walls and patted into balls before a barrage of them sent the two parish constables scuttling back whence they had come. Some were to say later they retreated too quickly and too thankfully: the constables were to say they did it in fear of their lives.

The events should have ended there, but, unhappily, they did not. Spurred on by the fact that no one had opposed them and, surprisingly, still a considerable number despite the few defections,

Will Ponder and a small group consulted in the middle of the street on what to do next. They had reached the end of the long High Street by that time: the dark of open country lay ahead. All they could do was return to the Black Bear and resume their drinking or melt away to their homes.

'Let's have a goo at Melchborough,' someone suggested.

'Aye, let's wake the buggers up there,' agreed another. 'If we set out now, we can be there by morning. They on't be expecting us neither.'

A chorus of 'Ayes' greeted the suggestion: and, with that, forty-five of them decided to march on the county town, eight miles to the southwest, seat of the Assizes and the county's senior magistrates. A small cart was commandeered from the nearby White Hart Inn and some others then mounted upon it two seven-feet-long fowling pieces which they had taken from one of the ransacked houses and which the owner normally fixed upon the prow of his punt when he went shooting amid the salt marshes of the Langwater estuary. Then, with shouts of abuse at the figures peeping nervously from behind upstairs curtains, they moved off towards the county town, pulling the cart with them.

The inhabitants of Hamwyte, those at the top end of the town, watched them go with sighs of relief.

THIRTY-EIGHT

IN MELCHBOROUGH, they agreed as they marched, their business would have to be of a more serious nature. There was to be no rollicking fun there, no ransacking of houses, no smashing windows, no throwing splintered furniture into the road, no terrorising old ladies or demanding men give them money: there, they had proper business to negotiate.

The hope was that no one in the county town would know of their coming: that way, it would be more effectual if a resolute body of forty-five or so suddenly appeared in the market square, knocked upon the door of the chief magistrate for the county and demanded, respectfully, that he fix wages at a proper level of, say, two shillings or two shillings-and-threepence a day for ordinary labourers, with an extra threepence or sixpence for artisans. They would respectfully demand also that he fix the price of a stone of flour that was reasonable to them all and so give them hope of a daily loaf of bread to ease their children's hunger: and also compel the begrudging overseers to carry out their duties without exception or prejudice, extracting from the rich as much money as was wanted and giving sufficient relief to whoever was in danger of perishing of hunger.

Their hopes of surprise were dashed before they had got halfway: for the fleeing vicar, the Reverend Greene, had persuaded the neighbour with whom he had sought sanctuary to lend him his pony and trap, since he feared to go back for his own, and he had set out for the county town via a back way as fast as he could travel. He arrived soon after midnight and drove straight to the home of the chief magistrate of the county, the Reverend Spencer Barker, and informed him of the riot: in consequence, a messenger was dispatched to summon a troop of the First Royal Dragoon Guards, encamped some fifteen miles to the south of the town, at Gatstone.

In the meantime, even though it was the middle of the night, several gentlemen were knocked up by the magistrate and summoned peremptorily, despite the bitter weather, to the Half Moon Inn at the end of the market place where they were sworn in as special constables: and there they waited till the 'rebel mob' was sighted some hours later, just as the dawn came up, plodding through the mud a mile from the town in their determination to secure a victory for their cause, unmindful of the bitter wind blowing across the open countryside.

The Reverend Barker was not an intolerant man, even though, as a magistrate, he had sentenced twenty or thirty men and youths during that winter to varying periods on the tread-wheel for a variety of misdemeanours and felonies. He considered that, if he listened to the men and learned the causes of their actions, he could placate them. Men do not commit riot and affray for nothing, he told himself: there was always a cause. So, with a half-dozen of the special constables at his side, he bravely rode out to meet the column, which he did a half-mile from the town's boundary.

It was six o'clock in the morning by then: the men had been walking all through the night and, understandably, they were cold, tired, hungry, bedraggled and thirsty and keen to get out of the streaming wind. So when the Reverend Barker reined in his horse and raised his hand to command them to halt, they did as he requested and none offered any response while he read them the Riot Act, other than muttering amongst themselves, bunching together against the cold and shuffling their feet in the mud to keep warm. However, as he put away the scroll of paper, none dispersed.

'What is it you men want?' the Reverend Barker asked, concentrating his gaze upon the stocky, broad-shouldered man, with pale blue eyes, red hair and a freckled face, who had been marching at their head and had a pistol sticking from his belt.

'All we ask is that you give us work and pay us a living wage and reduce the price of a stone of flour to no more than two shillings so that we can at least buy it to make our bread,' was the blunt answer given by Will Ponder. 'And for those on relief, we want a decent sum that a man can live on, not one he starves on. Our children go hungry day after day for the want of a bite of bread.'

The fact that Will Ponder did not yet have children was, of course, not known to the chief magistrate. What was clearly evident to him, however, was the men's hunger and their despair: no one would march that far in such weather and in such a state of mind if it were not true.

'If you men will return to Hamwyte peaceably, I will see that your promises are put to the other county magistrates,' the Reverend Barker told them quietly.

Some of the men, seeing that the clergyman appeared to be sympathetic to their plight, would have done as he asked: indeed, at the rear of the marchers several, having delivered their appeal, were about to turn back along the road to Hamwyte when Will Ponder suddenly shouted: 'No going back! We are nearer to Melchborough than we are to Hamwyte. We have not come this far to be put off by a clergyman reading a piece of paper! How do we know he will keep his word? I know these people, they will keep us standing here all day if it suits them. No, I say we all go on. We could wait till doomsday for an answer. We've had a go at Hamwyte, now let's have a go at Melchborough!'

The fierceness of his shout rekindled their defiance. Pitchforks, cleavers and the two pistols were waved in the air again, the faint-hearted returned to the fold and forty-five laughing and jeering men and youths streamed past the startled clergyman with renewed hope, those hauling the cart with the two fowling guns moving even faster now, while the disappointed reverend wheeled his mount around, signalled for the half-dozen constables to do the same and, taking a wider path, along the edge of the muddy road, cantered back into Melchborough.

As the Hamwyte men entered the town and approached the market place, a number of the poorer inhabitants, roused by their cheering and shouting, appeared at their doors and, on learning of what the newcomers intended, hurriedly dressed and ran to join them, claiming a sympathy with their cause and shouting as loudly as did they for the magistrates to meet their demands.

By this time, the magistrates, now five in number, had quit the Half Moon and had retreated farther up the market place to the larger Spread Eagle, where they held a hasty conference, guarded on the outside by a line of nervous special constables.

As the mob, now numbering upwards of two hundred, came up, the Reverend Barker flung open an upstairs window, leaned out and, from this vantage point, informed the throng milling below that he, as the senior county magistrate, and the other county magistrates had agreed that they would ensure that the overseers of the poor at Hamwyte paid to each family 'on the parish' two shillings per head per week when flour was half-a-crown a stone and that this sum would be raised in proportion when the price of flour was higher. They also agreed that the price of labour in the town and on nearby farms should be set at two shillings a day, whether a man were married or single, and that the farmer himself should pay the labourer his full weekly wage and not just give him six or seven shillings and leave the parish to make up the rest.

The good reverend was cheered all round: indeed, all of the magistrates were cheered: everyone smiled happily and the relieved magistrates put their heads together again, came up smiling and ordered free ale to be given to everyone in the crowd.

The majority of the Hamwyte men, forty to be exact, feeling that they had done a good deed that day in the name of all their fellows, after drinking a celebratory mug or two, turned and started the eight-mile tramp back through the cold and streaming wind to their homes. However, five of the more hot-headed of them remained in the vault of the Spread Eagle, two who were not yet eighteen years of age, a third who was nineteen years and a fourth a twenty-year-old, newly married. The fifth who remained with them was the oldest of them, the red-haired Will Ponder, still with the pistol stuck in his belt, smiling with delight at the success of their mission and the steady flow of free ale being poured into his tankard. The magistrates were toasted, the Union Flag was toasted, even the Prince Regent was toasted.

Unfortunately, as such events always do, the dispensing of free ale also attracted all of Melchborough's own collection of ne'er-do-wells: in consequence, a second barrel was demanded of the innkeeper and tapped, to be followed by a third, all on the magistrates, with the inevitable result that several of the local malcontents got drunk on the free ale, as did also the five from Hamwyte who had remained behind.

When eventually the five set out to return late in the afternoon, they found themselves accompanied part of the way by a dozen or so of their new Melchborough drinking companions, all of them in a state of obvious intoxication: and, sadly, on their way out of town, emboldened by their drinking, they perpetrated further acts of violence and robbery against several tradesmen with whom they had no quarrel other than with their apparent prosperity. A baker's shop on the High Street was again looted for bread, various other shops were entered as they passed, the customers terrorised to make them scuttle away and the shop owners forced to hand over whatever money they had in their drawers, in some cases as much as ten pounds. Further, the agent for a bank whom they came across on the pavement was stopped and forced to hand over his leather satchel containing ten golden guineas, which, along with their other loot, was divided between them and their new-found friends when they parted.

Even then, the drinking of Will Ponder and his companions was not over. At one of the roadside inns on the way back, the four entered flourishing their pitchforks and cleavers while Will Ponder showed his empty pistol. Free ale was again demanded and, what they did not drink of the barrel which they tapped and drank sitting in the road, they allowed others to join them in drinking as their 'brother workers.' Having seen the others passing back, many of the nearby labourers came out of their cottages to watch the antics of the five drunken stragglers and to laugh and to drink with them.

THIRTY-NINE

THE MAIN BODY of the rioters had arrived back in Hamwyte in the early evening and immediately sought out the warmth and comfort of their own favourite hostelry, the George, where the drink flowed freely, paid for with all the money they had garnered the previous day. The law-abiding citizens of Hamwyte scurried to their homes at the first warning of their approach, the two parish constables amongst them, and there they all remained, behind closed doors, with the shutters closed tight and the curtains drawn across and not a sole on the street after seven o'clock.

Indeed, the curious quiet, the number of broken windows and the amount of glass and splintered furniture still lying in the street was remarked upon by several of the passengers on the coaches which continued to come rumbling down from Wivencaster and up from London, though when they learned the reason why from the stable lads and yard boys at the Black Bear, the White Hart and the Angel, they, too, waited nervously inside, listening to the raucous noise emanating from the George, till their coaches were ready to depart and they were glad to be out of the place.

It was not till around midnight that four of the stragglers came staggering up the High Street, pushing a barrow which they had stolen for the purpose of transporting the fifth. When Jem Stebbings stepped out of the shadows across the road from the George, the four were so taken aback that, in attempting to manoeuvre round him with their cumbersome load, they tipped poor Will Ponder into the mud and would have left him there and fled had Jem not reassured them. 'Hold there, I'm not the constable,' he cried, which was enough to halt them. 'I'm a friend of Will. He's my brother-in-law. I am married to his sister.'

He eyed the prostrate form of his brother-in-law stretched out upon the ground, oblivious to where he was and the fact that he was lying in ankle-deep mud. 'Drunk is he?' Jem asked with a sigh, yet knowing the answer full well.

'Aye, he's had a few too many,' replied the nineteen-year-old, lurching unsteadily and grinning inanely himself.

'More than a few too many,' giggled one of the eighteen-year-olds, 'about twenty too many!'

'You would all do best to slip away back to your homes,' Jem told them. 'They won't let you forget what's happened here. The militia and the specials will be here, I have no doubt.'

'Know what, friend, we don't give a damn!' cried the lurching nineteen-year-old, waving one hand dismissively as the others sniggered, 'not a damn, not a bugger, not a sod!'

It was defiance borne out of drink: but Jem knew that what had happened was too serious to be overlooked. Robbery, riot, mayhem and near-murder had been perpetrated, according to the wagoner Daniel Gate, who had brought the news of it all to the village, which was how Jem had come to be waiting in the shadows. Mary-Ann had guessed rightly that her brother was most likely a part of it and had sent Jem hurrying into the town to talk some sense into him. He had arrived just as the main body of men came straggling back from Melchborough in the early evening. When he found that Will was not with them, he had decided to wait, not in the George with the others in case the townsfolk thought he was a part of the mob. Instead, he had walked a little way down the High Street and had sat under a tree for hour after hour, well away from the inn and hidden in the shadows, occasionally rising to stamp his feet and clap his chilled hands and to peer up the High Street towards Melchborough in the hope that his brother-in-law would appear.

'I'll take him now,' said Jem, pulling Will to his feet and lowering him back into the wheelbarrow. 'I'll take him back to Hamwick Dean. His sister, Mary-Ann, lives there. I'll take him to our place.'

It was at that moment that Will Ponder opened his eyes: whether or not it was hearing the words 'sister' and 'Mary-Ann' that brought him to his senses, he realised immediately who was holding him and knew exactly what was happening.

'No, no, Jem, old friend, no, I'm with my mates. I'm staying with them,' he protested, struggling to rise from the wheelbarrow. In fact, so violent was his struggle, wriggling and wrestling, that, in the end, Jem let go of him and he lurched unsteadily to his feet and, as drunks will, performed a stumbling circle in the road as the world whirled before his eyes.

'No, no, Jem, I'm with my friends, old mate,' he declared again in a slurred voice, managing eventually to steady himself with the help of two of them. 'We're all going into the George. Come and join us, old mate. Come and have a drink with us. I ain't going to no bloody

Hamwick Dean. There'd be no fun in that, not with my sister there. She'd only start her caterwauling. You know Mary-Ann, you know what she is like about my drinking. Gawd, you married her, old mate! No, me and the lads, we have a heap of drinking to do yet. We ain't finished by a long chalk. We're celebrating, Jem, celebrating. We put one over on the nobs today that'll stick in their craws for the next twenty years or more. Me and the other lads did it and they're all in there – ' He gestured vaguely towards the George's front door and, unbalanced, staggered a short way after his own pointing finger before managing to steady himself. 'Come on, Jem, come and join us. Have a drink with us.'

'You've had a skinful already, Will, you don't need any more,' Jem told him forcefully. 'If you have half a brain in your skull, you'll come home with me right now and lie low for as long as you can manage and just hope that no one has recognised you because there is going to be trouble over what has happened here, mark my words. You know it and I know it. They'll call the specials out on this one, that they will. They won't let this rest.'

He knew nothing, of course, of what had happened at Melchborough or on the return journey. Will Ponder, however, was in no mood to listen. Now that he was aware of the world again, he was just eager to join his brothers. Staggering across the high road with his companions, he somehow managed to locate the latch on the entrance door to the George and lurched through it, one hand on the doorjamb for support. 'Huh! Bugger'em!' was his retort. 'We ain't afraid of no parish constables or specials! Come on, Jem, join us. There's plenty of beer for everyone and we've got plenty of money... '

The other four followed him inside, laughing, and a great shout went up as they were greeted by their fellows. With a sigh, Jem watched them go in, then turned away: he had done his best, but he knew Will Ponder of old, knew that he would have put up his fists and the two would have had to fight before he would go where he did not want to go: so he turned for home.

When, at about three o'clock, he quietly lifted the latch on the cottage door so as not to wake Mary-Ann, he found she was still awake: and when she realised he had returned alone, her face fell.

'He wouldn't come. He was drunk. He wanted stay with his friends,' Jem told her with a shrug. 'He knew what you would say. If he doesn't want to come, I can't make him. I tried. I tried to bring him here in a wheelbarrow, but he broke free. He just refused to come.'

'You should have hit him on the head and carried him back here!' Mary-Ann declared, tears in her eyes. 'You should have knocked him out. Oh, my God, what will happen now, what will happen now?'

Nothing Jem could say that night would placate her: all he could do was to sigh and to listen to his wife's tearful lamenting as she sat all night in the parlour, while he lay in the bedroom, trying to snatch what sleep he could before the dawn came.

In Hamwyte, meanwhile, while Jem had been trudging back to Hamwick Dean, Will Ponder and his four friends had been supping again on their stolen money and regaling all the others with details of the mayhem they alone had caused on the way back: it was all a great lark and they were slapped upon the back and cheered for it.

The celebration in the George went on into the small hours. Four full barrels of best home-brewed ale were drunk dry that night: unsurprisingly, all were very much the worse for it when the last of them settled down to sleep. Few were capable of going to their homes and every chair, table top and square foot of the floor in the taproom, the vault, the passageway and the small meeting room upstairs was covered by snoring men, deep in the sleep of the drunken. Such were their throbbing headaches that those who awoke to a loud shout from outside cursed first the one who had shouted to awaken them so early and only secondly did they curse the brightness of the morning sunlight streaming through the windows.

The same shout awakened Joly Cobbold and brought him padding to the widow of his bedroom at the front of the Black Bear. Across the road, a clergyman – the Reverend Barker, the chief magistrate of the county – was standing in the middle of the High Street outside the George, calling upon the men and youths inside to come out and give themselves up: for ranged behind him were sixteen troopers of the First Royal Dragoon Guards, under a Captain Thomas Henry, retired. He lived midway between Hamwyte and Melchborough, in a mansion in one of the small villages, and, on hearing of the disturbances, had ridden into county town to take charge. Till then, all that had arrived in answer to the messenger's summons was the small troop of dragoons under a mere corporal. Now, however, they had a captain at their head, a member of the gentry, ready to give orders and, further, supported by twenty of the special constables sworn in at Melchborough, gentlemen all and all armed with everything from pistols and muskets to a blunderbuss, with both of Hamwyte's two parish constables joining them, eager to redress the embarrassment of their earlier show of timidity.

An upstairs window was flung open and a youthful head popped out which Jem would have recognised from the previous night as that of the nineteen-year-old: the reply to the reverend's call came before half the men had had time to rub the sleep from their eyes, not with words, but with the discharge of a pistol, the ball shattering the forearm of one of the troopers, a survivor of Waterloo, so that the poor man was thereafter disabled and became a drain upon the county town at a pension of twelve shillings a week for the rest of his life. Somehow, the nineteen-year-old had obtained ball and powder and had loaded his and Will Ponder's pistols against just such an eventuality.

The other dragoons, drilled to return fire, did so at the captain's command, wreathing the street in smoke: ball crashed through each of the four windows on the inn's frontage, wounding two men in the act of rising to their feet, breaking the bones in the arm of one and tearing off the edge of another's ear. Other than that, the remainder of the shots ploughed high up the far walls or into the ceilings.

Inside, there was immediate pandemonium: the Hamwyte men had not expected to have to fight the military. Though one or two shouted that they should resist, the majority quickly pulled open the front door of the inn before the dragoons could reload and ran out with their hands in the air, calling for the soldiers not to shoot. Even then, when the troopers and special constables went into the George to rout out the rest, they found several still asleep: not even the sound of the guns firing could awaken them from their deep slumber: the troopers had to kick them awake and prod them into the street with their musket barrels.

The first tragedy happened while the men who had first run out were being held under guard on the road: one of the younger youths, thinking himself likely to be quicker than any other, tried to seize a trooper's musket and, when he failed, ran off in panic: the trooper called out for him to stop, but was ignored. The running youth had not got thirty yards when the soldier calmly raised his weapon and shot him through the back of the head.

Only two of the rioters sought to resist arrest: Will Ponder, who was used to sleeping through such cacophonies and who had escaped many a Frenchman's slashing sword on the Peninsula and at Waterloo, struck out when he was kicked awake by one of the special constables and, for his pains, received a sabre cut which took off part of his chin. The other was the nineteen-year-old who had fired from the upstairs window: he was desperately seeking to reload from a stolen pouch of powder when he was seized and dragged down the stairs.

A few of the rioters managed to evade capture by going out the back way as the soldiers and special constables stormed in at the front, climbing a fence behind the stables, and so were not taken that day: some were caught later, for it was known who they were, but three of the younger men managed to avoid capture altogether. Being more fleet of foot, they fled across the fields and did not stop till they reached the next town, Levendon: two of them did not return to Hamwyte till years afterwards, having made their way to London, and the third was never seen again.

Those taken, numbering forty-four in all, were marched off under guard with their hands in the air: twenty-four were locked in the bridewell, while the cellars of the Moot Hall had to be pressed into service to hold the rest, which was inconvenient for a number of reasons, particularly the smell emanating from below as there was only one latrine for them all: to deter escape, two dragoons patrolled outside.

Over the following days, during which the freezing rain gave way to a bone-numbing cold, the fates of twenty of the men, deemed somehow to be the lesser of the rioters, that is, those causing the Moot Hall latrine to overflow, were dealt with summarily by the Hamwyte magistrates, eager to put behind them the affair which had so sullied the good name of their town in case it damaged trade by deterring visitors. Thirteen were severely fined, mostly sums of five pounds and ten pounds: seven received terms of imprisonment ranging from three months to twelve months in the Steadleigh House of Correction with hard labour. The twenty-four others in the bridewell were committed for trial at the next Assizes in Melchborough.

All of Hamwick Dean was agog at the sensational news, that so many men and youths from the supposedly staid town should be placed on trial for riot, robbery, criminal damage, highway robbery and threatening to kill a poor servant woman with a meat cleaver. Save for the bitterly cold weather and the never-ending rain, no other subject received so much discussion amongst the men who sat in the smoky haze of the Wayfarers' parlour and the vault of the Carpenters' Arms with the rain dripping off their clothes. It was the same at the Shoulder of Mutton on the main Maydun-to-Wivencaster highway, the Green Man at Lower Rackstead, the Bull at Merchant Staplers, both the Ship and the Anchor at Inworth, the Compasses at Greater Tottle, all seven public houses at Shallford, the three at Levendon, indeed every inn and ale house in every town and village within a radius of twenty miles of the market town.

On the following Tuesday, a packed Vestry meeting of the good and upstanding parishioners of Hamwyte, unanimously agreed that the thanks of the meeting should be publicly extended to the Reverend Greene for his action in giving warning to the county's chief magistrate. Thanks also were expressed to the Reverend Barker for having 'accompanied the military to this place and for having, in the most spirited and determined manner, oppressed the tumultuous proceedings which were going on here, threatening danger to the neighbourhood.' The town's gratitude was also publicly expressed to 'the Melchborough gentlemen, who came in the night, to the Hamwyte constables who joined them, and to Captain Henry for his assistance and laudable exertions.'

It came as no surprise to Jem, as he stood in his fields, watching the rain teeming down and collecting in the furrows he had ploughed, that one of those who was marched in chains and under guard to the old Melchborough Gaol along with twenty-three others to await trial at the next Assizes, to be held in the fourth week of June, was his brother-in-law, Will Ponder.

The good judge who tried them, Mr. Justice Christian, was known for his harshness and as one who often prescribed the death penalty: indeed, he had done so in another county the year previously. It was as if he were trying to live down the ignominy brought on by the fact that his younger brother was lost somewhere in the South Seas and had been for twenty-eight years, ever since he had seized the *HMS Bounty* and disappeared with half the crew to no-one knew where.

On three separate days, Jem and Mary-Ann took the carrier to Melchborough and joined the throng outside the Shire Hall, where the Assizes were held, hoping to be there on the day that Will was put to the bar, but, due to the crush, the infamy of the trial and the likely sentencing, they were unable to get into the courtroom. The seats had all been allocated to the good and worthy of Melchborough and Hamwyte and the surrounding district and there were more than enough of them feeling aggrieved to have filled the place twice over without the 'lower orders' joining them.

The twenty-four were brought into the dock in three batches of eight. The trial took two days to complete: at the end of it, twelve – a 'goodly round dozen,' as the upright judge commented – were left for the hangman when he and the other judges, lawyers and clerks departed for the next county. Mercifully, however, in the days that followed, the kindly authorities of the town petitioned the Prince Regent, with the result that the powers that had sentenced them had second thoughts and reduced the number for execution to only five – the same five who had remained behind in Melchborough to rob its citizens and cause mayhem on the road home. The seven spared the gallows joined the others in the old Melchborough Gaol, awaiting transportation to Van Diemen's Land – the old name for Tasmania, named after Anthony Van Diemen, the one-time Governor of Java. Their terms were set at seven or fourteen years, the severity of the sentencing depending as much upon their demeanour before the judge, their display of contrition or otherwise, the manner in which they questioned the witnesses, whether too boldly and too disrespectfully, and whether they had a past conviction or convictions, for felonies or otherwise, as it did upon the evidence given against them.

In truth, there was never any real hope for Will Ponder and the four others who had straggled back with him. The authorities were in no mood to allow leniency of any kind: for that same June of 1817, even as their trial was under way at Melchborough, news came of a similar uprising in Derbyshire. There, three hundred half-starved stockingers, weavers, quarrymen, ironworkers and a few agricultural labourers had gathered at the White Horse Inn in the village of Pentrich, a few miles north-west of Ripley, motivated the same as the Hamwyte men by feelings of anger and despair at the lack of work, by the lack of food and by the indifference of the Government and local worthies to their ever more desperate plight and by ever-changing economic forces over which they had no control.

Led by a volatile stockinger named Jeremiah Brandreth and armed with a few ancient firearms, blunderbusses, pikes, scythes and bludgeons, they set out in the dark to walk the fourteen miles to Nottingham before morning in the hope that others there would join them in a march on London as part of a national uprising against the Government. Urged on by their leader, they tramped all night through pouring rain, calling at farms and houses en route and demanding arms and support: sadly, at one place where they were told to 'Clear off!' the mercurial Brandreth fired a shot through a window and killed a farm servant.

As it turned out, no one would join their insurrection and there was to be no march on London: they had been misled by a Government spy. By the time they reached the outskirts of Nottingham, so many had deserted in the darkness due to the cold and rain that, when a small force of hussars rode up, most of the marchers dropped their weapons and ran. Many were rounded up within hours and the Government, determined to make an example of them, put thirty-five on trial at Derby accused of treason and levying war against the King. Most were given sentences of transportation or gaol, but three, including their leader, Brandreth, were sentenced to be hanged, drawn and quartered, but, mercifully, their sentences were commuted to just being hanged and beheaded.

FORTY

HAD ANY of Hamwick Dean's inhabitants been standing at the cross-roads at the top end of The Street at about noon one early July Saturday, they would have seen a very ashen-faced and somewhat distressed Parson Petchey come up the long hill from Hamwyte in his pony and trap as if fleeing from some terrible vision. There was about him a look of shock almost akin to terror: for that morning the good and religious parson had just witnessed the well-to-do's answer to the solution of pauperism and riot: and, while he did not disagree with their methods, the carrying out of it had shocked him to the core. After all, it was his first execution and, worse, his first mass execution.

As a magistrate of Hamwyte and a clergyman of the Hundred, Parson Petchey had been obliged to witness the hanging together of five male inhabitants of the town, not only to witness it but as a priest to take part in the hideous ceremony of it all. The five doomed men had been brought from Melchborough's old gaol to the town's bridewell to be lodged in chains overnight: and he had gone to the bridewell that morning to act as the ordinary, that is, the priest of the prison, as the replacement for his friend from the town, the Reverend Greene, who, as a victim of the riotous mob, felt himself unable to perform the religious offices in the gaol with the prisoners under sentence of death and had called upon his good friend to officiate.

The crowds from the town and the other towns and villages had been gathering on the High Street outside the small bridewell since the previous evening, as much to show their unity with the doomed as to keep vigil with them. In fact, so great was the throng by the early evening that dragoons and special constables had come over from the county town to mount guard all night around the bridewell, as much to see that order was kept as to ensure no rescue was attempted.

Poor Mary-Ann, despite her pregnancy, spent the whole night standing in the drizzling rain, as close up to the ring of dragoons and constables as she could manage in the crush, her shawl wrapped over her head, weeping quietly to herself, sometimes managing to call out to her brother: 'Have faith, Will, have faith. We will pray for you, we will pray for your soul to go to Heaven.'

The sympathetic corporal of the guard made allowance for them, letting those who were relatives of the doomed stand closer to where the bridewell's solitary barred window looked out on to the High Street: but, close as they were, no audible reply came from within to her calls or to those of the other mothers, fathers, sisters and brothers who stood with them. For his part, all Jem could do was to place an arm about his wife's shoulders and to comfort her throughout the long night, holding her closer and tighter in the hope of stifling her quiet sobbing as the first light of day began to streak the eastern sky.

The five condemned had been brought to Hamwyte for execution, rather than being hanged at the usual place, on the gibbet at Melchborough, so that, come the morning, the rich and the robbed from the town would be present to see justice done and vengeance taken without having to trouble themselves with travelling to the county town in bad weather along poorly maintained roads. A cold wind was blowing spatters of rain along the High Street when, a half-hour after the great bell of All Saints' church had tolled the signal hour, the five were brought out through the low door, blinking in the brighter daylight, each with a white cap upon his head, tied with a black ribbon. Unhurriedly, each climbed without assistance on to a cart covered with black cloth and seated themselves on the benches on either side, staring at the crowd all around them as if surprised by its vastness.

There had, the district's older inhabitants agreed, never been an execution like it in their memory – five all at once: the last multiple hanging had been a hundred and seventy or so years before when the so-called 'Witchfinder-General,' the half-mad Matthew Hopkins, had ridden through, dragging eight wretched old women in chains to Melchborough, to be tried and hanged for witchcraft, consorting with the Devil and for having 'teats' on their bodies to suckle the Devil's brood, which, in effect, were no more than common moles.

As the five were trundled slowly along the High Street, westwards towards the top of the town and the place of their execution, in the same direction as they had marauded a month earlier, the same dragoons and special constables rode immediately ahead and immediately behind the cart. Behind them came the grim-faced and somewhat fearful Hamwyte Justices, who had willingly committed the five to the more severe justice of the Assizes at Melchborough and so felt it necessary to follow the black-shrouded cart. Parson Petchey, being the ordinary who had performed his duty at eight o'clock on that Saturday morning, led them in his own pony and trap, with the rest of the melancholy Justices in procession behind him.

To ensure that the dignity of the occasion was properly maintained, three hundred of the most respectable inhabitants of the town came next, four-dozen of them on horseback, riding solemnly six abreast, to act as some form of ceremonial escort, each rider holding a white wand upright in his hand, with the mane of his horse similarly bedecked with white ribbon. After all of them came the four chief parish constables of the nearest towns, one from Hamwyte itself and the others from Maydun, Shallford and Levendon, all with their staffs of office covered with black crepe and all wanting to take part in the great ceremony of execution as if it were a religious rite on some holy day.

Behind them were ranged the carriages of the respectable townsfolk, almost sixty of them, the gentlemen and ladies all dressed in their finest as befitted a gathering of that Hundred and the Hundreds either side, respecting the solemnity of the occasion by tying white ribbons of their own around their hats and their horses' manes. Afterwards, they had arranged to return to the Moot Hall, where a mid-morning luncheon would be served, with punch, wine, beer and spirits: indeed, at that very moment, the carcass of an ox was being turned on a spit in the Moot Hall yard by one of the cooks from the White Hart, awaiting their return.

Tramping after the gentry, the magistrates, the dragoons, the special constables and the cart and the leading constables came the labouring classes of the town and the surrounding villages, two thousand of them in total, amongst them, of course, Jem and Mary-Ann, her eyes fixed upon her brother, a small figure fifty yards ahead, barely visible between the many riders in front. Though the families of the condemned had begun their walk at the head of the 'common procession,' they had not gone fifty yards when some of the more ghoulish element had hurried past them to get ahead, all the better to get as good a viewing place as they could when the drop was made, since the gentry and the other 'nobs' would take the best spots anyway.

Indeed, such was the number and such was the crush of carriages along the muddy, rutted and pot-holed way out of town to the place of execution that it took almost a half-hour to reach the area of open, furze-covered heath to the west, where a gallows had been erected close to the road so that no one would have to trespass too far on to what might prove boggy ground, especially given the continual rain of the past weeks.

The good Reverend Doctor found himself greatly moved by the display of faith of four of the five: for, upon their arrival on the heath, all except the stockily-built, red-haired man had knelt in prayer before him as he blessed them. The chief of the two hangmen had looked at him briefly to see whether he wanted him to force the other man to his knees, but such had been the defiance showing in those cold, pale-blue eyes that the parson had shaken his head, though it was imperceptible to the crowd. Even so, despite the defiance of one, it had brought a lump to his throat that at least four of them should, in the very hour of their death, ask for God's forgiveness for their sins, even though the troopers and the constables surrounding them and the gallows above their heads ensured that there could be no forgiveness from the legal authorities on this earth and that sentence would be carried out regardless of the moaning and agitation and wailing of those all around.

Parson Petchey felt only sympathy for the five, three of whom he knew were not above the age of nineteen, saddened that they should be leaving the light of the day so young, but buoyed by the knowledge that their souls would rise up to see the beatific vision amongst the righteous and faithful and stroll forever through the golden streets of Heaven, as described in Revelations, after due time in Purgatory, of course, where the souls of those dying penitent are purified from venial sins.

He had been much surprised that all five could read and was most moved by one of the youngest of the condemned, aged only eighteen two weeks before, who, when prodded forward by the senior hangman to say his piece, had, as instructed, declared in a loud voice so that the many hundreds gathered there could hear that they had all confessed to the crimes for which they were about to be hanged.

'All you who are witness to this, my disgraceful end,' the condemned youth had shouted in a quavering, reedy voice, reading slowly from the paper held up before him by the second hangman, 'all you who are witness to this, my disgraceful end, I exhort you in the name of God – that God before whom I must shortly appear, before whom we must all shortly appear – I exhort you in His name to avoid drunkenness, Sabbath-breaking, whoremongery, and bad company. I pray you also to avoid rioting and in every respect refrain from breaking the laws of your country, for the law of the land will always be too strong and those who defy it will in the end be forced to submit to its justice or its mercy.'

The hangman nodded his appreciation and tapped him on the shoulder: and, as he stepped back to the stand upon the mark where the two hangmen had first positioned him, it was the turn of the twenty-year-old to be prodded forward.

'We stand here a melancholy example of the power and justice of the law,' the twenty-year-old declared in a shivering high treble, again reading from a piece of paper held before him. He had a wife aged seventeen years and a child of three months and, catching sight of them both near to where Jem and Mary-Ann stood, he was unable to hold back the tears and unable, too, to brush them away as his hands were manacled behind his back: mercifully, his eyes would be covered when the black-ribboned hood was pulled over his face.

'I most sincerely warn you all,' he went on, weeping, 'to avoid those sins which have been the cause of bringing me here and I freely forgive those who gave their evidence against me and may the God of mercy forgive me and have mercy on my soul.' With that, he stepped smartly back into his place to await death, still unable to brush away the tears rolling down his cheeks.

And so, in their turn, the next two came forward to give penitence and absolve themselves of their sins, both reading slowly and laboriously from statements held up before them.

If Mary-Ann were hoping to hear some final declaration of contrition from her brother, she was to be disappointed. When the second hangman pushed Will Ponder forward, he had to give him a much harder push than the rest and, when he held up a piece of paper for him to read, he turned his face aside so as not to see it, shook his head and mouthed something at the holder, who simply lowered the paper with a shrug of indifference. They then all prayed again with Parson Petchey, though once again Will Ponder's head had to be forced down and held there by the hand of the first hangman.

As they prayed, their final act in life upon this earth, Mary-Ann's weeping grew louder and more uncontrollable. In the end, Jem had to tighten both his arms around her shoulders and hold her to his chest, at the same time whispering, unheard by anyone, his own farewell to his friend: 'Cheerio, Will, old friend, cheerio.'

Since it was his duty, as a magistrate and the ordinary, Parson Petchey then read out the confession of them all, which he and the other magistrates had had them sign that morning at the bridewell so that all was morally tied up and none need have a conscience about taking part in the proceedings. Such was the dampness in the air at that spot, he found it necessary to clear his throat several times before beginning and was thankful that he had had long training in voice projection at the cathedral in Oxford to be able to deliver his words to the greater part of the crowd with a steadiness that belied his own inner turmoil.

'We poor, unfortunate, suffering creatures,' he read, lifting his voice and articulating clearly, 'beg leave to present the public with this our last dying acknowledgement of the justice of the sentence which has condemned us to die for the violent outrages we have committed and hope it will be a warning to all who may see or hear of us to avoid this course. We acknowledge and confess our sins in general and we most sincerely beg of God to pardon our sins; fervently hoping and trusting that God's almighty will, for the sake of all atoning merits of the Redeemer, receive our precious and immortal souls into his favour, though we have delayed their interests to this late hour, most earnestly entreating that the Almighty may grant us all our sufferings in this world and none in the next.'

Upon the next sentence, he raised his voice to an even greater pitch, for he was particularly pleased with the wording of it as it was entirely his own: 'We poor unfortunates, further implore you, by all means at your command, to avoid irreligion and vice of every kind, particularly our shameful neglect of the means of grace, the only means through the merit of Christ, of our soul's salvation. We sincerely recommend to you that you attend the public worship of God, particularly on the Lord's Day, and most sincerely pray that all our friends and relations will not put off their repentance to their death-bed, lest that God, whom they have neglected to serve while in health and strength, should say unto them at last, as He does to every neglecter of salvation, "When I called thee, ye refused me, when I stretched out my hand to thee, ye regardethed me not, but set at nought all my counsel and would have none of my reproof. Therefore, now I also will laugh at your calamity and mock when your fear cometh." – Amen.'

Hardly had the good parson finished than the two executioners went along the line behind the five condemned, pulling down their hoods to hide their trembling mouths and wide-staring eyes and adjusting the ropes around their necks: then, upon a signal, the wedge was pulled, the drop fell and all five left this world, each twisting and turning for few seconds before they gave up the struggle.

Mary-Ann's face was still buried in Jem's shoulder, but he forced himself to watch. To do so was to him like holding a dying man's hand, but even he, a man who had himself laid the dead in rows in pits, could not prevent the tears moistening the corners of his eyes. He saw the old parson standing stock still before the swinging bodies, his face raised to them, and marvelled how he could be so calm in a moment like that. He did not know that, on hearing the platform wedge pulled, Parson Petchey had simply screwed his eyes shut and then had stood there, tensing himself to remain stationary, counting first to thirty, then opening one eye for a peep, before closing it and counting to a second thirty so that when eventually he opened both his eyes, it was mostly over except for the twitching of the legs of two of them: and the shouting and wailing of the women, of course, but the military simply closed their ranks to forestall any foolishness on anyone's part.

The parson was pleased to note that the ladies and gentlemen of the town were far more reserved and, in general, tended to observe the whole business in a quiet and respectful manner, upholding the dignity of the occasion, which he was pleased to see. The horrible, heart-piercing, unladylike shrieks at the moment of the drop came from the 'common masses': clearly, some of the women had lost their calm.

As was the custom in that county, the bodies of the executed were required to hang for eight hours: so by the time they were taken down in the early evening, placed in cheap coffins and given to their relatives for interment, Parson Petchey was back in Hamwick Dean, in his study writing his sermon for the next day, with a cup of tea and a buttered scone beside him. The bodies were finally taken on a cart to a cottage in the poorer part of the town and laid in a row in the parlour, as again was the custom, so that all night long a steady procession of tearful women and silent, white-faced men could shuffle through to view them and pay their last respects.

Mary-Ann, Jem, the young wife of one of the hanged and the mothers, fathers, brothers and sisters of the others kept vigil with them till morning came. Later that day, they were buried together in a common grave in the old parish churchyard on Cannium hill, though there was some disapproval that, as was the custom of the church towards those hanged, the sexton would allow only one seven-foot deep grave to be dug for all five so that they would all have to be buried upright and, therefore, could never 'lie at rest.'

So genteel Hamwyte on the chill, damp July morning when they hanged five of its sons from the 'lower order.'

FORTY-ONE

EVEN as Parson Petchey was writing his sermon, some two hundred or more of his own parishioners who had been at the scene of the executions, men and youths and some women, too, came walking wearily back into the village, subdued and sad-faced, stunned by the mercilessness of it all. For months afterwards, the riot and the hangings were the sobering topics of many a sad conversation in the Wayfarers' and the Carpenters' Arms, indeed in every village inn and ale house in that Hundred and throughout the Eastern region, though they were mentioned only in hushed whispers, for men would talk of them in low tones only and never loudly or carelessly if there were others within hearing whom they distrusted or did not know. Such was the gloom in Hamwyte and the villages around, it was as if a great dark cloud had descended over the whole landscape: men could scarcely believe what had happened. There was a lingering sense of shock and despair which only time could disperse: a year or more afterwards some men would still have moist eyes when they talked of it.

Parson Petchey, however, on the Sunday, delivered the sermon which he had hurried back to write, trusting that by concentrating upon it he would put the sight of the five swinging corpses from his mind's eye. He had laboured long at it because he was keen to impress his concern upon the congregation, in particular those who met in the Wayfarers' and still availed themselves of the villagers' own sick benefit society, the Teapot Fund.

Despite the Reverend Doctor's part in the proceedings, Mary-Ann held no malice towards him: indeed, she was thankful that, despite Will's obvious reluctance to pray, he had at least 'bowed his head' at the end to receive the parson's blessing so that he would, if nothing else, appear before the gates of Heaven in a state of some grace. Jem, however, was not so convinced of Will's unexpected return to the faith, but, knowing that it mattered to her and comforted her, did not say so. What he had seen was five men, one of whom he had known well, his own brother-in-law, put to death by the unforgiving system of a country for whose King he had fought in war. He knew the crime of the five was great and realised that they had to be punished, but, like most, he had not expected to see them hanging from a gallows while a crowd numbering three thousand or more looked on: it had shocked even the hardened soldier in him.

Not unexpectedly, that first Sunday 'afterwards' – as people began to refer to it without actually saying after what – the church was packed almost to overflowing. It was as if the sudden extinguishing of five lives had jolted the villagers into considering their own mortality and they wished to show those who were above them and ruled over their lives that they were pious, peaceful and law-abiding, faithful to King and country – or, as it was at that time, to the Prince Regent and country, as King George was in dispose again.

Mary-Ann, of course, was keen to pray for the departed soul of her brother and so, clutching her grandmother's tattered prayer book and despite her condition, she was the amongst the first of the congregation into the church that Sunday morning, falling upon her knees as soon as she had entered the pew, screwing up her eyes and clasping her hands so tightly that they made small, jerky movements as the words of her prayer tumbled through her brain. Jem accompanied her as usual, just as he had done every Sunday since their marriage, though that morning he went more to be beside her and also because he dared not refuse rather than out of a wish to put himself in a state of grace with a God in whom he had now begun to doubt.

All of the four hundred and fifty seats in the centre of the nave and along the side aisles were taken when the parson climbed to his pulpit and ran his gaze along each row of faces in turn as he did each week before beginning, almost as if her were seeking to assure himself that each was sitting in his and her allotted place. Of course, it helped with church attendance that four hundred of the seats were free: only the likes of the late lamented squires and the three larger farmers, Amos Peakman, Joshua Godwin and Marcus Howie, and one or two others who had lived in the village at various times, were God-fearing enough to pay for their seats in order to ease their path to Heaven. The three larger farmers were each seated expectantly with their families at the front of the church as Parson Petchey began his sermon to his sheep, or more precisely, his harangue of the bemused inhabitants of Hamwick Dean, apart from one who had a fit of coughing.

His object that morning was nothing less than the complete suppression of the Hamwick Dean Teapot Fund, which he had failed to do on the earlier occasion. Now, however, he had a cause with which to berate them, an example of what could happen if people tried to set themselves up in opposition to the Church's care when they had seen no other object in the Teapot Fund than its stated intention of helping the needy when they desired it.

'You will all know of the terrible executions which took place only yesterday less than five miles from here,' the hook-nosed parson began, 'when five young men, labourers of the soil like yourselves, were hanged upon the gallows. These young men and others took it upon themselves to riot and to rob and, in so doing, wilfully imperilled the peace in both Hamwyte and Melchborough in an orgy of criminal destruction, saying they were not paid enough wages by the landowners and farmers for whom they worked or received enough from the poor rate. As you know, in the first instance, twelve of those who were tried and convicted were sentenced to the gallows, though, mercifully, the kindly judge, who had sentenced those twelve, had second thoughts and, through his good offices, His Royal Highness the Prince Regent was pleased to reduce the number for execution to only five, which were duly carried out in my presence and the presence of many of you yesterday morning. The nineteen others who were convicted with them of crimes of robbery, of menace, of burglary and thieving and riotous assembly – they were spared the gallows and are to be transported in due course to Van Diemen's Land, on the other side of the world, some for seven years, placing a great burden of hardship and struggle upon their loved ones left behind – and some for fourteen years, they perhaps never to see their wives and children again, a terrible, terrible fate for any man. The remainder of those convicted, numbering some twenty in all, have been sent to the county gaol and the House of Correction for the next twelve months to labour at the tread-wheel and some have been heavily fined and all because their anger rose up at a meeting of what they termed was their benefit club – ' He paused and again ran his eyes along the rows of faces, this time as if seeking to ascertain the guilty amongst them by a change in their looks, a sudden reddening of the cheeks or by them casting their eyes down and a needless shifting of their positions. ' – Brethren, brethren, let the terrible events of yesterday serve as a warning to you all. Once again I must plead with you, in the name of good common sense, to cease and desist from the foolhardy enterprise which exists in this village out of which no good ever will come. If you would not heed me before, heed me now...'

There were smiles upon the faces of the three large farmers and they could not help themselves but turn their heads and glance back at the sullen, resentful faces of the fifty or so husbandmen and day-labourers seated behind them who were still paying into the benefit society. Suffice it to say, after the parson's sermon, the cowed and despairing villagers of Hamwick Dean bowed to his wishes: the Hamwick Dean Teapot Fund was disbanded without delay and the pot shared out amongst those who had continued with it.

At the end of July, a month prematurely, Mary-Ann gave birth to a sturdy son, whom father and mother gazed upon with pride: there was talk, of course, of naming him after her deceased brother, but, in the end, they named him Jed, for no other reason than Jem liked it. In the weeks which followed, as soon as she was able, Mary-Ann left the baby with a village woman who had also given birth and so could suckle him, and made her pilgrimage to Will's communal grave, walking the three miles into Hamwyte and up Cannium hill through the rain which persisted all through the August, with barely a day when it did not fall, waterlogging the ground and stunting the growth of the corn.

The gloomy, sunless days further delayed the harvesting of what was, by any standard, a meagre crop yet again. When eventually Jem and Mary-Ann, with the new-born Jed laid in a bushel basket for a cradle, did go into the fields to mow their corn, they found themselves beset for seven consecutive days by an early autumnal frost and a chilling fog further damaging their yield –weather once again more akin to January or February than late August. It was to be another fortnight before they were able to gather up the last of their sheaves and, in the end, they harvested only half the yield of the crop that he would have got two seasons before.

Jem fared little better with the turnip crop he had sown on the Badger's Hole part of Long Field: a plague of black caterpillars, called 'black jacks' by the labourers, invaded large breadths where he had planted his turnips and he and Mary-Ann, with Jed in his 'cradle' nearby, had to spend long hours walking the furrows seven or eight times a day, drawing a heavy cart rope held between them over the tops of the leaves to sweep away the caterpillars, as did all the other husbandmen and small farmers, of course. Even the three large farmers, Amos Peakman, Marcus Howie and Joshua Godwin, were plagued by the caterpillars, the sweeping away of which gave five days of unexpected work to two-dozen or so day-labourers from the village.

When the new year came, Mary-Ann was two months' pregnant again. As her second pregnancy swelled and the cold of January and

February came, Mary-Ann's visits to Cannium hill became less frequent, from once a month at the start to none at all by her seventh month. Whether guilty at not being able to visit her brother, she suddenly began to speak of him again, whereas, since his execution, she had barely been able to mention his name aloud, though Jem knew that she spoke it in her head every night at prayer, kneeling beside the bed, and every Sunday in church, kneeling in the pew.

In the late July of 1818, a girl was born, whom they named Thirza, after Mary-Ann's grandmother: as well as the blessing of Thirza, that year also they were at last able to cut a good harvest. Though gales and rain blew along the estuary in the March when Jem was broadcasting his seed, making the scattering even more haphazard, the summer itself was the longest, driest and warmest in living memory, which gave all hope that the dismal and peculiar springs, summers and autumns and hard winters of the past three years were mere aberrations of the country's weather. It bolstered the both of them, for a good harvest would at last put back into their flour jar some of the money which had dwindled markedly since Jem had begun his enterprise, more than he had expected it would.

Further, he was able to pull his turnips from Thornbush a month after the corn had been gathered-in and this time there was no plague of 'black jacks' to concern him. The work kept himself and Mary-Ann busy till the end of October when he flailed his corn in the same barn in which he had rented space before. It meant that they had a good load of winnowed wheat and barley dried and sacked to take to the corn market at Hamwyte: that way he was always busy.

Unhappily, though Jem did not know it then, his way after that was to be downward, ever downward: and the simple event which was to precipitate all the trouble for him was a change in the administration of the village's Vestry.

FORTY-TWO

SINCE MEDIEVAL TIMES, responsibility for parish administration in Hamwick Dean, Lower Rackstead and Merchant Staplers had always lain in the joint Vestry, which met every Easter Monday and thereafter as required, perhaps up to four times a year. By custom, it had the right and power to provide the inhabitants of the village and the two hamlets with whatever services or regulative ordinances were deemed necessary.

In addition to its principal responsibilities of maintaining the fabric of the three churches, managing parish property and bequests, meeting statutory requirements for the maintenance of the poor, repairing local roads and, vitally, appointing parish officials and overseeing their duties, it also set the local poor rate in all three places. Like other villages and hamlets, the amount of shillings and pence in the pound which a person paid was based upon the value of their owned or leased property: and, if more money were needed to support a growing list of poor, then the Vestry could, and sometimes did, increase the number of times per year that the poor rate was collected, to the inevitable upset of all ratepayers.

By far the largest payers into the poor rate and other taxes then were the labour-hiring farmers, such as Amos Peakman, Marcus Howie and Joshua Godwin in Hamwick Dean, along with the two larger farmers in Lower Rackstead, Silas Kempen and James Allen, and the largest of the farmers in Merchant Staplers, Thomas Godbear. Their taxes far exceeded what was paid by the lesser labour-hirers, the small farmers, the husbandmen, tradesmen and artisans.

Though at one time, its Easter Monday meetings had been open to all, the joint Vestry of Hamwick Dean and the two hamlets by that time consisted solely of the rate-paying farmers, the rate-paying tradesmen, the rate-paying husbandmen and any others from the three places subject to paying the poor rate by virtue of what they owned, leased or produced.

From amongst those same ratepayers, the parish constable was nominated to serve all three parishes, the hamlets being too small to warrant one of their own. It was not a well-liked appointment since his responsibilities were many – primarily to apprehend malefactors, perhaps having to keep them in the village's stocks opposite the Wayfarers' till they could be marched to the bridewell at Hamwyte and put up before a magistrate. It was also the constable's duty to expel vagrants and unlicensed hawkers, with force if necessary, collect and deliver to the appropriate authorities any taxes, remove back to their parish of origin any poor of other parishes who had fallen on hard times, attend Quarter Sessions to support prosecutions, check for weak and watered beer at the four hostelries, the Wayfarers', the Carpenters' Arms, the Green Man and the Bull, keep the parish armour, provide men for the militia if required and take charge of the parish gun. Whoever was elected was allowed, as a sign of his authority, to fix the constable's staff outside his door for all to see. However, with alternative appointments limited, he usually found the staff remained there for a number of years: though, when he finally did retire, the concession was granted that he would not be prevailed upon to serve again for another seven years.

The most disliked of all appointments made by the Vestry, however, was that of the surveyor of the highways or the 'waywarden,' as he was called by most, who was responsible for overseeing the maintenance of roads and byways of the village and hamlets. But since, apart from The Street in Hamwick Dean, the other roads (particularly those from Lower Rackstead and Merchant Staplers) were used mostly by through traffic from other places going to and from Hamwyte and Maydun rather than by local vehicles themselves, there was little incentive and much resentment to do so. For this reason, one of the most dispiriting tasks was having to exhort reluctant householders to fulfil their legal obligations to pay the tax to keep the roads of their parish in good repair and also to coax villagers to give a few days of free labour each year, digging, breaking or carting stones from the village's gravel pit, collecting brushwood to fill the potholes or perhaps just lending a team of horses free of charge.

Also elected from amongst the members on a rota basis were two churchwardens for St. Bartholomew's and one each for St. Cuthbert's and St. John's, the latter positions, of course, filled from amongst the few ratepayers of those hamlets. Traditionally, for St. Bartholomew's one warden was chosen by the vicar, which was how Joshua Jaikes had come to be elected, to the chagrin of everyone, while the other was elected by the people, the other ratepayers. The stipulation was that they serve for three years, but, as was often the case, invariably it was for longer, like Andrew Norris, who had served two terms amounting to six years by then and who was at last asking to be relieved of the onerous duties since he was into his fiftieth year and the host of duties took up too much of his time and wearied him. For example, other than overseeing the normal maintenance of the church fabric, ornaments, decoration and the churchyard, provision of books, candles, beeswax, wine, et cetera, the churchwardens were also required to remonstrate with absentees from church services, collect alms, allocate pews, collect pew rents from those who paid them, help to collect the poor rate payments and other taxes and set and collect burial and bell-ringing charges.

As watchdogs of the parish, they also had to ratify the accounts of the overseer of the poor, pay the parish clerk, present to the bishop a list of 'irregularities' in the parish, such as adultery, incest, whoredom, drunkenness, swearing, ribaldry or usury, and deal with the destruction of collected vermin – the sparrows, rooks, crows, hedgehogs, moles and the like – though, so as not to upset Parson Petchey again, these were no longer brought to the Vestry for payment, but were left at the constable's office.

At the same joint Easter Monday meeting, the chief overseer of the poor and an assistant were also elected, again to serve all three parishes, both posts, like the others, being 'voluntary' and unpaid. It was the chief overseer's task to set the valuation of each householder's property to determine what his legal contribution should be to the parish poor rate, then to present his list to the Vestry for its approval. Not unexpectedly, it exposed him to much grumbling from his fellow ratepayers at every Vestry meeting: for whatever poor rate was set to provide for poor relief, it was always too much for those from whom it was collected, namely the landowning gentry if they lived in a village, but, in the main, the large and middling farmers and anyone else with a property of a value above fifty pounds per annum, like the shopkeepers, the innkeepers, tradesmen and others who had to pay it by law. And, since the churchwardens had the power to grant reductions and exemptions from the list, it gave scope for all forms of machinations and grumbling.

The overseer had to collect the money and distribute it according to the Vestry's directions, keeping an account of all the transactions: again, the relief given out was never enough for those who received it and he was subject also to a great deal of abuse from the parish poor, whom, married or unmarried, having no means to maintain themselves, he set to work. The overseer also supervised the poorhouse, if a village had one, set aside for its destitute, perhaps acting as a visitor or guardian to look after the welfare of the usual long-term inhabitants, the old crones and the deserted wives and children (who paid him lip service to his face and spoke scathingly of him behind his back). Sometimes the overseer was called upon to give relief in regular or casual small cash doles, or sometimes larger loans, supplemented by grants of clothing, shoes, bed linen, cloth, fuel, soap and, occasionally, tools for work. Sometimes, too, he was asked to pay a pauper's weekly or six-monthly rent, or his rates, or the fees for his burial, such as the coffinmaker's, the gravedigger's and the parson's charges, or the apothecary's or surgeon's bill for attending him or her before they died.

On occasions, he also paid for 'nurses' to sit with the dying, 'midwives' to sit with those giving birth and made payments to many an unmarried mother, as well as recording what payments were made by the fathers of the bastard children. Amongst the many extraneous duties foisted upon the overseer from time to time were the provision of a mortuary, perambulation of the boundaries, taking of censuses, supervision of the labour of rogues and vagabonds and the apprehension of lunatics: it was in effect, almost a full-time position.

At that time, voices were beginning to be heard throughout the Eastern Counties, indeed throughout the kingdom, declaring that the poverty amongst the labouring classes was more the result of their own fecklessness, immorality, idleness and drunkenness. Such complaints were particularly prevalent where the number of farmers paying into the poor rate had been drastically reduced by the abandonment of so many farms at the start of the depression as the folly of their borrowing during the war years caught up with them.

In the village of Salter, not five miles from Hamwick Dean, for instance, to reduce the relief given out to the poor of that place, the rate-paying parishioners had held a meeting to appoint a man to the office of overseer of the poor who was distinguished for his extreme parsimony and his hardness of heart, the result of which was a cruelty and oppression to the paupers of the village which they had not experienced before. One of its older inhabitants, a man named Moses Sack, was so regularly refused relief that he starved to death.

In this regard, the poor of Hamwick Dean and the two hamlets fared marginally better than those in many other places, though the begrudging of compassion was no different and the higher payers of all three places, the larger farmers, were frequently heard to observe that, since the ending of the war, the relief being doled out was far too readily given and merely encouraged these vices and discouraged honest labour by allowing the able-bodied day-labourers who were fit to work to draw on the poor rates. They complained, too, that what the unemployed labourers were given in money anyway they spent most of it sitting in the Carpenters' Arms or the Green Man or the Bull all day rather than on food for their families: and then went back a second time with their hands held out. It also encouraged the young men and girls to marry earlier than they might have done, the grumblers said, with the inevitable result that it increased the population too quickly because couples started their families earlier and over time had more children, seven, eight and nine in the same number of years, not caring if the fathers were out of work through being laid off in wintertime or through sickness as their wages would always be made up to subsistence level by the weekly dole.

Invariably, at the Easter Monday meetings, one or other of the ratepayers from the three parishes – several together sometimes – would complain that their contributions as a percentage of the poor rate were forever rising. For instance, in the past two years, the levy set on the Easter Monday had twice been raised in the summer and the autumn, they pointed out: further, the number of claimants for relief in the three parishes had also increased markedly, till it seemed half the males in each place were living 'on the parish.' Something needed to be done.

What was becoming clear to the non-farming ratepayers, if to no one else, was that, well intentioned as was the Speenhamland system of subsidising wages through poor relief, all it had succeeded in doing since the war had ended and the hard times had begun was to push down wages and subsidise the mean practices of the large farmers. In short, it encouraged an attitude amongst the six farmers that whatever they paid their labourers, no matter if it were not enough to keep body and soul of a man and his family together, the parish would still make up his wage to a level allowing subsistence at the very least.

It was the same all over. The country at that time was still far from being at peace: the disturbances around the nation caused by the despair of the Corn Laws were continuing. In Manchester, cotton spinners had gone on strike in the July and August of 1818 and there were riots in the nearby town of Stockport by power loom weavers, with yet more squatters' riots at Rhydoldog in Caernarvonshire: and in the November, there were food riots amongst colliers at Whitehaven in Cumbria. In the July of 1819, there were Orange riots against Catholics in Liverpool: then on August the sixteenth of that year came the so-called 'Peterloo massacre' in Manchester's St. Peter's Fields when untrained – and, some say, drunken – local militia and the Salford Yeomanry rode into a crowd of many thousands gathered on St. Peter's Fields to hear 'Orator' Hunt and other leading radicals demand the reform of Parliament. The troopers and mounted militia laid about the people with their sabres, resulting in nineteen dead and around five hundred wounded. There were other reform disturbances in the North at the silk-weaving town of Macclesfield and again in the cotton town of Stockport and, in the October, disturbances during a keelmen's strike at North Shields.

As it turned out, in that year of 1819, more and more of the day-labourers of Hamwick Dean, Lower Rackstead and Merchant Staplers were to go 'on the parish.' It was again wet and miserable and cold for the most part and the grain harvest was again poor and the market depressed as farmers and husbandmen everywhere harvested and rushed to market what grain they could in an attempt to get some return on their depleted product before the prices sank even lower, which invariably they did. The peculiar weather continued into October: indeed, on the very morning that Jem and Mary-Ann rose with the dawn to lift his patch of turnips, he found the ground unexpectedly covered by three inches of snow and lost a quarter of his crop.

That snow presaged a bitter winter: snow fell again heavily in the December and the January of 1820 was so cold there were ice floes in the Langwater estuary, while the Thames was frozen as far downstream as Kew, west of the capital, and ploughing was once again delayed. It was during this year that five of the husbandmen finally admitted defeat and surrendered their land to the Little Court at the Lady Day session: they no longer had the earnings to pay the rent or the will to continue. From then on, they would either go day-labouring, taking what work they could, or live off the parish as did so many others, sixty in Hamwick Dean alone at any one time, thirty in Lower Rackstead and twenty-five more in Merchant Staplers.

FORTY-THREE

THE CHANGE in the administration of the village's Vestry which was to affect Jem and many others had come about in the June of 1818, when an Act for the Regulation of Parish Vestries, applying to all vestries outside of London and Southwark without relevant local Acts or peculiar customs, had been passed by Parliament. It set rules for the conduct of meetings, disenfranchised persons who had not paid their rates, gave votes to non-resident occupiers and introduced a plural voting system, depending upon the rateable value of a man's or woman's property. Under it, a landowner with property worth fifty pounds or less, say, so long as he contributed to the rates, was eligible for one vote at a Vestry meeting and, for every further twenty-five pounds worth of property, he was awarded another vote up to a maximum of six.

The following year, 1819, a further Act to Amend the Law for the Relief of the Poor was also passed by Parliament, which added a resident clergyman to the ex-officio members of the Vestry, that is, those who became members by virtue of their office. The 'select' Vestry was now to consist of the parish incumbent, the churchwardens and the overseer of the poor, along with between five to twenty other parishioners elected annually by the 'open' Vestry. They were to be responsible for the operation of the Poor Laws in the parish.

Further, these 'select vestries,' as they were called, were told to distinguish between the 'deserving' and 'undeserving' poor, the latter group being deemed to be idle, extravagant or profligate. The Act also demanded better-kept accounting and either the enlargement of the existing poorhouse or the building of a new one, with the grouping of several parishes to provide the funding as well as the inmates. Under this legislation also, two Justices of the Peace would be required to administer poor relief, rather than only the one Justice as before, the object of which was to prevent 'generous' Justices from helping too greatly the poor who appealed to them for assistance, especially the 'undeserving poor.'

As was to be expected, the very first election meeting of the new select Vestry of Hamwick Dean and the two hamlets, held on the Easter Monday of 1820 in the nave of St. Bartholomew's, was attended by all the more prominent inhabitants of the three parishes. Amos Peakman, Marcus Howie and Joshua Godwin from Hamwick Dean were there, as were Silas Kempen and James Allen from Lower Rackstead, and Thomas Godbear from Merchant Staplers, all puffed with their own importance in view of the numbers of votes they held and all taking the main seats at the table either side of the Reverend Waters, who, as the chairman and Parson Petchey's representative, had seated himself in the middle.

It meant that Josiah Bright, who also served as the parish clerk as well as the Little Court clerk, was forced to one end with his pen and ink and minute book. Peter Sparshott led the smaller farmers and husbandmen, including Jem, Dick Dollery, Enos Diddams and others from the village, plus several from Lower Rackstead and Merchant Staplers. When they entered, they found themselves ushered into the pews along the south wall by Joshua Jaikes, he not wanting to antagonise the farmers by allowing them into their paid pews in the centre: it was an awkward start.

They had settled the matter of the next people's churchwarden for St. Bartholomew's, which was to be Peter Sparshott, who surprisingly volunteered his services to replace the retiring Andrew Norris. The baker did not say it, but serving alongside Joshua Jaikes over the two years had been the cause of his weariness, especially as Jaikes had indicated his willingness, indeed his determination, to continue as the parson's warden, which was only to be expected of him. It was too much for Andrew Norris. 'I can't work with the man,' was all the explanation he had ever given in the Wayfarers'. 'I just can't work with him!'

It so happened that the new Act now provided for the employment of a full-time overseer of the poor to give such relief as was ordered by the select Vestry in place of the previous 'volunteers' like William Hurrell. The long-serving revenuer, like Andrew Norris, had indicated his wish to retire from the position due to age and increasing infirmity: indeed, he had sent his apologies for absence that evening as he was too unwell to walk there from his ridge-top house. He had no wish to take over the post 'full time.'

It was for that reason that the meeting was so well attended. Now that the post of chief overseer of the poor was to become salaried at thirteen pounds and thirteen shillings per annum, with all expenses incurred repayable by the Vestry, there was someone who was very willing to take up that role full-time, one not so old and forgetful. The man nominated by Amos Peakman, seconded by Marcus Howie, supported by Joshua Godwin, the Reverend Waters, on the direction of the parson, even the larger farmers from Lower Rackstead and Merchant Staplers, was none other than the bailiff of the church's Glebe farm, Joshua Jaikes. In view of the ever increasing poor rate, the farmers in particular wanted to ensure the new overseer would be one who would not be too generous with their money.

When it was questioned by Caleb Chapman, 'as a matter of interest,' how Joshua Jaikes, as the bailiff of the Glebe farm and the holder of several acres on the open-fields, could take up the role 'full-time' – how he would even find the time – Marcus Howie jumped to his feet to claim that, apart from milking a dozen cows and providing cream for the parsonage and cheese and butter for the Tuesday market at Hamwyte, the bailiff of the small Glebe farm, which was only twenty-eight acres, after all, could easily combine the two and still continue as a churchwarden and verger as well. The butcher, William Hoskins, had managed to do his part as assistant overseer well enough while carrying on his business and performing his other tasks, he declared, as had the landlord of the Wayfarers, he recalled, when he had been the assistant. Besides, much of the work on the strips which Joshua Jaikes leased from the Church was done by his Glebe farm labourer, Lemuel Ring, as everyone well knew.

Believing he had satisfied everyone's concern, Marcus Howie sat down. However, the presence that evening of a Dissenter in their midst was to cause a rift within the Vestry and within the village and the two hamlets: for, though the Act specifically added a resident clergyman to the ex-officio members of the Vestry, meetings were not confined solely to Anglicans.

Dissenters, too, could also take part in the discussions and decision-making: and the Dissenter that evening was none other than Mr. Able, who had turned up at the meeting much to everyone's surprise, since it was the first time in a long time that he had been seen in the church. He had, in fact, ceased to attend St. Bartholomew's soon after Parson Petchey arrived in the village, preferring to drive himself and his wife in his gig over to Hamwyte each Sunday morning to attend the prayer meetings there of one or other of the 'Independents' rather than have to listen to the Reverend Doctor's long and painful sermons.

The portly lawyer was then approaching his sixtieth birthday and so had begun to think of giving up his practice in Hamwyte since his appearances at the various magistrates' courts and the Assizes and Quarter Sessions at Melchborough were becoming increasingly infrequent and tedious. He had, he said, served the dusty business of the law for more than thirty years, was comfortably off financially and he thought the post of overseer of the poor, combined with his continued stewardship of the Little Court, would serve to occupy him for several years to come till he went to meet his Maker – 'always assuming that He will want to meet me!' he would say with a twinkle in his eye when he sat in the Wayfarers' parlour.

Immediately, Mr. Able's nomination was proposed by Caleb Chapman, who perhaps saw a use of an empty outbuilding being made again if he were elected, since he passed all requirements, Amos Peakman was on his feet to oppose him. 'If the other members of the Vestry have any regard to their pockets or their characters, they will vote for Mr. Jaikes as overseer,' he declared. 'Respectable as he might be, Mr. Able is the last man we should choose to hold the office since he alone of all the villagers has turned away from a Christian church to join those who sit together without so much as a proper altar to pray at and who declare consecrated buildings like churches and ordained ministers like parsons irrelevant to people seeking God and, worse, do their spouting from their own chairs.' With that, he sat down with a thump.

Unusually for a peace-loving man, it was Peter Sparshott who started the rumpus. 'Is not a Dissenter a Christian like us?' the new people's churchwarden enquired. 'I see nothing wrong with belonging to a congregation which makes its own decisions about its affairs, independent of any higher authority such as bishops and elders. It makes sense to me. Sometimes I think it is a pity we cannot do the same in Hamwick Dean – ' There was a stifled protest from the Reverend Waters, but Peter Sparshott ignored him. ' – I see nothing against those who preach the gospel of brotherly love and regard all humans as being equal before God,' he went on. 'Mr. Able here has always been scrupulously fair and honest in his stewardship of the Little Court. Whether he be an Independent or not, he would make a fine overseer, in my opinion, and is more of a "substantial householder" than your nomination, who lives in a glebe farmhouse.'

Amos Peakman was on his feet again immediately to point out that the ratepayers of the parish had never voted Mr. Able into the stewardship of the Little Court: the husbandmen had done that themselves when the previous steward, Reuben Johnson, had given up the task several years previously and no one else had come forward to volunteer as his replacement. 'And there's another thing,' declared the red-faced farmer, 'there is a deal of fining going on at the Little Court for so-called wrongs by one against another, but none of you, so I am told, has ever been given the chance to examine the books the lawyer is supposed to keep of the money he collects in rent. I am told by someone that he has not seen hide nor hair of those books for nigh on four years and yet the lawyer is always drinking money away at the Wayfarers', so I am told.'

It was a blatant inference, almost an accusation, that there could be irregularities being concealed about which the other husbandmen knew nothing: that the money taken by the Little Court steward had probably been spent over the counter of the Wayfarers' or at other inns in Hamwyte, such as the White Hart, where Mr. Able also frequently liked to dine with his brother lawyers, as his rotund figure showed.

When called upon by Peter Sparshott to reply, the portly lawyer, though amused by all the fuss which was being caused, nevertheless, declared somewhat solemnly that he could not allow aspersions which had been cast upon his character and his honesty to go unchallenged, even when they were spoken in 'the heat of the moment' at a Vestry meeting amongst 'friends' by one seemingly totally ignorant of the laws of slander, for which he was prepared to forgive him, even though he was a lawyer himself and such words were actionable.

'Be that as it may,' he went on, calmly and quietly, 'the ledgers containing the details of rental collections by me over the past several years are available for inspection at all reasonable hours in this very church since they are kept in the parish chest. And, with regard to my appointment as steward of the Little Court, I did not elect myself. The post was vacant through the inertia of the members and might well have remained so had I not been requested to take up the position by the Squire himself before his sad demise and by my good friend, the Reverend Burlingham himself, before he also died, because no one else in the village was willing to put themselves forward and take on the onerous task. It was done as a favour to them as much as anyone. As to the fact that I am a Dissenter, it is well known that persons who have been Dissenters have, in the past, held the office of people's churchwarden without complaint.' Which was true: the Vestry had elected a previous Dissenter, one William Cracknall, as a churchwarden during the first Peace and he had performed all his duties save attending the church for services.

To stop them arguing further, the matter was put to the vote: it was expected that Joshua Jaikes must win in view of the numbers of votes which Amos Peakman and the other larger farmers could cast due to the value of their property, but Mr. Able also had his supporters, notably Peter Sparshott, Caleb Chapman, Andrew Norris, Ephraim Simms and Jack Tickle, who each had two votes, plus all the husbandmen and small farmers.

Though the result was a clear victory for Joshua Jaikes, by forty-nine 'votes' to thirty, with the Reverend Waters abstaining, Mr. Able's supporters were not to be silenced so easily. Noting the absence of several of the Lower Rackstead and Merchant Staplers ratepayers who had a vote each from their holdings, they argued that, as not all the members of the Vestry who could attend were present, a poll of all three parishes should be taken as that would be more fair, which succeeded only in sparking another furious argument about 'waste of time and money' and 'gerrymandering' and cries of 'pigswill.'

They might well have come to blows there and then had not the Reverend Waters intervened. 'Order, gentlemen, order!' he cried.

Only when tempers had cooled was it decided that a poll should be taken of the whole village and the two hamlets, opening at noon on the Wednesday and closing at eight o'clock on the Friday evening so as to give everyone plenty of time to vote: every male cottager above the age of eighteen was to be allowed to take part, including the day-labourers, but not the women, of course, unless they were landholders or ratepayers themselves. Caleb Chapman was appointed the returning officer since they would have to file into the bay-windowed parlour of the Wayfarers' to make their mark, which was likely to be most of the adult males in the joint parishes: the scrutiny and counting would then be done in the taproom by Peter Sparshott, with Caleb Chapman, the Reverend Waters and Joshua Godwin assisting, and the result so far declared each evening.

The next day, Tuesday, supporters of both candidates began their campaigning, though Mr. Able adamantly refused to canvass on his own behalf and, on the first day, drove off to Hamwyte in his gig with a wave of his hand, saying he had business to attend at the magistrates' court: and, as Caleb Chapman could not canvass for him either as he was one of the scrutineers, the actual campaigning was left to his supporters, who, as it turned out, were Jem, Dick Dollery, Enos Diddams, John Romble and a few others. They gleefully entered into the spirit of the lark: Jem wrote out a dozen placards, with 'Vote

Able,' printed large on them, some of which they tied to trees and others they speared with a stake cut from the hedgerows and planted firmly in the verges along The Street and Forge Lane and by the guidepost: they even went over to Lower Rackstead and Merchant Staplers to plant them there. Mysteriously, some were knocked over in the night or disappeared altogether to be replaced by ones proclaiming 'Vote Jaikes': it was obvious to Jem and the others that it was the work of Joshua Jaikes's cohort, Lemuel Ring, along with some of his friends, day-labourers also, who sometimes worked on the Glebe farm at hay-making and so were protecting their future livelihoods whether they wanted to or not.

In return, of course, their placards were also 'blown down by a wind in the night' or 'stolen by thieves' and replaced with ones for Mr. Able again. Curiously, not everything was down to Lemuel Ring: there were others, it seemed, who did not want a Dissenter as their overseer and, not knowing the difference between a Congregationalist and a Quaker, lumped them all together and wrote out their own placards, 'No Quakery here!' and even 'Damn all Popery!' and there was even some night-time scuffling and the splintering of wood as placards on both sides were uprooted and the sticks broken.

The result of the first day's polling, though not the final result, was announced from the yard of the Wayfarers' on the Wednesday evening by Peter Sparshott before a large crowd from all three parishes: loud cheers greeted the news that, on the first scrutiny, Mr. Able was ahead by a majority of thirty. The early hours of Thursday saw more planting and uprooting of placards and, when in the evening another large crowd gathered outside the Wayfarers' to hear how the voting had gone that day, Parson Petchey was called upon to declare the state of the poll, in the hope that his presence would show that, since it was being conducted in the presence of God's representative on earth, all was fair and above board, even though the parson did not go inside the inn, for to do so would have been a breach of his long-standing moral values against drink and ale houses – 'dens of iniquity,' as far as he was concerned.

'The vote is still in favour of Mr. Able,' was all he said, in a surprisingly sour-faced way when Peter Sparshott handed him the sheet of paper recording the count that far: and then he stalked off in something of a huff: his partiality, clearly, was for his bailiff. Dick Dollery called the parson a few names that night, though they were growled under his breath.

As it turned out, the actual state of the voting, announced by Peter Sparshott, was that Mr. Able's majority was down to only ten and, though the announcement was greeted by slightly muted cheers, Jem and the others consoled themselves that so far only two hundred and had voted and there were still more than a hundred who might be persuaded to make their mark for their candidate and they had the whole of Friday to do it.

However, when the final result was announced on the Friday evening, by some peculiarity, Joshua Jaikes was declared the winner by fifty votes: why so many had voted against Mr. Able at the last, when they had promised Dick Dollery that they would vote for 'his candidate,' puzzled them all.

A jubilant Joshua Jaikes sent Lemuel Ring to pin a notice on the church door for everyone to read, which at least proved to a scornful and doubting few in the Wayfarers' that the bailiff could write: '*At the close of the poll on Friday evening, the majority of votes recorded in my favour was a margin of fifty, notwithstanding all the influences which have been used against me by certain parties in this parish,*' he wrote, making no mention of his own supporters' activities. '*In standing as a candidate for the office of overseer of the poor, I was induced to do so by a number of respectable ratepayers, who have entertained a favourable opinion of my services as bailiff of Glebe farm and my service as verger and churchwarden. The dictates of my own conscience prompt me to promise to maintain the order and decorum of the parish office and to respect the existing laws and institutions of this land. It remains only for me to return my sincere thanks to those who have done me the honour to record their votes on my behalf.*'

Mr. Able read it with a smile and a sigh and resumed his drinking in the Wayfarers'.

The only heartening news for the majority of the villagers was that, though the Act allowed also for the appointment of a salaried assistant overseer, the members of the select Vestry baulked at paying a second man to replace William Hoskins: Jaikes would have to do it alone. No one doubted that Jaikes would have pressed for Lemuel Ring to be made his assistant, but the Vestry decided to leave the position vacant until such times as circumstances improved. However, as a consolation, at the very next Vestry meeting, Lemuel Ring was elected as the part-time 'pinder man,' that is, the one who rounded up any cows, pigs or sheep straying from the various areas of common pasture and impounded them in one of three fenced areas in the 'pinfold' or pound. He also became its dog-whipper, chasing off any dogs harrying animals on the common, and also ensuring that all pigs were ringed so they did not dig too deep and spoil the grass on the common!

The previous pinder man and dog-whipper, old Tobias Jacks, who had been the sexton, had been bitten by dogs more times than he cared to remember and had been knocked down a dozen and more times by charging pigs when he tried to ring them: there was hope in the Wayfarers' and the Carpenters' Arms that the same fate would befall Lemuel Ring.

Sadly, Old Tobias had had a kick from a heifer, which had broken his leg and, though he had been carried to a surgeon to have the bone splinted, paid for by the parish, everyone knew he was 'on his way out,' which was why Lemuel Ring got that job and why he became the new paid sexton as well, carrying out the more menial duties such as digging the graves for the burials, scything the grass in the churchyard and ringing the bell. The hope in the Wayfarers' was that he might accidentally fall into one of his own open graves one night…

FORTY-FOUR

AS A RESULT of the regime which the new, salaried overseer of the poor introduced, he became more hated than he had been before: for, with the appointment of Joshua Jaikes, the days when the overseer would provide the likes of old Hannah Hinchcliffe not only with her board and clothes but also with tobacco to smoke, or when he would pay a girl to go into one of the woods around the village to gather bluebells for the funeral of one of the aged paupers – as had been done by William Hurrell for old Samuel Cheney two years previously – those days were over, as they were, too, for the likes of Lizzie Tonkin, who relied upon the overseer for the occasional half bushel of potatoes, and the overly large Witney brood, who were frequently asking for a stone of flour or a round of cheese or an extra loaf of bread.

Over the next year, the new overseer was to be far more rigorous in implementing the Poor Law of the parish: the cost of operating it was to be combatted at every turn: abuses in relief were to be investigated: the labour test was to become more stringent: and the unemployed able-bodied men of the village and two hamlets who applied for relief were to be put to work breaking stones for road-building or cultivating land, going from farm to farm where and when they were needed under the roundsman system.

One thing Joshua Jaikes was determined on was that they would not be allowed to be idle and to while away their time drinking in the Carpenters' Arms or the Green Man or the Bull, or the Compasses and the Shoulder of Mutton, for that matter. He would see to it that his annual salary of thirteen pounds and thirteen shillings was well earned and he would ensure also that he would not give either the parson or the Vestry or the higher ratepayers of Hamwick Dean, Merchant Staplers and Lower Rackstead any cause for complaint.

Further, the deserving poor of the three parishes would no longer get their coal or firewood, old furniture or blankets, or half rolls of cloth to make a shirt or a working smock as a matter of right: in future, in view of the continually increasing demand upon the poor rate, the new overseer was required to be particular about every detail of his office, especially what he gave out in goods or money. Every pair of shoes, every petticoat, every blanket supplied or paid for was to be recorded and the recipient to be named as well: if he paid the rent of any paupers – and some had received weekly relief in money, food, medicine and fuel over the years, in some case over many years – then they, too, would be noted to see whether they were deserving or undeserving, whether they were able-bodied and able to work or not.

The mood of doling out relief was changing for the worse: and Joshua Jaikes was just the man to ensure things were done the way the larger ratepayers had always hoped they would be done. Indeed, one of his first acts was to have Lemuel Ring clear all the goods stored in William Hoskins's outbuilding and, with the permission of Parson Petchey, lock it 'for safe keeping' in a disused byre at the Glebe farm. So 'safe' was it, in fact, that not much was ever to be issued from it.

If it were actually possible, and the cynics in the Wayfarers' did not doubt it, the very act of doling out a pittance weekly to unemployed labourers with large families made Joshua Jaikes even more mean-minded than he was known to be, even amongst those who had worked for him on the Glebe farm. Day by day, week by week, he grew ever more resentful of the requests made to him from the impoverished day-labourers, dispensing the dole under degrading and ever harsher terms. It did not matter to him that people had large families of seven, eight and nine children and the men of the family and their sons of fifteen and sixteen, who were bachelors and still half-men, were out of work through being laid off in wintertime or through sickness.

Joshua Jaikes saw it as his bounden duty to relieve the ratepayers of the ever-growing burden of making up the wages of the poorly paid to subsistence level by a weekly dole: his way would be to break the poor of the habit of asking for relief, except for the most impoverished, who had nowhere else to turn, which, in effect, then was half the parish. They would still receive some relief, of course: he could always tell the parson he had given a man or a woman something to tide them over, but it would be at a level more akin to slow starvation, though, of course, he would never have acknowledged it as such, just that he had been able to reduce the amount doled out for such and such week by a certain number of pounds.

All that mattered to him was that, by reducing the amount of poor relief paid out, he reduced the grumbling of the larger ratepayers, his employers, in effect, and so earned their admiration for the way he conducted his business: if he did that, he considered that he was doing the job properly. Indeed, so severe was he that, during the first wintertime, he made poor William Abbott, an unemployed shepherd in his mid-fifties from Lower Rackstead, who had fallen ill with a hacking cough and a fever and had been laid off by Silas Kempen, walk to Hamwick Dean every day and back home again for six days a week just to collect each day's money of a sixpence to feed himself and his wife and five children.

Joshua Jaikes did not consider shepherding to be proper work and so, in rain, snow, hail and freezing fogs, he expected the poor shivering wretch to trudge into Hamwick Dean via the open ridge, down Heath Lane and Parsonage Lane and to wait at the church gate till he deigned to arrive to unlock the Vestry, get out the parish cash box and dispense relief from the parish's money. For four weeks that winter, the poor man came coughing and shivering and bent almost double into Hamwick Dean to receive his daily sixpence, till one day he did not appear and the villagers learned a short while later that he had died of pneumonia.

The most destitute of the paupers, the idiot 'Prickle' Witney, who was barely employable and reliant totally on the parish, he sent traipsing from house to house around all three parishes for six months, ordering that he remain one week and a night at each place, be given no money for the work he did, but was merely to receive food and lodging, the latter, as it turned out, in barns, stables, on one occasion in a pigsty and another in a kennel, for no one would have him in their house. He also deemed the young orphan girl, Mariah Cudmore, idle and slothful for living on the parish and sent her round to each of the five larger farmers in turn for them to give her work in their fields or kitchens so she would at least earn what little he allowed her.

Since much of an overseer of the poor's time and expense was spent in dealing with the problem of policing the Settlement issue, he offered, too, to keep out of the parish, at a bonus of sixpence a person, every 'rogue poor of other places' then abroad on the roads who might come trudging through the backlanes and byways of Lower Rackstead and Merchant Staplers, hoping to find work in Hamwick Dean.

Thus the man who that Easter became the overseer of the poor for Hamwick Dean, Merchant Staplers and Lower Rackstead. There was much groaning because of it in the Wayfarers' and the Carpenters' Arms and the Green Man at Lower Rackstead, and the Bull at Merchant Staplers, but Parson Petchey, who had suggested him in the first place and had enlisted the assistance of the larger farmers to elect him, seemed to be oblivious to what he had foisted upon the people of the three parishes.

He did not seem to know either that Joshua Jaikes was also a drinker. However, he did not drink in the village with the other men as none would have drunk with him anyway, but preferred to ride on his horse over to the Ship at Inworth, three-and-a-half-miles distant, away from the church and Parson Petchey's prying eyes, away from the curates, and away, too, from his fat, childless wife, where he could indulge and spit and display his callousness of mind and his coarseness of speech at will.

In fact, so callous and indifferent was the man that, when he heard the news that four Irish vagrants had been found dead in a ditch over at Levendon that winter, frozen to death while they slept, he had laughed. 'And a damned good job, too!' he had declared and then had jested aloud, much to the disgust of the landlord, Samuel Chaplin: 'I'd be happy to see a plague break out amongst all the damned Irish because they are nothing but a thieving bunch of wastrels. To my mind, their carcasses would make right good manure for the turnips I grow on my ground!'

'Me, I am for the old system,' he trumpeted on, 'when the young and the beggars found wandering abroad and begging off honest hard-working men were shipped off to the Colonies or otherwise got rid of or put into trade as apprentices. People are too soft now, too soft by half!'

It was to be to the dismay of the poorer labourers of the three parishes that Joshua Jaikes was to be re-elected to the same post the following year and the year after that and the year after that, each time at closed meetings in the church Vestry, for an open meeting with the whole village taking part would never have agreed to it. The sad part for many was that, rather than have to work with Joshua Jaikes any longer, a similarly wearied Peter Sparshott gave up his post as the people's churchwarden at one of the Easter Vestry meetings, like Andrew Norris 'unable to work with the man,' as he said in the Wayfarers'. Worse followed when, on the recommendation of Jaikes and the overwhelming votes of the Vestry of farmers, the vacancy was immediately filled by his cohort, Lemuel Ring.

It did not help matters that the peculiar weather appeared to have returned, though the cause of it was still unknown to those in England. The grain harvest of 1820 had been as poor as that of 1819 and the summer was equally as cold and wet: with no money to spare to hire anyone to help from the auction of roundsmen by the new overseer, Jem and Mary-Ann again did all the work themselves, labouring from sunrise to sundown, with hardly any benefit or profit to show for it.

Ahead, though they did not know it, lay further trials: snow fell again in late May of 1821 and lay for two days on the ground when Jem was getting in the last of his hay on the common pasture: then the rains of summer caused rivers and ditches to overflow and the land to flood and continued all through the late autumn when he was again lifting his vegetable crop of carrots and turnips on Third Field.

However, the day dawned clear and dry when the inhabitants of the three parishes gathered together to celebrate the coronation of the Prince Regent on the nineteenth of July, 1821. In its magnanimity, the Vestry, like others throughout the kingdom, voted to pay for a hogshead of ale, which the villagers duly drank dry, Jem and Mary-Ann joining Dick Dollery and his wife, Lizzie, and Enos Diddams and his wife, Emma, as well as Nathaniel Newman and William Stubbs and their wives, Ann and Aggie, in toasting 'the new King' a half-dozen times, till they forgot to do it and just drank the ale anyway. The village's celebrations went on late into the evening until the great bonfire built in the front yard of the Wayfarers' had collapsed to glowing embers and the last of the pig roasted on it had been eaten and the barrel had been emptied, of course, and most of the younger children were asleep in their parents' arms.

Hamwick Dean's celebrations with the two hamlets, however, were nothing compared with those in London. The coronation of George the Fourth, who had actually become King eighteen months before on the death of his father, George the Third, in the January of 1820, was one of the grandest ever seen, outdoing even the tyrant Napoleon's coronation as Emperor of the French. Parliament had voted a hundred thousand pounds for the costs, with an additional sum of a hundred and thirty-eight thousand paid out of money received from France's war indemnity under the Treaty of 1815.

The coronation itself had a Tudor-inspired theme, the new King himself selecting the costumes for all the main participants. His coronation crown itself was adorned with more than twelve thousand diamonds and twenty-four thousand pounds was spent on his coronation robe of crimson velvet with gold stars and ermine trim, the latter alone costing eight hundred and fifty pounds. The train stretched a full twenty-seven feet and required eight pages to carry it, all the eldest sons of peers of the realm, assisted by the Master of the Robes: following them in procession to Westminster Abbey were the barons of the Cinque Ports, carrying a cloth of gold coronation canopy, but, instead of covering the King with it, they walked behind the pages so that those at windows overlooking the route would be able to see their new monarch and marvel at the gold embroidery of his train, which was purposely held spread out.

After a five-hour service and ceremony in the Abbey, a coronation banquet for three hundred guests was held at Westminster Hall, with hundreds more, the families of the guests, looking on from the galleries. Dishes included turtle soup, salmon, turbot and trout, venison and veal, mutton and beef, braised ham and savoury pies, daubed geese and braised capon, lobster and crayfish, cold roast fowl and cold lamb, potatoes, peas and cauliflower: there were also mounted pastries, dishes of jellies and creams, over a thousand side dishes and nearly five hundred sauce boats brimming with lobster sauce, butter sauce and mint. Unhappily, the wives and children of the guests, who were seated in the galleries, could only watch their husbands and fathers feasting, for they had not been invited and so remained famished till His Majesty, having finished eating himself, departed for Carlton House – except the family of one enterprising peer, that is, who tied a capon in a napkin and tossed it up to his famished wife and children.

The only event to mar the day was when the King's estranged wife, the fat and ugly Caroline of Brunswick, having returned from abroad, tried to enter the Abbey and had to be prevented by prize fighters dressed as pages: that night, curiously, she fell ill with vomiting and an erratic pulse, almost as if she had swallowed poison: three weeks later she was dead.

During his banquet, the King responded to the good wishes of the dukes and other peers by standing and raising his glass to do them the honour of drinking their health and that of his 'good people.' When his 'good people' in Hamwick Dean and the two hamlets attached in the Hundred of Hamwyte awoke the following morning, still with sore heads and upset dispositions, they discovered that nothing had really changed, not even the peculiar weather: the harvest was again interrupted by heavy rains and did not provide the usual employment upon which whole day-labouring families relied in order to pay their rent and purchase new boots and other clothing and such items as meal, tobacco, coals, candles and soap.

Then, in the November and December, gales and the sodden state of the ground prevented sowing or 'fallowing' the land at the proper season. Resigned as he was to accept all this as his lot in life, since he had chosen the way himself, what Jem found hard to accept was that, in the two years following Thirza's birth, two other children were denied to him: in the first year, Mary-Ann gave birth to a still-born boy, whom they christened Daniel before the curate, the Reverend Waters, prayed him into his grave: and in the next year, he did the same for a girl, christened Mary-Jane, who was also still-born. After that, Jem knew there would be no more children: after that, his only joy would be in watching young Jed and little Thirza grow: all else seemed too hard for him to comprehend.

FORTY-FIVE

MARY-ANN knew for a fact that, after the deaths of Daniel and Mary-Jane, if Jem could have avoided it, he would not have gone to church as regularly as he felt himself forced to go: just once or twice a year, at Christmas and Easter Sunday, say, would have suited him: enough to keep faith with the Almighty and make sure he was not forgotten on Judgment Day. Other than that, like most of the men in the village who worked in the fields ten hours a day, he felt the Church was for women and the well-to-do, not for poor labourers like himself. It was a source of sadness to Mary-Ann that her husband should query his faith in the Almighty and sometimes question the wretchedness of the lot of a husbandman after so many poor harvests, so much bad weather, their continual lack of money, none of which had ever been intended when he had first set out on his venture.

It was not that Jem had become an atheist: just that, as he saw it, the Almighty did not provide for his family and the poor of other families in their hunger and wretchedness any more than he did for the negroes he had heard about on the sugar plantations of the West Indies and the Southern cotton fields of America, but He seemed more inclined to take away their children to the graveyard on a whim, which was a thing he could never understand.

Neither could he understand how those in high places, the gentry, the bishops, the archdeacons, the parsons and such, who had the means and could have tried to raise up him and his kind, instead did their utmost to keep them down in a state of wretchedness akin to serfdom: they were of the very class of men who sat as magistrates and who had sent Will Ponder and twenty-three others to the Assizes at Melchborough for judgment and who rode off to the next Assizes leaving twelve of them for hanging, notwithstanding that seven were reprieved.

Jem defied anyone to comprehend it: and yet he was expected to pray to Him to grant health and wealth and long life, not for himself and his family, but for a King who did not even know he existed, yet who was included in all the parson's prayers: and also expected him to to pay an annual tithe of several pounds, which he could scarcely afford, for the upkeep of a man who, then approaching his sixtieth year, was known to be one with a considerable inherited fortune, enough to have kept every villager in plenty for the whole of their lifetimes and yet, though having no children to whom he could pass it on, kept it all to himself and had no actual need to accept the substantial living which the parish of Hamwick Dean provided him.

Mary-Ann, however, was not one to complain of her lot: being a woman, she saw no sense in blaming the Lord for the lowliness of their state or the privations and misery they suffered: she reasoned, humbly, that the Lord must have other things to do than always to be spending His time watching over the poorest of his flock. Perhaps He was busy with more deserving cases elsewhere, like the poor despairing people packed five families to a house, from cellar to loft, in streets of squalid terraced dwellings in the grimy, smoky, soot-smothered mill towns of the North: and He would provide for them all in His good time.

Just as the other women sat with their husbands in church at Sunday communion so she liked to sit with her husband: and, like them, she responded as willingly and as fervently as they to the chants, lifted up her eyes to the Lord to sing the hymns of praise as tunefully as any of her sisters, recited her catechism better than most and, kneeling on the bare pew stool, screwed her eyes as tight shut as anyone and furrowed her brow as deeply as them all to ensure her prayers for her husband and children and for the souls of her two still-born and her hanged brother winged their way straight to Heaven.

So Jem continued to accompany Mary-Ann to church, not because of the chiding of his wife or because he feared the wrath of God or because the Reverend Doctor had said from the pulpit only a month before that everyone should attend at least one Sunday service, communion or evensong, to save his or her soul, but solely because, like others in the village, he had no wish to fall foul of the man who held the rental of the land he farmed and the cottage in which he and his family lived: but that is exactly what he was to do.

If there were one thing which irritated him, it was how the churchwardens, as well as being responsible for ensuring everyone remained throughout the service and did not slip out before it was over or the sermon had ended, were responsible, too, for seating each person in his or her place, according to their status and, in the case of women, according to their age, whether young or old, married or single. The church pews of St. Bartholomew's then were separated into 'islands,' so to call them, first by two aisles running the length of the nave from the chancel to the bell tower and then by a wide cross-aisle by which the congregation entered and dispersed to their places. Two of these square 'islands' were down the centre of the nave, in front of and at the back of the cross-aisle, two were to the left or north side of the church and divided from each other by the cross-aisle and the entrance, and the other, the longest, lay all along the south wall running almost the full length of the nave.

The prime section, of course, was directly in front of the chancel in the centre of the nave: that was where the rector's wife and the larger farmers and their wives and children always sat in their 'paid' pews, for it gave a clear view of the chancel and all happenings at the altar. The next most favoured section was again at the front, being the first half-dozen pews of the long and narrow 'island' lying all along the south wall, which was reserved for the churchwardens, the parish officers, the small farmers and the tradesmen of the village and their families. To the left side of the church, in front of the cross-aisle, there was a small section of pews where the aged widows and the latest residents of the village's poorhouse were placed, though a person sitting there had the misfortune of being close to the small, hand-pumped organ, which the parson had introduced after ejecting the Rackstead Players years before, and which was played for hymn-singing by his wife, though not well, with many missed keys. Anyone seated there was under her disapproving gaze whenever she crossed to the organ to play it and no fidgeting or whispering was possible.

The majority of the husbandmen and day labourers sat at the back of the church, some in the rear half of the long 'island' by the south wall, some in the square 'island' which lay immediately behind the cross-aisle and the font, which at least gave them a distant view into the chancel, and the rest in the pews along the north wall where the view of the chancel was obscured by a broad pillar. It was no surprise to Jem and Mary-Ann that, right from the start of their going to church together, they should find themselves directed by Joshua Jaikes to the front pew in this section, immediately inside the door, where their view was not only blocked but where, on gusty days, they were subject to every draught that came whistling in, even when the door was closed: their only consolation was that they shared it with Dick Dollery and his wife, Lizzie, and their girls.

'I think Jaikes has got a down on thee and me for some reason,' a grinning Dick Dollery remarked, tongue in cheek, in the Wayfarers' one evening, knowing full well what that reason was and, since most in the village despised the man, revelling in the fact that it was confirmation to him that he was one of the many.

In Jem's case, what Joshua Jaikes was making abundantly clear from all his surliness was that he had not forgotten or forgiven Jem for taking the parcel of land which 'Bunny' Hebborne's widow had surrendered six years previously and which he had wanted so badly, especially as he had had to wait a further two years before the next surrender, when a mere acre, a half-dozen roods and nine perches came up and not where he hoped it would either.

In the six years since, Jem had hardly had occasion to exchange a civil word with Jaikes: but since he accompanied Mary-Ann almost every Sunday, he was unable to avoid the surly gaze of the new senior churchwarden as he stood by the door ushering the people in. All during that time, neither he nor Mary-Ann ever received a 'Good morning' or a 'Good day' from him when they arrived or left the church, though, to Jem, that ostracism was worth the relief of never having to reply.

At that time, too, the churchwardens also controlled the order in which the male parishioners went up to the communion rail for Whitsun communion: for that simple act defined a man's position in the village. The three largest farmers, Amos Peakman, Marcus Howie and Joshua Godwin, went first and only when they had sat down did the small tenant farmers, like Peter Sparshott, Jonas Bunting, Reuben Frost and Peter Hull, with their lesser acreages, stand up and go to the front. Once they had returned, the tradesmen, the butchers and the bakers, the innkeepers, the wheelwright, the blacksmith, the cordwainer, the rakemaker and the wagoner and the like all went forward: and when they were back in their places, the lesser husbandmen, like Jem and Dick Dollery, if they were so inclined, went forward. Finally, after them, from the very back of the church, came the landless day-labourers, the drinkers in the Carpenters' Arms, again in an order decreed as those employed first, even if only temporarily in work, ahead of those unemployed and 'on the parish.'

Year after year, Jem had watched this happening, taken part in it, accepted the tradition, unbothered by it all: after all, the happenings in St. Bartholomew's were no different from the happenings in thousands of other churches throughout the land. But after the still-births of his two babies, the utter unfairness of how men 'supped at the Lord's table,' as the villagers regarded it, began to rankle with him: the more he thought of it, the more irritated he became. To him, it seemed, as if the day-labourers, particularly the unemployed day-labourers, were regarded as unworthy. Why should the poorest, those 'on the parish' without work, always be the last to go up, he asked himself.

'I was always taught all men were equal in the eyes of God,' Jem would argue with Mary-Ann, 'but we have created our own order of righteousness, starting with the parson and the bigger farmers like Peakman, Howie and Godwin and putting the poorest of the village last of all.' It needed someone to challenge this false hierarchy, this assumed order: at the next communion, Jem determined it would be him.

Come the fateful Sunday, as the three larger farmers, Amos Peakman, Marcus Howie and Joshua Godwin, rose to go to the rail, Jem pushed open the door of the pew and strode purposely towards the front, intent upon joining those who were men of the land like himself and whose only claim to a higher righteousness was that they each farmed twenty times more land than he and possessed greater wealth than he. If that were the criteria for deciding the order in which men received God's sustenance and Jesus's blood, then there was something wrong with it!

When the time came for the first of the farmers to go up, Joshua Jaikes would always station himself in the cross-aisle in front of the font, the better to direct the flow of communicants: thus, before Jem had taken a half-dozen steps, Jaikes stepped forward with a raised arm.

'They are not done yet,' he hissed. 'You are too soon. Go back to your seat and await your turn.'

'Why?' demanded Jem. 'Why should I wait my turn? Why should the poorest of us have to go up last? We are supposed to be drinking the blood of Jesus and eating the body of God, so we are told. Are we not all equal in God's eyes when we do that?'

The congregation behind saw instantly what was happening: the congregation in front only heard, but heads were quick to turn: an altercation in church was not to be missed, especially one which involved Joshua Jaikes.

As voices rose, so Lemuel Ring came hurrying over to assist. 'Be quiet! Be quiet!' he, too, hissed at Jem. 'You are in the House of God!'

'I know where I am well enough!' snorted Jem, still trying to push forward, 'but do you know where you are because it doesn't look like it to me the way you are acting?'

At that, the two seized the lanky husbandman by his arms, intending to propel him back to his seat: it was too much for Jem and with one heave, he threw off the both of them, not so much in anger as in irritation at being handled. Joshua Jaikes was thrown against the side of a pew and Lemuel Ring was sent stumbling backwards over the step of the font and finished up sitting with a hard bump on the flagged floor.

At that moment, Parson Petchey found himself forced to pause in administering the host: so many heads were turning to look back down the nave where voices were being raised that he could not help himself: whatever was happening there, it must end. What he did manage to see was Joshua Jaikes, his verger and senior churchwarden, holding one arm, his face contorted with pain, and Lemuel Ring, his other churchwarden, climbing to his feet and limping back to his place, rubbing a bruised backside. Unfortunately, he also saw Jem returning to his pew so he knew who had caused the commotion if not what it was all about: he would learn that later from his churchwardens.

Poor Mary-Ann. When Jem as reached the pew and sat down with as much dignity as he could muster following a violent rebuff, he was conscious that, beside him, Mary-Ann had bowed her head in embarrassment and shame, her cheeks as red as plums, aware that the eyes of the whole church were upon her and her husband, which even Lizzie Dollery's reassuring patting of her arm and the sympathetic looks of her friend's girls could not dispel. For their part, Dick Dollery, alongside, and Enos Diddams, behind them, were laughing fit to bust as were the other husbandmen and day-labourers behind, but all marvelling at his audacity in seeking to present himself as an equal of the other more well-to-do farmers.

The other womenfolk simply pulled their shawls across their mouths and tittered and looked at each other with eyes that spelled out the thought: 'See, no good ever comes of trying to ape your betters and him a man with just eight acres, one horse, five cows, a half-dozen scrawny sheep and ten geese grazing on the waste common and just the same as the rest of us!'

Though nothing was said then, for the remainder of the service, both Joshua Jaikes and Lemuel Ring glowered at Jem, the one massaging his arm, the other rubbing his backside, while Jem sat in his pew as stony-faced as a contented man could be. He had not achieved what he had intended, but he had challenged the unfairness of the system and given Jaikes and his sidekick, as well as the whole congregation, something to think about and so felt all the better for it.

Mary-Ann, however, was not so happy. Worse for her was the fact that, because of their placement in the church, they were always the last to leave and she had to stand in the pew beside her fool of a husband and wait while the rest of the congregation filed past out of the door, the greater number still smirking as they went.

There was not much Christian forgiveness in Joshua Jaikes's eyes when eventually they left: for he knew that he would have to make his report to Parson Petchey in the vestry as soon as the church was cleared. 'Be warned, Stebbings,' he hissed just before he closed the door on Jem and Mary-Ann. 'I won't be made a fool of in front of the parson and his lady and the whole village. So you be warned.'

Suffice it to say, after that, Jem never accepted the host again or was expected to and would not have been welcomed had he done so:. What did happen was that he did not go to church for the following three Sundays, though Mary-Ann went. However, before long, he was to have another brush with Joshua Jaikes and Lemuel Ring.

FORTY-SIX

ANOTHER OF Joshua Jaikes's actions on becoming the overseer for the three parishes was to persuade the members of the select Vestry to adopt a means of adding to the parish's coffers, one which he had brought from his home village in Lincolnshire, that of renting the grazing or mowing of the grass verges around the dozen or so lanes and roads of the village, it being far better grass than that on the trampled common pasture. His idea was to divide each length of verge into thirty 'gates' or lots at a cost of a pound per annum, with preference supposedly given to 'labouring men' of the village to keep a horse or cow on the verge, provided they kept them continually tethered by the head and ensured they were 'gated' by hurdles after sunset. Any cattle found wandering the roads or lanes during the hours of darkness were to be impounded in the pinfold as 'strays.'

The husbandmen and day-labourers of Hamwick Dean soon noticed that Lemuel Ring was impounding quite a number of 'straying' cattle, for it was a lucrative source of income for the Vestry and helped to reduce the poor rate levy. For a first offence, the owner of straying cows or lost sheep had to pay a shilling for each, which was increased to two shillings for each on a second offence and subsequently rose for each offence after that.

In that first year, the amount raised for the parish purse by Joshua Jaikes's 'pinfold' fines amounted to almost twelve pounds and two shillings, which pleased Parson Petchey no end, though it brought more grumbling in the Wayfarers' and the Carpenters' Arms. Men, particularly the hard-pressed day-labourers who tried to provide a little more for their families by keeping a solitary cow or a couple of goats, could not afford to pay fines when they were barely able to buy bread, when they never saw meat from one month to the next and when they lived on a diet of cabbage and turnip and onions and potatoes and meal.

Those who pegged their animals on the verges found, to their surprise, no matter how deep the peg had been sunk, the animals would somehow 'pull it out' in their desire to graze better grass farther along. What disturbed the husbandmen and day-labourers was that there seemed to be a growing number of straying animals: and more and more men in the Wayfarers' and the Carpenters' Arms found themselves paying a fine into the hands of one whom they detested and who never failed to smile slyly when the money was being handed over. Strangely, when the same method of roadside 'gates' was adopted at Lower Rackstead and Merchant Staplers, the number of straying animals rounded up was, by comparison, very few and far between, perhaps because the distance was too great for Lemuel Ring to bother.

Jem himself had rented three of the 'gates' along the Merchant Staplers' road, since it was near to his cottage on Arbour Lane. Most times he would herd his cows back into his own fold of hurdles on the common pasture to the west of the village, but sometimes he would leave them overnight in situ in the 'gate,' as other men did. One morning, when Mary-Ann and the four-year-old Jed went to fetch the cows for milking from where they had been left in the 'gate,' they found that every one of them had strayed during the night. It did not take long to track them down to the pinfold, where, as it turned out, Joshua Jaikes himself had ushered them in, helped by Lemuel Ring. It was the third time in as many months that Jem's cattle had strayed, though he never knew exactly how and he could only guess. Previously, he had been able to pay his fines, but now he was short of money.

It so happened, however, that young Jed had risen during the night: the bright moonlight streaming through the window had fallen upon his face to awaken him and a noise outside had sent him padding to the window to find out what it was. In consequence, he had seen something which puzzled him: why would a man be driving cows along the road in the middle of the night?

The next morning when Mary-Ann found the cows had gone, young Jed innocently told her. 'A man has hid them. I saw him last night, driving the cows away.'

When Mary-Ann told Jem what Jed had seen, he knew immediately what had happened. Without waiting to eat his breakfast meal, he stamped out of the cottage, followed by his curious son, and marched straight along Forge Lane and Parsonage Lane to the pinfold, threw open the gate with such force that one of the bars split when it banged against the bank, whacked his five cattle there hard on their rumps and drove them back out on to the road just as Joshua Jaikes and Lemuel Ring came hurrying out of the churchyard opposite, almost as if they had been waiting for him.

'What do you think you are doing?' demanded Joshua Jaikes.

'I'm taking my cows back,' declared Jem as he and young Jed herded the cows up the lane.

'Those cows are in the pinfold,' the overseer-cum-bailiff protested, hastily jumping back as one of the beasts cantered past him, almost knocking him over. 'You can't take them, you haven't paid your fine yet. They were found wandering last night. You have to pay the fine to get them back.'

'Wandering be damned!' exclaimed Jem. 'I'll be damned if I'm going to pay a fine to a man who unties my hurdles and drives my cows out, then has the gall to tell me they were straying when I damned well know they were not! Your friend Mister Ring here was seen.'

'Who says he saw me?' Lemuel Ring wanted to know, looking nervous.

'My boy here saw you,' Jem told him, which only produced a laugh from Joshua Jaikes.

'No one will take the word of a boy that young against an appointed parish officer,' he snorted as he followed Jem along the road. 'Whatever you say, you'll have to pay the fine. I intend to report it to the Vestry committee and we will let them decide. I think you will find they will take our word against yours. Your cows were found straying and put in the pinfold by Mister Ring, as is his bounden duty.'

'They were not straying, they were driven there deliberately!' Jem shouted back, giving each of his cows a further whack to send them trotting along the lane even faster.

'Mister Ring says he found them wandering – ' Joshua Jaikes began, still following.

'Then Mister Ring is a liar,' declared Jem. 'They were penned in by me last night. The hurdles were tied. Cows can't untie a hurdle. They were let loose on purpose.'

'You would take the word of a four-year-old over a parish-appointed man?' Joshua Jaikes queried with a sneer.

'Aye, I would take the word of any four-year-old, particularly my own, before I would take either of yours,' Jem retorted. 'You are a pair of rogues together and I don't know which of you is the worst.'

Unfortunately, for Jem, neither his word nor that of his son was good enough for the Vestry members who heard the case, namely Amos Peakman, Marcus Howie and Joshua Godwin, who sat as his judges: they felt duty bound to accept the pinder man's word and did so, fining Jem ten shillings and sixpence: that is, two shillings for each of his five cows and sixpence to mend the broken gate, which left Jem sitting in the Wayfarers' that evening with a face, as Dick Dollery described it, 'black as thunder.'

'I would lend it to thee if I had it, but I don't have none to spare,' said Dick Dollery, who at the time was as hard up as the rest of them.

'No matter,' Jem told him. 'Mister Jaikes's time will come. His time will come.'

That was not to be Jem's only run-in with Lemuel Ring: it was just unfortunate for him that the surly Lemuel Ring still tilled, sowed and harvested the land alongside Jem's acreage on the Ash Grove part of First Field for the Glebe farm bailiff-cum-overseer. With the incessant rains continuing to fall at that time, drainage on the open-fields had become a cause of much dissension and there were frequent arguments between neighbours and complaints of flooding lodged at the Little Court: for, though a good husbandman might dig trenches and ditches to drain his land, his effort could easily be rendered inefficient by the neglect of another, lazier husbandman next to him who dug none and there were always a few of those.

The absence of any hedges and ditches to divide the plots and the high number of owners rendered any satisfactory system of drainage all but impracticable, though the Little Court had made an attempt in the years before the war, appointing a 'field reeve,' with the authority to make drains at the expense of those upon whose land they were sited. However, the poor man had received so much abuse that he had quit within the first two years and his successor had lasted no longer after an assault by one enraged husbandman which had resulted in him being fined five pounds and lucky not to have the matter sent on to the magistrates at Hamwyte. Thereafter, no one would take up the post and the matter of one man's drainage affecting another's land was never properly resolved, except by argument and anger at the Little Court.

Whatever competence Lemuel Ring might have shown as a labourer on the Glebe farm, he was somewhat careless with his husbandry on Ash Grove: and, after the fracas in the church and argument about the pinfolded cattle, curious things began to happen. There had been incidents before, but Jem had dismissed them as accidents, such as finding his grain trodden down just before harvesting and his sheaves fallen when he and Mary-Ann had stood them carefully in stooks: now other things began to occur elsewhere.

As it happened, his land on the Farthing part of Third Field lay almost on the flat and he had always taken care in ploughing his drainage furrows properly. Yet, on arriving at his strips there soon after his argument over the host, he found his land was little more than a lake: and, though he spent the whole day digging a new drainage system, when he went back a few days later, he found someone had purposely stopped up the main drain he had dug with a load of thick, pulled weed and turf tossed deliberately into his furrow. The result was the water had backed up and swamped his growing wheat crop yet again, 'drowning' the shoots. His neighbours either side were both competent husbandmen and friends, so he knew they were above reproach. Clearly, someone had done it, but who? Jem had his suspicions, but they could not be proved.

Wherever men farmed them, the common fields were proverbial for quarrels and constant strife: men would argue for want of a mound to keep cattle within their own boundary: fights were not unusual and litigation was commonplace, with pleas and counter pleas even being taken before the judges of Assizes on occasion. Herdsmen fell out, men stole their neighbour's corn and grass and turned their cattle loose on purpose to destroy the crops of their antagonists and then pretended they had broken their fetters.

The open nature of the lands and the precarious character of the landmarks led inevitably to trespassing, to confusion of boundaries, and to quarrels: landmarks could easily be pulled up and a part of a crop ploughed under by the carelessness of another or, on the pastureland, one man's grass mown by another for his own hay. Several times Jem found the balks between his arable land on Ash Grove and Joshua Jaikes's land alongside had been carelessly ploughed up by Lemuel Ring: further, the strips were too narrow to be cross-harrowed or cross-ploughed, yet it was with some consternation that he arrived one morning to find Lemuel Ring had turned his plough as if on a headland across Jem's growing corn and had cut up more than his own was worth.

Jem had to go to the Little Court to seek redress, which he duly received and which only antagonised his Ash Grove neighbour all the more. Though Joshua Jaikes might be lording it about the village as the salaried overseer as well as remaining the church farm's bailiff and the church's verger and senior churchwarden, he was still subject to the rules and disciplines of the Little Court so long as he held his land and so was subject to the same fines as all the others, though some, noting the shrug he gave when the fine was imposed, suspected it was more than mere coincidence what had happened – that it was, in fact, deliberate.

Not long after that incident, Jem found that someone who had been driving twenty cattle along the driftway on the part of Long Field where his strips lay close to a track – because it had rained and there was no good path – had walked them twenty yards off their usual route to detour on to drier ground right across his land and his growing corn yet again. One of the other husbandmen said he thought he had seen Lemuel Ring rounding-up cattle on the common meadow nearby and supposed they were from the Glebe farm, but again Jem had no proof since it was done late in the evening when the field was empty and the twilight was deepening.

For want of better drainage, like a common ditch, say, as soon as it rained, the paths and cattle ways running between and sometimes across the three large open-fields turned to mud and others, who knew no other highway, simply followed the wagon routes of their fellows in driving their wagons along the edges of a man's land. Even those husbandmen and small farmers taking wagons across the common fields would do so across another's strips. Thus, one day on the Barrow lesser field, Jem found the ruts of wheels crossing four of his strips and it did not take him long to realise that the wagon was heading in the direction of the Glebe farm yet again.

Again, none of his other neighbours had seen anything amiss so he was unable to say who the culprit was: he only had his suspicions and all he could do was to soldier on. To his way of thinking, the whole atmosphere in the village had changed since his return: he did not know it, but it was about to change again.

FORTY-SEVEN

THE FIRST the villagers of Hamwick Dean knew of Titus Broake was when they were informed by Parson Petchey in his parish notices at the end of the Sunday morning service a fortnight before Christmas that year that a new owner was to take up residence in Hamwick Hall. The late lamented Squire's moated mansion had lain vacant for twelve years by then and had fallen into decay, while the two hundred acres of parkland behind the high clay-brick wall, once grazed by the Old Squire's own cows and sheep and those which the Welsh drovers brought to fatten for the London market, had long since become overgrown with tussocked grasses, greenwood saplings, patches of weed and thickets of blackthorn, bramble and gorse.

The due processes of the Chancery Court in London had ground slowly, more slowly than any others, but had finally reached their end: after exhaustive searches, no heir to the Darcy-Harpriggs had been found in this land or any other, though there was a rumour that one of that name had gone to Virginia as one of the Jamestown settlers of 1607 when a party of a hundred or so had formed the first actual English settlement in the New World on the banks of the James River – thirteen years before the Pilgrim Fathers even set foot on Plymouth Rock in Massachusetts.

Unfortunately, though that Darcy-Harprigg had survived the terrible hardships of the settlement's early years, he had been one of the three hundred killed fifteen years later when the disenchanted Algonquians attacked the out plantations. No offspring of his was known to have survived: and since none knew of any other heir to the estate, in this country or abroad, all that was the manor and estate of Hamwick Hall had reverted to the Crown and, in due course, was put up for auction, which is how Titus Broake bought it.

What the villagers did not know was that pure chance brought him to Hamwick Dean. While passing through Hamwyte one day in his pony and trap, scouting for farmland to purchase just north of the market town, he had seen instead a notice nailed to a tree by one of the town's constables, announcing the sale – at last – of the late Squire Darcy-Harprigg's mansion of Hamwick Hall, in the parish of

Hamwick Dean, three miles distant from the town. For sale with it was the surrounding estate of two hundred acres set southwest of the village, all the furniture and effects of the Hall itself, all outbuildings, the stables, barn, buttery and kiln for brick and tile-making, its neglected apple and plum orchards as well as the rights attached therein, which the Old Squire, having no longer any direct or indirect heir, could not have willed on anyway. The notice was a month old by then: the day after Titus Broake saw it, a gale blew it away.

The men standing in the Ash Grove part of First Field, which bordered the lane running down to the Hall, saw a stranger of no more than thirty years of age, with a moon-shaped face, hollow-cheeks, cold blue eyes, receding hairline and high-domed forehead, driving a pony and trap somewhat furiously down the hill through the late November gloom one afternoon, but, not knowing who he was, supposed him to be someone lost or in a hurry and cutting across to the Langridge road as unwise strangers sometimes did. So no one took much interest in him, though they thought it strange when a few minutes later he came bowling back up Hall Lane and disappeared down the hill towards Hamwyte whence he had come.

It was rumoured, but never confirmed to the villagers – and certainly Titus Broake would never have done such a thing – that the deaths of, first, his two older brothers in the war, both in the service of the King, and then his grieving widowed father had given him an inheritance of a great house and more than a thousand acres of land in Yorkshire, which, though not of the best quality, the arable being heavy loam and the greater part of the rest moorland and suitable only for sheep, was owned outright by the family as a result of indiscriminate enclosure, or seizure, a century previously. Along with this land went several stands of good timber, a water-powered sawmill, a stone quarry and various workers' cottages, all of which the inheritor, Titus Broake, had promptly set about selling, completing his final transaction that very autumn.

With a sizeable fortune in golden guineas locked in a strong box and placed under the seat of his pony and trap and two pistols and a sword stick lying beside him in case he should have to deal with any footpads on the way, he had come driving south, first, to deposit his money in the new bank at Melchborough, which he had observed from a map lay not too far from the ready market of the burgeoning capital itself and handily astride an old Roman route directly to it. Then, with a letter of credit from the manager of that bank, he had embarked on a tour around the environs east of the county town, each day widening his circle, looking for an estate which he might purchase outright and so begin his farming the following spring. The Corn Laws were a chance not to be missed: great amounts of money were to be made in buying up good corn-growing land in the South and putting it to the plough to grow wheat and oats and barley now that the import of grain was so strictly governed that hardly any, if any at all, came into the country. Prices per quarter ton were high – a hundred and twelve shillings – and had remained high for the previous two years and the Government was adamantly refusing to lower them: for that reason, he had sought a farm as near to London as he thought fit and, when he saw the Hamwick Hall estate advertised for auction, he had not hesitated.

He was keen to get to work as it was mid-winter already and for that reason, if he were to make a spring start, he did not want to waste too much time going round and round the county: he had found what he wanted within three days and that was good enough for him and, further, it was up for auction that very week and close enough to London for transport to be only a matter of a day's journey by wagon.

During the latter years of the war, he had attempted to persuade his father of the value of buying good corn land in the South, all to no avail, even though others were making fortunes from owning land: the old man was Yorkshire-born and bred and would have no truck with Southerners.

His death from typhoid after drinking contaminated well water earlier that year while walking through a village near to his estate could not have been more fortuitous, if somewhat overdue, in the son's opinion. Of course, it meant Titus Broake had probably missed the best bargains which had come on to the market around the capital a half-dozen years before when farms were being thrown up and foreclosure notices were being delivered by the score in Hundred after Hundred and great numbers of tenant farmers were not even waiting for those but were disappearing overnight. Still, Hamwick Hall suited his purpose so he took it.

No sooner did Titus Broake take up occupancy a fortnight later than a band of workmen appeared at the Hall, all strangers to the villagers, men from Melchborough, who seemed always to have a smirk on their faces when they saw the husbandmen trudging along the lanes to their fields as if they themselves were better men than those of Hamwick Dean, whom they regarded as 'nought but country bumpkins, swedes, clod-hoppers, straw-chewers and turnip eaters!' They chipped the arms of the Darcy-Harpriggs off the Seventeenth

Century carved stone fireplace in the great hall, removed two of the old gables on the frontage, pulled down the old timbered entrance porch and substituted one in brick faced with stone with a crenelated parapet, while at the eastern end, they began building a two-storey brick and timber wing, higher even than the main Hall itself though in keeping with it. Within the span of that spring and summer, they would rebuild, too, the farm's dilapidated barn and two of its outbuildings, which had been roofless and open to all weathers for several years simply because, after the death of his only son, the Old Squire had not had the will to maintain them.

Once the work on the Hall was under way, the new owner set about clearing and refurbishing the venerable pile: he dragged out the Squire's worm-eaten oak tables, his elmwood chairs with their faded coverings, his darkwood cabinets and squat, heavy-legged beds, and set fire to the lot in the yard. In so doing, he sent up such a pall of smoke that, with the breeze from the west, it drifted over the village and, it being a Monday wash day, the women had to rush out of their cottages and gather in their sheets and shirts and under things from where they had draped them on the hedgerows and fences.

Having endeared himself thus to the good folk of the village, Titus Broake had then − ostentatiously, some thought, though none used that word or knew of it − brought in furniture of his own on three carrier wagons chartered in London and trundled the whole thirty-eight miles to Hamwyte and then right through the centre of the village, with the tarpaulins either lifted up of blown up as they came up Chantrey hill on a sunlit early April evening so that all were able to see the goods for themselves and marvel at them. For it was furniture such as the villagers had never seen before, delicately-shaped, curved and carved pieces of polished red walnut, with coloured veneers and gold inlays, nobility's furniture, in their simple eyes, the very latest in fashion, ordered especially from the London workshop of a 'good Yorkshireman,' as Titus Broake called him in someone's hearing, a man by the name of 'Chippendale,' of whom no villager had ever heard and would have thought the name a funny one anyway.

Soon after, he sent for his young and pregnant wife and, as was to be expected, once she was in residence, Parson Petchey was quick to call with his wife to extend the church's welcome. Knowing the new owner to be 'a gentleman, he was keen to gauge what type of gentlemen he was − that is, monied, classically learned or hereditary, of which Titus Broake was the first and third but never the second:

and, thirdly, the call was made in the hope that he and his young wife would attend divine services at St. Bartholomew's when her confinement was complete and eventually, by their regular attendance, swell the church's coffers with a donation or two. However, even he found himself treated almost as an irritant by the new owner, who seemed to want only to get away and get on with his business about the estate and so excused himself from the drawing room within five minutes of the parson's arrival, leaving all discussion to his wife, which the Reverend Doctor, used to long, genial chats with others of his status at Oxford, thought the height of poor manners, though he did not say so, of course.

Parson Petchey was learning what a number of the Hundred's small and middling farmers of twenty to forty acres had already discovered when they had attended an auction of implements and stock of one of their own at Lower Rackstead a month after Titus Broake had moved into Hamwick Hall – and that was, the tall, fair-haired newcomer might be a gentleman by his birth, but he was certainly not at all one in his demeanour. A small farm of twenty-five acres, with house and outbuildings, known as Coppice farm, right on the hamlet's western edge, a stone's throw from Hamwick Dean's eastern waste and common pastureland, had come up for sale on the death of its actual owner, old Samuel Ruffle.

What quickly became apparent to the other yeomen farmers of the Hundred, who, having a little money to jingle in their pockets, had gathered in the yard, was that 'this newcomer chap' standing amongst them was wealthier than all three-dozen of them put together: and that he intended to spend it to get what he wanted. For when the bidding started, first for the farm's implements, a plough, a harrow and three scythes, Titus Broake so easily outbid them for each lot as it came under the hammer that eventually they stopped bidding altogether, at which point Titus Broake marched to the front and brusquely informed the auctioneer that he had not 'come to bid separately for each pail and pitchfork,' but that, if an agreement could be reached there and then, he would buy the farm outright, lock, stock and barrel, house, outbuildings, animals, everything, if their total worth could be assessed on the spot to the satisfaction of all concerned, that was himself. 'Auction or no auction,' he was not going to hang around in a farmyard while they put up every item separately.

Of course, with such a deal on offer, the auction was suspended there and then and eventually, after some blunt negotiation, Titus Broake and the auctioneer spat on their hands to seal the deal in the empty yard and the farm and all that went with it was his, all livestock, the implements of husbandry, the household furniture and other effects, nine useful dairy cows either in or with calves, three two-year-old heifers, one sow and twelve pigs, two ditto in farrow, one draught mare in foal, one two-year-old colt, one yearling colt, one new North Norfolk light swing plough, one cast-iron harrow, one narrow-wheel wagon, one ditto cart with head and tail ladders, a pair of extra six-inch-wide wheels to ditto, milk-carriage, five cow-cribs, six ladders, sheep-cribs, flake-hurdles, three sets of harness, bridles and saddles, chaff-box and knife, pig-troughs, hog-tubs, two single cheese-presses, two ditto tubs, double whey lead cheese-vats, tacks and stands, barrel-churn, bucket and yokes, three dozen sacks, cover for a cart, mash-tub, oval kivers, eight iron-bound casks, washing-tubs, brewing-copper nearly new, wagon-line, garden-tools, hay-knives; also a two-wheel neat and useful chaise with head and harness and sixteen tons of prime meadow hay.

It did not endear him to the other smaller and middling yeomen farmers of the Hundred, who had already stood for an hour in an exposed yard in the wind-streaming cold in the hope of picking up something cheaply, a couple of good milk cows, say, a half-dozen of the pigs, the old draught mare or Old Samuel's narrow-wheel wagon perhaps, though quite a few had their eyes on the new North Norfolk light swing plough with its cast-iron, self-sharpening share and improved mouldboard, which was far better than their own: though, if the prices were low enough, they would have accepted a cast-iron harrow or a two-wheeled cart or a set of horse harnesses or a grindstone or a turnip-cutter – anything so long as it was cheap.

The manner of Titus Broake's purchase of Coppice farm and all its contents was a talking point in the Wayfarers' and the Carpenters' Arms for days after, as was the fact that, within two days of the sale, most of what he had bought had been carted over to the manor estate by Daniel Gate ready to be put to use there.

FORTY-EIGHT

TITUS BROAKE'S ideas on farming were to prove vastly different to those still adhered to by Jem and the other husbandmen and also the large and small farmers of the three parishes: the great improvements which had been made in farming over the previous hundred years – new crops, crop rotations, selective breeding, new buildings and drainage, the use of new implements – played little or no part in any of their husbandry or, indeed, of many others throughout the whole of the Hamwyte Hundred. Jem, like all others on the great open-fields, still mostly followed the old rotation of wheat-barley-fallow, except when, in its wisdom, the Little Court thought it time they planted peas or beans or white turnips again along with the wheat: they had always done things that way and saw no reason to change.

The new owner of the ancient manor estate, however, did not intend to lag in his adoption of the new methods in agriculture. From the very first day of his arrival, things were to be done differently on the manor estate: and to ensure they were, he brought with him a bailiff, a Northern man like himself by the name of James Heginbotham, who had worked on his father's old Riding estate and was as blustering and strange-talking a fellow as his master, with the same driving, abrasive manner about him. Titus Broake set up him, his wife and two children in the bailiff's chambers at the Hall which the old squires had turned into a cattle byre, diverting one of the Melchborough bricklayers to rebuild the fireplace and chimney at one end and to knock a hole in one wall to fit a larger window even as the new bailiff and his family moved in. It was typical of the man, the villagers noted, that while he lived in the splendour of the Hall with his wife, his two dogs and the two maids he had quickly employed from amongst the village girls, his bailiff lived in a converted cow byre and was accorded as much respect by his master as was a day-labourer – to their way of thinking, none.

It was a measure of the man, too, that, on the simple premise that grass was good only for raising milk cows and at that time there was more profit in growing wheat for bread or barley for beer or oats for animal feed, he should immediately set about ploughing up the greater part of the two hundred acres of the park meadowland, which hitherto had been unploughed, even though it lay amid good corn-growing country. Johnny Thickbroom and Ned Munson, working full-time throughout the whole of the wet March and April, turned most of it within the span of that spring so that the smaller husbandmen, who themselves had land to be ploughed and who normally relied upon the village's two ploughmen to do it, had to hire ploughs and horses from the small farmers and do it themselves.

Even before the two ploughmen had completed their work, ten day-labourers from the village were hired for a whole fortnight to follow behind with horses and harrows and even wooden hammers to break up the clods on the newly turned acres: and four of the same men were then retained over a further week to drill half of the harrowed land with grain seed and the rest with turnips and beans and peas, using a new seed drill, which Titus Broake had bought and which James Heginbotham had trundled through the village for all to see. Everyone knew the benefit of a seed drill, of course, without his need to do that: a seed drill sowed in straight lines, which facilitated weeding and harvesting and was less wasteful than broadcasting seed by hand the old way: it was the cost which deterred Jem and the others from buying one, even between themselves: that, and each man being jealous of another.

Nor did the new owner of the manor estate leave any of his land fallow after the same gang of village men and their wives and children had taken his first harvest of wheat from the fields: instead, he had the land from which the corn had been cut ploughed again by Johnny Thickbroom and Ned Munson and then, under the watchful eye of his bailiff, who was as pushing as his master, sown with a vegetable crop under a system of crop rotation, of which Dick Dollery and a few others had heard talk and knew was called the 'Norfolk four-course,' though they had not much time for it themselves.

Dick Dollery had had it explained to him once by a man he had met in the snug of the Green Man at Lower Rackstead and so was able to explain the workings of it to all the others when he, Jem, Enos Diddams and the rest sat drinking their pots of ale in the bay-windowed parlour of the Wayfarers' discussing the goings-on at the manor estate. As Dick Dollery told it, a viscount named Townsend – 'called "Turnip" Townsend on account of his liking to grow turnips' – and another landowner, named Thomas Coke, whom he knew little about, had a few years back during the previous century evolved a system, whereby they did away with leaving a field fallow and rotated their crops over four years and got better produce as a result: it was called 'the Norfolk four course' simply because both men lived in Norfolk where it was first tried and it involved four rotations of crop.

The viscount and the other landowner, Dick Dollery explained, had encouraged other farmers around them to rotate their crops as well and the idea had spread. In fact, he had heard of it being used by several of the 'dunderheads' up in the next county – 'those who were strong in the arm and weak in the head – so there must be something in it.'

In the first year, they would grow wheat: but in the second year, instead of leaving the field fallow because the wheat, which was an exhausting crop, had taken too much out of the soil, they would grow beans or peas or vetches or turnips in the same field just like Titus Broake was doing – 'hitching the fallow,' as they called it. When they 'hitched the fallow,' they found the beans, peas, vetches or turnips they had planted mysteriously increased the yield of the crop which was planted in the field in the following year. Dick Dollery could not have explained it, but what they were doing, in effect, was taking nitrogen, an essential nutrient for all plants, out of the atmosphere and 'fixing' it in the soil even if the actual chemistry of it all was a complete mystery to the likes of him, Jem and the others.

In the third year, Dick Dollery went on, continuing his explanation, a spring corn, barley or oats, which were just as exhaustive to the soil, could again be sown in the same field: and, in the fourth and final year of the rotation, a mixture of clovers or temporary 'ley' grasses could be planted and they would again provide a restorative period in place of the fallow and, further, could be mown for hay, grazed or both.

It would not be a bad thing if jurors of the Little Court agreed to adopt it themselves, he suggested. It sounded as if it were all very scientific: perhaps they ought to make a point of mentioning it at the next meeting of the Little Court? All in good time, some answered, all in good time.

But as much as the newcomer's ways impressed the husbandmen and small farmers, they impressed even more the village's three large farmers, Amos Peakman, on his hundred and fifty-two acres of Goat Lodge farm to the east of the village, Marcus Howie, with his hundred and thirty-three enclosed acres at Smallponds, southeast of the village towards Merchant Staplers and Joshua Godwin, with his hundred and fourteen acres at Milepole farm along the Maydun-to-Wivencaster road, for after the first year they were induced by Titus Broake to adopt the same methods and ploughed, harrowed and dibbed turnips in their fields, hiring a few more of the day-labourers to do it, though still paying poor wages and laying them off when the work was done. In that respect, nothing had changed.

While the cultivation of the manor estate gave work to more of the village's day-labours, albeit sporadically and temporarily and poorly paid, it did not do for a man to complain: he needed to be grateful and simply to get on with the work, as the villagers learned in the early summer, just as the corn weeding got under way.

One disgruntled day-labourer, who had toiled for the new owner of the manor twelve hours that day, declared rather rashly within the smoky confines of the Carpenters' Arms: 'This Titus Broake chap will screw you down to the lowest penny of your wages same as all the others. If he can set you on at seven shilling when he ought to pay you seven and six, then seven shilling is what you will git and no arguing over it either!'

'A more tight-fisted, screwing, hard-set fellow I have never known in all my born days,' the day-labourer went on, his normal caution overcome through drink. 'He don't care so much as a gnat's eye about his workers – all he cares about is making money and then making more of it. He and that bailiff o' his works us from dawn till dark and there is never a thankee or a helping hand for anyone. And Gawd help the man who don't turn in a-cause he has a fever from being out in the rain – you either goos in or you don't goo in at all ever agin. He en't no different from the others – he'll lay you off same as they to suit his convenience and damn everyone! "If you don't like it, you can always go and work elsewhere. There's others willing to take your place!" is the only answer he and his bailiff ever gives.'

Some callow fellow must have reported what the man had said to the bailiff, Heginbotham, for when, at seven o'clock four mornings later, the day-labourer, his two sons and three others trudged the mile down the long hill to the manor estate together to begin work, they found Titus Broake seated in his gig blocking their path and, in front of him, Heginbotham, standing at the gate, barring their way, with a bull mastiff on a rope at his side.

'You men who complained about the wages, there's nothing for you here any more,' Titus Broake declared as the complainer with his two sons and the others halted. 'I won't be wanting any of you men again. You can all go, the lot of you. I shall be hiring other men to take your place.'

'What us, too?' asked one of the innocent companions, who had not even been in the ale house.

'Yes, all of you,' was Titus Broake's answer. 'You're with him so you go, too.'

'But how are we to manage?' pleaded the innocent man, almost in tears from the shock of it, and with four other children under the age of ten to keep and rent to pay. 'How am I to feed my family? How are any of us to do that?'

'Go on the parish,' Titus Broake told him. 'Now get off my land, the lot of you, or I'll have Heginbotham set the dog on you!'

As if out of spite, rather than going into the village to hire others, Titus Broake sent his bailiff riding the thirteen miles to Wivencaster with the wagoner, Daniel Gate, where he hired on the spot six Irish from a camp of them on the westernside heath there to take their places, employing them alongside the others from the village who remained for the whole fortnight of weed-picking at a shilling a day.

As far as the Irish gang were concerned, they were simply hired as extra labour, knowing nothing of the circumstances and not understanding the sullenness displayed towards them by the other men and lads, though they gave as good as they got when a fight broke out one night in the Carpenters' Arms and Jack Tickle had to send for the new parish constable, Elijah Candler, the cooper, an honest and respected man, who had been elected at the last Easter select Vestry meeting: he was content to let them fight it out and not to intervene. When eventually the fighting stopped and the reason for the villagers' hostility was explained to them, the Irishmen did say they had known nothing of it and had come simply because they were near to starving themselves and any work meant bread.

Titus Broake even billeted the Irish in the barn on straw and deducted fourpence a day from their pay for that, so that, in effect, he paid them only eightpence a day for their labour and they still tipped their hats to him and called him 'Sir' and 'Master.' It was work which, at the time, other village men were in desperate need of and, despite the grumblings of one, would have been prepared to take a reduced wage to do it.

No one then had a guarantee of employment. What the twelve men and three 'half-men' of the parish who had become dependent on Titus Broake and the manor estate for occasional day labour were learning was that the new owner of the manor had no sympathy for the sensibilities of the locals. He seemed to care nothing for the village itself or the well-being of those who lived there: they were simply a source of labour which he employed from time to time to arrive at his annual profit return. Indeed, he seemed more concerned over the quality of a crop and its rate of growth than he did over how the day-labourers he employed fared in their daily lives. In that, of course, he was no different from the likes of Amos Peakman, Marcus Howie and Joshua Godwin and three score other middling and large farmers in that Hundred and fifty score throughout the county and a thousand score elsewhere.

Jem's concern that year lay elsewhere, however, for the floods in the December had continued into the New Year and, in the February, a severe gale came roaring up the Langwater estuary, damaging several of the cottage roofs and uprooting many old trees in the woods surrounding the village because the ground was too sodden with rain to hold the roots. The cold and wet spring was followed by a summer which was again one of the coldest that people could remember and a harvest which was mediocre for all the husbandmen and small farmers – Titus Broake's first gathering-in included – and Jem's expenditure on seed, time, threshing and flour-milling turned out to be greater than his income from the milled flour.

FORTY-NINE

NOTWITHSTANDING having the greater part of the two hundred acres of his manor estate ploughed and sown with corn, turnips, peas and beans and vetches to his satisfaction and the purchase of Samuel Ruffle's twenty-five acres at Coppice on the boundary with Lower Rackstead, also sown the same, as if spurred on by some great need to establish himself above all others, once the harvest had been gathered in, Titus Broake also had a notice of eviction served on old Zeikiel Jaynes from Redhouse farm.

Redhouse had always been the 'home farm' for the Hall all during the time of the bishops and then the succession of Darcy-Harprigg squires who followed them and had continued right up to the Old Squire's death. All the time the wheels of the Chancery Court in London had been grinding away, old Zeikial had continued to farm it as his father had done before him and his grandfather before that. However, when the new owner of the manor arrived, he was the first to fall victim to his uncaring disposition.

Titus Broake employed a lawyer from Melchborough, by the name of Mogg, partner in Lilley and Mogg, to go through the deeds of the estate to establish that it had been ancient demesne to the owners of the manor from Norman times and, therefore, the farm was his to do with as he pleased and so he had his lawyer serve the eviction notice on old Zeikial, his wife and their thirty-five-year-old idiot son. They were given two days to gather their things and then were sent on their way with no more than a shrug of Titus Broake's shoulders as to where they should go and were last seen heading along the ridge-top road towards the poorhouse at Inworth with their possessions loaded on a farm wagon since the small pair of cottages on Forge Lane, which the Hamwick Dean Vestry maintained for the destitute poor of the village, were taken by two deserted wives and their nine children.

Hardly had Zeikiel and his wife and son gone than the new owner of the Hall brought in a half-dozen labourers from Hamwyte and paid them a shilling and fourpence a day to pull down the old three-roomed, timber-framed farmhouse and its barn and buttery and dairy, to burn its five-hundred-year-old oak beams and to cart away everything else, leaving no trace whatsoever of human occupancy on the site.

The old farmer barely lasted a twelve-month over at Inworth: he died of a broken heart, his wife said, but no one in Hamwick Dean knew for sure. They just blamed the callousness of Titus Broake for the old farmer's death: and there were some who even said aloud that it was a great shame to have demolished the old timber farmhouse, for it made a pleasant picture surrounded by its small grove of trees. It was even said by someone who saw him that a young artist had once come walking all the way from the next county, a mill owner's son, who had learned his painting in London, just to sit in a cornfield there and to paint the old place in water colours amid the rippling corn. All that remained by the time Titus Broake had finished was the small grove of trees which had ringed its pond and they were cropped hard that winter to provide fence posts for the ploughed land and in time would be felled altogether and the pond they ringed filled in and ploughed over.

It was not merely that the new owner of the Hall had replaced the benevolent Old Squire, it was the character of the man which so irritated the villagers – his abrasiveness, his unsympathetic ways:. For he spoke sharply and brashly to everyone and with an accent queer to them, who, being used to their own vernacular, found it vexing to hear such a strange dialect in their midst, one which, it was rumoured, was derived from Old Viking or Old Norse rather than Anglo-Saxon. And to have one of them come amongst them made it doubly disconcerting in view of the defeat the East Saxons had suffered at Maydun nine hundred years before to the ravening wolves of Norsemen.

It galled them particularly to find that the speaker of such a queer tongue was a bludgeoning, bull-headed, pompous, grasping, self-centred type of a man to a degree they had never experienced before: one who seemed to possess an amount of wealth far greater even than that of the late lamented Squire and greater even than some of the ermined estate owners in their grand hundred-year-old mansions built in the rolling hills to the north of Hamwyte in the times of the Second and Third Georges, yet he had none of the old world manners or gentleman's character or learning of the Old Squire.

For instance, he did not trot along the narrow lanes and byways on a grey, dappled hunter as if he were some feudal earldoman, but bowled around the village and the narrow high-banked lanes in his pony and trap as if he had to get everywhere in a hurry and would not stop for anyone, shouting at any who unwittingly impeded him, as he did to twelve-year-old John Thirkettle, herding a flock of sheep, who blocked his way coming along Hall Lane one day.

'Idiot boy!' Titus Broake shouted, standing up in his gig. 'Out of my way! Come on, out of my way! Get those damned sheep off the road!' At the same time, he flicked his whip across the flanks of his pony and drove straight through the flock, scattering them everywhere and breaking the leg of one ewe.

He said much the same to a half-dozen others: 'I'm in a hurry! Get those damned cattle...' or 'that damned horse...' or 'that damned wagon...' or 'those damned cows off the road and let me pass.'

From which of the Yorkshire Ridings Titus Broake came, none knew, but even before the first year was out many were already muttering under their breath that they wished he would go back there. Unfortunately for them, yet more was yet to come...

The concern of the husbandmen and small farmers, especially those who drank in the Wayfarers', was not so much the character of the newcomer but what would happen on the open-fields and the pastureland: for, by his purchase of the Hall, Titus Broake had, of course, also assumed ownership of all leases on the Old Squire's sixty or so acres spread throughout the three great open-fields in acres and half-acres as well as his acreage on the meadowland.

At one time, the lords of the manor, the various squires, had owned almost the whole area of the village, receiving it as part of their purchase of the bishop's old lands from the Crown in the Sixteenth Century, thus becoming also the proprietors of almost all the strips in the First Field, Long Field and Third Field. Then the Darcy-Harpriggs had been prosperous, having been shrewd enough in the middle of the following century to buy up a considerable number of building plots and timber-framed Tudor houses along the High Street in Hamwyte and for a while were the town's major property owners.

One black sheep sent their fortunes into rapid decline. Eighty-five years before, in the early years of the Eighteenth Century, the grandfather of the Old Squire had taken a liking to the dissolute attractions of London, particularly the gaming table, and, no sooner had he inherited the manor from his own father, than he had set off back to the capital in a coach, leaving the manor estate to be run by his aged mother, his wife and his young son, returning only now and again to sell off piecemeal another parcel of a few acres in Hamwick Dean or a property or building plot in Hamwyte to supplement his gambling needs. So over the years, the land which the villagers rented had gone to some two-dozen or so absent landlords, amongst them the dean and chapter of one of the colleges at Oxford University and the others people in a dozen other places and not a single one in Hamwick Dean. The Old Squire's father had restored the family's fortunes as best he could when he came of age, but, of course, had not farmed what had remained of the scattered strips himself, but had continued to rent them out at two shillings an acre: they were a part of his legacy to his son, the late lamented Old Squire, though they were greatly diminished in number.

Over the years, the various small parcels of land first sold by the black sheep of the Darcy-Harpriggs had been sold on by one landlord to another, almost entirely without the knowledge of those who tilled them, so it was not uncommon for a small farmer or husbandman to be called into the Little Court by the foreman and informed that, come the next Michaelmas, the tenure of the land they worked would pass into new ownership. Not that it bothered the men so long as the rents did not increase too greatly: they simply continued to pay their rent to the steward of the Little Court and to farm the land much as their forefathers had done.

The husbandmen got their answer when Titus Broake had Mr. Mogg write to the foreman of the Little Court, Peter Sparshott, giving notice that, in time, he intended to foreclose on any leases on 'manor land' right across the open-fields as he saw fit. For the present, since the acres and half-acres were so scattered, starting the next Michaelmas, those whose leases were due to expire then on land he owned as a result of and who would be seeking to renew them would be able to do so only annually rather than seven-yearly, fourteen-yearly or twenty-one yearly as before: in time, the yearly leases would apply to everyone on manor-owned land.

Unfortunately for them, yet more was yet to come.

FIFTY

THOUGH he was the owner of the Hall and its estate, Titus Broake required an Act of Parliament to grant him the actual lordship of the manor and the appurtenances and impropriatorial tithes attached: as such, within a month or two of taking up residence, he had instructed his lawyer, Mr. Mogg, to draw up just such a petition. Parliament took its time and none in the village knew of the petition till Parson Petchey climbed into the pulpit one Sunday in the late autumn and blandly announced that Parliament had approved it, an Act was in force and, in consequence, the new owner of Hamwick Hall was officially titled the lord of the manor: it caused groans in the church and much debate later that evening in the Wayfarers' and the Carpenters' Arms.

By an ancient statute, the property of the soil of the waste of Hamwick Dean had always been vested in the squires as lords of the manor. Under certain terms, they were allowed to make whatever enclosures, fencing, hedging and drainage they cared to make on the waste common, though the Old Squire had never done so and neither had his antecedents since the time of Henry the Eighth, when his family first came into them and the bishops lost them. For, under the terms of the statute, they would have been obliged to leave enough of the waste for the needs of their tenants and so just had not bothered, seeing no reason to incur an expense of fencing or hedging such rough, gorse-covered ground.

To the villagers, therefore, the waste land had always been theirs to roam freely, to keep their animals and their geese and ducks upon and even the place to go blackberrying and rabbiting, to pick hips and haws and to cut furze for their gardens and turf for their fires – which was why Titus Broake's next expansion came as such a shock to everyone: for by becoming the actual lord of the manor, he was also able to assume his rights over the waste which encircled the whole parish on its fringes – which he did.

Having completed the conversion of most of his two hundred acres to arable and done the same on Redhouse and Coppice, the new lord of the manor took up his rights to fence off the waste adjoining his estate to the west and northwest of the village along the banks of the Langwater stream, showing no concern whatsoever for the opposition of the villagers who depastured their goats and geese on the flood plain there and who one day found men from Hamwyte whom they did not know erecting hurdles across their path with the authority of the lord of the manor. No amount of arguing altered the fact and all they could do was to turn their animals around and drive them elesewhere.

At the same time, he also had Mr. Mogg write to the absentee owner of a consolidated five-acre parcel on the lesser Barrow field of First Field, offering to buy his land 'at a good price,' especially as it lay closest to the defunct Redhouse farm, divided from it only by the hedge, and he had heard that its fourteen-year lease was due to expire at the Michaelmas. The landowner was only too pleased to accept as he himself had no use for the land, which he had inherited from an antecedent anyway and he was being offered a price well above what he would have expected for it: selling it on was of no consequence to him.

The transaction was completed away from the jurisdiction of the Little Court and, come the autumn, the new lord of the manor blithely announced the purchase and had his bailiff, Heginbotham, plough up the balks and half-balks which separated the various strips and to fence it all off to form a single field as suited his purpose, without a care for poor Shadrach Johns, who had farmed it for thirty years and whom he had deposed and reduced at one stroke to a day-labourer.

In the months which followed, still more letters went out to other owners of land on Barrow, particularly those owning acreages on which the longer leases were nearing their end: no land was too small for Titus Broake to make an offer. Some land he bought was of a single acre only, some a mere dozen roods and fifteen or so perches, bought up even if scattered about the lesser field. Ownership, perch by rood, half-acre by acre, half-yardland to full-yardland was what mattered to Titus Broake: consolidation would come later: for now, the husbandmen would be offered one-year leases only.

It was abundantly clear to everyone that, given the opportunity, the new lord of the manor would willingly have bought up the whole of the parish little by little, or at least all the lands of the parish that suited him. Thus, a man who had farmed his two acres, twelve roods and eighteen perches or one acre, nine roods and twenty perches, say, or as much as eight acres, five roods and twenty perches all his life, suddenly found the means of his livelihood threatened, his future, before so assured, now uncertain, all through the expansion and greed of one man, an incomer and a Yorkshire one at that!

Titus Broake's acquisition of land was not to be confined solely to Hamwick Dean: in the summer of his second year, he bought up a small abandoned farm of fifteen acres on the southwestern side of Lower Rackstead parish, close to Samuel Ruffle's old Coppice place, where the boundary adjoined the northeastern corner of Hamwick Dean. Like others, unable to pay his tithes and taxes and payments on his mortgage, the bankrupted farmer had simply piled his furniture on to a cart, locked the farmhouse door and departed north to the cotton mills of Lancashire and ruing the day ever since as he lived now in a cellar dwelling in a street of terraced houses, it was said by someone who had received a letter from him by the post service.

Though Coppice and the new acquisition were separated by a tract of some ten acres of waste, no one doubted that in time it would be swallowed up and fenced and hedged off to form one farm of forty acres and Heginbotham or another bailiff installed. In a short time, by his takeover of Redhouse and Coppice farms, the waste land, which he had divided off for his own purposes with hurdles, and other purchases, not to mention his two hundred-acre manor estate, the new lord of the manor had become the holder of almost one-sixth of the total acreage of the parish – such was his wealth in comparison to the poverty of the villagers.

Fortunately for Jem, his acreage was all glebe land, which, is one of the reasons why eventually he went back to church of a Sunday: first, to placate Mary-Ann, but also so as not to upset Parson Petchey any more than he had done, though determined still not take the host and adamantly refusing to say 'Amen' at the end of all prayers. Nor would he join in any responses and no longer sang hymns either, though his voice was no loss, as Lizzie Dollery remarked, for she had a fine voice.

To some who sat and drank in the Wayfarers', the new owner of Hamwick Hall seemed bent on encircling the village: but no matter how great his wealth, one thing was assured, they would never regard him in the way they had regarded the old Darcy-Harpriggs, particularly their esteem towards the late Sir Evelyn.

An incomer he would always be.

FIFTY-ONE

IT WAS PERHAPS inevitable that, once Titus Broake had begun to acquire more and more of the lease-held land on the Barrow field, he should cast his eye towards the glebe land there and the glebe on the Thornbush and Ash Grove parts of First Field, where Jem farmed his separate acres-and-a-quarter, simply because of their proximity to the manor estate: the glebe was the next obvious acquisition. The problem for Titus Broake was how to acquire it. In the end, he concluded that the only way to achieve anything was to write directly to Parson Petchey, which he did in the April of his third year there, offering to purchase outright, at three pounds an acre, the twenty-six acres, sixteen roods and twenty-eight perches of Glebe farm down Mope Lane, adjoining the northern boundary of his manor estate, as well as the whole of the Church's thirty acres, ten roods and eighteen perches of glebe on the lesser Ash Grove field and any on the Thornbush and Barrow fields, too.

Jem and the other husbandmen, who were most threatened by this offer, remained in ignorance of it: they continued to farm their lands as usual, though Dick Dollery was to remark in the Wayfarers' long after that he had seen the new lord of the manor standing up in his pony and trap on Parsonage Lane one morning and peering over the bank on to the Glebe farm land: he thought it strange at the time, but gave it no further thought.

In his letter to the parson, Titus Broake simply declared that he had 'hopes of acquiring certain acreages within the parish,' which he expected were soon to come up for surrender, and, respectfully and humbly, he was asking if the parson could see his way to pursuing the matter of the sale of the glebe when next he attended His Grace the Bishop of Melchborough and 'having every hope of us reaching a mutual agreement beneficial, as well as satisfactory, to us both.'

The timing of his offer was not haphazard: for the new lord of the manor had read in the *County Weekly* that the tower of the ancient Gothic cathedral church in Melchborough was in danger of collapsing. Eighteen years before, in 1805, when the good citizens of the county town had learned of the great victory of Admiral Nelson at

Trafalgar, they, like the inhabitants of towns and villages throughout the country, had rung the bells of their medieval cathedral church in jubilation, even though, because of the war, it was in a state of some neglect – except they had rung the bells for several days in succession, resulting in a crack some ten feet long appearing down one side of the bell tower.

Even that might not have mattered had they repaired it, perhaps pulled down the old masonry and built it up again: but, due principally to the constraints caused by the war, that was not done: all the Church authorities did was to abandon ringing the tower bells, purchase a cheaper bell, mount it on an axle behind a wrought-iron railing in the churchyard and have it rung by the sexton turning a handle, though it was a poor substitute. For a start, the new bell, being cheaper, was far inferior: it had been carelessly cast, its tone was decidedly off and it had no range of which to boast when compared with the rich peel of the four great bells in the tower, which could be heard five miles off.

Ten years later, in their exuberance to mark the Duke of Wellington's great victory at Waterloo, the happy inhabitants of Melchborough had been so cheered by 'bloody Boney's' defeat that they had forgotten themselves and, ignoring the 'tuneless' smaller bell, had rung the four tower bells again. The outcome was to be expected: the crack widened and, what was worse, had lengthened also to thirty of the tower's eighty-five feet. As a precaution against collapse, the tower was hastily buttressed and had remained buttressed ever since and the sexton continued to summon the townspeople to holy observance by means of the less than melodious bell in the churchyard.

Then, that very winter, as the rains fell and soaked into the ground yet again, some workmen, digging a vault for one of the town's more prosperous and laudable families in the angle of the tower and the front wall of the nave, had dug their pit too close to the foundations, no more than two feet from the base of the tower, with the result that the tower had shifted on its foundations in a fierce gale and was in danger of complete collapse.

So immediate was the danger, in fact, that the upper blocks of stone on the embattlements had been removed for safety's sake lest they plummeted on to the heads of the congregations passing to and from divine services below. The desperate need was for money to demolish the tower entirely and rebuild it. Collections had been taken about the town and donations given by the wealthier citizens, to which the parsimonious tradesmen had added their guinea or two: but, in those straitened times, they were still a long way short of the Bishop's 'Tower Fund,' which had so upset him that he had gone off in a huff to Bath earlier than he normally did, before the season had even begun, 'to take the curative waters.'

Parson Petchey, in his first letter of reply, thanked the new lord of the manor for his 'sincere concern at the state of the cathedral church at Melchborough' and his kind offer 'to help with the restoration funds by offering to make a donation and also to help further by offering to take off the Church's hands the twenty-six acres, sixteen roods and twenty-eight perches of Glebe farm on Mope Lane and the thirty acres, ten roods and eighteen perches sited on the Ash Grove part of First Field and any other parcels on Barrow and Thornbush at present rented to the husbandmen.'

'I shall be pleased to place your kind offer before His Grace at the earliest convenient moment,' Parson Petchey had written. 'His Grace is away from the diocese at this time, but I can assure you his attention will be drawn to the matter immediately upon his return from Bath, which I do not expect to be before May or June at the earliest, when, I am sure, all due consideration and thought will be given to your generous offer to purchase the glebe acres, along with buildings and implements at the farm, all stock, dead or alive, et cetera, subject to there being no hindrance. Should His Grace, when he hears of your kind offer, decide, after due consideration, to go ahead with a transaction, he will, I am sure, expect the full remuneration to be paid immediately upon the completion of the transaction and I would, therefore, propose that you ensure you have the means to hand, perhaps a letter of credit worthiness from the manager of your bank, to convince His Grace that the matter is worth proceeding with. In the meantime, I will gladly forward your offer to His Grace and have no doubt that, when he hears of your kind suggestion, he will give the matter much thought and prayer so that we are guided in our deliberations not only by our own needs but by the hand of Him on High.'

Titus Broake was not too pleased with the reference to his 'credit worthiness,' but took heart from the fact that it was not an outright refusal: and so, in preparation, set aside a whole day from the time he devoted constantly to the management of his farms and the manor estate to drive in his pony and trap to Melchborough to obtain the very letter of credit worthiness which Parson Petchey had suggested he obtain for the Bishop, though it was to him a waste of time as he had enough funds in the bank to buy the Glebe farm and seven others like it outright. But he had no wish to flout the wishes of the stickler parson: if he wished for a letter of credit worthiness from the manager of the new bank in Melchborough High Street, then that is what he would be shown.

He even visited the cathedral church while in Melchborough and was seen by the verger to kneel down and to utter a quick prayer: not that Titus Broake was a man who prayed overmuch or sought spiritual guidance for what he did: he did what he did and everyone else could go hang! But he was visiting the cathedral church and he knew that someone would probably be watching and wondering who he was, the dean or the verger perhaps, and, if there were any further developments from his offer, they might also remember him, so he thought it best to look as if he were communing with 'Him on High' just in case, when, in fact, it was just an unintelligible mumbling, with not a religious word spoken as part of it, just a rapid moving of the lips. He had even walked backwards from the altar and, in doing so, had nearly tripped over the worn carpet in the aisle.

In fact, had he been required to categorise himself in matters of religion, Titus Broake would, if anything, have described himself as a strong agnostic, who, ever since he had arrived in the village, had attended divine services at St. Bartholomew's as few times as possible: indeed, the only time he had gone without protest had been for the christening of his son, Robert, in the first summer, but then that was an event to which any man would go.

Apart from that, once the business of his wife's 'churching' on the fortieth day after giving birth was dealt with, she rode up alone in her carriage to the church every Sunday morning and conspicuously sat in the front pew where the Old Squire had once also sat, almost as if it were a 'churching pew.' Titus Broake himself was rarely seen, except at the Christmas and at Easter and forty days after the latter for the Rogation Sunday blessing of the crops by the parson, or, as it was, by one of his curates, and then really as no more than a reminder to the clergy of his presence in the village, as well as a certain precaution against what might happen in the after-life – if indeed there were an 'after-life.'

Then, curiously, since the February of that year, he, too, it had been noticed by the villagers – without knowing the reason why – had suddenly become more frequent in his church attendance: and, as befitted his station, sitting in the front pew beside his wife, ahead of the parson's wife and the other farmers and their wives, who had all had to shift back one row to accommodate them, though Mrs. Petchey remained still in splendid isolation in a pew of her own and continued to play the small organ – poorly. Titus Broake was even pausing at the porch door to nod his head, smile and to say 'Thank you, Doctor' and compliment him on his sermon as he left. No one knew, of course, that he did so because he wanted to keep on the righteous side of the pious, hook-nosed clergyman, simply declaring that in the past the pressing matters of the restoring the estate and the two farms and seeing to his other land had kept him away and now that all that was in order he had more time to devote to spiritual matters.

In the same way, Titus Broake's visit to the cathedral church was simply to ascertain with his own eyes how close the tower was to actual collapse: he was pleased to learn from the same gloomy verger that, thanks to the stupidity of the excavators, the danger of collapse was indeed imminent. The diggers, it turned out, were Irish navvies and, being Catholics, there were quite a few who suspected them of sabotage in revenge for something Oliver Cromwell was supposed to have done at a town called Drogheda a hundred and fifty or so years before, though none could prove it. One glance upward revealed that, buttressed as the tower was, it would not do for a man to linger under it, especially if he heard a rumbling of any kind, though how a person was expected to differentiate between a collapsing tower and the sounds of wagons, coaches and carts rumbling past along the High Street not thirty feet away the verger did not say.

Titus Broake was pleased to learn that the trustees of the church had already made an application to Parliament for permission to rebuild the tower: indeed, they had made an application to take down and rebuild the greater part of the five-hundred-year-old church as well, nave, vestry and three side chapels: and for that they would require a great deal of money, even more than previously planned. Hence his offer to the Bishop via Parson Petchey to provide a modicum of that amount by purchasing the small Glebe farm to the north of his estate, as well as the many strips the Church owned in the Ash Grove, Barrow and Thornbush fields, responding as would any 'true Christian' to the Church in its hour of need and, as he had said in the letter, willing to pay above the market price.

Unfortunately, though Parson Petchey put the matter to His Grace in the April, by the June, the Bishop had still not returned from his gout-healing sojourn in Bath, which he had already extended on medical advice from two to five months and which he showed little signs of interrupting even then, despite the pressing needs of the cathedral church which he had left in the capable hands of the archdeacon. Further, in a second letter to Titus Broake, summarising His Grace's decision contained in a missive sent from the Bishop's lodgings in Bath, Parson Petchey had written that 'for the present, His Grace feels he must politely decline the offer.' However, he added that he did not see that this should be a closure of the matter and, should the sale of the Church's glebe land in Hamwick Dean become a matter of likelihood rather than necessity in the years ahead, he, Titus Broake, would certainly be 'considered as a potential purchaser and given every opportunity to make an offer.'

The lord of the manor had received his reply and, for the moment, he was prepared to bide his time: but not for too long: time was precious and he had a greater scheme in mind and had already begun to draw in those whom he deemed required to be drawn in.

FIFTY-TWO

THE TALK OF THE VILLAGE that June was that the new lord of the manor, or 'Squire Broake,' as they now grudgingly and somewhat sneeringly called him, had written to Hamwick Dean's three large farmers, Amos Peakman, Marcus Howie and Joshua Godwin, and the three substantial farmers of the two other parishes, Silas Kempen and James Allen in Lower Rackstead and Thomas Godbear in Merchant Staplers, inviting them and their wives to an evening dinner at Hamwick Hall, 'the gathering of the swine,' as some villagers called it and smiled at their own wit and sarcasm. They heard all about it afterwards from the two village girls who worked at the Hall as maids and who told their mothers on the following half-Sunday visit and, in due time, of course, the news was passed on in the Wayfarers' and the Carpenters' Arms and discussed in the same sarcastic and disgruntled fashion.

The six farmers' traps, all washed clean of muck and mud and their wheels freshly painted yellow and blue and red, rolled up the Hall driveway just after seven o'clock on a fine warm evening, when the peacocks which Titus Broake's wife had introduced to his grounds were sounding their piercing cries just as a blood red sun was setting beyond Maydun hill. A thin, reedy adolescent, dressed as a liveried footman, who answered to the name of 'Hepplethwaite,' who was said to be an orphan and whom Broake had, like Heginbotham, also brought down from Yorkshire, and whom, like him, no one liked or spoke to overly much, helped the womenfolk down, something which their husbands had not done since before their marriages, if at all then. Titus Broake and his wife were themselves waiting on the steps of the Hall to welcome each of them and conduct them inside.

On the great dining table, the sixteen-foot one in the panelled hall itself, two great silver candelabras were lit and there was an array of silver cutlery such as lesser folk never used: the food came in on silver platters carried by the two maids in white aprons, with the footman, now acting as a butler to serve the guests their wine and soup.

'Four different wines were on the table, as well as a jug of claret,' one of the girls told her mother, 'and all the cutlery was silver, five pieces either side of the plate, even a separate spoon for the soup. I have never seen anything like it in my life before and I expect I never shall again.'

The food itself was of a kind a normal farmer and his wife would never have dreamed of cooking: five courses – or was it six? – soup, salmon, goose, 'some things called entrees,' ice cream and two puddings, after which the women were taken on a tour of the Hall to see all the new furniture in the morning room and the sitting room as well as the drapes in the bedrooms and all those things which interest women, while the men retired to what had been the Old Squire's study to talk, to drink port wine and to smoke their pipes, before the evening ended with hearty goodbyes, handshakes and smiles amongst the men and flushed faces amongst the wives that they should have been treated so royally: and, just by being invited to the Hall, having their status confirmed as being well above the small farmers and their wives and so far above the lesser husbandmen and their wives as not to be worthy of mention.

The reason for the dinners was to reveal itself later: for the fact was that the three Hamwick Dean farmers, Amos Peakman, Marcus Howie and Joshua Godwin, all held their farms on copyhold, which was a medieval form of land tenure by which a parcel of land was granted to a person by a lord of the manor, say, in return for agricultural services: the transaction was recorded on the rolls of the manor by the steward, who gave the tenant an authenticated copy of the record: hence copyhold. In past times, leases from the lords of the manor were usually for the lifetime of the man, his wife and one other – perhaps their son – though a man could extend the family's occupancy of the farm to succeeding generations by buying a 'reversion,' though this was costly at five times the annual commercial value of the estate. Usually, too, transfer of lands held by copyhold was achieved by 'surrender and admittance': that is, the copyholder surrendered his land, to a baronial court, say, and the steward admitted the person designated by the previous holder – the son, say – to the land by recording the transfer on the rolls and issuing a copy to the new tenant: if nothing were done, the copyhold would revert to the lord of the manor, whoever he was.

It just so happened that, through the neglect of their fathers and their own neglect, due to the death of the Old Squire and the length of time the estate was in chancery, the three Hamwick Dean farmers needed to obtain reversions of their copyhold from the new lord of the manor, in the cases of Amos Peakman and Marcus Howie on a sizeable part of their land and in the case of Joshua Godwin on all of it. Tenure under copyhold was at the will of the lord of the manor, but there was at that time no lord of the manor!

Amos Peakman had been heard to say once in a rash outburst sometime after the Old Squire had died that his copyhold document had been lost in a fire during his father's time. 'I can't prove I ever had it,' he had snorted with a laugh. 'It is gone, lost, so perhaps it is as well the business of the estate is tied up in the courts in London because I don't know what I'd do if I were challenged on it. I don't have it.'

Everyone supposed that some kind of deal must have been done at the Hall that evening because Titus Broake did not seek to end or to challenge the copyholds of the three or insist upon a reversion payment being made: rather, he would seek the support of the Hamwick Dean farmers, as well as Silas Kempen, James Allen and Thomas Godbear, for a venture he had in mind, on condition that they undertook not to oppose it: indeed, if they joined him, they would benefit greatly from it.

FIFTY-THREE

TO TITUS BROAKE'S way of thinking, the open-field systems of Hamwick Dean, Lower Rackstead and Merchant Staplers were a lamentable waste: it irritated him beyond measure to ride past such great tracts of good corn-growing land which lay still in open-fields, knowing full well that, by the very way they were farmed by the husbandmen and small farmers, they were under-productive and, therefore, under-profitable, at least in the way which he regarded profitability. Too much of the land lay in acres and half-acres quite disjointed, with tenants under the same landowner crossing each other continually in performing their necessary daily tasks.

In his Riding, these defects of the ancient system of open arable fields and common pasture had long since been remedied: the land there had been enclosed and parcelled into farms of four hundred, five hundred and even a thousand acres since the middle of the previous century, some of it legally done by Act of Parliament, but much of it illegally done by the simple act of a titled landowner assuming a right to enclose the common waste and to bring it into production as nature intended: the land his father had left him had been enclosed that way by his grandfather and great-grandfather.

Too often, on his journeys around the three parishes, he had seen that the open arable fields were in a bad state and the common pastures in a neglected and unimproved condition, as were the numerous driftways for cattle and wagon ways crossing the area: and common-field arable, wherever it was, was always let for less than half the price of any enclosed arable adjoining it, while the common pastureland and common waste were seldom reckoned to be worth anything when valuing an estate that had a right on them.

Titus Broake had seen in his native Yorkshire that the advantages to be gained from enclosing open-field acreages were considerable: for example, where enclosures had been completed twenty to thirty years previously in his Riding, property had trebled in value, especially once the wastes had also been drained. Commons overrun with furze and ant-hills and worth only eight shillings an acre unenclosed, such as was the waste around Hamwick Dean and the heathland at Merchant Staplers and Lower Rackstead, would be worth from eighteen to twenty shillings an acre if converted, according to his estimations: and, even if the land were not converted to pasture but continued to be farmed as arable, the production of grain from the 'new' land would be increased greatly and, even where converted to pasture, the stock of sheep and cattle depastured on it would be improved markedly.

He could cite examples where a village's whole annual production of corn had been increased threefold by enclosure: for only on enclosed land could a man be the master of it all, unlike a husbandman and a small farmer, who, in truth, were only half-masters of the land they worked. For someone else owned it and others, like the Little Court, which they all attended so readily, especially on Lammas Day and at Michaelmas – they directed how a man should farm every single acre of it, what he should grow, when he should plough, when he should harvest, when he should turn his animals on to it: and then punished him if he transgressed any of their rules.

That was not the way to farm, in his opinion: a man needed to be able to make his own decisions on what he planted and where and when, following nature's good guidelines, of course, incorporated in the 'Norfolk four-course' system or the seven-year rotational system, if it suited his ground better, as it had on his father's land, whereby a three-year ley of grassland for pasturage was followed by two years in which wheat was grown upon it and then two years in which barley was sown, before the land was returned temporarily to grass once more, thus allowing the grain crops to grow on more fertile soil built up during the period under grass.

It irritated him, too, that those who farmed the open-fields of the various villages rarely had more than two or three acres contiguous and he had convinced himself that, as far as Hamwick Dean and the two hamlets were concerned, the local husbandmen and small farmers needed to adapt their inconvenient system of occupation to the improved practices of the new agriculture, of which he alone seemed to know the advantages.

To Titus Broake, the rotation of the crops still practised showed the villagers' ignorance: indeed, there were even fools amongst them who left their land to Nature's ravages, the worst acres simply being left to pasture and whatever seeds drifted in on the wind or were deposited by birds and animal droppings. These husbandmen on their scattered strips occupied some of the best land of the Hundred and yet areas of the ploughed land, where the soil was rich red marl, were completely exhausted and some years were simply left to weeds and became overgrown with furze, gorse and nettles through neglect. If enclosed and ploughed and properly drained, the land would yield far more bushels to the acre than was being got by the men he saw working it at present.

It was, he told the six farmers whom he invited to dinner at the Hall, simply 'barbarism' to allow the open arable fields to remain in their present 'open, unproductive and disgraceful state, solely owing to the expense of enclosure': he had said the same thing many times to his wife during his first year in the village and also to other large farmers and landowners of the Hundred whom he had met at the Farmers' Association meetings in the White Hart at Hamwyte or the Blue Boar at Maydun. Another thing: a man on enclosed land did not have to contend with the failings of a neighbour, which he had witnessed time and again on the open-fields: it made him despair at times to see how the neglect of one could ruin all the work of another alongside him, whether through a neighbour's laziness, his incompetence or his downright carelessness, such as ploughing up another's sown corn, driving a wagon across another's crops, neglecting to plough a drainage furrow or allowing a drainage furrow to silt up and flood everywhere.

It was because of its dreadful state that he had hurdled off the common waste on the flood plain of the Langwater stream to the northwest of the village: little or no provision was ever made for the support of the animals which grazed upon it in the winter, the ground was often churned by deep cart-ruts, it was perpetually in want of draining, was subject to pools of water forming and entirely spoiled in places by deep patches of mire created by the tread of the many hundreds of animals, where a man could sink to his calves if he were not careful.

The rest of the common waste, which encircled the parish on its outskirts was no different, to his mind: the cattle and sheep depastured on it were a miserable breed, pitiful, starved-looking creatures of a very inferior sort, subject to rot and scab in wet seasons, with little if any care being taken either in the breeding, feeding or preserving of them. The sheep, in particular, were kept solely for the sake of two or three fleeces and their meat, which was the last return most lived to make. To the east of the village, in fact, the common waste was so overstocked with sheep that cows would have starved if put upon it as the sheep ate every blade of grass and nothing was left for the cattle. Livestock, Titus Broake knew from his own experience in the Riding, thrived best and cost least on enclosed land: why could not the common-field farmers realise that, if a farmer had a long lease of his land, it paid him to go to the expense of fencing it off in separate fields with hedges and ditches?

For that matter, most of the waste was capable of being converted into tillage of the first quality, in his opinion: it needed only to be done as he had done with the parkland of the manor estate. Those parts of the common waste which were unsuitable for the plough – and there were some, he acknowledged – could be improved by management and drainage to a state whereby, instead of the ill-formed, poor, starved, meagre animals of little or no value that were depastured on them after harvest, there would be flocks of healthy sheep, providing an abundant supply of wool and mutton to send to the capital. In fact, the drainage was so little attended to in general on the common waste that, of at least a thousand sheep annually depastured, not more than forty on average were annually drawn out for slaughter or for other uses because infectious diseases swept the rest away.

Where there was a large common waste, like at Hamwick Dean, enclosure would be an advantage to the village's population, he reasoned to himself, since, instead of a horde of pilferers who built their cottages in back lanes overnight and used the common waste without rights and with no care for the use of others, as happened in other places, there would be a skilled band of agricultural labourers to till the turned earth and care for it and produce from it. Such were the times, in fact, that he suspected that some of those who depastured their cattle on the outer waste were 'certificated incomers,' men from nearby parishes which in the last few years had been enclosed allowed to come on to Hamwick Dean's waste because it still afforded them the means of keeping a cow and poultry, allowed them, too, to gather furze for fuel and put their pigs into the woods to eat the acorns: that needed to be stopped!

At the outer edges of the village, lost amid the narrow, high-banked back lanes which branched off from the main ways, particularly down the narrow, twisting route towards Lower Rackstead, he had seen the primitive and haphazardly built dwellings which had been thrown up overnight by squatters working hurriedly through the hours of darkness with whatever material came to hand – long branches cut from a nearby wood perhaps and furze gathered hastily for thatching from the heathland – so that, come the first light of dawn, simply by emitting smoke from his 'chimney' hole, a man was able, by an ancient law of that region, to claim the right to remain in a community. Even though most were abandoned after their inhabitants had been escorted back to their own places by Hamwick Dean's succession of parish constables, one or two remained, the poachers, the likely thieves: obdurate.

Enclosure – enclosure of the whole parish – even the three parishes as one – that was the only answer, he was convinced: he had no worries about the cost of such a thing: he had the means to fund his part of it: he needed only to ensure that other parties were brought on board. On that score, his lawyer in Melchborough, Mr. Mogg, had already set the wheels in motion. The cost of enclosure, the cost of the Bill to go before Parliament, the meetings which would be required, the lawyers to be hired, the commissioners to be paid, the fees for the surveyors and the printing of the plans, not to mention the post-enclosure costs of the fencing and hedging, the labourers to dig the ditches, the rerouting of some roads and the building, if necessary, of other roads – all of it, he knew, needed to be paid for, just as he understood, too, that the cost of it all varied from parish to parish, the amount depending upon the size of the parish and whether it was the whole parish being enclosed or merely the common and waste land.

Nothing he had heard from Mr. Mogg had deterred him, not for a second: indeed the more he considered it, the more his ambition grew: though there were those amongst the husbandmen in the Wayfarers', in particular, who, had they known of it, would have said the more he considered it, the more his greed grew.

FIFTY-FOUR

AS FAR AS the costs of enclosure were concerned, Titus Broake and his lawyer, Mr. Mogg, adjudged Hamwick Dean and the two hamlets to be in the middle grouping, neither overly large nor small: perhaps fifteen hundred to two thousand pounds, they estimated, would be the overall cost of it, if the examples witnessed in other places were anything to go by: and he and the other parties could easily manage that, he was convinced. It was for that reason, as a beginning, he had invited Amos Peakman, Marcus Howie, and Joshua Godwin, as well as the two farmers from Lower Rackstead and the one from Merchant Staplers who mattered, to dinner at the Hall, to sound them out: if they wanted to expand their own domains, they would have to contribute, for every farmer who received an allocation of land under an enclosure award was obliged to pay a share of the costs of everything.

The reaction of the six had pleased the new lord of the manor: they had been flattered to have been asked to the Hall and none would do anything which might upset their wives' new prestige: so they had listened to his views and generally were in agreement with them. For example, it appealed to them that the expense to be incurred in fencing and hedging-in enclosed land, while it might be excessive in one year, after that, they would have no further expense at all.

However, they baulked somewhat at the cost which the making of any new roads might entail, though they accepted that such a provision would be necessary under enclosure since the old public roads had been nigh impassable for too long. The roads, for the most part, were unmade and rutted, potholed and puddled, mired in the winter by the rolling of the wagons and the tramp of hooves and poorly repaired each spring by those on parish relief by the simple expedient of drawing a wheelless wagon along them to flatten the ridges and depressions and then throwing down sand and gravel from the village's pit and pounding it flat.

As Titus Broake had told them, good turnpike roads needed to be introduced, especially in a country where so much rain fell at almost any time of the year: and, if places like Hamwyte and Melchborough and Hamwick Dean could be more energetic in repairing their approaches, then enclosure and the improvements in cultivating the commonable lands need no longer be neglected, particularly with a major market less than a day's travel away.

Titus Broake aimed to ensure that all this was carried out and he could be a very persuasive man, especially when addressing guests flushed and languid after drinking between them three decanters of sherry and two of port. For example, he also told the six farmers – and they in their bucolic haze agreed wholeheartedly with him – that it was of no concern of theirs if some of the small farmers, 'the twenty-acre men,' who did not possess large amounts of capital, would find such costs too heavy a burden. Their concern should be that the land in Hamwick Dean, Lower Rackstead and Merchant Staplers was 'being wastefully, woefully and ruinously farmed by small farmers and incompetent husbandmen': and, if the smaller farmers and husbandmen could not afford to take up a part of the costs, then they would fall by the wayside. That was life: had it not ever been so?

The husbandman's and small farmer's yearly obligation to plough and crop all soils alike, the impossibility of improving sheep stock because of the crowded commons, the difficulty of growing food for their winter keep, the expense, trouble and excessive number of horses required to cultivate all the detached and dispersed lands – they were all disadvantages of open-field husbandry which must be swept away. What did it matter if it deprived cottagers of producing food for a few half-starved sheep and geese on the common? The loss of a few trifling advantages of individuals ought not to stand in the way of improvements such as they could make.

'Hear, hear,' echoed the six farmers amid the clouds of pipe tobacco. 'Damned right, sir, damned right!' But then what else could they say, since there was still the matter of the copyhold reversions to be attended to...

Enclosure, Titus Broake informed them, meant the creation of bigger farms of five hundred, six hundred and seven hundred acres or more which would provide incentives for investment, which would allow the owner control over exploitation and, in general, ensure that resources would be put to their most efficient use. It would also mean that more grain would be grown, more sheep and cattle raised, and, therefore, fewer people would starve in the long run, he informed them, blithely forgetting those villages in Cambridgeshire and Bedfordshire, where good arable land had been enclosed just before the war and turned into pastureland for thousands of sheep and great herds of cattle, which meant that the villagers who had been denied their livelihoods had not even been able to go day-labouring since all sheep needed were a shepherd or two and cattle a herdsman or two – the villagers had starved anyway and the exodus to the towns had begun.

'We are farmers, it is our job to feed nation, the population is growing, it is time we acted,' he declared and the six farmers chorused their agreement. Indeed, everything the lord of the manor said made sense and pleased them: all six got into their traps and went home smiling to themselves, so the maids said later, though for reasons different from why their wives were also smiling.

Jem, meanwhile, knowing nothing of Titus Broake's opinion of the husbandmen and small farmers and their ways of agriculture, continued to work his land, though the weather was no better than before. The rains had poured down for days on end – weeks on end, it seemed: the crops were flattened in the fields, their growth stunted: everywhere the fields were waterlogged again where there was no drainage so that half the harvest was lost before it was even time to begin the mowing and then it was a race to gather in what there was.

On many a day, all Jem could do was to stand and watch as the rain teemed down and then try to dig channels to run off the water, but the furrow ditches were already overflowing and the rain kept falling, ruining the grain in the arable fields and on the waste causing an illnesses which decimated the sheep so that in one week he lost two-thirds of his small flock, as did others. His troubles, however, did not end there.

FIFTY-FIVE

HAMWICK DEAN had never seen an occasion like the great assembly in the churchyard which occurred one gale-blown Sunday morning in the August, not in the nearly seven hundred and fifty years of the village's history, not since the very place where the Glebe farm stood had received a visit from one of the Conqueror's scribes and two lines were given to the settlement on Mope Lane in the Domesday Book, of the farm being inhabited by one churl, six pigs, a horse and four cows, with dwelling, which was all Hamwick Dean was then.

The whole village, it seemed, were ahead of Jem and Mary-Ann as they struggled up the lane against the ferocity of the wind, the men clutching at their hats, the women drawing their shawls more tightly about them as twigs torn from the trees whirled about their heads. In fact, so many were there making for the churchyard that Jem and Mary-Ann had to take their turn to pass through the small iron gate and some, being more impatient than others, forced their way through gaps in the hedgerow to get ahead of their neighbours and discover for themselves what was the cause of it all.

What Jem and Mary-Ann found was a jostling and seething mass around the porch, those at the back craning their necks to see what was tacked on the church door itself and those at the front calling out what it was to those behind above the babble of voices in between. That something momentous had occurred was evident from the many small groups of women who by that time had detached themselves from the main crowd at the church porch and were standing with anxious faces in small sullen groups amongst the gravestones, uncaring of whether they stepped on the mounds covering the dead or whether their children were chasing across them, whereas in normal times they would have picked their way carefully between so as not to offend any living relative.

The cause of the fuss was a notice, printed in bold scroll italic, tacked to the church door and addressed *'to all those whom these matters shall come unto or concern,'* announcing that an application was to be made to Parliament for a Bill to *'divide, allot and enclose, or to divide and allot only; and also for draining and improving all the open and common fields, common meadows, common pastures and commonable lands and waste ground in the parish of Hamwick Dean, and in the hamlet or tithing of Lower Rackstead, and also in the hamlet or tithing of Merchant Staplers, all in the Hundred of Hamwyte in the said county, with power to divide and allot, with consent of the respective owners and upon just and reasonable allowances, any homesteads, gardens, orchards and old enclosed arable, meadow and pasture land and other ancient enclosures and lands lying in all of the said parishes...'*

There were thirty-eight signatories to the notice of petition: and the name of Titus Broake was at the very top. Yet it was no surprise, it was almost to be expected of the man and many now declared they had suspected that was his intention since first coming to the village and taking over the Hall. After all, had he not incorporated Redhouse farm, taken Coppice and another small farm at Lower Rackstead, and then roved around the parish looking at other places to buy-up as well as threatening to foreclose on land owned by the Old Squire on part of Barrow field? And was he not always openly disdainful of their husbandry practices and their village ways? In retrospect, it was no surprise at all, they said to themselves, that he should make such a move which now threatened their freedom and security.

Nor was it a surprise, though it stoked the anger of many on that blustery Sunday morning, that three of the names below that of the lord of the manor were 'Amos Peakman, Marcus Howie and Joshua Godwin, farmers of Hamwick Dean', indeed: it was as if the three did not care that there was hardly a man or a half-man or lad in the village or the two hamlets who had not worked at some time for one or other of them, some for their fathers even and one still living aged eighty-seven for the grandfather of one, ploughing, broadcasting, weeding the crops, dibbing the peas and beans and turnips, gathering-in the harvest and helping with the threshing and winnowing in the barn. No one had ever disputed that there was land enough for all around the village: now Titus Broake and the sons of the old farmers were seizing an opportunity to extend their holdings at the expense of others and with it their wealth and authority: for their object, all recognised, was the complete enclosure of all the land in the three parishes.

Of the other names on the petition, most were unknown to them, for their owners lived either in London, Oxford, Melchborough, Wivencaster or a string of other places: one, a Lady Amelia Blight, for instance, who owned a good third of the land at Lower Rackstead, amounting to several hundred acres, lived in Somerset and they supposed it to be in some great country house with servants and footmen and gardeners, though no one knew exactly where or, for that matter, what exactly her connection was to the hamlet other than she had inherited all her lands by the marriage she had made. Another name was that of the Dowager Marchioness of Thrapstone, who lived somewhere in the Midlands and who owned most of the rest of Lower Rackstead's acreage.

Two knighted gentlemen on it were known to them, however: for Sir Gentry Giblin and Sir Benton Brierley, prime landlords at Merchant Staplers, with three hundred and eighty acres and three hundred and twenty acres of the arable and common, respectively, were the two Members of Parliament for Hamwyte, though they were rarely seen in the town, except at General Election time when they needed to canvass for votes, and never at all in Hamwick Dean or the other parishes that anyone could remember, preferring to live their lives in London where life was more cultured and the society immeasurably more sophisticated.

That the sympathies of the village's three self-elevated farmers should lie not with the misfortunes of the poor husbandmen and small farmers but with those with whom they supposed themselves equals was to be expected: the greater disappointment was that Silas Kempen and James Allen, in Lower Rackstead, and Thomas Godbear, in Merchant Staplers, had allowed their names to be appended as well since their fathers had once been husbandmen themselves and in the old days had attended the Little Court with their grievances the same as everyone else. All Jem and the others could do was to shake their heads in disbelief and assume the sons could only have been coerced somehow into signing by the simple fact that Lady Amelia and the dowager marchioness and Sir Gentry were their landlords and most likely had had some lawyer write to them informing them of their copyhold and what they should do and why they should do it. Such happenings were not unknown: proprietors and freeholders who declared that their estates would be totally ruined if an enclosure Bill were passed into law, could be, and often were, induced by threats and menaces to consent to things which they knew would be to their future disadvantage.

By Standing Order of Parliament, the law of the land then decreed that notice of any such petition should be affixed to the church door in each of the parishes affected for three Sundays in the month of

August or the month of September before the ploughing and, in some cases, the drilling for the next year began: in such a way, the Government prevented the process of enclosure from being completed in secret, though it did not give the villagers affected any kind of voice in their own destiny. Titus Broake and his prime cohort promoters, Her Grace Lady Amelia, the dowager marchioness and the two Members of Parliament for Hamwyte, along with the dean and chapter of Christ Church at Oxford, had laid their plans well before: only when their arrangements were agreed amongst themselves had they given notice to the parish itself, in accordance with the requirements of the Standing Order.

The cursing now was of 'utter betrayal' – betrayal by the three yeomen farmers, betrayal by the Lower Rackstead and Merchant Staplers men and, worse for Jem and them all, betrayal by the last name appended – that of the Bishop of Melchborough himself. The shrewd Bishop had been persuaded in a second letter from Titus Broake, sent to him directly so as to circumvent Parson Petchey and any delay, that the Church could accumulate more land in one year by enclosing Bills than it would probably do in fifty years from charitable legacies.

'Your Grace will, I hope, agree with me,' the lord of the manor had written, 'when I say that I see no actual difference between allowing the clergy a share of the products of the land and giving the Church the land itself, especially if it is a seventh or an eighth of the one instead of a tenth of the other. After all, the land received by the Church would be in lieu of your tithes, to which you have a legal right and every good minister has a right to a living from his parish.'

That the Bishop of Melchborough would add his name to such a document and, by it, include the glebe lands in the enclosure Bill – that, they said, was 'the Judas betrayal': to them, the Church was declaring that the cold stones of its cathedral church took precedence over the fortunes of living men, women and children.

It was a sullen, angry and bewildered crowd who milled about the gale-whipped churchyard that first August Sunday morning, not knowing really what the fates held out for them, but fearing the worst by the example of other places and by rumour of other places.

FIFTY-SIX

ALL THIS TIME, Parson Petchey had been in the small vestry off the bell-tower, putting on his vestments, at the same time ordering the four choirboys from the Dame School, who were putting on their cassocks, to stop their chattering and whispering, while notifying the two churchwardens, Joshua Jaikes and Lemuel Ring, on certain church matters for the service that morning. He seemed oblivious to the tumult outside, either that or he did not consider the notice nailed to his church door to be a significant enough diversion to detain his congregation when he was ready to begin the service and neither did he appear to consider it likely it would deter the greater number from even attending communion.

Thus, when the two churchwardens, Joshua Jaikes carrying the gilded cross and Lemuel Ring holding the small gold incense burner, formed up ahead of the four candle-holding choir boys and all were ready to proceed down the aisle, there came a sudden whisper from the front: 'The church is empty, Reverend Doctor!' Which it was – except for the parson's wife, of course, Amos Peakman and his wife and two grown-up daughters, both still unmarried, Marcus Howie and his wife and four girls and Joshua Godwin and his wife and three sons, two of whom were home from the school at which they were 'parlour boarders' as their father once had been. Apart from them, not another solitary soul had entered.

The fact was they had all arrived exceptionally early for the service, a good half-hour ahead of normal time, and thus well before the first villager was likely to trudge, willingly or unwillingly, up the lane: and all the better, too, of course, to be able to put up the notice unobserved and then to seek the sanctuary of the church. Now all sat in their usual pews, furrows on their brows, concerned at the tumult outside, heads turning continually to look towards the door as if expecting any moment that an angry, yelling, fist-waving mob would rush in upon them. Even Joshua Godwin's ten-year-old boy sensed the nervousness about his father and mother and stared wide-eyed from one to the other and back again – all except Amos Peakman, that is, who sat bolt upright in his pew, stony-faced, gazing straight ahead at the altar for the most part and only turning his head to the side to glower down at his small, dark-haired wife and two frumpy daughters nervously following the gazes of the others.

'Empty? Empty! We shall see about that!' Parson Petchey exclaimed, pushing through the procession of choirboys and churchwardens and pulling back the church's main door to find himself facing a crowd of fifty or so congregated in and around the porch and a further two hundred or more standing about the churchyard in groups of tens and twenties and yet more still arriving.

'What is all this?' the Reverend Doctor demanded imperiously and then, as if commanding children, shouting loudly to those in the porch: 'Inside, all of you! Inside!'

The clamour stopped instantly: the villagers in the porch all looked at one another and several dropped their heads as if mortified to be caught there, while others at the back ducked and slipped away.

However, when none at the front moved forward to enter, the hook-nosed parson let out a snort of exasperation and began to push in amongst them. 'You must come into the church if you wish to hear about all this,' he cried. 'You must come into the church and all will be explained to you. The first reading of the notice is this morning. I am obliged to read it on three consecutive Sundays. You must come into the church if you wish to learn about it.'

Still no one moved to obey him, though a few stepped aside to give him a path: the rest remained rooted where they stood. The Reverend Doctor somehow seemed unable to understand and made a show of craning his neck to peer over the heads of those crowded around him, as if expecting that way any who wanted to attend church, on seeing his face and hearing his voice, would make their way forward. None did: so with a final loud 'Harrumph,' he turned on his heel and strode back towards the porch, a sour look on his face, not even considering or understanding that the villagers that morning had more on their minds than lifting up their voices to sing in praise to the Unknown in the Sky above them when the unknown they now faced on the earth was of far greater moment.

It was Dick Dollery, standing by the stone stoup for holy water fixed to the wall beside the church's main door, who answered him. 'Begging your pardon, Doctor Petchey,' he said, taking off his hat and clasping it respectfully to his front as Parson Petchey brushed back past him, 'but we have read the notice already, those that can read, that is, and those of us that can't so well, we have had it read to us by those who can, so we know what it says. And we know what it all means, especially for the likes of us. It don't need no explaining, begging your pardon, Parson. We understands exactly what it means. So we 'on't be coming to church today, not this morning, if you please. The men have too much to talk over, begging your pardon again, Parson.'

It had been a cheering surprise to the husbandmen and small farmers that day that even the day-labourers, on reading the notice or having it read to them, had turned back and had refused to enter the church: showing solidarity with their fellows, they, too, were standing about the churchyard talking amongst themselves.

'What of your wives and your daughters?' Parson Petchey demanded, rounding on Dick Dollery as if he were the instigator of the villagers' refusal to enter the House of God. Clearly, to him, the need to save one's mortal soul and to ensure a place in Heaven after death was of greater importance than the daily needs of life on earth.

'I can't answer for the other women, I can only answer for my own and she en't going in,' Dick Dollery informed him with a shrug, a half-smile of satisfaction playing on his lips as he observed the parson's reddening face. 'If the others want to goo in and pray along o' thee and the farmers that has done this, I can't stop'em. But if they don't want to goo in, they 'on't and there's none that can make'em.'

The women, however, answered for themselves: even as the parson glowered at them, as if his look alone would shame them into obeying, those at the front turned their backs to him and retreated behind their menfolk.

Defeated, the hook-nosed parson gave Dick Dollery a final angry glare. 'You shall hear more of this. I won't be insulted so,' he cried huffily and strode back inside, banging the door shut.

No sooner had the door been closed than a grim-faced Dick Dollery reached up and tore the notice down and set off back along the road to the Wayfarers' Inn: and, as if by unspoken agreement, the other two hundred or more men followed him and were, in turn, followed by the two hundred or more women and youths and girls, though there was no bright chatter, just grim faces and mutterings of impending doom.

In the Wayfarers', all those who could squeezed into the beamed bay-windowed parlour: those that could not overflowed into the taproom and even into the vault, till the whole place was packed with people: and such was the sense of anger and despair amongst them that Caleb Chapman, who himself had followed them back to the inn, broke all his previous rules on Sunday observance, first by not going into the church himself with his wife, and, second, by serving them ale without fuss while a divine service was being held, as much out of sympathy with their despair as a desire to forestall a further eruption. He even tolerated Jack Tickle's presence in his hostelry since he had three acres, ten roods and fifteen perches of land himself in the open fields and kept sheep on the common waste and so was as entitled to attend as anyone else.

Back in the churchyard, once the bulk of the people had gone, a few faint-hearts did steal into the church because they felt duty-bound to attend, if only to pacify the hook-nosed parson: they slipped into their seats just as the procession finally reached the chancel and the nervous choirboys, sensing a division in the village and not exactly knowing why, crept to their places in the choir stalls. For their trouble, the faint-hearts, as they hurried to their seats, received an icy reprimand from the Reverend Doctor about the need to 'put the Lord first' and to 'save their souls.'

In the Wayfarers', Daniel Gate, the wagoner, the most travelled of the villagers, spoke up first, having on his many journeys passed through a particular village. 'I have seen the effect of enclosure and what it does to a village and it en't a happy picture,' declared the wagoner, standing alongside Jem and Mary-Ann. 'There is a village up in the county north of here which lies on a regular route I take – I have passed through it enough times to know every bump and hollow on the way and every church and inn on the way, too, so I know what I am talking about. I have been through that village more'n two score times – a real lively little place, it were years agoo, with an inn and a church and all that was busy about village life – till it had its fields enclosed five or six year agoo.

'A couple of years back, I was up there agin and I stopped at the inn there and asked about it and they told me none of the cottagers now keeps cows because they has nowhere to pasture them – their land is gorn and their rights are gorn with it. The land they used to use is all gorn to the farmers and, where there were fifty or sixty husbandmen and small farmers making their livelihoods by their own employment, like there is here, there now are just three farms, all of a grand size, with fences dividing off the new fields and new hedges growing everywhere so a man can't roam anywhere n'more. All around there was nothing but corn as far as the eye could see, great long fields of it, with no hedges, and the barns, I should think, they were two hundred feet long and ricks of enormous size, too, and crops of wheat, five quarters to an acre, on the average; and a public-house without either bacon or corn. The labourers' houses, all along the road

I travelled, were beggarly places and the people who I had knowed when they was bright and smart, like, they now was poor-looking and all dressed in raggedy clothes. They told me, too, that the poor rates has increased to an amazing degree because of the numbers who was now wanting and had nothing. And the new farmers, they weren't sympathetic – t'is all a business for them. I tell you, there weren't a village there n'more, not what I'd call a village – just half a village. Where there was once, by my reckoning, ninety houses, there were not above fifty when I passed through afterwards, if I counted'em right. Half the houses that was left was tumbling into ruins and the rest had all been pulled down. I was told some rich lord from one of the big estates, a duke or a baron or somesuch, had bought up all the land, arable, meadowland and waste heath, barns and cottages, too, because he had the money to do it, and the next hamlet adjoining it, too, and that he had thrown the one into four farms and the other into three farms over five hundred acres apiece, and when I asked what had become of the farmers who were turned out, the answer I got was that some of them was dead, so it didn't matter about them, and the rest has become labourers. And that is what will happen here if this is not fought, that is what will happen here in this village.'

He paused to take a swallow from his tankard: his listeners sat in shocked silence, eyeing each other, knowing the worst was upon them, yet feeling powerless to prevent it: finally the old wagoner banged down his tankard. 'Enclosure is worse than ten wars for the harm it does,' he cried angrily. 'It will be the ruin of England. T'is the great, big bull frog grasping everything. Things is changing and not for the better for us. Every inch of land is being grabbed by the rich. Soon there will be no commons for us to plough for ourselves, no pastureland to graze our cows, the whole a country will be divided into great farms, with a few trees surrounding the great farmhouse and all the rest bare of trees, like I have seen up in the next counties, and the labourer will not have a stick of wood to his name and no place for a pig or a cow to graze or even to lie down.'

The villagers had no reason to doubt anything he said and a gloomy silence fell over the company: they had experienced the contempt with which the new lord of the manor regarded them almost from the day of his arrival when he had ignored their rights merely to enforce his own. It so happened that Hamwick Dean had always intercommoned with Lower Rackstead on twenty acres of land on the east side of the parish from hay harvest to Lady Day, with a so-called 'bite' on Easter Sunday, which by custom lasted from six in the morning to the end of church service. The villagers in the Wayfarers' remembered the previous year how Titus Broake had purchased a herd of twenty cattle at Wivencaster market, brought them back to the village and, exercising his right as the new owner of Coppice farm, had driven so many on to the commons there that all chance of a hay crop for that year had been destroyed. That was one small instance of the meanness of the man.

Now he had persuaded six of the area's large farmers to join him and others in the petition to enclose the whole of the three parishes of Hamwick Dean, Lower Rackstead and Merchant Staplers, which meant the only opposition could come from the husbandmen and small farmers themselves.

FIFTY-SEVEN

THE MEN remained in the Wayfarers' till just before twelve o'clock, at which time there was a sudden exodus and they all ran back along Heath Lane and Parsonage Lane, arriving at the church gate just as the main door was pulled open and the three farmers came out into the porch with their wives and families. By then, the villagers' numbers had swelled to five hundred or more, though the majority were day-labourers who drank in the Carpenters' Arms and had followed just to see the fun. For the most part, they remained at the back of the crowd, leaving the husbandmen and the small farmers to confront the three larger farmers, since it was their interests more than anyone else's which were threatened.

It was perhaps with a certain calculated bravura, as if knowing they would come to no actual harm, that the three farmers, after eyeing the crowd for a few seconds, began to push their way through towards where their ponies and traps were tethered some thirty yards away along the lane verge.

Amos Peakman led them, calling out sharply to his plump wife and two frumpy, spinster daughters to 'Follow me and keep close,' to be followed in turn by a wary Marcus Howie and his skinny, overtly fashionable, though limping wife and their four equally fashionably dressed daughters of seventeen, sixteen, fifteen and nine, with Joshua Godwin and his wife and their three young sons, aged fourteen, thirteen and twelve, bringing up the rear.

At first, a narrow path obligingly opened up for them, as if the villagers did not actually want to impede them, but, as it turned out, so narrow was it that a woman leaning forward over the shoulder of one in front could easily shriek her abuse into the ear of whomever she chose, which, since the three farmers were the cause of it all, was to be each of them as they passed.

Enos Diddams's wife, Emma, near to hysterical, began it. 'Thieves! Robbers! Murderers!' she screamed into the face of Amos Peakman as he forced his way past her: and, when he pointedly ignored her, attempting to maintain as dignified a calm as was possible under the circumstances, she flew into an even greater rage, picked up a stone off the path and flung it straight at the farmer's head. Fortunately, it struck him on the shoulder, though with no great force. However, he still whirled round, his silver-topped cane raised menacingly, and would most likely have laid about those nearest to him had not his white-faced wife reached between their two petrified daughters and given him a vicious push to propel him forwards again.

Others, meanwhile, had begun to shout epithets of their own, such as 'Traitors!' 'Judases!' and 'Blackguards!' so that spittle flew from yelling mouths and splattered the cheeks of farmer, wife and children alike.

'Scoundrels! Rascals! Rogues!' You're stealing our land and our livelihood!' Dick Dollery's wife, Lizzie, shrieked into the ear of the second group pushing their way through, Marcus Howie and his fashionable wife and daughters.

Dick Dollery, taking a cue from his wife's boldness, thrust a great clenched fist under the nose of Marcus Howie and shouted: 'Damn thy soul, Howie! Thee will rue the day thee did this deed.'

'And damn your soul in return, Dollery!' the farmer shouted defiantly back.

'Have a care, have a care!' came the plaintiff plea from his wife behind, though it was not concern for her husband that made her half-turn and look back in anguish: someone's foot had trodden on her gown and there was the sound of material ripping.

'What's one dress to thee? Thee've got plenty more,' sneered Nathaniel Newman's wife, Ann, alluding to the frequent carriage rides which the farmer's wife made to the milliners and dressmakers in Wivencaster: the fat blacksmith's wife had deliberately done the deed, stamping her foot on the hem as the crowd pressed in around them.

William Stubbs's wife, Aggie, standing with her, added her twopenn'orth of scorn. 'Don't worry thyself, thy husband'll buy thee another with all the money he has saved from paying his men poor wages,' she sneered, uncaring of the fact that her husband was a harnessmaker and only a small husbandman and only occasionally needed to seek day-labouring to supplement his earnings, that is, if he could find any: now she was most likely casting that hope to the wind.

So close had the villagers now squeezed in upon them that all three farmers were having to push back at the crush just to make headway and such was their exasperation that each farmer had raised his cane as if prepared to strike at the heads and shoulders of those in their path if needs be.

Suddenly, from the rear came the anguished cry of Joshua Godwin's wife, who was attempting to herd her three boys through: 'Give us room, for mercy's sake! These are children! You are crushing them! Give us room!' Her plea, however, was drowned by the shouts of abuse of some and ignored by others who did hear it.

By chance, Jem and Mary-Ann had taken up a position near the gate and so were directly in the path of the three farmers and their families as they forced their way through: neither had joined in the shouting, preferring to leave that to the hotheads and the hysterical, like Dick Dollery and his wife, Enos Diddams and his wife and Nathaniel Newman and his wife, as well as others. But, with the threatening crowd so close around the farmers and their families, it was clear to Jem that, unless someone did something and quickly, one or other of the younger children, Marcus Howie's nine-year-old daughter or Godwin's youngest son, could well be injured, or worse: for it needed only one to stumble and he or she would be trampled under the feet of those pressing from behind, all eager to shout their abuse at the farmers.

'Be careful of the children!' Jem shouted, moving forward a few paces and pointing with an outstretched arm towards Joshua Godwin's wife and children at the back of the throng. Unfortunately, it was at that moment that he came face to face with a near apoplectic Amos Peakman: so virulent and hostile had the abuse hurled at him become that, seeing a man pushing towards him and shouting, the farmer feared he was about to be physically attacked and, in his own defence, struck out with his upraised silver-topped cane. The blow caught Jem on the temple and for an instant he saw only a red haze and reeled back. The next thing he knew was that Mary-Ann was helping him away from the baying crowd and there was blood trickling down his face: after that, he remembered little till he was seated on a chair in his cottage and she was bathing a gash some two inches in length and his head was throbbing painfully.

What did happen was the sudden emergence of Parson Petchey and the two churchwardens from the darkness of the church deterred an outright assault upon the three farmers. For when Dick Dollery, Enos Diddams, Nathaniel Newman and William Stubbs saw their friend, struck and helped away by his anguished wife with blood pouring from his wound, they were all for having a go at Amos Peakman, but were deterred when Joshua Jaikes and Lemuel Ring plunged into the crowd and forcibly threw aside anyone who did not get out of the way quickly enough: and, since Joshua Jaikes was the overseer of the poor and doled out relief from the poor rate and none wanted to get on the wrong side of him, there was a general drawing back.

Into this vacuum stepped Parson Petchey with a withering harangue, which was enough to disperse them further and to allow the three farmers and their families to climb into their traps with as much dignity as they could still muster, flick their whips about their ponies' ears and trot off with the jeers of the crowd echoing in their ears. Out of sight of the parson, the fist-shaking resumed and some of the younger village boys ran a little way after the departing traps and threw small stones, but with no real effect.

Joshua Godwin's three sons, with their tongues out, were staring defiantly from the seats of their trap as it disappeared along Forge Lane, and Amos Peakman almost galloped his vehicle through the crowd towards Heath Lane and the ridge-top, unconcerned whether he bowled anyone over, to the consternation of his plump wife and their tearful daughters, while, Marcus Howie's skinny wife was still complaining about her torn dress as they too escaped down Forge Lane, as if that were the only matter of importance, which, of course, it was to her.

The crowd was still milling about The Street a half-hour later when Mr. Able's gig trotted back into the village from Hamwyte, where he had been worshipping with one of the bands of Dissenters in their chapel off the High Street. When Dick Dollery handed him the notice of the petition which he had torn down, he read it with a grim face.

'I fear the worst for you all,' he said. 'I do not see how I can help overmuch, but, if you wish to, I will call on the Doctor and Mr. Broake and see what comes of it, though I fear it will likely be nothing.' Then he gave a gentle tug on his reins and trotted away up his drive, leaving Dick Dollery and the others all the more disheartened.

What did happen was that later that evening, Jem, still sporting the blood-stained bandage which Mary-Ann had torn off a shirt and wrapped around his head, answered a knock at his cottage door and opened it to find his five friends standing there.

'Mr. Able has been to see the parson and has got him to call a meeting to be held in the church so everyone can goo and have their say,' Dick Dollery informed him, having been nominated as their spokesman. 'This business of enclosure is all to be thrashed out in the church next Monday. We'd be obliged, Jem, if, thee, as a friend and a husbandman like ourselves, would do a bit of speechifying for us. Lead us like. Thee's a good talker, leastways thee tells a good tale in the Wayfarers' – ' Behind him Enos Diddams, Nathaniel Newman, William Stubbs and John Romble all smiled, as did Jem himself, for he had told many a tale of his doings on the Peninsula, sitting amongst them in the Wayfarers' and they had appreciated the broadening of their own minds that it brought.

' – We need a leader,' Dick Dollery went on, 'someone who can talk back at Titus Broake, Peakman and the parson and his ilk and put our case proper like. Half on us can't read or write properly because we en't had the schooling. Thee went to the parish house till thee was eleven, afore thy father and mother died, so thee was schooled proper to read and write. So we are asking, if there is anything that needs to be read and said, then will thee do it for us and we won't look like fools? Thee are used to talking to other folk, gentry folk like officers and that. We are asking thee to come as our friend, Jem, and put into words what we want to say and into writing, too, if needs be.'

FIFTY-EIGHT

A HUNDRED YEARS before, in the time of their great-grandfathers, half the arable land of England had been held in open-field strips: but over that same century, too, square-mile by square-mile, village by village, enclosure had begun to change the landscape of England. In a span of twenty to thirty years, more than three-million acres of arable strips, waste and common had been enclosed as a result of twelve hundred Enclosure Acts being passed by Parliament. A further two thousand had been passed during the years of the French Wars from 1793 to 1815 as men sought to benefit from the high cereal prices which followed a series of poor harvests, aggravated as things were by the restrictive Continental System, with even marginal waste land being enclosed and high loans and mortgages taken out by foolish farmers to do it.

Land had even been enclosed in and around Hamwick Dean two centuries previously by the enterprising ancestors of the late lamented Squire, though done in a piecemeal fashion: like many others with money and influence, the Darcy-Harpriggs had made good use of it to enlarge their manorial estate illegally at a time when the procedure had been open to abuse.

In the time of the First Charles, the fourth squire had exercised what he deemed to be his manorial rights and privileges to make what was, in truth, an illegal encroachment on the waste, enclosing by formal agreements with himself as the lord of the manor some thirty acres along the meandering Langwater's eastern bank, thus extending his hundred-acre estate southwards and westwards towards Hamwick Dean's boundary with the parish of Langridge. Over the next half-century, other piecemeal enclosures by similar 'agreement' had been made by his successors, such as fifteen acres of rough pasture, again to the south towards the Maydun-Wivencaster road, enclosed and then rented out to a small farmer to plough and to seed: and a decade after that, the sixth Darcy-Harprigg had enclosed a further twenty-five acres adjoining the manor estate to the north of the Hall, displacing several cottagers, again done supposedly with the 'agreement' of the holders of the rights, notwithstanding the fact that the Old Squire's grandfather at that time owned the very cottages in which the holders lived. A decade after that, his son had ten further acres incorporated, dispossessing an independent small farmer on them and then had added another twenty acres farther to the north, till by the time the last Squire inherited it, the manorial estate had doubled in size to two hundred acres and all of it done without the whisper of a challenge from any of the villagers of any of the places or the other holders of commonable rights and all ratified in Chancery Court so that over time the memory of the land as it had been was forgotten and the land it had become prevailed.

After 1750, however, it had become accepted procedure to obtain an Act: by that, each enclosure had legal documentation and certification: in theory, it allowed opposition to be heard, but it also allowed for the whole of a village to be enclosed at the same time, that is, open-fields, common meadowland and wasteland.

In addition, in an attempt to correct the fact that, in some places, many small tracts of common land were left unenclosed because the cost of it alone threatened to absorb the possible profits of the undertaking, a general Enclosure Act was urged. Unsurprisingly, it was opposed by private interests more concerned with what would become of the 'poor but honest' attorney, the officers of Parliament and the long train of others who obtained their livelihoods from the 'trifling fees' of individual enclosure Bills: no thought was given to the victims of enclosure, the shadowy poor, who inhabited a place lost in some dim and distant haze.

The opposition of titheowners wrecked a further Bill, introduced in May of 1797. One of the chief advantages of enclosure was the 'commutation of tithe' by which tithes were extinguished by an allotment of land in lieu: but, though the first Bill passed the Commons, the lords and bishops of the Upper House seemed to think it hostile to the Established Church and it was rejected: again no thought was given to the poor who would be thrown out of their cottages and livelihoods by this revolution.

Four years later, however, in 1801, the first General Enclosure Act was finally passed for consolidating in one Act certain provisions usually inserted in Acts of Enclosure and for facilitating the mode of proving the several facts usually required on the passing of such Acts. No alteration in the machinery of enclosure was made: private Acts of Parliament were still required: but they were simplified and to some extent the expense was reduced. The first Bill dealt with the commons and subsequent legislation dealt with the open-fields, but the effect was at once seen in an increase in the number of private Acts and a diminution in the size of the areas which each enclosed, which allowed the likes of Titus Broake and others like him to proceed with their petitions for enclosure at an affordable cost.

The various stages of the proceedings were always costly. There were considerable fees to parliamentary officials to be paid, for a start: and if by chance several parishes claimed rights over a tract of common land to be enclosed, say a large heath, fees were charged for each parish. For example, in enclosing certain areas of Fen in Lincolnshire, forty-seven different parishes claimed rights and so the single general Act was charged as forty-seven separate Acts, with fees in proportion for the 'honest' attorneys and the train of others who fed off the enclosure petitions.

As all this had coincided with an increase in the population, the effect had been increased poverty in the countryside because the smaller farmers and husbandmen, deprived of their land and their common grazing rights, had been unable to feed themselves. This is what the inhabitants of Hamwick Dean had feared as they read the notice that wild Sunday morning.

FIFTY-NINE

THE MEETING to debate the matter of enclosure of the village's lands and those of the two hamlets was held a week later in the nave of St. Bartholomew's, on the Monday as arranged, so that there was time enough for word to go around the three parishes and allow those who wanted to attend to make their preparations.

When approached by Mr. Able – 'a Dissenter of all people!' – Parson Petchey had agreed, somewhat reluctantly, to open the church for the meeting, but really he had no option since five hundred, and maybe six hundred, perhaps even seven hundred, not only from the village itself but from Lower Rackstead and Merchant Staplers, were expected to attend and would need to be seated in some comfort, particularly if it were to rain, though even then the Reverend Doctor acceded only on the conditions that the people conducted themselves with decorum and respected the House of God. He further stipulated that there was to be no blaspheming and no foul language of any kind used and anyone guilty of either would have to be ejected: he would be there himself to ensure that decorum did prevail: and, of course, the place must be swept and cleaned afterwards.

Caleb Chapman was prevailed upon, equally as reluctantly in view of the trade he would lose, to lend two of the Wayfarers' longer tables, which were carried from the inn by Jem, Dick Dollery, Enos Diddams and the others and put end to end just in front of the chancel to form one long table, with a line of vestry chairs placed behind, facing down the nave.

The question of who would or should act as chairman was a point of some debate in the Wayfarers' all during the preceding week: what was obvious to any overhearing the talk in the bay-windowed parlour was that none of the husbandmen wanted Parson Petchey to chair the meeting, not solely because of his usual imperious manner at such times but also because they did not think he could be or would be fair in his deliberations. In consequence of the Bishop of Melchborough having appended his name to the petition, the Reverend Doctor was considered as much a signatory as His Grace. Further, he profited from the glebe rental in all three open-fields and the tithe and they suspected, too, that he was also a supporter of enclosure anyway, since he would always do his Bishop's bidding: and in that they were correct.

The matter of compensation for any lost tithe had been the good parson's main concern ever since the subject of enclosure had first been broached, but that had been solved to his and the Bishop's satisfaction in a further letter from Titus Broake, setting out the advantages of an enclosure rather than the disadvantages of open-field cultivation, which were of no great concern to a man of the cloth worrying as he was about the rebuilding costs of his cathedral church now that the bills for the stonemasons and surveyors were starting to come in and the Archbishop was writing from his palace to ask how the work was progressing. That was of more concern to the Bishop, especially as the townsfolk seemed to be giving far less of late and were complaining of exhausted pockets.

'I am informed by Mr. Mogg,' Titus Broake had blandly informed him, 'the tithe of the common field will benefit considerably after enclosure, especially when the quantity of the waste, which is now worth scarcely anything to the tithe, is also enclosed and brought into cultivation. The landowner can expect higher rents from enclosed land as it will be Your Grace's right to commission his agent to renegotiate leases since all leases are annulled by the Act and, therefore, new terms and conditions can be introduced, if Your Grace is desirous of improving the Church's glebe. In places of which I have experience, where much common ground and waste has been brought under cultivation from enclosure, I venture to inform Your Grace that rents have doubled within a year of the awards being made. Your Grace will know for himself from your agent that unless a division and enclosure of the open-fields is carried into execution, the property will ever remain in the same unimproved state which it has been in for centuries past, to the disgrace of this part of the county, which is so much behind in the improvement of agriculture compared with so many other counties.'

It took a week for the two sides, one opposing the petition and the other supporting it, to agree on the chairman: Mr. Able was proposed by Peter Sparshott, still the foreman of the Little Court's jurors, precisely because the portly lawyer was also still its steward and was known to be a fair-minded man, as well as also being a Dissenter and, therefore, unlikely to be influenced by the Church and any opinion the hook-nosed parson was likely to give. But his nomination was objected to strenuously by Titus Broake and the three other Hamwick

Dean signatories as well as by Parson Petchey himself: it was felt he was too close to the husbandmen since he was 'known to frequent the same inn and to sit and drink with them,' as Amos Peakman wrote sniffily in his round-robin sounding out the opinion of the other petitioners.

In the end, as a compromise, the vicar of Inworth, the Reverend Finias Coleman, a short, fussy little man with puffed cheeks and curled white hair hanging about his ears, was prevailed upon to take the chair: he, it was hoped, would at least be more independently minded than the village's own parson since he lived 'outside' all three parishes. Also, his presence would be more likely to maintain the peace and to quell the tempers of any hotheads attending, of which there were likely to be many if the sounds of fury emanating from the smoky interiors of the Wayfarers', the Carpenters' Arms, the Bull at Merchant Staplers and the Green Man at Lower Rackstead were anything to go by.

Further, since it was not a formal church meeting and the church was simply the venue, the parish constable, Elijah Candler, was named as the assistant steward, designated to sit at one end of the main table so that, if the temper of any became too heated or their action or words too hostile towards any of the petitioners particularly, or the chairman or any others at the main table, he was empowered to eject them, especially if they would not calm down when told and interfered with the progress of the meeting.

To the glee of the villagers, it did put Joshua Jaikes's nose out of joint slightly, for, as he was the current senior churchwarden as well as the full-time overseer of the poor for the three parishes, he had expected that keeping order in the church would be solely his prerogative. He would however, be present 'to assist,' though there were some who would have preferred any other than him: for so great was the enmity in which the overseer was held by then that the only place most wished to see him was at the bottom of a six-feet-deep hole lying in a long polished box with brass handles!

There were even some who, when they saw he had put himself up with the dignitaries suspected that he had done so to impress others of his status, as those who sit a top tables believe they impress others and are more important than those who sit at lower tables. Of course, his other task, as he saw it, was to protect his reverend employer and the 'House of the Lord' and for that he had called upon his cohort, the weasely Lemuel Ring, to assist him in turn.

Though it was planned that the chairmen should sit in the centre of the table, dividing the two opposing camps, the Reverend Coleman could not have done so had he wanted to: for, there was such an uneven balance at it, with only two seated to the right-hand of the Inworth rector – Peter Sparshott and Mr. Able, representing the interests of the Little Court and the husbandmen and small farmers. The Reverend Doctor placed himself to the left of the Reverend Coleman, with the supporters of the petition, Titus Broake, Amos Peakman and the other large farmers all seated to the left of him.

Titus Broake had arrived at the church in his pony and trap just as the crowd was congregating and had pushed his way into the porch with the aid of the lanky, lean-faced Heginbotham, glowering at everyone as he did so and ignoring the insults hissed at him by unrecognisable female voices from the back of the crowd.

Once he had taken his place, which was at the actual centre point of the table, as if that were his right, he lounged lazily in his chair, a sour look upon his face and seemingly uncaring of the hostility which he knew would be directed at him, passing his time while he waited by idly tapping a silver-topped cane against his polished boot and looking bored before the proceedings had begun. Alongside him sat his lawyer from Melchborough, Mr. Mogg, who had arrived in his gig much earlier, before even the crowd had begun to assemble.

Amos Peakman, Marcus Howie and Joshua Godwin, too, and the three other large farmers from the hamlets, Silas Kempen, James Allen and Thomas Godbear, had also slipped into the church well ahead of the scheduled starting time and were all seated together in a comforting group. Amos Peakman was already somewhat chagrined and more red-faced than usual: for, on entering the church, he had forgotten himself and taken out his clay pipe and was about to light it when a curt reprimand from Parson Petchey deterred him. 'Not in here, Mr. Peakman, if you please,' the hook-nosed parson had chided him. 'This is the house of God, not a cow byre!'

The proceedings were somewhat delayed by the pernickety Mr. Mogg, who spent a considerable time shuffling various sheets of paper which he unrolled one by one from a bundle he had brought in his satchel and then proceeded to flatten each carefully on the table before placing them in an order of importance known only to himself. They were copies of documents from the representatives of each of the other petitioners not present, namely Lady Amelia, the dowager marchioness, the Oxford dean, the two Members of Parliament, Sir Gentry and Sir Benton, as well as several of the city gentlemen, who had all sent letters empowering him to represent their interests since they themselves could not be bothered to attend, which the lawyer was happy to do since he had done the same thing in four other places in the county where the same enclosure meetings had been held. By his diligent work at those, he had made a name for himself amongst certain of the gentry as being a 'thoroughly reliable attorney,' which boded well for future business.

The protests at the four other meetings had all been to no avail and he saw no reason to suppose that the outcome of the business at Hamwick Dean would be any different since the value of the combined holdings of those whom he represented, her Ladyship, the marchioness, the lord of the manor, the Honourable Members and the dean *et al*, when added to those of the Church, exceeded by three hundred times the combined value of any acreage actually owned by any of the small farmers or husbandmen of all three places opposing the petition. The whole exercise was, as his client, Titus Broake, had grumpily pointed out, patently futile, though he would not say so, of course: it had to be gone through: his task was merely to point out the differences in the value totals as the law required and as such to continue with the process of drafting the petition for the Bill.

'Well, gentlemen, we had better let them in,' declared the Reverend Coleman, finally, for there had already been several impatient shouts for the door to be opened from the throng outside: now, as Elijah Candler, who had been guarding it, turned the great key and then the ringed handle which lifted the latch, Amos Peakman, Joshua Godwin, Marcus Howie and the other 'turncoat' farmers, as Dick Dollery called them in the Wayfarers', all shifted uneasily in their chairs: the three local men, in particular, had not forgotten the hostility of villagers only a week previously and the other three had heard of it.

Notwithstanding the drizzling rain which was falling that August evening, the whole population of Hamwick Dean and Merchant Staplers, it seemed, were waiting outside: six hundred and more in total: the men and youths in their working smocks, the women in their aprons and shawls, the young girls in their caps, aprons and patched dresses, some of the very young children barefoot, some booted, but all uncaring in their handed-down tatters: all were there. Even the old men and the old women with their sticks had struggled slowly along Parsonage Lane, determined to be present: for there had not been an event like it in all their born days that they could remember: it was a making of history in their own village: even they recognised that.

The disappointment was that only forty-seven of the hundred expected from Lower Rackstead had turned up, some put off by the weather, others unable to come because, it so happened, the village was in isolation at that time. Two weeks previously, the curate and the select Vestry, quite innocently, had decided that every one of the hundred and fifteen inhabitants of the hamlet, men, women and children, should be inoculated against smallpox. It was just an unfortunate coincidence that it should occur at that time.

It was not an uncommon happening and almost every village in England was inoculated at one time or another: villagers were pricked with the cow pox in two 'shifts,' so to speak, which meant the inoculated half had to spend three weeks in isolation, generally in a farmer's barn, though, in the case of the first fifty of Lower Rackstead-ites, they were all still cooped up together in a brick stable well away from the rest of the village, who took food, water and fuel to them, but left it at a safe distance. Thus, only the non-inoculated half was able to attend the meeting, though the curate of the place, Reverend Snetterton, had set a good example by taking part in the inoculation himself and was also confined.

Despite Parson Petchey's hopes of decorum being observed and respect being shown for the House of God, when the porch door was eventually swung back, the whole six hundred and more surged forward in a great rush, happy at last to get out of the rain and also eager to get to the front pews ahead of everyone else so that they almost knocked over poor Elijah Candler, who shouted hastily for them to 'Hold there! Hold there! Walk! Walk! You're in church! You don't run in church!' One or two did barge 'accidentally' into Lemuel Ring, standing across from Elijah Candler, sending him staggering backwards a short way before he recovered himself, but that was to be expected in such a crush: besides no one cared about that.

The cooper's shouts were of little avail: as were his directions shouted at the backs of the jostling mob which barged past him: 'The front pew is to be left for them that wants to say something and has something to say. If you don't have anything to say, take the other pews and hold your peace!'

Human nature being what it is, people not wanting to hear him did not hear him, or pretended they had not heard him, and there was scuffling and pushing and some arguing as the first fifty or so hurried down the aisles to the front: a child fell and had to be snatched smartly out of the way of the trampling feet coming behind and such was the impetus as the good people of the three parishes surged forward that they almost knocked over the eagle Bible lectern standing beside the pulpit. Indeed, the clatter of nail-shod boots on the red-and-black tiled aisle and on the bare wood floors of the pews caused such a din that Parson Petchey himself eventually jumped to his feet and, in as stentorian a tone as he could muster, furiously commanded: 'Quiet! Proceed quietly, please!'

While waiting outside in the churchyard, Jem and Mary-Ann, Dick Dollery, Enos Diddams and the other husbandmen from the Wayfarers', accompanied by their wives and several of their children, had managed to push their way to the front of the crowd and, though they were amongst the first through the door, they were beaten to the front pew by twenty or so others, who all crammed themselves in and were mightily pleased to find themselves occupying the very pew where the lord of the manor's wife sat, even if he seldom did: that was a great thing to them and they were in no mood to give it up.

Jem and the others missed out, too, on the second pew, where the parson's wife sat, for it was taken by, amongst others, three of the village's small farmers, Jonas Bunting, Reuben Frost and Peter Hull and their wives and children, for the matter affected them as equally as it did the husbandmen. Jem and his friends had to be satisfied with occupying the pew in the third row, where Amos Peakman and his wife and daughters normally worshipped, though it was still in the central section of the church and thus still directly in front of the chairman's table.

Even then they had to defend it from an attempted incursion by a dozen others, who would have forced their way in to join them and overcrowd it had not Dick Dollery and Enos Diddams blocked them, shouting: 'We're full up! There's no room!' and 'No more! No more! We're full!' The rejected dozen then began a haranguing match with those seeking to occupy the pew behind: angry exclamations – all vulgar if not blasphemous – were exchanged as villager jostled villager, good naturedly at first, but then tending towards open hostility: everyone, it seemed, wanted the novelty of sitting in the front pews where, in normal times, they were never allowed to sit.

It was all too much for the poor Reverend Coleman and a horrified Parson Petchey: both leapt to their feet again. 'Ladies and gentlemen, please! Please!' cried the stocky vicar of Inworth in his thin, piping voice.

Parson Petchey's remonstrance was a deal angrier: 'Behave yourselves or I shall have you put out! Churchwardens, restore order and stop this mayhem!'

At his bidding, Elijah Candler, Joshua Jaikes and Lemuel Ring rushed forward to block both aisles, pushing back those still seeking a place at the front where there were none to be had and physically 'directing' them into other pews at the rear and sides of the nave.

'The pews at the front are full up. The rest of you will have to take your places at the back and listen from there,' shouted a red-faced Elijah Candler, at that moment wishing he were not the parish constable. 'Anyone who has anything to say that is different from what is being said up there on a particular matter need only call out and we will make way for him. You'll all have a say if you wants it.'

At last, order was restored and the Reverend Coleman and Parson Petchey resumed their seats: Mr. Able sat smiling through it all like a benign father watching children at play, amused that there should be such enthusiasm to enter the church when there was generally little enough of it on a Sunday. Peter Sparshott looked on aghast, the farmers appeared unsurprised, as if they expected nothing less, and Mr. Mogg appeared to be totally indifferent: if people wished to conduct themselves in that manner, then so be it, his face said. The only person who seemed to find if all openly laughable was Titus Broake, who sat in his chair with a knowing smirk on his face as if to say, 'What else is to be expected of these people!'

Gradually, the scraping, the chattering, the curses, the bustling and clattering and jostling at the back of the nave subsided and those still hoping to push their way forward a part way towards the front finally gave up and settled to sit in the side pews or to stand in the aisles towards the back of the church: it was a relieved Elijah Candler and Joshua Jaikes who finally retook their seats at either end of the table, leaving Lemuel Ring to guard the aisle.

With a reprimand to the congregation from Elijah Candler to 'Keep this civil, it 'on't do no good to start a fight. We need to discuss this business like civilised people,' the meeting was finally handed over to the chairman to get it under way, though the cooper's remarks were greeted with murmurings of disagreement rather than agreement from certain parts. The men were in a mood to state their case in the hardest terms, whether in church or out of it, and, if shouting and waving their fists and calling out were required, then so be it, that is what they would do: the niceties of democracy and decorum were not suited there that evening, in their view.

Still the affable Reverend Coleman did his best. 'We are here to debate the matter of the enclosure, the division and the allotment of the commonable lands of this parish and the adjoining parishes of

Lower Rackstead and Merchant Staplers,' he informed them, with a faint smile as if most of those there had not already sensed the inevitability of it all, but were there anyway, just as they had been at the five hangings over at Hamwyte seven years previously to see the doomed fall.

'I ask, gentlemen, that you put your views honestly and without rancour,' he said, 'so that all views for and against, of which I am sure there are many on both sides, can be heard, if not to make a decision here this evening, at least to allay the fears of some and – ' He gave a slight cough as he paused. ' – to temper the views of the others with as much Christian charity as we would wish upon ourselves.'

The floor was then given to Parson Petchey, who made no speech, or attempt at sermonising, which was unusual for him since he had as big a captive audience as he had ever had for any sermon he wished to preach, but instead, behind the safety of the table, he bowed his head to pray 'for the guidance of God' and asked all in the church to do the same, which all did except Titus Broake. He spent the time while the heads of the others were bowed, regarding the throng with the same disdain as he always regarded them, particularly as he was smartly dressed in town clothes: a navy blue surcoat, gold-patterned waistcoat, with a crimson cravat tucked into the neck of his white shirt: his leather boots were polished to a mirror shine, his stiff-brimmed hat lay upon the table alongside his silver-topped cane.

It all contrasted with what passed as the 'Sunday-best' of the 'lower orders' before him: the same faded smocks, the same worn boots, the same dowdy dresses and the same plain shawls as they always wore. It irritated him having to attend at all, which, of course, the parson seemed not to notice as he invoked the 'blessing of the Lord upon these proceedings that we may go forth into the future in harmony and in hope.'

Though when he said 'Amen,' it was noticeable that, amongst the six hundred and more in the church, only a few dozen mumbled their repeat: most remained silent, including those in the third pew, Jem, Dick Dollery and the rest. God's judgment, it seemed, was not required that night: men would decide the matter for themselves.

SIXTY

PETER SPARSHOTT was first to speak: as the foreman of the Little Court and used to dealing with its many and varied proceedings, he was not one to be fazed by any hostility emanating from Titus Broake and the other farmers: when a man has suffered curses as regularly as he from men fined for dragging a plough across another's corn or flooding another's land or for not keeping cattle or sheep hurdled properly, he becomes inured to that hostility.

'Not a solitary man or woman in the body of this church, save the petitioners, is in favour of the intended measure,' the lanky, dour-faced bachelor declared, and, looking straight at Titus Broake, he boldly went on: 'That gentleman there has, ever since his arrival in these parts, been working in an underhand manner to conceal his intentions from us. Before the notice went up on the church door a week agoo, he never so much as asked any one of us if we had any objection to his application. No word of it of any kind has ever been received from him at the Little Court. I know that to my own knowledge. He has maintained his secrecy to the last. His lawyer and the representatives of others, I have learned only this week, have been holding secret meetings in Melchborough over the past several months at which no doubt they conspired amongst theirselves to agree on all matters regarding the enclosure of the lands of this and the two other parishes afore even the notice of the petition was nailed to the church door.'

Mr. Mogg appeared as if he were about to rise in protest, but then changed his mind and instead leaned forward in his chair and fussed with straightening his papers again, as if what the foreman said were of little or no consequence to him or to his clients.

Peter Sparshott, meanwhile, had turned to look at the two clergymen. 'It grieves me more than anything,' he went on in his normal doleful way, 'to learn that the Church itself saw fit to be represented at those secret meetings on at least two occasions, to my knowledge. It seems to me that this whole plan of Mr. Broake was settled between the lawyers of the main proprietors without even letting those who it concerns the most into the secret till they was called upon to sign the petition as a deal already done – ' The six farmers all looked at each other and their faces reddened, for they knew the words applied to them as much as anybody and that the whole village had guessed it, too.

' – The greater number of our holdings in the three joint parishes are small,' went on Peter Sparshott. 'There are very few on the open-fields or on the small farms of any of the three parishes who hold land for themselves – the greater part is owned by others, most of who live in distant places. Should this all be carried, even those who own an acre or two of what they farm – less than a half-dozen among a hundred of us – even those who might receive an award of land to replace their loss will be obliged to sell what they are given, small though it will be, for they will not have the means to do anything else, if the happenings in other places is anything to goo by. Mr Broake and his friends here, by the means they have and which others do not have – they will be in a position to become the purchasers on their terms and their terms alone, which is what I believe has been intended by him and them all along.'

Cheers and clapping rose up from everywhere in the nave, in which Jem and Mary-Ann joined, along with Dick Dollery and the others: the people had never heard the lanky foreman of the Little Court speak in such a manner before and were heartened to hear him. There was a buzz of excitement about the place: people were smiling and nodding agreement with everything that had been said. Titus Broake merely scowled, the six farmers looked decidedly uncomfortable, while Parson Petchey feigned disinterest and kept his eyes focused on the rows of pews as if to ensure that nothing untoward was happening there or likely to happen.

Buoyed by the 'congregation's' cheers and applause, Peter Sparshott plunged on: 'I have heard it is said by Mr. Broake – and no doubt he will say the same this evening – that the reason he gives for petitioning for this enclosure is that, with all the toil and pains of which a small farmer like myself or a husbandman is capable, he has not the time to make any proper improvement to his land in its open-field state. That is to say, he has more land for his money in the open-field than he can plough and sow in a season and his crops are larger than he can get in at harvest time. That, he says, is a good enough reason for enclosing the land, so the husbandman will not be overburdened with too much land to plough and too much corn to harvest! Such is the argument of the kind landlord, to consider the ease of the tenant farmer and, out of that kindness, to turn him out of his living to save him such troubles! – ' The smiles of the villagers broadened again: this was truly unexpected sarcasm from the foreman. ' – I say that the diligent husbandman and the small farmer – as am I – he will find both the year and the day long enough to do his work to good purpose, even in the open-fields. I say, too, for myself, if the hardworking farmer does not complain, if he is willing to follow his plough, goo muck-carting and do his dibbing and broadcasting a while longer, then ought he not to be allowed to goo on as he has always done? By his labour, he pays his rent – he supports his family – he produces what is needed to feed himself and his family and, in so doing, he provides for his fellow countrymen. If he don't complain at any o' that, what need to force this change on him? That is what I ask. What need?'

With that, he sat down, with the cheers and applause of all the villagers echoing around the church, which the Reverend Coleman was prepared to allow to run their course, but which Parson Petchey was not and stood up yet again to call for silence: 'Quiet please. Quiet.'

Mr. Able then rose, invited to speak by the Reverend Coleman, who was an old acquaintance, simply out of respect for one whom he knew to be a man of intelligence, one known, too, for his altruism and magnanimity during his many years as a steadfast steward of the Little Court.

'It is not because of any idealised romantic love of the land that the husbandmen and small farmers oppose enclosure,' the portly lawyer began solemnly, hooking his thumbs in the buttonholes of his topcoat as if he were addressing magistrates in a court of law. 'It is because they fear the loss of their customary rights. The most important common right these husbandmen and small farmers have is common of pasture, but they have other property rights which they do not wish to lose, but which they fear they will if enclosure is proceeded with – I refer to the rights of pannage, of estover, of turbary, piscary and soil, which are all matters defined by local custom over the centuries. Who can take what, when and where is inscribed in immemorial practice. They are their rights and they wish to keep them.'

He paused and gestured towards a still indifferent Titus Broake. 'The honourable gentleman there is, I am sure, well aware that proceedings of this sort are inconsistent with the maxim that "Every man has a right to do what he will with his own." It is my opinion – and I state it as a God-fearing man – that no man or body of men, however considerable, has a right to dictate to any of their neighbours whether his land should be enclosed or open, even though that neighbour has only an acre in a field in which they have five hundred. His one acre is as important to him and his family as their five hundred are to them and, if he chooses to enjoy his sole acre in an open-field state, as he has been used to doing, who can equitably oblige him to enclose it if every man has, as the maxim says, a right to do as he please with his own?' A murmur of agreement flowed around the nave as he paused to mop his brow with a large kerchief.

'Many small proprietors of land, the husbandmen and small farmers of this village and the two hamlets,' went on Mr. Able, 'the likes of Mr. Sparshott here and Jem Stebbings there and Dick Dollery there and Mr. Hull and Mr. Johnson there, men such as they – they would be greatly injured by enclosure. It is a fact, of which I know, that when a parish is enclosed, the labourers in it are deprived of the means of their support. They almost universally disapprove of enclosing and their number is as considerable in Hamwick Dean, Lower Rackstead and Merchant Staplers as it is in all other open villages – much greater than perhaps the several constituents of our legislature themselves are generally aware. Indeed, they cannot well know it when these unhappy sufferers are not able to make an opposition, but were the expenses of opposing these Bills in the House of Commons less and the prospect of success greater, perhaps the Parliament might know much more of the sense of the people on enclosing than they do at present.'

'It is well known, too, I think you will agree,' he continued, this time nodding towards Mr. Mogg, who was now listening more intently to a fellow lawyer, 'that all small estates are invariably much depreciated in value by an enclosure, to say nothing about the expenses that enclosure would place upon any who participated in it were it to go ahead. The expense of allotting Hamwick Dean and the two hamlets would be enormous, beyond the means of almost every man here save the chief petitioners, I believe. The Bill would greatly injure all the proprietors excepting Mr. Broake and the other prime signatories to the petition and completely extinguish those who have nothing but their land to depend upon. Every small farmer and husbandman is now able to cultivate his land as he pleases and the only inconvenience is that of the lands lying in small pieces, which can produce difficulties which I understand fully from my years as the steward of the Little Court. But they are not insurmountable. It is better, I say, that the husbandmen of the three parishes should submit to that than to have it remedied at the expense of their own ruin. Mr.

Broake is a large proprietor – he has now, I believe, upwards of several hundred acres in the three parishes – yet it would appear he is desirous of acquiring yet more land and proposes that the Bill should take power to sell the waste land as well as the arable and the common pasture. I venture to say that there is no waste land in any of these parishes which is not of some value to those who hold it in its present state.'

His voice now took on a darker, more sinister tone than before: 'Enclosure of the open-fields, the common pasture and the waste around this village and in the two hamlets of Lower Rackstead and Merchant Staplers, will, like other places of which I have heard, drive so many away because they are unable to find work in the villages in which they are born and raised. They will move to the towns or worse to the colonies, Australia, Upper Canada, even America. There will be many empty cottages. Enclosure, I say, sirs, will be the death of this village, the death of the two hamlets, too. I have no doubt of it. Indeed, in time it will be the death of old England as well, I fear. Mark my words, sirs – the death of old England itself.'

He, too, sat down to appreciative applause: the Reverend Coleman then looked about him to see if anyone in the body of the church wished to speak, clearly not expecting anyone, for he was about to turn to Titus Broake, to give him the floor, when Dick Dollery raised his arm and declared loudly: 'Begging your pardon, Reverend, but we would like to have our say. We have a spokesman who we have chosen and we would like him to speak for us.'

'Very well, let him stand,' the Reverend Coleman said with a slight sigh: he had not expected it, but it would do no harm to hear a third speaker. His acquiescence, though, drew sighs of exasperation from Titus Broake and the farmers at the table: clearly, they had hoped the villagers would sit quietly and be told what was going to happen to them and their open-fields, commons and waste: the proceedings would be over all the quicker if they did.

Nudged by Dick Dollery, Jem now stood up to show himself. 'I am asked to speak for the others,' he began, a little nervously. 'My name is Jem Stebbings and I have eight acres on the arable and I keep five cows on the stinted pasture and some sheep on the common and geese on the waste. I am known to Mr. Able and Mr. Sparshott and also to the Reverend Doctor Petchey. Mr. Broake and the others, I think, may know me as well – ' He paused and gestured at the rows of people in the pews behind and all around and the crush of two hundred or more gathered in a fidgeting, unsteady semi-circle in the cross aisle. ' – If you wish to know why we are here, sirs, you need only look about you. The whole village is here. Most of those who live in Merchant Staplers are here and half the village of Lower Rackstead is here, too. The others would have been here as well, but are unable because of the inoculation. We who are here, sirs, are here to ask these gentlemen not to proceed with their petition to enclose the common arable, meadowland and the common waste of our three parishes, for we do say, all of us here, that enclosing the commonable lands and removing them from general village use will take away all our rights and we are the majority here – '

'In number only, sir, not in annual value or in total of acres held,' Mr Mogg quietly interrupted with a smile, though not as a criticism, merely by way of a correction of fact.

The interruption, if meant to hinder Jem in any way, failed to do so. 'We are the majority in numbers of small farmers and husbandmen if not in value or total acreage,' he continued, calmly acknowledging the lawyer's point, 'and none is more industrious, none toils and labours so hard as the husbandmen and small farmers of this and the other parishes. We all have families to support – upon us depend the souls of at least five hundred others of every age in this village and a further hundred or more in each of the two hamlets. T'is a moral fact, is it not, your reverences, that a man should not steal the bread from another man, that he should not steal it especially from a poor man's or a starving man's mouth? It seems to me, sirs, that it is the avarice of one man and one man alone – an incomer, a stranger to everyone of us when he came here – a man different from us only in the amount of money he has – it is his avarice and his avarice alone which threatens all three of the parishes here with ruin.' His finger was pointing directly at Titus Broake.

There were gasps at his audacity: and, when Jem looked at the faces of Peter Sparshott and Mr. Able, they were smiling broadly to show their admiration: indeed, Mr. Able was leaning back in his chair, having taken off his gold-rimmed spectacles and was chewing the end of one arm as was his habit when he was listening more intently than usual. Titus Broake, on the other hand, remained sprawled on his chair, but now staring hard back at Jem, almost as if marking him out: while the six yeomen farmers shifted uneasily on their chairs and looked about them, three of them in particular as if they feared a resumption of the violence of the previous Sunday and three others trying to gauge if it were likely to begin. Even Parson

Petchey, who was still feigning impartiality, frowned and harrumphed at the last remark.

'We are opposed to enclosure, sirs, because we say that the meadowland ought to be left open as the right to it is attached not to land but to whoever lives in this parish,' Jem went on, feeling Mary-Ann's hand take his and give it a gentle squeeze of encouragement. 'There are those here who have stocked the meadowland with three, four or five cows, as they have thought proper, without any interruption all their lives and their father's and grandfather's before them. It is the say of all of us, sirs, that, under the pretence of improving lands – which is what we are told enclosure is supposed to be about – we, the husbandmen and cottagers and other persons entitled to right of common on the lands intended to be enclosed, we will lose our village right of access to the open places. The rights we now have of turning our cows and our calves on to the meadows, of pasturing our sheep on the stubble of the arable fields after harvest, and on the fallow field, of keeping our geese on the waste and our pigs in the woods round about – they will all be taken from us. These are hard times, sirs, hard times for everyone, especially the labouring man.'

There was a murmur of agreement at this from the back of the church, stifled immediately by a sharp word from Lemuel Ring, though it did not deter Jem, who continued impressively: 'Most of us who rent cottages and work little parcels of land in the open-fields are able to make a living or sorts – little as it may be – for ourselves and our families by our daily labour and the profits of a little trade. The land we farm gives us wheat and barley for our bread, beans and peas to feed a hog or two for meat, straw to thatch our cottages and wither our cows, which, in their turn, give us milk for nine or ten months of the year. From the wastes, we take fern and heather for litter and for bedding, turves for our fires, wood for our hurdles and our hoes and our rakes, acorns for our pigs, tree-loppings for our livestock to browse on in the winter months when there is not much else to be had. As Mr. Able has said, it is our belief that this enclosure petition will have a ruinous effect on us all and our way of life. Enclosing the commonable land of Hamwick Dean, Lower Rackstead and Merchant Staplers will deprive us not only of the livelihood which we have as husbandmen and small farmers, even if on small acreages, but it will bring hardships to us and our kind, our kith and our kin.'

'If the land is all enclosed,' Jem went on, louder now, 'we shall be denied all that we now have and all that we now do. Such rights and places that are ours to use by right either will not exist any more or the area of them will be so reduced in size and number as to be of no profit or benefit to the majority of us here in this church this evening. Even if a man was to claim and be granted a parcel of land because of the loss of his common rights, I have heard it said that the land that has been given in other places is little more than the size of another man's garden, even if he had a holding of some considerable size beforehand. And, if he has not, then it will be a very small garden indeed that he will receive. I have heard, too, that same garden, whatever its size, will attract a share of the costs of the enclosure and fencing afterwards exactly the same as a man who has taken up ten hundred acres and so will be not worth a man taking it up.'

Again Jem paused: a silence had fallen over the nave: mutterings from Dick Dollery and Enos Diddams alongside and more behind told him that men were beginning to understand the true nature of what enclosure would mean for them. Jem well knew, as all did many in the church that evening, from talking to travellers from other places passing through the village and through Hamwyte and general talk in the inns and ale house of the town on market days, that, in reality, enclosure costs, when the unavoidable monies for hedging and fencing and ditching and re-routing roads or constructing new ones were included, could be as high as twelve pounds per acre: and few, himself included, could afford any worthwhile parcel of land at that price. Most would not run to half an acre let alone a full acre or several acres.

Small wonder then that the talk in the Wayfarers' had been that, in other places, so they had heard, any who had common rights claims had sold up the land acquired at enclosure or shortly after to spare themselves those costs, to make a profit of some kind, no matter how small, but still the best for which they could hope. Thus, for the need of the money, those in other places lost all semblance of independence: they ceased to be independent husbandmen and small farmers and became dependant wage-labourers at the mercy of the whims of their employers, as are all dependant labourers.

'We cannot stand by helplessly while the land which has been the common property of the people of this village for centuries is fenced in by rich and greedy landowners and our only source of livelihood is taken from us,' declared Jem, his anger rising. 'If enclosure is forced on us, the greater number of us will have to give over farming and betake ourselves to labour for the support of our families. We shall all be landless, reduced as farmers, for we shall not have a sufficient amount of land attached to our cottages to enable us even to keep a single cow. And, if there are more men than there is work going day-labouring, then, as sure as night follows day, men will have to compete neighbour against neighbour, son against father, brother against brother even for that employment. Instead, we shall be driven into the towns in search of work, just as Mr. Able has said.

'T'is a plain enough case of class robbery, to my way of thinking, played according to fair rules of property and law and such as laid down by a Parliament which is itself full of property owners and lawyers. The law is being used to take the commons away from the poor. It is pretended that the law is impartial, but it will make the poor strangers in their own land. Landed wealth will lie in the hands of a few, I say, to the detriment of the many and we, sirs, are the many!'

The men and women in the church had listened to him in silence: now, when they realised he had finished, there was a great roar of acclaim and a swelling of applause and many were smiling broadly, delighted to hear their fears and their anger so well expressed. Surprisingly, in Jem Stebbings, veteran of the Peninsular campaign, the husbandmen, small farmers and day-labourers of Hamwick Dean and the two adjoining hamlets of Lower Rackstead and Merchant Staplers realised that they had found a natural leader, one who had long since learned that audacity and resourcefulness sometimes paid dividends.

SIXTY-ONE

ALL THE TIME Peter Sparshott, Mr. Able and Jem had been on their feet, Titus Broake had remained slouched in his chair: he would have jumped to his feet a dozen times to challenge them had not Mr. Mogg repeatedly laid a hand on his arm and shaken his head, as if to say, 'It does not matter what is said, the power lies with us. That is all that matters.'

However, he continued to eye Jem coldly and with interest: clearly, he had not expected anyone could rise and speak the way he had spoken, from the heart. It was if he had suddenly realised there was someone who could put a case against him, one that could have swayed matters in another way had not the values of the land associated with the various signatories far outweighed those opposing.

Now the lord of the manor, the chief petitioner, the chief instigator of all their anxiety, was rising to speak his piece: unsurprisingly, he was greeted with hisses and shouts from those at the rear of the throng and low mumblings from those closer to the front, who, nevertheless, still kept their heads down to ensure that they were not the ones recognised as doing it.

'You have had your say, Peter Sparshott, and you, Mr. Able and we have heard, too, from the husbandmen's spokesman,' Titus Broake began, with a sneer, 'now I shall have mine. You people have to learn that you cannot stick to the old ways forever. The old system has had its day. It limits us with all your bits and pieces of land all over the place. I have instructed my lawyer, Mr. Mogg here, and we have the authority and the support of the other major proprietors of the land in this village and the two hamlets to go ahead with the petition to Parliament whether you sign it or not, whether you accept it or not, whether you oppose it or not. It does not matter to us, it will go ahead and the land will be enclosed. Mark my words on that. It *will* be enclosed. We shall prevail no matter what you do. Your day is finished. It is the turn of the modern farmer now. Enclosure will come to this parish whether you like it or not. Open-field farming and commoning is wasteful and incompetent – ' The growls of disapproval, which had begun when he had risen to his feet, grew louder. ' – The whole country is having to change and I and the other petitioners for the Bill intend to see that we change here. The population of these islands has to be fed. It is growing faster year by year and we farmers must grow more food so the people can be fed. That means there is but one way forward now – and that is for bigger farms, with proper-sized fields where crops can be grown according to the farmer's direction and to meet his market and not be governed by some old-fashioned methods dictated to him by the likes of your Little Court, as is now done to you. As far as all those little lands you have, we need to think of big enclosed fields of many acres, as big as a man needs to have them. You may think it right for the small farmers to go on the way they do and it may be enough for you cottagers with a half-dozen acres to keep yourselves in corn and milk and butter, but it does not make sense any more. We need to parcel up the land, all together and make farms bigger. We need farms the size of three hundred, four hundred, five hundred acres – a thousand acres, if need be!'

There was an instant surge of anger throughout the nave: a thousand acres was almost two-thirds the size of Hamwick Dean parish itself, not that most there knew it, only that it was an exceptionally large holding: too large for one farmer. The greed which proposed that one man only should think to own so much land shocked them. Dick Dollery was on his feet in an instant, shaking his fist. 'You're robbing us of our land, thieving it from under our noses!' he shouted.

Others, too, were shouting and waving their fists: indeed, had not the Reverend Coleman and Parson Petchey jumped to their feet yet again, hands raised in an attempt to calm the incensed gathering, a riot might well have ensued there and then, House of God or no.

'You are in a church! You are in the presence of God! Behave yourselves! Behave yourselves!' cried an alarmed Parson Petchey, as though he expected a bolt of lightning to pierce the vaulted ceiling and smite the wicked shouters – or, worse, that the outburst might put him in a bad light with his Maker. The Reverend Coleman restricted himself to a more simple but effective, 'Please, please! Good people, please!'

Even Joshua Jaikes and Elijah Candler were on their feet to ensure that none rushed up the aisle to strike at the lord of the manor or any of those sitting with him:. Not that any of it bothered Titus Broake: he remained standing throughout and, when the shouting and the rumpus had subsided and the two clergymen had retaken their seats, he resumed in the same contemptuous vein. 'This village is backward and needs a good kick up the arse!' he snorted, uncaring, too, of the fact that he was in a church or how his crudeness might affect the sensibilities of the two parsons, who both reddened visibly, but made no attempt at censure.

'We need to do away with all your little lands of perches, roods, half-acres and acres. It is too much of a waste. We need to enclose the land, divide it up, common arable, common meadowland and common waste, too, if it can be drained and ploughed and cropped. We need to modernise and enclosing the land is the only way for us to do it. A farmer needs his fields to be hedged and fenced so his cattle and sheep can be penned away from other men's diseased stock. You have had too many losses of your sheep on the common. It is but three years back since you lost a quarter of the whole flock on the common with rot – ' Which was true. ' – The superiority of the new agricultural ways over the old commonable ways cannot be disputed. I notice no voice is raised against enclosure on any other grounds than the injury it will inflict on wasteful and incompetent open-field farmers and commoners – ' There were growls of disapproval at that remark, too. ' – The economic gain it will provide is admitted to by everyone but you. In other places, it has been demonstrated beyond a doubt, beyond argument, that consolidating the land is a far better method over commonable fields. And since we out-value you all, there is no way we can be opposed. The petition will go-ahead whatever you do, whether you sign or not.'

With that, the lord of the manor sat down amid boos and hisses, glowering at Jem, Dick Dollery, Enos Diddams, Nathaniel Newman and the rest who had challenged him.

Silas Kempen, who was also dressed in his Sunday-best, sensing that Titus Broake's bluntness had angered the congregation more than was necessary, now rose and somewhat nervously attempted to placate them. 'My friends, I know how angered you are,' the heavy-set, florid-faced Lower Rackstead farmer began rather foolishly, for it was a remark almost guaranteed to stir up the same barrage of discord as the previous speaker, which it did. He was not an unliked man, in fact the best liked of the six large farmers, and, in past times, they might have listened to him: but he had thrown in his lot with the petitioners, willingly or no. Anonymous shouts from the back of the church, all recognisably Lower Rackstead accents, bluntly informed him that he no longer had any friends, not even amongst the day-labourers there, and they were as prepared to show him the fact the same as the men of Hamwick Dean had shown their three 'turncoats.'

'Let us approach this like sensible men,' Silas Kempen tried next, but they were in no mood to be sensible either: they would listen to him, but if he said anything with which they disagreed, then they reserved the right to shout out and tell him so in honest terms, or some amongst them would and not care tuppence about it either.

So Silas Kempen tried reassurance. 'The benefit of enclosing can be seen the other side of Wivencaster, in the village of Yearton Breal, which was enclosed ten years ago,' he informed them. 'I have passed through it many times on my way to Witchley and can vouch for the fact that the heathland there, which was covered with gorse, furze and bramble and which produced very little, has been changed by enclosure into profitable, sizeable parcels of consolidated arable farmland, with two new farmhouses built on it, as well as barns and other buildings. Enclosure has brought prosperity there. The landlord and occupier have both benefited, the one in an advance of rent, the other in the increase of crops, and many hundreds of acres once neglected have been brought into cultivation, which before were productive of little more than furze and a few scanty blades of grass. By the enclosure of common fields, lands have been laid together, rents have risen on the heath and the farmers are much better off. They grow more crops, the numbers of cattle and sheep have increased, and more of the men are employed – '

His voice trailed away: throughout his discourse, there had been a persistent shuffling on the pew seats, though no one had shouted out: they were not the least interested in the success of others in other places, most particularly farmers who had become better off through enclosure: and they were in no mood either to heed reassurances. They were concerned solely with their own livelihoods and the effect enclosure would have on them: so they just stared blankly back at him till he sat down.

Amos Peakman got to his feet next: to his way of thinking, there was no point other than being absolutely blunt. 'You cannot hold back progress,' he declared with a sniff. 'You cannot stop the future. It comes towards us and we cannot stop it. It would be like trying to stand in the way of a bull in full charge and only a fool would try to stop a bull running straight at him. What good does it do a man if he has his hay lying in so many parcels in balks and loads and at such a distance from each other that it costs near as much gathering in the hay as it is worth? It does not make sense either that, when several of you are all under one landlord, you must continually cross each other as do you for no good or sensible purpose than to get from one land to another in another part of the same field. The same way, you pay no heed to the improved methods of arable farming and the proper use of roots, clover and grasses to help put the good back into the earth as we do now on our farms. Your land is not put to the best use by the proper interchange of arable, which is the new way and has been for a long time. The greater part of your holdings is still used only for corn-growing and you persist with the fallow when it has been proved ours is a better way. We all need to modernise, as Mr. Broake has said, and enclosing the land is the only way for us to do it, to feed the nation. The people of this parish will be three times better off when enclosure is done. For a start, it will stop all the strife and arguing which goes on and causes so much trouble at the Little Court. It is time the Little Court and all its rules and practices were done away with once and for all. That is what I say.'

He, too, sat down, amid hisses and low grumbling: and when the Reverend Coleman turned to the four remaining farmers and asked if any of them wished to speak, none accepted his invitation: besides, the people had listened long enough and, church or no church, they wanted their say now, spoken their way.

Jonas Bunting, a small farmer of some twenty acres, rose to his feet in the pew ahead of Jem, to begin it. 'Enclosing will be fatal to us small farmers and cottagers and the like,' he declared. 'If thee strips the small farms of the benefit of the commons, then we are all levelled to the ground at one stroke. Our common rights are worth more to us than anything we are ever likely to receive in return. T'is our anchorage, is the land. T'will be a sad day for this village if you encloses our land.'

'There is a revolution going on in agriculture and we intend to be a part of it,' said Marcus Howie, jumping to his feet and looking as angry and frustrated as Titus Broake and Amos Peakman had been. 'You can't hold it back and why should we be held back? You have only to go over to Inworth, not four miles from here, to see why. The common land there is overrun with thistles, the field land is badly managed, some of the fallow has not been ploughed for two or more years. It is still farmed on the fallow system the same as here, with all its loss of time and expense. It needs a new hand if it is to prosper under the new farming methods as does the land around Hamwick Dean.'

'The lord of the manor will do best out of this, the small man will get nothing but worry and trouble, mark my words,' shouted Dick Dollery, pointing a finger at Titus Broake, who stared straight back at him, as if to say, 'Do not attempt to impede me.'

Unfazed, Dick Dollery continued to point his finger directly at the lord of the manor. 'He, for one, will receive the most in lieu of his rights and what he will get will be far more valuable than the rights he has to give up. It will be the same with the tithe-owner,' he went on, shifting his gaze and his pointing finger along the line to Parson Petchey. 'He and the Church stand to gain from the higher rents they will be able to charge on the cottages and the tenanted land they own.'

His finger now targeted Amos Peakman, Marcus Howie, Joshua Godwin and the three hamlet farmers. 'They are the same because they have the money to take up the acres, which we do not have. There are no rich men amongst us. T'is us, the husbandmen and the cottagers, who stand to lose by this. What they propose is for themselves and themselves alone and for no other, least of all us.'

Immediately several shouts went up of 'He's right!' and 'He speaks the truth' and 'What he says is true.'

'T'is our rents which will leap up now,' someone shouted from the standing throng filling one of the rear aisles.

Joshua Godwin then rose to speak. 'Enclosing the land can only bring improvement,' he began, glowering somewhat contemptuously at the rows of angry faces before him. 'The old ways are a restraint on good productivity, as Mr. Broake has said. Too much is lost due to trespass, due to the employment of wasteful fallows and the inefficiency of having scattered holdings. Scattering is the evil of bad cultivation and common-field husbandry does not allow a man to have proper turnipping or any of the other late improvements in agriculture, which some of us here have learned about and have adopted to our benefit. We all here know there can be no real improvement when the occupier of the land, whether it be open-field or hedged, is obliged to depend on the whims of others and where the awkwardness or ill nature of one bad neighbour can defeat the best intentions of a whole parish. It is a nonsense and you know it. I ask, what will you lose by enclosure when you have everything to gain?'

The question was a slight, a casual dismissal of everything for which any husbandmen had ever worked. Benjamin Dixon, who was not a man angered easily, answered him: 'I farm five acres and keep nine cows and two-dozen sheep,' he retorted. 'If the parish land is to be enclosed the way it has been done elsewhere, when three or four takes the whole lot for themselves, then I shan't be able to keep so much as a goose! Thee asks me what I will lose by it, Joshua Godwin! I'll tell thee what I shall lose – I shall lose everything. Everything I have ever worked for. Everything I have ever held. I shall lose my whole way of life and thee asks me what I shall lose!'

The truth of his words and the anger in them drew more voluble support from the villagers at the back and the insults of 'Robbers!' and 'Thieves!' and 'Villains!' began to be shouted down the length of the church, though none stepped forward to identify themselves or to make a speech of his own, but hid behind the backs of others.

'Gentlemen! Gentlemen!' The Reverend Coleman and the Reverend Doctor Petchey were on their feet for a third time.

Enos Diddams ignored them: he was too angry. 'We may only be small men compared with you, but we have our own cattle and we get our own milk and make our own butter and cheese from it,' he shouted. 'That is one thing in our favour – that we have the sheep to manure our land.'

Titus Broake now leapt to his feet. 'You arable farmers may well be dependent on sheep for fertilising your soil,' he shouted back as the chorus of dissent and opposition persisted, 'but in winter, your animals, even when they are reduced to the lowest possible number, barely survive on straw and tree-loppings. The miserable condition of your livestock on the open-fields and the commons exposes them all to the scab and the rot and your cattle to the murrain. The first things I saw when I came to this village was the head of an ox impaled on a stake by the highway as a warning that the cattle here were infected by murrain – as they were! You can't go on farming like that. The new methods are being used in other places. They are revolutionising farming – '

'T'is a revolution of the rich against the poor!' exclaimed Daniel Gate, the wagoner, also speaking up for the first time. 'The lords and nobles are breaking down ancient law and custom. They are robbing us poor of our share in the common. I am a wagoner and I have been to places where the land has been enclosed and I have seen where they have torn down the houses and taken away the villagers' rights, which the poor had long regarded as their own and, in time, would pass to their heirs. The ruins of villages not forty miles north of here testify to the greed of the revolution you speak for – a revolution against us. Enclosure will overburden the soil and turn it into dust and, by it, decent husbandmen will be turned into a mob of beggars and thieves. I myself have seen parishes which have been enclosed and every one of them has been in a manner depopulated.'

From the back of the church again came outright blasphemies, boos and yet more cries of 'Robbery!' 'Thievery!' and 'Stealing!' so much so that the red-faced Reverend Coleman and Parson Petchey had to stand a fourth time to quell the disorder: however, by then the tenor of the meeting had become so openly hostile that it was time to end it as no further good would be served, no minds would be changed, no agreement reached.

Even before the meeting, a list of all the owners of property in the parish, based on the land tax returns, with, as well, a description of the properties, acreages and value and whether they would be 'for' or 'against' the enclosure had begun to pile up in Mr. Mogg's office in Melchborough. All through the meeting, the lawyer had listened quietly without a word and with barely a flicker of emotion, casually turning a fob watch over in his fingers, allowing the parties to have their say. Now, however, it was time to put an end to all the argument.

'Gentlemen,' he said, calmly, rising from his chair alongside Titus Broake, 'I speak for my clients here and I speak also for those who are not present. Between them, they hold more than threequarters of the value of the lands of the three parishes combined. I am obliged to state their view, but it is one with which I concur, even though I am not a farmer, but a lawyer. The changes they seek in the Bill which we propose to present to Parliament are, in my opinion, justified, if not made necessary, by the very progress of farming in this modern day. I ask those opponents of enclosure what they say to the enclosures in the counties of Norfolk, Nottinghamshire, Derbyshire, Lincolnshire and Yorkshire and many other counties, of which I know myself, and which my client here, Mr. Broake, also knows, and all the northern counties which yield corn and mutton and beef from the force of enclosure alone? I ask them what say they to the Wolds of York and Lincoln, which, from barren heaths at one shilling per acre, have been rendered into profitable farms by enclosure alone? I ask them what they say to the vast tracts in the Peak of Derbyshire, which also by enclosure alone have been changed from black regions of peat and heather into fertile fields of grass pastured with cattle? I ask them what they say to the improvements of the moors in the northern counties of Northumberland and Cumbria, where enclosures alone have made those counties flourish whereas before they were dreary as night? I say to you open-field farmers that you ought yourselves to recognise the advantages of enclosure and embrace it as have others.

It would make sense to agree amongst yourselves to consolidate your holdings intermixed everywhere and extinguish your reciprocal rights of common, for it is the intention of my clients to proceed with their Bill to Parliament and it is their belief that they will succeed and that enclosure will come to this parish and the two other parishes whether the common field farmers wish it or not. The law and the values are in my clients' favour.'

With that, he declared rather peremptorily: 'I am finished, Mr. Chairman. I have no further views to air on this matter, either for myself or my clients. I thank you for your courtesy.' And with that, he and Titus Broake pushed back their chairs, bade the others at the table a 'Good evening' and walked boldly down the left-side aisle, followed by Amos Peakman, Marcus Howie, Joshua Godwin, and the other three farmers, with Joshua Jaikes, Lemuel Ring and Elijah Candler rising quickly from their own chairs to force a passage for them through the stunned and quietened throng.

As far as Titus Broake and the others were concerned, the matter was settled and further argument was useless. The small proprietors of land, the small farmers and husbandmen, the likes of Jem, Dick Dollery, Enos Diddams and all the others who had tried to resist, they had been informed bluntly that the success of the enclosure petition was certain and that, in the final award, those who obstructed it would suffer just as those who assisted it would gain, a clear intimidatory attempt to stifle all opposition to it there and then.

It was too much for the villagers to let the departing petitioners go so peaceably: they were booed and jeered and jostled as they made their way to the door. Unfortunately, the venue being the church, none had thought to remove the three vases of flowers which Joshua Jaikes's wife kept always before the font behind the cross-aisle, an innovation she had dreamed up to 'beautify God's House' to please the parson, but one which gave three of the more devil-may-care youths weapons which they did not shirk to take up. Two vases were emptied over the heads of Amos Peakman and Marcus Howie as they pushed together through them and the third was flung over Joshua Godwin and the other three farmers: Titus Broake and Mr. Mogg escaped unharmed, having already passed into the porch.

Had it not been for the presence of the parish constable and the churchwardens, as well as the two reverends, the latter six might well have been strung up from the trees in the churchyard: indeed, some swore they saw Dick Dollery and Enos Diddams standing in the churchyard just after the meeting had ended and when the majority had dispersed to their cottages, looking up at the trees as if ascertaining which was the strongest bough to take someone's weight without it breaking!

SIXTY-TWO

NO MATTER how hostile the opposition, Titus Broake, as the instigator of the Bill, had never considered himself bound to accept the opinion of a meeting of small farmers and husbandmen, anyway: he had expected that they would be hostile to it. All that had ever concerned him was that no large proprietor should stand out against the scheme: and none had. They had all accepted it: the rewards which it promised them were too great to refuse. The petitioners were, therefore, masters of the situation in every sense, being ahead in their planning: indeed, the experienced Mr. Mogg had already drawn up their Bill, all according to law: and being all well-to-do landowners, they had the money to support the petition and all stages of the proceedings.

Just as Peter Sparshott had charged, the whole plan had indeed been settled between the various lawyers of the principal proprietors long before – before even the six farmers had been apprised of the details of it at the unexpected dinner party at Hamwick Hall. On that evening, the subject had first been broached by Titus Broake over the salmon, discussed further over the goose, parsnips, peas, potatoes and gravy and expounded upon in more detail still over the ice cream and spotted dick pudding, till eventually all had been persuaded – not that they needed much persuasion – and their full support was given amid much smiling and back-slapping as they each drank their third or fourth glass of port and smoked their pipes in the Old Squire's study, while the ladies were sipping their sherbets in the drawing room after touring the Hall.

What even Amos Peakman, Marcus Howie and Joshua Godwin and the others did not realise at the time, was that, in effect, Titus Broake had presented them with a *fait accompli*, an accomplished fact, and that wining and dining them had served only to secure a possible loose end, the lord of the manor reasoning it was best to have the six sign the petition believing they were all bold allies and as forward thinking as himself simply so that he would not have the embarrassment of the value of several hundred acres of the more than three thousand total for the three parishes counted against him. It was simply an exercise by Titus Broake to confound any likely opposition: if the six largest yeomen farmers in the three parishes all supported his enclosure petition, then so much the better: though it would have gone ahead without their agreement anyway because of the weight of the value of the other landowners. Their land contributed towards the eighty per cent by value to present the petition, but it was not totally necessary for its success. The need of three of them to obtain reversions of their copyhold from the new lord of the manor had helped, of course.

Parson Petchey was made an unwitting party to the deception though the Bishop of Melchborough's agreement that the glebe lands should be included in the mix, which was duly communicated to the Reverend Doctor by letter a fortnight beforehand, though not a word of it was said by him in any of the parish notices subsequently delivered at the end of the two following divine services. He was told by the Bishop 'not to reveal anything until the notice of the petition is advertised so as not to excite agitation,' an instruction by which he abided: and only when the arrangements were all agreed upon did the participants, in accordance with a Standing Order of Parliament, tack the notice of the intended petition for an Enclosure Bill to the church door for the villagers to read – those that could read, that is.

Once a petition for enclosure of open-fields and commons, signed by threequarters or four-fifths of the owners of the land value, by the lord of the manor, by the owner of the tithes and by a majority of the persons interested – once that had been presented to Parliament by persons locally interested, then, by leave of the House of Commons, a Bill was introduced, read a first time and a second time and then referred to a committee, usually of selected Members.

The committee, after receiving counter-petitions, if any, and hearing evidence, if any, reported to the House, that the Standing Orders had, or had not, been complied with, that the allegations were, or were not, true and that they were, or were not, satisfied that the parties concerned had consented to the Bill. The parliamentary committees generally took as a guide in their deliberations the values of the landholdings as well as the numbers which were represented on the petition for enclosure: and, upon its report, the Bill either was rejected or was read a third time, passed, sent to the House of Lords and, finally, received Royal Assent.

However, there being no fixed rule on the consent necessary to satisfy a committee on the precise distribution of land, in the case of the three parishes of Hamwick Dean, Lower Rackstead and Merchant

Staplers the consent of three-fourths was required, not of persons, but in terms of ownership of property – and adding to that manifest unfairness the necessary value to be taken into account was to be calculated in acres, rather than in annual value held.

By that time, the lord of the manor of Hamwick Dean himself owned an enclosed and extended manorial estate of three hundred acres, two farms, parcels of meadowland, arable strip-holdings and waste totalling together some three hundred and fifty of the one parish's seventeen hundred and thirty-four acres alone (with the Church, through the Bishop, and the dean and chapter at Oxford and certain others holding the rest of the acreage on the open-fields).

Titus Broake further owned seventy of Lower Rackstead's near nine hundred acres by then (with five hundred other acres of open-field and meadowland being owned by Lady Amelia, who, it turned out, was the daughter of the old dowager marchioness, who herself held two hundred and eighty of the other acres in that parish, with the remainder leased on part-copyholds by Silas Kempen and James Allen, and three small farmers).

The tenant of Hamwick Hall also held sixty acres of Merchant Staplers's nine hundred and fifty acres (with the dowager marchioness again holding a hundred or more and Sir Benton and Sir Gentry and the Church, with several others, sharing the rest, save for the likes of the yeoman farmer Thomas Godbear). The lord of the manor, of course, also had rights on the pastureland and the waste in all three places: thus the substantial acreage of these proprietors, all signatories to the petition, swamped the entire community of small farmers, husbandmen and cottagers in all three parishes. The petitioners had easily achieved the required four-fifths majority in determining whether the open-fields, common pastureland and the waste should be enclosed or not: in Mr. Mogg's lawyers' terms, it was *chose jugée*, a judged thing.

In theory, of course, anyone in Hamwick Dean and the other parishes wishing to revise a clause or clauses in the Bill, even if to their own advantage, or anyone opposed totally to enclosure, was free to object as others had done in other places and, in some instances, had been successful in achieving the changes they sought.

Two days after the church meeting, a committee was formed to oppose the petition, with Jem, Peter Sparshott, Jonas Bunting, Dick Dollery, Enos Diddams and Nathaniel Newman elected by mutual consent of the other drinkers in the Wayfarers' to represent Hamwick Dean and two husbandmen from Lower Rackstead and Merchant

Staplers to represent the hamlets. Their first act was to call a meeting in the bay-windowed parlour at which all those objectors from Lower Rackstead and Merchant Staplers were invited to join with the men and women of Hamwick Dean. A blue banner, emblazoned with the words 'May Hamwick Dean Flourish Free and Ever Protect Her Rights,' was hung across the front of the Wayfarers' yard on the Wednesday evening upon which the meeting was held.

Their next duty was to ask Mr. Able, in his official capacity as a lawyer, to draw up a petition which they could send to Parliament to show the strength of the opposition, that is, if they could find someone to present it. The lawyer readily agreed to their request, charging a modest fee of a guinea for writing it out in his best hand, for which a collection was then taken up to pay for it: the wording of it was left to the committee.

'We needs summat that'll tell'em how hard it will be for all of us,' Dick Dollery told the lawyer, and proceeded to list his suggestions, which they all agreed since none felt they could better them.

A week later, Mr. Able brought them their counter petition, all written out on parchment in his neat hand: the whole village, it seemed, was thronged outside the Wayfarers' that Saturday afternoon when Jem climbed gingerly atop a table brought out of the inn to read it to them. Even the publican at the Carpenters' Arms, Jack Tickle, had walked up The Street again to listen: the only upset was that, for some reason, very few from Lower Rackstead and Merchant Staplers came.

'The petitioners beg leave,' Jem read, speaking as loudly as he could so his voice would carry over those at the front, who were loudly 'shushing' those behind, who, in turn, were 'shushing' those standing at the back, *'the petitioners beg leave to represent to the House that, under pretence of improving lands in the said parishes herein named, the cottagers and other persons entitled to right of common on the lands intended to be enclosed, will be deprived of an inestimable privilege, which they now enjoy, of turning a certain number of their cows, calves, and sheep, on and over the said lands; a privilege that enables them not only to maintain themselves and their families in the depth of winter, when they cannot, even for their money, obtain from the occupiers of other lands the smallest portion of milk or whey for such necessary purpose, but, in addition to this, they can now supply the grazier with young or lean stock at a reasonable price, to fatten and bring to market at a more moderate rate for general consumption, which they conceive to be the most*

rational and effectual way of establishing public plenty and cheapness of provision; and they further conceive, that a more ruinous effect of this enclosure will be the almost total depopulation of their village, now filled with bold and hardy husbandmen, from amongst whom, and the inhabitants of other open parishes, the nation has hitherto derived its greatest strength and glory, in the supply of its fleets and armies, and driving them, from necessity and want of employ, in vast crowds, into manufacturing towns, where the very nature of their employment, over the loom or the forge, soon may waste their strength, and consequently debilitate their posterity, and by imperceptible degrees obliterate that great principle of obedience to the laws of God and their country, which forms the character of the simple and artless villagers, more equally distributed through the open countries, and on which so much depends the good order and government of the state: these are some of the injuries to themselves as individuals, and of the ill consequences to the public, which the petitioners conceive will follow from this, as they have already done from many enclosures, but which they did not think they were entitled to lay before the House until it unhappily came to their own lot to be exposed to them through the Bill now pending.'

All agreed it was fine wording, of a kind they could never have written themselves, and would make them all sound very educated and law abiding and loyal to the realm: not that sending a petition against a Bill for Enclosure to the House of Commons would have mattered or altered things.

SIXTY-THREE

IF A PETITION against an Act of enclosure emanated from a lord or a lord of the manor even, or perhaps from a tithe owner, who for some reason or other was dissatisfied with the contemplated arrangements, it would, of course, receive due attention, especially if supported by the local Member of Parliament, who could speak and lobby for it. If necessary, the titled objector could get a friend in Parliament to attend the committee and introduce amendments so the Bill could perhaps be altered to suit him. However, with a petition from a group of cottagers and small landholders, the committee was, as a rule, able to neglect any petition they might send. If a Bill were being promoted by the powerful of the land, whether national or county, objectors often found it a waste of their money to appeal to Parliament against it: in many cases, it was not worth the trouble and the expense to be heard on Second Reading.

However, of the petitioners against the Enclosure Bill for Hamwick Dean and the two hamlets, two-thirds were the husbandmen and small farmers who sat in the Wayfarers' and the Green Man and the Bull and did not themselves own or let any land, but leased it from others, and so were never likely to receive the least consideration. Others signed it, too: the blacksmith Nathaniel Newman signed, as did the Wayfarers' innkeeper Caleb Chapman, and Jack Tickle at the Carpenters' Arms, and the flour miller Abel Tedder, the cordwainer Matthew Cobbe and the wheelwright John Romble, who were tradesman and artisans, but who also rented and tilled small plots.

Another who willingly signed against enclosure was the cattle herder, Tully Jordan, and the village shepherd, Isaac Coulson. Thirty others who were cottagers and who drank in the Carpenters' Arms boldly put their names to it, claiming they did so because of the rights attached to their cottages – the same rights over which they had provoked an argument years before, that was, 'to depasture a horse and ten sheep as well as a cow into the harvest fields without paying a fee the same as their fathers and forefathers before them.' Last of all to sign were several of the younger day-labourers, a lodger, a housekeeper and two servants of Mr. Able, who had appended his signature as the very first.

One evening, at a further crowded meeting of the small farmers, husbandmen and cottagers in the Wayfarers', Dick Dollery did ask in all innocence: 'How much is all this petitioning business going to cost us?'

'About five hundred or six hundred pounds, I suppose,' replied Mr. Able, casually, thinking they would already have surmised that for themselves. For, just as it cost several thousand pounds to launch a petition and achieve enclosure, so it cost far more than the poor villagers of Hamwick Dean, Merchant Staplers and Lower Rackstead could ever have mustered to present a petition to oppose it.

There was an immediate intake of breath from everyone and it stopped the conversation for a full twenty seconds before the hubbub resumed and thirty or so voices all discussed the simple fact that there was no hope – and really never had been – that they, a band of husbandmen, small farmers, tradesmen and day-labouring cottagers, could ever raise such an amount.

Sometimes Bills for enclosure were introduced and passed without discussion and, while it was true that Bills were referred to a committee, the sittings of those committees generally were attended only by honourable Members who were interested in them, some being lords of manors themselves: the rights of the poor, though they might be talked about, were mostly taken away. Further, only the pressure of the powerful interests could decide whether a committee should approve or disapprove of an enclosure Bill: it was the same pressure that determined the form in which a Bill became law.

In effect, it enabled rich men to fight out their rival claims in Parliament and left those who could not send counsel to Parliament without a voice: and, if there were no lawyer there to put their case, what prospect was there that an obscure band of small farmers and husbandmen and cottagers, who were now to be set adrift with their families by an enclosure Bill launched by the lord of the manor, supported by two titled ladies, a bishop, the dean and chapter of an esteemed university college, two knights and various esquires and promoted by one of those very same Members of Parliament – what prospect was there that they would ever trouble the conscience of a committee of landowners? The answer, of course, was none.

Nor was a committee composed mostly of landed proprietors likely to bother to elicit the opinions of small claimants: inhabitant cottagers had no votes or the means of influencing either an election to

Parliament or a committee of the House, particularly one hearing a Bill for enclosure, because, by the very fact of their poverty, they were unable to go to London to fee counsel, to produce or pay for witnesses or to urge their claims themselves before the committee.

Any witnesses who wished to speak against an enclosure Bill had to attend the committee in the House of Commons and, subsequently, in the House of Lords, incurring the expense of travel and lodging and time away from their land. There might well be postponements, delays and protracted intervals to be accounted for and, if so, the witnesses had either to find lodgings in London each time or make costly journeys to town. For opponents of Bills, such expenditures were generally prohibitive and they had to be content with drawing up a counter-petition such as those at Hamwick Dean had done, but which, if delivered, might not even be referred to the House committee.

On such matters, the rights of the poor were largely neglected and the committees often remained in ignorance of their claims: nor was much time spent in worrying about their fate. To the landowning Members of Parliament, who sat smoking their pipes and taking their snuff in the panelled walls of the old Palace of Westminster, they were merely the poor inhabitants of a village about to be enclosed, mere 'paupers and potwobblers,' who most times were not even listed amongst those opposing the Bill. Indeed, the *Journal of the Commons* generally listed only the total sum of land owned by the opponents of the Bill, not the actual opposition of husbandmen with land in the open-fields and a right of common on the waste and pastureland.

Thus, when Titus Broake's petition for a Bill to promote the enclosure of Hamwick Dean, Lower Rackstead and Merchant Staplers was presented to Parliament, the opposition of seventy-six husbandmen and six small farmers from the three parishes and a hundred others who owned no land worthy of taxation and whose only property was common right to put a cow on the pasture free and, for a fee of a few shillings per annum, to feed it on the corn stubble, went unnoticed.

So the fine words which Mr. Able had penned so expertly languished in the dusty recesses of his office at Hamwyte all during the hearing of the Bill. The grumblers in the Wayfarers', amongst them Jem himself as well as Dick Dollery and Enos Diddams, and all the others in the Carpenters' Arms and the Bull at Merchant Staplers and the Green Man at Lower Rackstead, as poor countrymen, they all knew in their hearts that the only way of making any impression at all upon the intransigence of Titus Broake and the others, indeed to repay them for the downright scorn they had shown towards them, would have been to carry out some daring act of sabotage or incendiarism on some dark Saturday night after they had left the inn and everyone else was abed.

'Enclosure is the robbery of the poor by the landowning class,' growled Dick Dollery at a meeting of all the husbandmen and small farmers convened in the Wayfarers' the following Wednesday. 'We shall all become landless, working as day-labourers for whatever wage the farmers decide to pay us.'

'Even so, I'd sooner that than gooing to one o' they new towns up North to be worked to death in one o' they factories up there,' declared Enos Diddams glumly.

'We should fire their ricks. That'd make'em think afore they acts agin us next time,' suggested Nathaniel Newman, not appreciating that there would be no 'next time.'

No one did, of course, though feelings remained high for a long time afterwards. Curses were muttered against the lord of the manor and the other petitioners at almost every drinking evening in the Wayfarers': and there was as much blaspheming against the Church and anger against Parson Petchey from amongst the day-labourers in the Carpenters' Arms as there was in the Wayfarers', for they were men all drawn together in a common cause and all wanting to put in their tuppence worth.

Despite the anger generated, not to mention the sale of ale which Caleb Chapman made, all knew that any attempt at disorder would be met firmly by the forces of law and order, as represented by the local Justices of the Peace, namely Parson Petchey and Titus Broake himself. Indeed, the rumblings of discontent were noted by the one man who made it his business to note such things – not the parish constable, Elijah Candler, who, had he been asked, would have agreed with the sentiments of Jem and Dick Dollery and the others anyway, but by Joshua Jaikes, the overseer of the poor, senior churchwarden and bailiff of the Glebe farm, who still lived in the farm house there and so was still beholden to the parson.

Exactly who informed on them to him, no one knew for sure, though most suspected Lemuel Ring. Jaikes then took it upon himself to report 'expressions of revolt overheard in the Wayfarers' Inn' to Parson Petchey, who immediately let it be known in his parish notices after divine service the very next Sunday that, if necessary, he would summon the Melchborough Militia to quell any further meetings where there was such talk. In consequence, a plan to convene a secret meeting in the Compasses on the main Maydun-to-Wivencaster road at Greater Tottle, in the hope of getting the Lower Rackstead and Merchant Staplers small farmers and husbandmen to attend, was abandoned.

Unbeknown to Jem and the others, the protestors in Lower Rackstead and Merchant Staplers had already wavered: Richard Shadwell, John Dicker, Henry Sweetapple and Widow Snook, all small tenant farmers in Merchant Staplers, had been prevailed upon to sign the petition just before it was presented to Parliament, as had Jonathan Hartless, who had twenty acres in Lower Rackstead, Thomas Crawley, with twenty-two acres, and Thomas Templeton, who farmed twenty-six acres. Further, fifteen cottagers in Lower Rackstead had been coerced to do the same and thirteen in Merchant Staplers were likewise coerced by their landlords or lose their homes, for their landlords were Sir Benton, Sir Gentry and the dowager marchioness – not that their desertion affected the matter one way or another.

Other who also signed secretly in the hope of not being found out were the three disgruntled contributors to the poor rate, William Hoskins and Francis Clutter, the butchers, and Samuel Thorn, one of the bakers, who each did much business with the lord of the manor at the Hall, the parson and the three larger farmers…

SIXTY-FOUR

THE PETITION for a Bill to enclose the common arable, meadowland and waste of the joint parishes of Hamwick Dean, Lower Rackstead and Merchant Staplers was heard almost as a matter of course: leave was granted for the introduction of the Bill and instruction given to one of the Members for Hamwyte, Sir Benton, who would present the petition, to prepare it, which, of course, the principal promoter, Titus Broake, had already had Mr. Mogg do in advance.

The Bill was submitted in late November, read a first time a week later and a second time in the following January and then referred to a committee, the members of which were as prejudiced in favour of enclosure as the proposers of the Bill, judgment upon which was given by the very kind of landowners who were themselves to profit by other acts of enclosure.

'The supposed advantages derived by cottagers in having food for a few sheep and geese on a neighbouring common have usually been brought forward as objections to the enclosing system,' Sir Gentry began in his address to the committee, which sat in a small tapestry-hung room at the Palace. 'This question was much agitated with regard to the enclosure of Hamwick Dean and the adjoining parishes, but, if Honourable Members will refer to the example of the villages of Gooding and Whidding, in the north west of the same county, both enclosed some fifteen years previously, the state and appearance of them contrast so greatly as to what they were before, particularly in respect of the present produce of corn to the sheep that used to run over the land, that little doubt can remain of the advantageous result of enclosure. Thirteen hundred acres of wet and gorse-covered waste were enclosed and, in the first year of cultivation, the produce was calculated at twenty thousand and more bushels of wheat, or of some other crop in equal proportion, from seven hundred quarters to two thousand three hundred quarters in one place and from six hundred and ninety quarters to two thousand one hundred quarters in another.'

Sir Gentry concluded: 'Even if it could be proved that some cottagers were deprived of a few trifling advantages, the small losses of individuals ought not to stand in the way of improvements on a large scale.'

The committee was most impressed by Sir Gentry's revelation that the common waste of these three places was worth only a few shillings an acre in their unenclosed state when overrun with furze and ant-hills, but that, if enclosed, cultivated and converted, they would be worth upwards of two to three times as much per acre: there was much nodding of heads at the marked rise in values and the sense it made in enclosing such unproductive land in the three parishes.

Sir Benton, in his address to them, was equally convinced of the advantages of enclosing common wastes. In his humble opinion, like his 'honourable friend,' the common waste lands of these three parishes were seldom stinted to a definite quantity of stock in proportion to the number of acres occupied and the cottagers claimed by custom the right to stock equally with the largest landholder. 'It is justly questioned whether any profit accrues to either from the depasturing of sheep,' declared Sir Benton, 'since the common wastes, being under no agricultural management, are usually poisoned by stagnant water, which corrupts or renders unwholesome the herbage, producing rot and other diseases in the miserable animals that are turned adrift to seek their food there.'

The honourable Sir Benton did add, as an afterthought: 'In the two villages along the northern boundary with the next county, which have already been enclosed, scarcely a farmer can now be found who does not possess a considerable landed property and many whose fathers lived in idleness and sloth, on the precarious support of a few half-starved cows or a few limping geese, are now in affluence.'

He made no mention of those who, having been deprived of their rights, deprived of their livelihood, deprived of their independence and, in some cases, where they had been unable to find work as day-labourers and where the parish overseer had decreed that there were too many for the parish purse to keep and it could no longer afford to pay their rents, deprived of their homes – that they had been evicted and at that very time were tramping the roads towards the towns, hoping to find work of any kind there.

To Sir Benton, in such circumstances, the most effective solution to the country's population problems was to get rid of the surplus mouths: an exodus of the landless and the incompetent poor by assisted migration to New South Wales, as was the Government's policy, was the answer, he thought: and he regretted that it was not popular due to the stigma which was attached to it simply because of the transportation of convicts to the same place.

Such was the mood abroad amongst the great landowning classes, who formulated the laws which governed the land, that nothing was ever going to stop the inexorable march to the near total enclosure of the former common lands of England. Progress demanded it, as Titus Broake had said: and there was little the poor could do to promote their opposition to it.

Not that there was much prospect of a successful opposition when those ranged against them were the powers that appointed the commissioners who were to make the ultimate awards, namely the wealthy lord of the manor, two wealthy titled ladies, two wealthy knights who themselves sat in the Commons, a bishop more concerned with the rebuilding of his cathedral church than the trivial happenings in a small part of his diocese, the dean of an Oxford college who was so far removed from ordinary life that he had not actually spoken to anyone outside his cloisters for ten years, plus another who supported the petition and was the beneficiary of the great tithe, and various others of means, including several large farmers of the very parishes included.

SIXTY-FOUR

PARSON PETCHEY was feeling satisfied and at ease as he stood in the pulpit at St. Bartholomew's that June of 1825 looking down at the blank, upturned faces, though failing to discern – indeed totally unaware of – the relief showing on them that the service and the sermon were finally over: for that mid-June morning, the black-gowned Reverend Doctor had read to them all forty-two chapters of the Book of Job. *'There was a man in the land of Uz, whose name was Job; and that man was perfect and upright, and one that feared God, and eschewed evil. And there were born unto him seven sons and three daughters. His substance also was seven thousand sheep, and three thousand camels, and five hundred yoke of oxen, and five hundred she asses, and a very great household, so that this man was the greatest of all the men of the East...'*

They had listened in despairing silence as he had read to them of how Satan had gone up to Heaven to appear before the Lord with the other angels and God had told him of Job: *'Hast thou considered my servant Job, that there is none like him in the earth, a perfect and an upright man, one that feareth God, and escheweth evil? Then Satan answered the Lord, and said, "Doth Job fear God for nought? Hast not thou made a hedge about him, and about his house, and about all that he hath on every side? Thou hast blessed the work of his hands and his substance is increased in the land. But put forth thine hand now and touch all that he hath and he will curse thee to thy face." And the Lord said unto Satan, "Behold, all that he hath is in thy power: only upon himself put not forth thine hand".'*

The tragedies which befell Job they received with great sorrow that so much could happen to a God-fearing man: how, as Job's sons and daughters were eating and drinking wine in their eldest brother's house, his oxen and donkeys were taken by the Sabeans, how a fire fell from heaven and burned up his sheep, how the Chaldeans stole his camels and how the servants minding all his animals were slain with the edges of swords and how, finally, *'a great wind came from the wilderness and smote the four corners of the house'* wherein his sons and daughters were eating and drinking wine '*and it fell upon them and they are dead.*'

Despite his great grief, Parson Petchey told them, Job did not blame the Lord, but '*... arose and rent his mantle and shaved his head and fell down upon the ground and worshipped and said, "Naked came I out of my mother's womb and naked shall I return thither: the Lord gave and the Lord hath taken away: blessed be the name of the Lord." In all this Job sinned not, nor charged God foolishly.*'

They learned, too, that Satan then struck Job with '*loathsome sores from the sole of his foot to the crown of his head*' and how Job's wife reproached him for his continued reverence to God, saying '*Dost thou still retain thine integrity? Curse God, and die.*'

'But in all this did not Job sin with his lips,' the parson intoned solemnly

Then the Reverend Doctor read out to them the many chapters detailing how El'iphaz the Te'manite, Bildad the Shuhite and Zophar the Na'amathite, the friends of Job, went to mourn with him and how they rebuked him for his piety, saying it was all a judgment of God and he must have sinned: and how Job answered them and how he replied, too, to Elihu, the son of Barachel the Buzite, and how at last Job cried out to God to ask why a good man like him should suffer so and how the Lord answered him out of the whirlwind, saying: '*Who is this that darkeneth counsel by words without knowledge? Gird up now thy loins like a man, for I will demand of thee and answer thou me. Where wast thou when I laid the foundations of the earth?...*'

And mortified, Job had answered seventeen chapters later: '*...Therefore have I uttered that I understood not; things too wonderful for me, which I knew not. Hear, I beseech Thee, and I will speak: I will demand of Thee, and declare Thou unto me. I have heard of Thee by the hearing of the ear: but now mine eye seeth Thee. Wherefore I abhor myself, and repent in dust and ashes.*'

There he ended the lesson, omitting, lest the congregation, should misinterpret, the last verse: '*...and the Lord blessed the latter end of Job more than his beginning: for he had fourteen thousand sheep and six thousand camels and a thousand yoke of oxen and a thousand she asses. He had also seven sons and three daughters and he called the name of the first, Jemima and the name of the second, Keziah and the name of the third, Keren-happuch. And in all the land were no women found so fair as the daughters of Job: and their father gave them inheritance amongst their brethren. After this lived Job a hundred* *and forty years, and saw his sons, and his sons' sons, even four generations. So Job died, being old and full of days.'*

The sermon was very apt, Parson Petchey thought: the sufferings of Job were something upon which they might well reflect to help them through the changes which were about to come to the village. No matter what their sufferings, none would be greater than those which befell poor Job: therefore, they must rise above it all and, like Job, must not turn away from the Lord, but must bless His name always.

Now, clearing his throat with his usual solemnity before announcing the parish notices, the hook-nosed parson peered along the lines of incomprehensible faces, trusting that only a few miles away the curate at Merchant Staplers, Reverend Waters, and the curate at Lower Rackstead, Reverend Snetterton, would be standing in their pulpits before their congregations, small as they were, and would be doing the self same thing he was about to do before his flock.

'I have to tell you,' Parson Petchey began calmly, reading with a certain stiffness of manner from the notice in his hand, 'that the Act to divide, allot and enclose the open and common fields, common meadows, common pastures and commonable lands and waste grounds in the parishes of Hamwick Dean and in the hamlets of Lower Rackstead and Merchant Staplers has received Royal Assent.'

There was an immediate hubbub of conversation as startled neighbour turned to startled neighbour in the pew beside them: gasps and cries of despair came from some of the women, while from the men, knowing what it meant, there were deep groans and angry muttered curses and not a few blasphemies, while some just put their heads in their hands and sniffed and wiped at the corners of their eyes with a thumb and forefinger.

'Please be quiet! We are in God's House!' cried Parson Petchey sharply, giving out his usual admonition to still the sudden restlessness amongst his congregation: besides he had not finished making his announcements.

As was to be expected of a Bill for enclosure supported by so many of wealth and position, the report of the committee followed a stereotyped formula, stating simply that everything was in order, '...the Standing Orders having been complied with and the committee having examined the allegations of the Bill and found the same to be true and that the parties concerned having given their consent to the Bill to the satisfaction of the committee...' It had passed in the House of Commons on May tenth of that year and one month later, on June the ninth, the Act of Parliament for the enclosure of the three parishes, affecting the livelihoods of several hundred cottagers, small farmers, husbandmen, tradesmen and their dependants, had received Royal Assent.

Under the terms of the Act, the parson now blandly informed them, since it was their right to know, all leases on land were annulled: further, three commissioners for enclosure would soon be visiting the parishes, where they would hold meetings in the nave of each church and all claims for land must be lodged with them at one of those specified meetings. The appointed commissioners, Parson Petchey added, would be legally responsible for executing the enclosure by valuing the land and all legally demonstrable common rights and also for re-allocating the existing landholding distribution. In truth, from the moment when the decision to enclose was taken, all power passed to the commissioners: the husbandman and small farmer, indeed all farmers, no longer had a stake in the land they were farming.

What he did not tell them was that, in common practice, the lord of the manor selected one commissioner, the holder of the great tithe selected another and the third was selected by all the other proprietors, in this case her Ladyship, the dowager marchioness and the two members of Parliament, with the dean of the university and others concurring. Nor did he state that the three commissioners required to be named in the Act had already been approached even as the Bill was in the committee stage. Or that, in effect, the commissioners would be free to act as though they were some kinds of despotic lords into whose hands the property of all three parishes had been invested, to recast and distribute at their will and whim.

In his announcements from the pulpit, he failed also to inform his congregation that a few days previously, while they had been working unsuspectingly in their fields, he had been in the mayor's parlour at Melchborough with two other county Justices of the Peace to witness all three of those commissioners take the oath, in accordance with the requirements of the Act, the very first of them an old friend, who had recited: *'I Doctor Charles Honeywood-Jones, of Little Pestlesham, in the county of Oxford, rector, do swear that I will faithfully, impartially and honestly, according to the best of my skill and judgment, hear and determine all such matters and things as shall be brought before me as a commissioner by virtue of an Act for dividing and enclosing the open and common fields, meadows and other commonable lands in the parishes of Hamwick Dean, Lower Rackstead and Merchant Staplers in the said county without favour or affection to any person whatsoever.'*

The Reverend Honeywood-Jones, though recommended by Parson Petchey, had, of course, to be sanctioned by the Bishop, who had the final say by virtue of the fact that all the glebe land in the three parishes was also being given up as a part of the enclosure scheme and, therefore, it was the Church's right, as the great titheholder of the three parishes, to nominate one commissioner, supposedly to look after the interests of the poor and allotment of charity lands, but also, at the same time, to look after the Church's interests. The fact that the Reverend Honeywood-Jones had no experience of surveying or of acting as a commissioner for enclosure was not mentioned. 'He is considered a very judicious, candid and respectable clergyman, well known by his many public writings,' Parson Petchey had written to the Bishop of his old friend.

The second to take the commissioners' oath at the mayor's parlour that morning had been a lean, high-domed, Roman-nosed lawyer from chambers in Lincoln's Inn Fields in London: Tobias Grint was the appointee of Titus Broake, solely to represent his interests, which he was also allowed to do under the laws of the Act as the lord of the manor and a lay impropriatorial titheholder: the London lawyer had been personally recommended by Mr. Mogg and was an acquaintance also of the two Members of Parliament, Sir Gentry and Sir Benton, and had served three times as a commissioner on enclosures in Berkshire and so brought valuable legal experience to the task, the gathering was told.

Third to take the oath, nominated directly by her Ladyship, with the agreement of the dowager marchioness and the others, was a red-faced, retired naval captain, William Bushnell, of Yarmouth, who had taken up commissioners' duties since the end of the war as a way of supplementing his half pay and improving his parlous finances: and had been delighted to find that he could make a more than useful living at it. Indeed, he had already served twelve times as a commissioner, six times in Hertfordshire, twice in Cambridgeshire and Huntingdonshire and once each in Buckinghamshire and the Isle of Ely, as well as acting as an umpire in Norfolk, for it was not unusual or unknown for a person to act as commissioner on a score of successive enclosures and so develop considerable expertise: and being a man used to vast open spaces – namely the sea – he saw no difference between mapping unboundaried open-fields and commons and sighting the sun aboard ship with a sextant or determining a vessel's longitude with a chronometer. He was also hoping, if the enclosure were carried forward successfully, to put himself in the grace and favour of the dowager marchioness and, it was to be hoped, receive her patronage in seeking a seat in Parliament for the Whig Party.

That Sunday morning at Hamwick Dean, Parson Petchey examined the surprised and bewildered faces of his congregation. 'The commissioners appointed, I know to be reliable men of standing and probity, who possess an understanding of land tenure, farming and the relevant legal matters,' he told them, as if that would satisfy all their concerns and convince them, just as those who stated again and again that enclosure would be good for them and provide more of them with work in the long run, hoped it would appease them and subdue their anger against those pursuing the scheme.

Once appointed to carry out the enclosure, the commissioners – usually three or four, but sometimes as many as twelve, depending on the amount of land involved – were free to nominate surveyors and clerks: a plan of the village with its open-fields and strips was drawn up and the owners of the strips recorded on it. Following that, it was then the role of the commissioners to call a series of meetings at which the landowners could make a claim as to how much land they should be awarded under the enclosure: the commissioners had to decide on the validity of each claim and come to a decision as to who was actually entitled to receive land in the award. When, finally, the land had been allocated, the surveyors drew up a new map displaying the new enclosures, boundaries between each section of land and the location of new paths and roads: and with the new enclosure map went the award, a list of all the landowners allocated land in the enclosed village.

The Reverend Doctor did not tell his congregation that mid-June morning either that, at their first meeting, before they proceeded in the execution of their powers, the commissioners had solemnly taken the oaths for consolidating into one general Act certain provisions for facilitating enclosure which normally would have required the passing of several Acts: in short, the commissioners had powers over every aspect of the enclosure: they were, as was said, the masters of everything.

He also failed to tell them that two surveyors from Berkshire would soon be arriving in the village, indeed sooner than he himself had expected, to conduct a survey and undertake measurements and also to make a map of all the lands and grounds directed by the Act to be divided and allotted and also to make a plan of all previously enclosed lands and titheable tenements within the parishes. Nor did it enter his head to inform them of the appointment of a neutral umpire, a certain Reverend Jeremiah Cuthbert Pole-Carew, from Wivencaster, another old friend, who would determine any dispute or difference that might arise.

Money was always a factor throughout any enclosure scheme: the cost was heavy and the money sometimes had to be raised by periodic rates levied on proprietors: sometimes, too, special rates to pay for drainage and for the fencing and ditching of the new allotments were required to be levied and the work undertaken by contractors, who then sent their bills to the commissioners.

There were, of course, bills for the commissioners' own expenses, especially for regular meetings at local inns, of which two had been held already in the White Hart at Hamwyte, for which the usual expenses, coach travel, lodgings, meals drink, time and 'sundries' would be charged in due course. Further, two clerks, supplied by Mr. Mogg's partnership, had been appointed to keep a record of all their decisions taken at the various meetings which the commissioners deemed it necessary to call. There were the charges, too, of the lawyers in proving or contesting claims, preparing the awards themselves, and other miscellaneous business. On top of these were the not inconsiderable future outlays on roads, gates, bridges, drainage and other expenditure necessitated by the enclosure of a village's land.

Thus, there was a need for the commissioners to obtain finances to administer the day-to-day running of the enclosure proceedings, so a source of finance had to be found until such time as the proprietors were ordered to contribute to a commissioners' rate. In consequence, even before the three commissioners had been sworn in, the banker at Melchborough had been drawn early into the plan so that credit could be drawn: for it was not unusual, once the Bill had received Royal Assent, for the self-same commissioners who were to oversee the scheme to draw an advance of eight hundred pounds, say, from the bank before any money had been levied on the proprietors, the money being used to pay the parliamentary fees and lawyers' fees for the soliciting stage of the Bill.

It was common, too, before an Act was passed, for a lawyer to conduct the business with his own resources, for which service he would be granted interest of five per cent: it was also common for the enclosure to be deeply in debt to the banker and a general rate levied on the proprietors to defray that debt.

Sometimes during the latter stages of an enclosure scheme, it was not uncommon either for a letter from one of the commissioners' clerks to be sent to the bank stating that a road could not be completed or fencing erected unless some of the principal proprietors consented to advance the money which the commissioners requested so that they would be able at their next meeting to discharge the several bills of expenses: men had to be paid their expenses, especially the commissioners, the surveyors, the lawyers, the clerks and the contractors.

Even as Parson Petchey spoke to his flock that Sunday, the banker at Melchborough had already been required to fee, to an amount of seventy pounds, sixteen shillings and fourpence ha'penny in total, the costs of the interminable meetings of the various lawyers who over several months had drawn up the petition for Parliament.

The Reverend Doctor did add that mid-June Sunday morning that 'all agriculture, whether husbandry or on enclosed lands, is to be carried on as normal.'

However, it was his reading of the Book of Job which was to be recalled in the Wayfarers' bay-windowed parlour that summer: for it was almost as if the perverse Fates were mocking them. After a hot spell in the July growing season, when the temperature reached ninety degrees or above during one week and there was hope of a last good harvest, 'God' sent violent gales in the August to punish them just as the gathering-in got under way so that the hope of Jem and the others of having a profitable year to compensate for the insecurity of what lay ahead vanished in strong winds and driving rain.

SIXTY-FIVE

IN THE MID-SEPTEMBER of 1825, the husbandmen and small farmers had only just finished harvesting the grain from the ravages of the gale and the sheep had been on the stubble for only a few days when the two surveyors from Berkshire, appointed by the commissioners, came riding on horseback into the village and took rooms at the Wayfarers' Inn, requesting full board and lodging for themselves and stabling and feed for their horses for a month, and perhaps even longer. Nothing was known of them other than the names they gave: William Cole, large and easy-going, in his forties, the chief surveyor, and Thomas Shuttle, serious-faced, in his early twenties and the older man's assistant, both from Amersham in that county: and in all the time they were in lodging at the Wayfarers', which was to be five weeks, as it turned out, so as not to be influenced by any in the village, they never mixed at all with the men who drank in the bay-windowed parlour of an evening, but preferred to sit by themselves in Caleb Chapman's own back parlour to drink porter and ale and to talk and smoke their clays.

They were pleasant enough men and Caleb Chapman said he could find no fault with either: they bade him and his wife 'Good morning' at breakfast and 'Good evening' at supper and smiled at the children who followed them on that first morning along the ridge-top road to the eastern boundary with Lower Rackstead where they began their work to establish the extent of the parish. They had promised three of the village children a sixpence to share between them at the village shop if they would show them where to find the old boundary posts, the children knowing exactly where they were since they accompanied the churchwardens and the curate from Merchant Staplers, Reverend Waters, around them every two years 'beating the bounds.' Parson Petchey did not go because he did not care for such 'heathen practices,' though all the jurymen of the Little Court attended and finished up in the Wayfarers' afterwards, which was more likely why the parson did not go.

What the two surveyors got was a whole procession of village children, twenty or more, once the news of their largesse was circulated and, in the end, it cost them a shilling to find all the markers, though, only the bigger boys were still with them by the time they had measured with two poles and a chain link all the way down to the boundary post with Merchant Staplers, the girls, more curious about the younger Thomas Shuttle, having had to return unwillingly to whatever tasks their mothers had set them to do.

Even the bigger boys did not bother to follow them on the later days as they circled chain by chain south of Captain's wood, westward along the Maydun-to-Wivencaster road, which there forms the boundary, till on the fifth day, they were moving along the banks of the meandering Langwater stream, the western boundary edge, the boundary, too, of Titus Broake's estate, which they followed round on the sixth day, the Saturday, to the small hump-back bridge halfway to Hamwyte. From there, on the Monday, at the start of the second week, they climbed the long slope through Chantrey wood back to the ridge-top point at which they had begun their circumnavigation of the parish, recording everything in a large leather-bound book which the younger assistant, Shuttle, carried in a canvas satchel slung over his shoulder.

Over the next three weeks, they were to be seen everywhere, in wind and rain, in sunshine and shower, mist and murk – and peculiarly again even in fall of snow which blanketed the land in white for two days in the early-October. They seemed to be measuring every last yard and even going over the same ground twice sometimes, but always writing it down or sketching and discussing with themselves or calling out numbers and measures which were incomprehensible to those who heard them.

'They're thorough, I will say that for them,' declared Enos Diddams after the two surveyors had spent the whole of seven days, excepting, of course, for the Sunday, again measuring all the roads in the parish and recording every foot of every track and path, it seemed, beginning at the cross-roads where the road from Hamwyte climbs past Chantrey wood and making the queerest of arrow marks on the road with a lump of chalk, before setting off back along the ridge-top road to the parish boundary again, this time measuring both the road's width and length and plotting its direction with the aid of a compass.

Having done that to their satisfaction, they ambled back to their mark at the cross-roads and set off down the hill to the hump-back bridge again: then it was back up to the cross-roads mark and off in another direction, this time down The Street to its five-way junction at Forge Lane, where they made another mark in the road and went on down the long slope all the way to the triangle at Merchant Staplers, before returning to their fiveways mark and going westward along Forge Lane to its junction with Parsonage Lane: another mark with chalk on the road and then it was sharply left at the corner of the triangle and back up the slope of Heath Lane to the cross-roads mark again. In time, they had traversed the whole village and a dozen other lanes and paths branching off the main throughfares, even as far down Parsonage Lane as Hamwick Hall itself.

'Making a map of the whole village, so they say,' Caleb Chapman solemnly informed his regulars during the third week, which drew laughter from everyone in the bay-windowed parlour who heard it as it would have been evident even to a blind man what they were doing. 'Doing it so they can change the roads and paths and cattle drives if needs be and maybe build new ones,' Caleb added once the laughter had subsided: and that was enough to cause surprise and make the men talk for the rest of the evening of which road, lane or driftway might benefit from being straightened and which they would not mind if it were lost altogether.

Having made their plan of the village's roads, they went into every orchard, close and back field, measuring with their pole and chain and writing it all down again. Nothing, it seemed was being left to estimation: every cottage, barn, byre, stable, even the churchyard, the blacksmith's forge, the two butchers' sheds, the two bakers' shops were measured for length and depth and written down by Shuttle in the leather-bound book, while his master plotted them on a great sheet of rolled paper. Even Titus Broake's estate was surveyed over two days in the fourth week, along with Amos Peakman's Goat Lodge for another day and then Marcus Howie's Smallponds and Joshua Godwin's Milepole and finally the Glebe farm. Everything was to be recorded to the last foot, including the Parsonage grounds and the churchyard itself and, after that, the areas of Chantrey, Likely, Captain's and Milepole woods and the other smaller woods around the village.

'They spread the map on the parlour table and work on it all evening, measuring and ruling their lines,' Caleb Chapman informed everyone in the bay-windowed room on another evening. 'In there doing it now, they are, and if I or the wife so much as goos near, they rolls it up to keep it secret like. I still had a peek, though. They aren't leaving much out, I can tell you, not a darned thing as far as I can see.'

When they moved on to the three open-fields, Peter Sparshott, who was still the foreman of the Little Court, was summoned to bring his books and papers to a meeting at the Wayfarers'. The two surveyors were very interested in the map of the strips on the open fields as well as the allotted areas on the meadowland, which the Little Court foreman had always kept with meticulous care as an aid to settling the frequent disputes more easily, as well as recording what acres, roods and perches each small farmer or husbandman leased.

On the fifth week, accompanied by Peter Sparshott and several of the jurors of the Little Court, they went up and down and along and across the various open-fields, starting with Ash Grove lesser field at eight o'clock in the morning and measuring till the light faded, still writing down every division, every location and measure of every furlong, balk and headland. Then over the following days, they walked over Barrow and Thornbush, then Snook's, Badger's Hole and Partridge on Long Field, finally finishing at the Reeve's, Farthing and Gravel Pit lesser fields, before crossing and recrossing the meadowland and the waste, even digging at the soil, running it through their fingers and making yet more notes in their leather-bound book.

It caused some amusement in the Wayafers' when Enos Diddams declared: 'There weren't no need for'em to go digging all over the place. I could have told'em which was the best land and which was the worst and saved 'em all that bother since I seem to have more than my share of the worst!' The men laughed because he was sometimes lax in his husbandry and sometimes his turnip crop or barley or wheat did not grow too well, even in good weather.

Then suddenly one evening in the late October the two surveyors declared themselves 'finished' and walked back to the Wayfarers' for their meal of potatoes, mutton, suet and flour dumplings and gravy: and the next morning they had moved on to the Green Man at Lower Rackstead and eventually, three weeks after that, to the Bull at Merchant Staplers, where they spent a further two weeks, completing their task a week before Christmas, which passed in the usual way, with rain falling for most of the day.

At the same time, a notice was again tacked to the church door stating that the commissioners had charged and assessed certain sums upon the several persons who were subject and liable to the provisions contained in such clause of the said Act 'viz the sum of a hundred and three pounds, nine shillings and sevenpence upon Titus Broake, lord of the manor, the sum of seventy-three pounds and fourpence upon the Honourable Lady Amelia, the sum of sixty-four pounds upon the dowager marchioness, the sum of eleven pounds, twelve shillings and sixpence upon the Reverend Doctor Wakefield Petchey, the sum of eleven pounds, eight shillings and ninepence upon Sir Gentry Giblin, Esquire, and the sum of ten pounds, sixteen shillings and one penny upon Sir Benton Brierley, Esquire, and further sums of fifteen pounds apiece upon Amos Peakman, Marcus Howie and Joshua Godwin – ' and the other petitioners ' – all such sums to be paid into the hands of the treasurer appointed to receive such monies and have been applied towards payment of the charges and expenses as directed by the said Private Act.'

At least, it gave those crowded before the fire in the Wayfarers' and the other hostelries of the district something to smile about, for the weather had turned bitter once more: snow had come blowing in after Twelfth Night and did not melt until the third week of January and there was again thick ice on the Langwater stream.

SIXTY-SIX

'T'IS LIKE DOMESDAY all over again,' Dick Dollery growled in the Wayfarers' one evening, though from where he had heard of the Domesday survey made under William the Conqueror eight hundred years before none knew and all were impressed by the remark. 'It will be the same as then, mark my words. The rich and powerful Norman buggers who took over our country got all the land then and the same blighters are doing it again. We shall end up becoming serfs just like our Saxon forefathers all those centuries agoo. We shall lose our land and others will take it.' No one challenged his comment: all knew he probably spoke the truth.

It was several weeks after the surveyors had left that the first of the commissioners deigned to put in an appearance. One afternoon in late-February, a small gig, pulled by a small chestnut mare, came struggling up the hill from Hamwyte, swung right at the guidepost and went bowling down Heath Lane and Parsonage Lane, before slowing where the road swings sharply left by the start of Mope Lane and turning into the gateway of the Parsonage.

As its driver, a bony, slim-faced man in his middle-fifties, with a wildly sprouting mane of disorderly grey hair, climbed out, the Reverend Petchey and his wife came hurrying down the steps to welcome him, smiling and extending their hands in greeting: his bags were carried inside by the parson himself and he was shown into the drawing room where the jolting tedium of his journey, all the way from Oxfordshire, was banished with a full glass of port and a half-hour of rest in an armchair.

He was then shown upstairs by Mrs. Petchey herself, where a small bedroom overlooking the orchard had been prepared for him and fresh towels laid out: after all, the Reverend Honeywood-Jones, friend of Doctor Petchey from his old college, could not be expected to sleep in a place like the Wayfarers' Inn, where the smell of stale beer and pipe tobacco permeated every room each morning and where the evening fare was as likely as not to be yesterday's greasy meat reheated by the simple expedient of pouring hot gravy over it.

So the first of the commissioners for the enclosure of the joint parishes of Hamwick Dean, Lower Rackstead and Merchant Staplers, took up lodging with Parson Petchey and his wife, as was to be expected of a bachelor brother clergymen, though there were some who grumbled that not only was he 'not a fit person for the business' of land assessment but that he should not even think to lodge with one of the proprietors and supporters of the Bill.

The Roman-nosed lawyer, Tobias Grint, and the red-nosed Captain Bushnell had earlier that same day taken rooms at the White Hart in Hamwyte so as to be at a stopover for the daily *Flyer* running between London and Wivencaster and the other Eastern Counties since they did not expect their business in Hamwick Dean and the two other parishes to last overly long. 'A week at the most,' they told the innkeeper, 'though we expect we shall have to return from time to time to complete the business.'

The next morning, riding in a hired coach and pair, they joined the Reverend Honeywood-Jones, Parson Petchey, Titus Broake, and the three farmers, Amos Peakman, Marcus Howie and Joshua Godwin, touring the village in a procession of gigs and traps, seemingly oblivious to the curious gazes of the inhabitants whom they passed on the road and in the fields or who came out of their cottagers to watch them go by.

The various aspects of the landscape were pointed out to them: the three open-fields, subdivided into three lesser fields, the area encompassed by the walled manor estate and that part extended by the incorporation of the old Redhouse farm, the meadowland of the 'hams' or stinted pastures, where the grazing was superior, lying between the arable fields and the east-west run of Forge Lane and the village itself, the other common meadowland to the north and west of the village and the common waste which encircled the parish at its outskirts where it met the boundaries of Lower Rackstead and Merchant Staplers and the waste part which encircled those two hamlets.

They were also shown the gravel pit and had the names of the various woods pointed out to them and, while none was near enough to hear what passed between them, there was much vigorous pointing and sweeping of the arms, particularly by Titus Broake and Amos Peakman, as they commented on the various landmarks and points of interest, and much nodding of the heads from the three strangers as they stood looking out over the expanses. They declined an offer to dismount and to walk along the balks between the strips in the Ash

Grove lesser field for a closer inspection owing to the muddiness of the ground and the fact that it was late afternoon by then and a grey, February gloom had settled over everything, obscuring the distance by its murk so that the whole landscape appeared particularly barren and bleak.

The next day, they all went off to Lower Rackstead to meet the Reverend Snetterton and the two farmers there, Silas Kempen and James Allen, then on to Merchant Staplers to meet the Reverend Waters and Thomas Godbear, where they performed the same tour at both places, making no contact at all with the small farmers and husbandmen whom they saw working in their closes and on their lands there either, but simply following the sweeping arm of one or other of the larger farmers who had supported the petition.

They returned to Hamwick Dean late in the evening and their same carriages were later seen going down Parsonage Lane towards the Hall, where, having completed their tours, they had all been invited to a dinner, which, according to the two maids who helped to prepare it, was even more sumptuous than the one Titus Broake had given to the six farmers and their wives on the night he presented them with a *fait accompli* of the petition. This time, the women were not invited since there were too many matters to be discussed in male company only.

A month later, Parson Petchey finally announced in a chilly church that a notice was to be put up on the porch door again after divine service, so that this time it could be read as they were all leaving, proclaiming the surveyors in their offices in Berkshire had finally transferred all their measurements and findings of the 'messuages, cottages, orchards, gardens, homesteads, ancient enclosed lands and grounds within the three hamlets' to a plan of the open-fields and strips of the three parishes to be divided, allotted and enclosed, the said map of the three parishes showing *'such public carriage roads and highways as they judged necessary and also such private roads and footpaths as appeared to them requisite were to be straightened before they proceeded to make any of the divisions and allotments of the lands.'*

Therefore, *'All persons who might be injured or aggrieved by the setting out of such roads are required to attend at the meeting so holden that such highways, roads and footpaths be finally set out and confirmed with the entire approbation of the parties who attend such meeting as aforesaid in such manner and directions as the said commissioners in their judgment consider upon the whole most convenient to all the parties interested.'*

A copy of the map was duly deposited with Messrs. Lilley and Mogg, solicitors of Melchborough, the clerks to the said commissioners, 'for the inspection of all persons concerned' and notices announcing this were fixed to the doors of all three churches as well as being inserted in the *County Weekly* with the various alterations to the roads and pathways outlined. However, since it was doubtful anyone would bother to travel that far to the county town to view it, the surveyors, being impartial, while adding to their charges, also drew up a second map, which they posted to Parson Petchey.

As it turned out, when the Hamwyte post boy delivered it to the Wayfarers' post office as usual, the Reverend Doctor and his wife were just setting off for Oxford to visit the dean and his wife and, rather than have a long queue of the curious traipsing through the church all day while he was absent, he decided to leave it there and gave the parish constable, Elijah Candler, instructions to put it up in the bay-windowed parlour, since he could not do so himself, and to send word to Lower Rackstead and Merchant Staplers that it was there.

Consequently, Caleb Chapman did a roaring business for three days afterwards as some three hundred curious viewers eventually shuffled through to peruse it, at least a hundred tramping over from the two hamlets, and most making the same smiling and delighted remarks on seeing the detailed map which showed every building and boundary, path and road, wood and pond and plot and close. 'There, that's our cottage!' one would exclaim delightedly, while another would add loudly: 'That's my land there – there – and there!' One or two did think to themselves, however, 'For how long?'

The landlords of the Green Man and the Bull complained bitterly at the sudden drop in their business, but found it picked up later as a fierce debate blew up at both places over the accuracy of the map, despite what the commissioners said, as to why their parishes seemed so much smaller than that of Hamwick Dean. 'Only half the size,' as someone in Lower Rackstead put it. 'No wonder they are lumping the three parishes together! They aim to get us all out of the way at one goo because it is cheaper for them to do it that way and they'll make more from us and get more land by doing it.'

The Reverend Honeywood-Jones then returned once more to stay at the parsonage and Mr. Grint and Captain Bushnell again took rooms at the White Hart in Hamwyte and all were eventually introduced by Parson Petchey at a meeting to hear objections to the proposed straightening and widening of the roads as outlined on the map, the meeting being held not in the Wayfarers', because of Parson Petchey's objections, but again in the nave of St. Bartholomew's. However, it drew less interest than he and commissioners and their clerks anticipated since none knew how he or she would be affected personally by the eventual awards since they had yet to be made. The most prominent alteration in the village plan was that, from the junction of Goat Lodge Lane and the Merchant Staplers road, a new road was to be constructed, cutting diagonally across both the Reeve's Croft lesser field of Third Field and Partridge lesser field of Long Field, then in between Likely and Milepole woods to join the Hall road a half mile south of the manor estate's entrance gates, all for the convenience of the lord of the manor, of course.

'I can't see the sense in it,' said Dick Dollery with a sniff. 'T'is a road to nowhere. Who is going to pay for it? That's what I'd like to know. It costs money to build a road. It 'on't be me because I can't afford it. It'll have to be some other poor bugger!'

Other straightenings and widenings, mostly on the Lower Rackstead roads, as well as several curtailments of traditional tracks and bridleways, drew equal head-shaking. 'This business will take longer than it took Moses to lead the Children of Israel out of Egypt!' exclaimed Enos Diddams in an aside to Jem. 'And don't expect to get anything out of it. T'will all goo to the gentry, they'll see to that. T'will all goo to them and we shall be left with nothing.'

It was early-May before the next notice of the commissioners was posted in St. Bartholomew's porch, declaring: *'To all whom these presents shall come unto and concern, We the said commissioners do hereby give notice that in fourteen days from the posting of this notice on the ninth day of May do intend to hold a meeting in the house of the said Caleb Chapman, known as the Wayfarers' Inn in the parish of Hamwick Dean in the Hundred of Hamwyte in the County aforesaid, for the purpose of the execution of the above named Act. All persons claiming any land, common right or interest whatsoever in or upon the lands and grounds within the said hamlet of Hamwick Dean aforesaid and the lands and grounds within the said hamlet of Lower Rackstead and the said hamlet of Merchant Staplers, both also in the Hundred of Hamwyte in the County aforesaid, or who are otherwise in any respect interested in the execution of the said Act, we give notice not only in writing affixed upon one of the doors of the parish church of Hamwick Dean, and also of Lower Rackstead and Merchant Staplers, all aforesaid, but also by an advertisement inserted in the "County Weekly" previous to such meeting. At such meeting claims are to be delivered to the said commissioners on the part of the several owners and proprietors of the homesteads, gardens, orchards, old enclosures and other lands and grounds within the aforesaid hamlets of Hamwick Dean, Lower Rackstead and Merchant Staplers from which claims and from other information and evidence by them received, we the said commissioners having fully informed themselves of the rights, properties and interests of the several persons interested in the said intended division and enclosure, will in obedience to the directions of the said general Act make our judgments ...'*

Thus it was, one wind-blown Wednesday Jem stood huddled with the others in the front yard of the Wayfarers', all waiting to be called in to register their claims one by one before the three strange commissioners, with the parish constable, Elijah Candler, controlling the flow. Her Ladyship, the dowager marchioness, Sir Benton and Sir Gentry, the dean and chapter of Oxford and the various others concerned had, of course, long since deposited their documents, supported by deeds, copyhold titles and other papers of transfers and purchases and maps and wills, as had Titus Broake for himself, and His Grace the Bishop and Parson Petchey for the Church. Ahead of the husbandmen and small farmers, Amos Peakman, Marcus Howie and Joshua Godwin and the farmers from Lower Rackstead and Merchant Staplers had also delivered in writing the schedule of their various lands and hereditaments and all had been dutifully verified, filed and recorded by the clerks and marked on a new and larger map, some five feet in width by four feet in height, drawn up by the same two surveyors and pinned to a board standing in front of the fireplace, upon which also were written the names of all the strip holders and small farmers which Peter Sparshott had provided from the minutes and maps of the Little Court.

As each husbandman and small farmer entered, he was required to point out which strips or close or half-yardland he currently farmed, the amount of that acreage down to the last rood and perch, whether he owned the land or leased it: whether, if claiming ownership, he held any documented form of possession. If so, how long he had farmed the land: if not, how long was his lease and how many years remained of it, now annulled anyway. They were asked, too, what cottagers' rights they assumed they had inherited, any documentation concerning such, the number of animals they kept on the common meadowland at that time, what number if any were granted a place each year on the stinted 'hams,' what 'doles' they had been allotted that year on the meadowland from which each man took his hay, the number of geese and goats they put on to the common waste, and when, if at all, they let their ringed pigs free to eat the acorns in the various woods around the village and, if so, which woods, et cetera, before signing the statement, if they could write, or making their mark if they could not.

When Jem entered he found the three commissioners seated at a long table in front of the blazing hearth for warmth, all three idly smoking their pipes and warming their hands before the flames, while the two clerks seated at a separate table to their left, farther from the fire, scratched away with their pens and took occasional sips of ale from the tankards set beside them. For his part, Jem claimed land in lieu of his eight rented acres and also of his common rights as a man who had fetched firewood, tethered his horse and grazed his cattle on the pasture and his sheep on the stubble and fallow field and his geese on the waste.

'Make your mark,' one of the clerks directed him matter-of-factly when he had finished registering Jem's claim. It was with an almost triumphant delight, to prove to the two surly clerks that he could write, that Jem took the pen, dipped it carefully in the inkwell and, with a flourish, wrote his signature on to the page of the book where his details had been recorded: then he sniffed in contempt at those who would take away his rights, the sullen lawyer, the red-faced sea captain and the strange punctilious parson, turned on his heel and walked out.

Of the many others who went in, however, few came out looking pleased. 'Why don't they just take our land and be done with it,' snorted Enos Diddams after he had made his claim, 'since that is what they intend to do, then I can goo and hang myself off the nearest oak tree and be done with it!'

Henry Eady, a landless labourer all his life, who had lived seventy years in the parish and had never left it, save for an occasional trip to Hamwyte market, followed him in. When he pointed out that every year after harvest the landless of the village had been able to buy additional field pasture for their animals, it was shrugged off by the lawyer, Mr. Grint, as of no use or value since he had no written record of it. 'I pay one of the fieldmen a shilling per head to let my sheep on to his land after harvest,' he exclaimed when the point was bluntly made to him. 'Now you say I am to lose it all because I don't have a piece of paper on which that is all writ down and you 'on't take my word for it nor his!'

'The right to the meadowland is attached to our living in the parish, not to land!' shouted old Frederick Easter, who had also laboured as a husbandman all his life. 'It should be left open not lumped in with the rest. I have stocked the meadowland with one, two or three cows as I have thought proper without any interruption all my life and my father afore me, as has every house dweller who could get a cow.'

'T'will take away from us poor a common of nearly a hundred acres which provides us with fuel and sustenance for our cattle and no compensation will likely be made to us,' a tearful James Sparkey declared, before he, too, stormed out, cursing as he went.

What the small farmers, husbandmen and cottagers did discern, slowly at first and then with a growing conviction and concern, was that, if they could not prove beyond a certain doubt their ownership of land or their rights to common on it by producing documents, leases, title deeds or such, a certain indifference surfaced in the manner of the good Reverend Honeywood-Jones, which was usually accompanied by a regretful sigh as each claimant left him. Captain Bushnell would give a slow exasperated shake of the head at times and the lawyer, Mr. Grint, would stare after them and pull a face, while the clerks would remain as non-committal as one would expect them to be as they calmly wrote down all that needed to be written down and assembled their documents and maps in neat piles.

What the villagers did not know was that Titus Broake, on behalf of all the landowners who had supported the Bill, had entered a general objection against all claimants on the grounds that many of them were, as he had told the commissioners, 'extravagant and unjust.' What that objection meant was that everybody had to prove their right and it was a source of much grievance by a large number of husbandmen, who fed their livestock on the meadowland and the waste, that they could not prove their rights, even though they supposed they had inherited those rights from their fathers, just as the father in his turn had considered he had inherited them from his line of forebears and had exercised those rights without giving a thought to them.

Eventually, after three days, having no further claims to register in Hamwick Dean, the three commissioners moved on to Lower Rackstead, where the notice had also been posted on the door of St. Cuthbert's, with the necessary alteration of the date being made, of course, and set up a table in the parlour of the Green Man so that over the two days each supposed landowner in that hamlet could make his claim as to how much land he considered he should be awarded: and after that, they went on to the Bull at Merchant Staplers and did the same.

In due course, the commissioners would decide on the validity of each claim and come to a decision as to who was actually entitled to receive land in the award: meanwhile they sent in their third requests for payment to the proprietors, who passed the matter to the banker at Melchborough.

At the same time, the commissioners were responsible for regulating the culture of the open-field land in what was the transition period before it passed into private ownership. To curb any deliberate exhausting of the land by cross-cropping by a small farmer or husbandman fearing he was about to lose it – especially if the enclosure were a drawn-out affair, as some were, even to five or six years in contested cases – under the Act, they had the control of the village's agriculture during the period between the Act and the award and were empowered to impose a five-pound fine per acre for cross-cropping or withholding manure from land and as much as ten pounds for any other specified offences.

They had, too, of course, the right to order which fields should be ploughed and sown and in what rotation, which previously had been the province of the Little Court: and they also were authorised to decide on payments if, say, turnips were planted by one owner, a small husbandman, say, but were harvested by another who, following the award, had taken over his land.

Jem and Mary-Ann, helped sometimes by young Jed and even Thirza, continued to farm their land. As it turned out, June, July and August of that year were persistently warm, making it the hottest summer that anyone could remember and they managed to achieve a reasonably good harvest, though there was little heart in anyone as many knew it was most likey the last they would cut and cart of their own.

Two days after the meeting, the three commissioners went off to Lower Rackstead to meet Lady Amelia herself and her mother, the dowager marchioness, who had travelled from Somerset and the Midlands, respectively, to stay with relatives in one of the large mansions built in the rolling countryside around Shallford. It was the first time that anyone could remember seeing either of their absent landowners: the two ladies wished particularly to have matters settled regarding the changes before they returned to their two homes. Titus Broake was also in attendance: afterwards, he and the three commissioners went to Merchant Staplers to meet Sir Gentry and Sir Benton to settle matters there.

SIXTY-SEVEN

WHATEVER WORRIES the husbandmen had about the threat which loomed large over them, it lay for the moment beyond the horizon of their knowing, so to speak: all they could do was to wait to find out what the Fates had in store for them. In the meantime, they had their land to tend, strips to be manured, ploughed and harrowed and sown, sheep to be birthed, grazed, marked and shorn, hay to be carted, arguments to be dealt with in the Little Court, rents to be paid: children were born, the eager young were married, the wearied old died. They went to church, Christmas came and went, the special days of the farming year were observed, Plough Sunday, Lady Day, Lammas Day, Rogation Sunday. Life in Hamwick Dean and the two hamlets went on in the usual way.

In fact, the only dispiriting note in all those long months of waiting was the sight of a surly Titus Broake bowling through the village in his pony and trap, still expecting everyone to get out of his way as usual and still ready to curse any who did not. Though none doffed their hats to him as they would have done to the Old Squire, neither did they show any outward hostility towards him, but kept their mutterings within the confines of the bay-windowed parlour of the Wayfarers' or the smoke-laden vault of the Carpenters' Arms, now, though, with a look first to see who might be listening. For all the warnings given, they were as unsure as any of what lay ahead: they could speculate, they could complain of the injustice of it all, they could curse the one who had brought it upon them and those who had supported him, but they could not alter one iota of it. The answer for them all came in the September of the following year, exactly three years and one month to the day since the petition had first been nailed to the church door.

By law, a written copy of the Enclosure Award, detailing those who had been successful in receiving allocations of land, along with the map delineating all new enclosures, boundaries between each section of land, routes of new roads as well as new paths to be created, had to be forwarded to the churchwarden or the incumbent of a parish and another copy had to go to the county's records in the county town. The copy of the Award and the joint map for Hamwick Dean, Lower Rackstead and Merchant Staplers, rolled up in a leather case and addressed to the 'Reverend Doctor Wakefield Petchey, incumbent,' was brought by the umpire, Reverend Pole-Carew, and handed over at the parsonage in the first week of that September. Drawn up at a scale of one inch to four chains and hand-inked on linen-backed paper, the map measured an unexpectedly large six-and-a-half feet by five-and-a-half feet due to the shape the three parishes presented, with the various parish all differently coloured.

The peculiarity was that none of the small farmers and husbandmen of the three parishes who were likely to be most adversely affected by the proceedings was present in the nave of St. Bartholomew's on the Friday evening of the first reading of the Enclosure Award. Peculiarly, too, when the allotments by the commissioners were read out by Parson Petchey himself, the front pew was occupied solely by Titus Broake, the second pew by Amos Peakman, Marcus Howie and Joshua Godwin, with the Reverend Snetterton and the farmers Silas Kempen and James Allen, from Lower Rackstead, and the Reverend Waters and the farmer Thomas Godbear, from Merchant Staplers, seated behind.

Equally peculiarly, after Joshua Jaikes and Elijah Candler had pinned the map to a board and set it down in front of the chancel, they took up positions by the main door, the churchwarden inside it and the parish constable outside in the porch as if to deter anyone else from entering. Lady Amelia, the dowager duchess, the two Members of Parliament, Sir Gentry and Sir Benton, the dean and chapter at Oxford were neither there nor represented: they had already learned of their successes through their lawyers.

Thus, only Titus Broake and company were in the nave to hear of their good fortune ahead of all the others, a decision which Parson Petchey had made as a means of avoiding any animosity which might be shown towards them, most especially of the kind which had been witnessed at the time the petition was first nailed to the church door three years previously.

It was not till the Sunday that a peculiarly hoarse-voiced Parson Petchey again announced in his parish notices from the pulpit that a copy of the written Enclosure Award and a new joint map of Hamwick Dean, Lower Rackstead and Merchant Staplers, drawn up by the two surveyors and 'commended' by the commissioners, had at last been received and would be displayed on a board in the nave from nine-thirty the following morning, at which time the awards would be read out.

Come the morning, unsurprisingly, word of the private reading for the lord of the manor and the six larger farmers and the three clergymen had got round the parishes already, spread by a sympathetic Elijah Candler, but none cared overmuch. The villagers, particularly the remaining husbandmen who trooped into the church on that bright sunlit Monday morning were more concerned with what the Award would reveal for them. No one counted how many attended from the three parishes, except to say later 'hundreds and hundreds': but they came streaming up from Merchant Staplers and trudging along the ridge-top road from Lower Rackstead almost from sun-up, it seemed, men, wives, youths, girls, children, even some of the shuffling elderly. Seven hundred or more was Jem's estimation after running his eye over the number waiting outside before Joshua Jaikes deigned to open the door, all determined to be there for such a momentous occasions and perhaps all fearing what they would hear.

Joshua Jaikes did not seem too pleased that Jem, Dick Dollery and Enos Diddams and their wives and children were the very first to enter and so were able to obtain seats in the very front pew, in Titus Broake's family pew. Not that being first assisted them overmuch: there were twenty or more crushed into it when at last they bowed their heads in prayer, though some might have wondered why the hoarse-voiced Parson Petchey chose to refer to the 'sacrifice of the Lord Jesus upon the Cross' and the fact that 'man shall find his reward in Heaven' and wondered, too, what that had to do with the matter in hand. The puzzled few who did take account of his words, such as Jem and Dick Dollery, glanced uneasily at each other and were filled with foreboding, even before the reading of the written Award began.

There was a noticeable apprehension when, after the map had been propped against the eagle lectern and Elijah Candler, instead of the croaking Parson Petchey, who had strained his voice at the earlier reading, stepped forward to read aloud the seventeen pages and nine thousand and six hundred words of the Award, all hand-written by the clerks at Mr. Mogg's offices: and, since no one had told him otherwise or attempted to stop him, the parish constable began naturally enough on the title page: '...*And whereas the said commissioners having completely finished the allotments of the messuages, lands and hereditaments by the said first mentioned Act authorised to be divided and allotted, have proceeded to form and draw up their Award agreeable to the directions of the said Act. And for the better observation of the several and respective matters contained in this their Award, they the said commissioners have thought it necessary and proper to cause a map and plan to be made of all the homesteads, gardens, orchards, old enclosed lands and grounds within the said hamlet of Hamwick Dean aforesaid in the Hundred of Hamwyte aforesaid, which said map or plan is annexed to this their Award...'*

The actual first part of the written Award detailed a description of the exact area of the three parishes as measured by the two surveyors, followed by a similarly detailed description of what changes were to be made to both public and private roads, bridgeways over streams and footpaths: each road and path in the three parishes, with their various junctions and meanderings, was named in turn and it took a good seven minutes to read out that part alone: and there was many a puzzled frown as each realignment or footpath closure was disclosed.

Even the announcement that a Wivencaster man had been selected to make the survey for the road and path realignments, and would also nominate a rate for the cost of the work and be later employed to keep them in good repair, elicited little comment, save half-stifled whisperings of impatience for the reading of the actual allotments, as if the rest of it had nothing to do with them.

Neither did they have much of an inkling of what it all meant. Indeed, though Jem listened as intently as anyone, the language was so strange and so convoluted that he was as perplexed by it as the rest of the congregation. Elijah Candler, too, struggled with some of the wording and several times stumbled over unfamiliar phrases and spellings, much to the chagrin of Parson Petchey seated on the choir's bench in the chancel. In fact, the more that was read out, the less most of the villagers comprehended and all longed to see the map: for only by viewing that would they ever be able to make sense of what was intended for each parish.

That, however, for the moment, was denied them. Parson Petchey wished all to remain seated or, as was the case for two hundred to three hundred, to stand at the back of the nave while the legal formality of reading out the Award was conducted. On his instructions, a glowering Joshua Jaikes stood guard over the board like the Keeper of the Crown Jewels, as if he feared someone might snatch it and run off.

Elijah Candler, meanwhile, droned on slowly and carefully, determined to read aloud every word. '*And the said commissioners, in allotting and awarding the said common and other commonable land, have had due regard as well to the situation of the houses and old enclosures of the said proprietors as to the quality and quantity of all and every part of the said land so far as was consistent with the general convenience of the said proprietors and in making the said allotments they have had particular regard to the convenience of the proprietors of the smallest estates in the said parish and they hereby certify that the several allotments hereby awarded are in full bar and satisfaction and compensation for their several and respective lands, grounds and other rights and properties in and over the open and common fields, meadows, pastures and commonable land and also of their respective tithes arising within and payable out of the old enclosures and titheable tenements in the said parish...'*

Finally, he paused: he was about to plunge into the wording of the allotments themselves: the whispering subsided, people froze on their seats, the scuffling of those standing at the back ceased as one by one the allotments were read out, beginning with Titus Broake: *'Unto the lord or lords of the Manor of Hamwick Dean and his or their heirs in lieu of the commonable part of his estate and right of common thereunto belonging... land situate in Ash Grove field... in Barrow field... in Thornbush field... in Badger's Hole field... and that part of Snook's field belonging and bounded by... Also all that parcel of land situate south of the manor estate bounded by the Maydun-to-Wivencaster turnpike amounting to ninety-five acres two roods and two perches... and all that parcel of land extending northwest from the manor estate and bounded by the Langwater stream on the west and the parish boundary with Hamwyte to the north ...'*

From 'first allotment,' it passed to 'second allotment,' then 'third' and 'fourth' and 'fifth': not till he had finished reading *'and the ninth allotment...'* did he pause. Gasps greeted each award: in one fell swoop, Titus Broake, as the instigator of enclosure, now owned more than eight hundred and fifty acres of arable open-field, meadowland, waste and woods in the west of the parish of Hamwick Dean alone. The commissioners' allotments had enlarged his three hundred and fifty acres of manor and other purchased and foreclosed lands by a further five hundred acres. It was staggering, almost incomprehensible to those who sat listening to the droning voice of Elijah Candler: they were struck dumb by it: all the warnings which had been given by the likes of Dick Dollery and the wagoner, Daniel Gate had come true.

Almost the whole of First Field, incorporating the lesser Ash Grove, Barrow and Thornbush fields, and half of the Long Field arable, incorporating large parts of Snook field and Badger's Hole field, had been awarded to the despised lord of the manor. Further, an allotment of waste bounded by the Langwater stream to the north of the manor estate had extended his land there right to the hump-back bridge and the parish boundary with Hamwyte itself. At the same time, an allotment of waste to the south extended the manor estate's acreage there all the way to the Langridge boundary to the west, so that the lord of the manor's land now extended from the south-east of the parish in a broad unbroken sweep up the western half of the parish, encompassing on the way also Milepole, Likely and Sparkey woods.

To the east, Coppice farm, which Titus Broake had purchased soon after his arrival in the village, lying just over the boundary with Lower Rackstead, had been extended northwards by a further hundred acres to encompass common waste along the Lower Rackstead road and, more importantly, to enclose the largest of the parishes' woods, Chantrey, which the lord of the manor had long coveted in a wish to be able to coppice it as and when he required and also to breed game birds since shooting was becoming all the rage amongst certain gentry in Hamwyte, including himself.

The next award read by Elijah Candler was to the Church: *'Unto and for the said curate of the perpetual curacy of Hamwick Dean, the Reverend Doctor Wakefield Petchey aforesaid, and his successor curates as aforesaid, all those several pieces or parcels of land, messuages, barn, stables and buildings next hereinafter mentioned and described...'*

As compensation for the extinguishing of certain tithes and giving up rights in the open-fields and meadowland, the award of seven allotments was made to the Church through the parson, the largest being of twenty-seven acres, five roods and thirty-seven perches to enclose the whole of the stinted 'hams' of superior meadowland lying between the open-fields themselves and the cottages on Forge Lane. A second allotment of sixty acres, nine roods and thirty-one perches of what had previously been common pasture on the ridge-top itself adjoining Glebe farm, plus other minor allotments on the waste there of twelve, six, four, three and two acres with the odd rood and perches attached, increased the amount of the homestead and consolidated the holding into a farm of a hundred and fifteen acres, give or take twenty roods and fifteen perches, which stretched from and incorporated the

Grove and Mope woods on the northern boundary, then crossed Parsonage Lane to enclose the stinted 'hams' alongside and below the church and parsonage. In due course, it would enable Parson Petchey to extend his parsonage grounds by two acres: the churchyard, too, would benefit by another half-acre for burials of the 'saved.'

The Bishop, who was in possession of a copy of the Award, was utterly delighted with the Church's allotment, since he had already agreed to sell seventy of its new acres to no less a person than the lord of the manor, just as had been discussed in their letters two years before: and which he duly did since it would enable him also to effect repairs not only to the cathedral church but also to the neglected parish church at the nearby village of Tirtlew Green, which was one of his favourites and which was greatly in need of restoration. Two of its bells were cracked and in need of recasting, the old bell frame was rotted and required replacing, while, in the body of the church, the carvings of the rood screen had been neglected and the galleries were in a poor state, as were the wooden benches at the west end: in the chancel, too, the few choristers who sat there of a Sunday did so on worm-eaten benches and frayed cushions. The Bishop was very pleased.

Meanwhile, Elijah Candler continued with his reading: *'Unto the Very Reverend the Dean and Chapter of the Cathedral Church in Oxford and their lessees...*

'Unto Amos Peakman and his heirs in lieu of the commonable part of his estate and right of common thereunto belonging...

'Unto Marcus Howie and his heirs in lieu of the commonable part of his estate and right of common thereunto belonging...

'Unto Joshua Godwin and his heirs in lieu of the commonable part of his estate and right of common thereunto belonging...'

The dean and chapter of the Oxford college also received four substantial awards, all in Hamwick Dean, taking up the whole of Reeve's Croft on Third Field as one parcel and adding to it much of the pastureland between there and the Merchant Staplers road, as did the other lesser landowners who had added their names to the petition. Amos Peakman was well rewarded for his loyal support, receiving in exchange for his rights most of the meadowland lying to the west of Goat Lodge between the farm and the village, as well as a further sixty acres of pasture and wasteland to the east and south of Goat Lodge, while the Farthing and Gravel Pit lesser fields of Third Field and the pastureland in between up to and across the Merchant Staplers road went to Marcus Howie at Smallponds. Joshua Godwin did not lose out: a sizeable portion of the common pasture in the southeast corner of the parish along with the whole of the waste along the southern boundary, as well as all of Milepole wood, were added to Milepole farm, along with twenty acres of the waste around Captain's wood.

It was no different in Lower Rackstead and Merchant Staplers: *'Unto the most honourable the Lady Amelia Bright who is entitled to…and for and in lieu of…'*

'Unto the most honourable the Marchioness of Thrapstone who is entitled to… and for and in lieu of …'

'Unto the said Sir Gentry Giblin and his heirs and the person or persons who are entitled to the same for and in lieu of …'

'Unto the said Sir Benton Brierley and his heirs and the person or persons who are entitled to the same for and in lieu of …'

In seven substantial awards, Lady Amelia increased her land in Lower Rackstead to six hundred acres, consolidated in one parcel, while the dowager marchioness received five similar-sized allotments at the same place, amounting to two hundred and seventy-nine acres, effectively placing the whole hamlet under the blood-tie of one family: at Merchant Staplers, Sir Gentry and Sir Benton received five allotments apiece, which, meant that, between them, they held almost two-thirds of the total acreage in that hamlet.

And still it went on, name after name of those whose claims had succeeded: *'Unto the said Silas Kempen… unto the said James Allen… unto the said Thomas Godbear…'* The two large farmers at Lower Rackstead, Silas Kempen and James Allen, both doubled their lands, while lesser but satisfactory ones of ten or fifteen acres went to the small farmers there, Jonathan Hartless, Thomas Crawley and Thomas Templeton, who had all signed the petition just before it was presented to Parliament. At Merchant Staplers, too, Thomas Godbear had five allotments amounting to ninety acres of ploughable heathland waste added to his earlier holding, Richard Shadwell, who had previously held a close of twenty acres, now had one of thirty, and John Dicker had a farm of thirty-five acres consolidated, while Henry Sweetapple also had twenty-five acres in all. Before the year was out, all three would lease more land till eventually they farmed double the acreage they had worked previously.

'Unto William Hoskins… unto Francis Clutter…unto Samuel Thorn…'

The Awards went on and three who had signed the petition in secret got their rewards, each being allotted several acres of waste and former common pasture, enough to make them all look pleased.

'Unto Jonas Bunting... unto Reuben Frost... unto Peter Hull...' The three small Hamwick Dean holders of closes of eighteen to twenty acres or so had cause to look woebegone: their holdings had been halved in size, but then they had not signed the petition.

Not till Elijah Candler read out Jem's name did he and Mary-Ann stir to show interest. *'Unto Jem Stebbings and his heirs in lieu of the commonable part of his estate and right of common thereunto belonging, all that allotment or parcel of land situate on the common waste...and containing five roods and thirty-four perches...'*

From the eight acres, ten roods and eighteen perches which he had farmed before, albeit glebe land which he had leased, Jem had been reduced to a parcel of land no bigger in size than a garden and a small garden at that. Both he and Mary-Ann were dumbstruck: Jem looked about him, thinking perhaps that he had misheard, and might well have convinced himself that he had misheard had he not seen Mary-Ann's face and the trembling of her lip as she fought back tears: he had not misheard.

It was the same for Dick Dollery: *'...in lieu of the commonable part of his estate and right of common thereunto belonging, all that allotment or piece of land situate on the common waste bounded by...and containing six roods and three perches...'*

And Enos Diddams: *'...all that allotment or piece of land situate on the waste bounded by...and containing two roods and seven perches...'*

And many others.

Finally, Elijah Candler cleared his throat for the last time: *'And the said commissioners further certify that they did in pursuance of the powers and authorities contained in the said second recited Act make a note in writing under their respective hands upon the several persons mentioned and contained in the schedule hereunto annexed not having or purchasing or otherwise being entitled to a sufficient quantity of the said open and common fields, commonable lands or other lands and grounds thereof directed to be divided, allotted and enclosed to make compensation for the tithes of their homesteads, gardens, orchards, home closes and other enclosed lands and grounds by such allotments and in such proportions as directed respecting the allotments for or in lieu of tithes for the several sums set opposite to their respective names and which said several sums of money were applied in payment of such parts and proportions of the expenses of obtaining and executing the said second recited act as ought to be paid by the respective persons whose land have been set out for discharging from tithes such homesteads, gardens, orchards and home closes or other enclosed lands and grounds.'*

As all had feared, the enclosure of the lands of Hamwick Dean had proved to be disastrous for the husbandmen and small farmers of the likes of Jem, Dick Dollery, Enos Diddams and thirty-eight others in that parish alone, as well as the greater number of those in Lower Rackstead and all in Merchant Staplers: and disastrous, too, for the landless day-labourers who had over the years struggled to get together a few geese or sheep, perhaps even two or three cows or pigs: they had lost everything.

Small wonder when the whole of the village crowded forward to inspect the map, some in tears, some questioning whether they had heard the words correctly, all desperate to see for themselves not so much what they had lost, but whether they had been awarded anything at all. All around, there were such cries of anger and disgust, tears and wailings, gloom and despair such as never had been heard or witnessed in all the thousand-year history of the village. Indeed, had Elijah Candler and Joshua Jaikes not been there to stand guard over the map, forcing the villagers to queue in line, it is certain that it would have been ripped into a score of pieces, irrespective of whether Parson Petchey was there in his two offices as God's representative on earth and Justice of the Peace at Hamwyte.

As it was, Dick Dollery kicked the board and stamped out and Enos Diddams walked off in a daze. For the rest of that day, till four in the afternoon, the greater part of the populations of the village and the two hamlets filed past the map, making their exclamations of surprise and indignation and fury, till eventually it was taken down early, rolled and carted back to the parsonage next door and put away in a drawer in Parson Petchey's study.

SIXTY-EIGHT

THE MOOD in both the Wayfarers' and the Carpenters' Arms that night was very subdued, as it was, too, in the Green Man at Lower Rackstead and the Bull at Merchant Staplers. For, impartial as they were supposed to be, it was not unexpected that there were some who would accuse the commissioners of malpractice, of favouring the rich landowners and the aristocracy, having been appointed by them, given them the best land and left the poor husbandmen with useless, near infertile plots. Other plots they had allocated to the owners of the cottages in which the husbandmen and day-labourers lived rather than to the tenants, leaving the latter with nothing at all and their landlords with more land still.

It seemed to them that, by an Act of Parliament made by the rich, only those who had bought part of the land or who had come into it by inheritance of a deceased parent or distant relative contained in a will and who had no other connection with it whatsoever – they were the only ones entitled by right to call the land their own. Those who had been bred on the land and whose forefathers had been bred on the land since before the Normans came – they were no longer entitled to work it for themselves, which is how it was in Hamwick Dean and the adjoining hamlets of Lower Rackstead and Merchant Staplers, where the poor had lost everything without any hope of redress.

When all was totalled and signed and sealed, the total cost of the enclosure of the three parishes – that is, the cost of the petition, the commissioning of the Act and the fees and expenses to everyone concerned over a period of three years – was a staggering five thousand, six hundred and ninety-four pounds twelve shillings and fourpence-halfpenny. The commissioners' fees alone amounted to twelve hundred and eighty-four pounds, the diversion and construction of roads and paths totalled a thousand and thirty pounds, surveyors' fees were nine hundred and thirty-four, with a further nine hundred and sixteen allocated for miscellaneous items, interest on bank loans, lodging fees, stabling, keep and the like.

The legal charges of Mr. Mogg and two other sets of lawyers and a barrister were eight hundred and seventy-six pounds in total. In addition, the three commissioners invoiced for two hundred and fifty pounds in other expenses, the parliamentary expenses themselves to see the Bill through the committee amounted to two hundred and nineteen pounds and there was a further expense of eighteen hundred and four pounds for stakes and fencing.

The wealth of Lady Amelia, the dowager marchioness, Sir Benton and Sir Gentry, the Diocese of Melchborough, the dean and chapter in Oxford and various others, combined with that of Titus Broake and the farmers, was more than sufficient. However, such were the gains, the outlay would always prove worth it: and, while they could easily afford to pay the five-pounds-an-acre cost of the enclosure, most others could not. Even Amos Peakman and the other farmers required a mortgage from the banker at Melchborough to meet their commitments, but it was a small price to pay for land which would always improve in value.

For Jem, Dick Dollery and the other husbandmen, however, it quickly became evident that it was not worth their while to take up their allotments: the burden was just too great. For one of the last things Elijah Candler had read out was: *'And the said commissioners do hereby further award, order and direct that the fences for enclosing the several allotments hereinbefore awarded shall be made within six months from the date hereof and for ever after be maintained and kept in repair by and at the expense of the respective owners of the allotments to which such fences belong with quicksets and ditches of four feet in width from the lower table and of sufficient depth to convey the water and with proper gates and stiles across the private roads and footpaths.*

'And the said commissioners have contracted with the said Benjamin Hayhoe, builder, of the parish of Hamwyte, for the making of the ring fences hereinbefore directed for enclosing the allotments herein awarded... '

Some thirty years before in 1796, when enclosure had been gathering pace in other counties, the promoter of a General Enclosure Bill before Parliament had proposed that the poor be exempted from the expense of fencing any land they received from a commissioner. However, a parliamentary Select Committee had disapproved of the idea: indeed, the outcome was that the only persons exempted were the lords of the manor or tithe-owners.

As a result, every small farmer, husbandman and cottager who received an allocation of land, however small, in the Award for the three parishes in the Hundred of Hamwyte, now found that the land they had received in lieu of his common rights attracted a proportion of the cost of the enclosure scheme. All land had to be fenced or hedged, even if it were little more than a large garden: and, though in Hamwick Dean and the two hamlets, it was five pounds an acre rather than the twelve they had feared as elsewhere, it was still too high for Jem and the others. For them, the expense of surrounding each allotment with a hedge or fence and ditch was greater than the value of the allotment they had received.

Had the portion which Jem received been large enough, he could well have sold a part of it to pay the costs of the hedging and fencing. As it was, Joshua Jaikes sat in the church porch for the rest of the week after the map was displayed, writing down the names of those who were not prepared to take up their land, but would accept two pounds an acre for it.

'We can't afford the fencing they call for. Who can pay that?' Dick Dollery snorted as Joshua Jaikes carefully wrote down his name.

'I have not been given enough to support a single cow, let alone myself and my family,' complained Enos Diddams. 'I have no option, I shall have to sell my cow and my land and the only ones who will benefit will be the rich farmers, for I shan't.'

'I have been left with scarce enough land to give me five day's work to take up my time,' protested another in abject disgust, 'and yet I am expected to bear the cost of hedging it. When I have done it, what am I to do with the rest of my time? How am I to live?'

So many in the three parishes received an acre or less that they had no alternative but to sell – and little to do with the money but to drink away their despair.

In the three years from inception to completion of enclosure, the dispossessed husbandmen and small farmers of Hamwick Dean were, effectively, removed from general village life: the enclosure of what had once been common land had irrevocably altered something in the make-up of the parish: the social fabric of its life had been torn apart.

In the weeks that followed, Marcus Howie bought up the land which Jem and Enos Diddams and five others had received because their separate allotments were contiguous with the expanded Smallponds along the Merchant Staplers road, while others, Dick Dollery, Nathaniel Newman and Caleb Chapman, with his three acres, amongst them, sold their allotments to Amos Peakman. Even one of the small farmers, who had proved his title to his ten-acre close and had received a compact holdings of twenty-five acres, also found the cost of hedging with the quick-growing thorn advocated was too great in the short time allowed. In no time at all, his parcel found its way into the hands of Titus Broake, as did several others in the ensuing months.

Before enclosure, Jem, Dick Dollery, Enos Diddams and the others had been labourers with land, albeit leased: now they were labourers without land. The basis of their independence had been destroyed: for they lost, too, their prescriptive rights of keeping a cow or sheep or geese or goats on common land, for which they received no compensation. Thus, ten years after launching his ambition, Jem Stebbings drove his half-dozen sheep to Hamwyte market one Tuesday and sold them for a poor price since there were so many animals being sold by others in the same plight. The following week he sold the cows and the week after that the old horse went to a knacker's yard at Budwick, for it was good for no other purpose by then. He found no takers for his single plough or the other implements he had accumulated at other sales and cast them into a ditch to rot and rust.

For long afterwards, Dick Dollery was to fume in the Wayfarers' bay-windowed parlour: 'We should have fought them. We have lain down and they have trampled on us.' He was all for some action, but, in truth, all knew that any form of protest was impossible.

A year later some did protest in their own small ways: one morning, when Amos Peakman and Marcus Howie went into the fields of their newly enclosed land, they found that someone had stolen out during the hours of darkness and smashed with an axe and a sledgehammer the new fencing they had just erected and also had trampled down the newly planted hedgerow shoots. Someone said it was women who had done it, for in the darkness the silhouettes they had seen were definitely the forms of women: but the whisper amongst some who seemed to be in the know of a secret was that some of the supposed 'women' had blackened faces and, if one had looked carefully enough, they might well have seen soot smudged on the collars and sleeves of the smocks and jackets of Dick Dollery, Enos Diddams and one or two others when they stood talking on The Street the following morning.

Whatever was done, it was done too late and influenced nothing: the great majority of the independent husbandmen of Hamwick Dean and the two hamlets had become common wage labourers for local farmers and any landed gentry who wished to employ them. For Jem Stebbings, his dream of living his life as a husbandman, independent of all others, was over...

The story of Jem Stebbings

is continued in

The Other Side of England:

PART II:

NO BREAD, NO WORK, NO HOPE

And in

The Other Side of England:

PART III:

LAW AND LAWLESSNESS

Made in the USA
Charleston, SC
02 September 2016